The Severed Finger

Other Novels by Arno B. Zimmer

☆ THE PARLOR CITY BOYS
☆ RETURN TO PARLOR CITY
☆ A MURDER IN PARLOR HARBOR
☆ DEATH COMES TO THE TORPEDO FACTORY

The Severed Finger

Copyright © 2019 Arno B. Zimmer

All Rights Reserved

No part of this publication may be reproduced, stored in or introduced into a retrieval system, or transmitted, in any form or by any means (electronic, mechanical, photocopying, recording or otherwise), without the prior written permission of the copyright owner, except by a reviewer who may quote brief passages in a review.

This book is sold subject to the condition that it shall not, by way of trade or otherwise, be lent, re-sold, hired out or otherwise circulated without the author's prior consent in any form of binding or cover other than that in which it is published and without a similar condition including this condition being imposed on the subsequent purchaser.

Cover Art By Mark E. Phillips

THE
SEVERED FINGER
A Thimble Islands Mystery

BY

Arno B. Zimmer

DEDICATION

To my sister, Rita,
for a lifetime of supporting and
encouraging my writing career.
I love her dearly but if
you don't like my novels,
please send your complaints to her!

ACKNOWLEDGEMENTS

I want to thank the readers and reviewers of my previous novels, including family, friends and former colleagues - but also strangers - who have urged me to keep writing after my debut novel, The Parlor City Boys, was released in 2015.

Special thanks to Cheryl Hardy, Dave Meinert, Phyllis Chillingworth and Rita Zimmer, faithful readers of all my manuscripts to date, including this one. They made helpful suggestions on clarifying the plot and timeline but also caught numerous typographical and grammatical errors that have, hopefully, all been exorcised (any remaining ones the sole responsibility of the author).

Finally, a special thanks to my artist (and nephew!), Mark Phillips, who has created the covers for all of my novels.

Contents

Prologue: Following Jerry Kosinsky 1
Chapter One: Casting A Wide Net 7
Chapter Two: Freak Street 11
Chapter Three: A Modern Day Don Quixote? 16
Chapter Four: From Bad To Worse 25
Chapter Five: Leaving Toronto 28
Chapter Six: Picaresque Man 38
Chapter Seven: A Little Encouragement Goes A Long Way 46
Chapter Eight: Jerry Starts Digging 50
Chapter Nine: Pudge McFadden's 58
Chapter Ten: Cyrus Trowbridge 68
Chapter Eleven: Quarry Island 76
Chapter Twelve: Dead Man's Finger? 81
Chapter Thirteen: No More Twitching 88
Chapter Fourteen: Woody Provides Counsel 94
Chapter Fifteen: The Reg and El Show 98
Chapter Sixteen: Fletcher Ladislaw 107
Chapter Seventeen: The Poe Enigma 111
Chapter Eighteen: "What's The Word?" 115
Chapter Nineteen: Buried Treasure 125
Chapter Twenty: Case Closed 131
Chapter Twenty-One: A New Twist 136
Chapter Twenty-Two: On The Road Again 146
Chapter Twenty-Three: The Cruikshank Connection 153
Chapter Twenty-Four: The Ring of Truth 161
Chapter Twenty-Five: The Wife's Lament 169
Chapter Twenty-Six: A Little Reprieve 176
Chapter Twenty-Seven: Smitty's Revenge 183
Chapter Twenty-Eight: Two Fingers? 187

Chapter Twenty-Nine: The Stake Out 191
Chapter Thirty: A Lightning Bolt 197
Chapter Thirty-One: The Color Of Money 202
Chapter Thirty-Two: Disappearing Act 206
Chapter Thirty-Three: Corpus Delicti 211
Chapter Thirty-Four: The Wig and the Ring 215
Chapter Thirty-Five: The Bonding 223
Chapter Thirty-Six: Toronto Comes Clean 227
Chapter Thirty-Seven: A Surprise Visitor 233
Chapter Thirty-Eight: Alibi Ike 236
Chapter Thirty-Nine: Back On The Tracks 242
Chapter Forty: A Legrand Time 250
Chapter Forty-One: Follow The Money 255
Chapter Forty-Two: Don't Bank On It 262
Chapter Forty-Three: Baxter DeCourcy 269
Chapter Forty-Four: Hanging By A Hair 275
Chapter Forty-Five: Anonymous Tipster 278
Chapter Forty-Six: The Patsies 284
Chapter Forty-Seven: The Shell 289
Chapter Forty-Eight: Road Runner 293
Chapter Forty-Nine: The Interrogations 298
Chapter Fifty: Slayer Beware 304
Chapter Fifty-One: The Great Escape 309
Epilogue 314

PROLOGUE:
Following Jerry Kosinsky

~~

It was the fall of 1967 when Jerry Kosinsky left Parlor City in Upstate New York and crossed the border at Rouses Point into Canada, just one day before his draft notice arrived in the mail. If Jerry had known this fact at the time, he would have considered it a fortuitous departure, a form of divine intervention. Sometimes, timing and blind luck are everything, but they don't always bode well, as he would learn.

He wrote a cryptic apology to his parents which he mailed when he was safely on the other side, in "neutral" territory, his estrangement from his homeland now a *fait accompli*. Actually, the letter was more an explanation than an apology. He wasn't a conscientious objector for religious or other reasons. He didn't believe that all war was evil or unjustified – or even avoidable, no matter how long people marched in protest and shouted slogans.

But Jerry was certain that the odds were overwhelming that should he enlist or be drafted, like his best friend Woody Meacham was likely to do, he would end up a grunt soldier on the front lines in Vietnam. Many would call his actions cowardly self-absorption but he simply refused to take the risk that his life might be snuffed out at the age of 22. Prof. Eyesmore at

Pythian College had convinced him that he was destined to be an estimable scholar and it would be sinful to throw in all away. It was this rationale that he struggled, unsuccessfully, to convey.

Even more than his parents, Jerry regretted leaving without telling his bosom buddy. The two had just been through a hellish summer in Parlor Harbor, the lakeside resort town only a two-hour drive from their hometown of Parlor City. Woody Meacham had been framed for the murder of a college classmate and, under the guidance of Woody's stepfather, the locally renowned Parlor City Police Chief Billy Meacham, Jr., Jerry played the role of amateur sleuth, helping to exonerate his friend. In the midst of his exhilaration upon crossing into Canada, it felt strange to Jerry that while he was on the run, Woody was probably in the process of volunteering for the very thing that he was fleeing.

It would take Jerry a long time, assuming they ever met again, to explain to his boyhood pal his unannounced but carefully-planned departure.

AT 6'2" TALL and over 220 pounds, Jerry Kosinsky might have been intimidating if not for his gentle nature and soft demeanor. He had double-jointed knees and occasionally walked with an exaggerated, awkward stride that made him look almost comical, a Don Quixote-type character in style and gait which belied his sharp, inquisitive intellect. He was reticent about imposing himself on others but was not shy about expressing himself when the occasion allowed or demanded. His thick, dark brown hair hung carelessly down his forehead to the top of his tortoise-shelled glasses. He had that puffy, pinkish skin that made his face look almost child-like. The full-blown mustache that draped over and dominated his upper lip saved him from this puerile ignominy.

Jerry was tired of being told through all his years at Pythian College that he was the spitting image of Mickey Dolenz of a rock group named The Monkees. He didn't even like their music. The mustache seemed to silence those who teased him about his "twin brother" and, in a way, it marked his passage into adulthood. When he left Pythian, he was determined to be taken seriously.

DURING THAT TUMULTUOUS summer of 1967 in Parlor Harbor after graduation from Pythian College, Jerry had stayed in constant touch with Prof. Eyesmore. This respected scholar of antiquities had high hopes for Jerry Kosinsky and could not accept the possibility that his prized pupil, his budding savant, would end up dead in some distant rice field, a "sacrifice to the war gods," as he put it. Eyesmore had resources and contacts at schools around the world. He pledged to underwrite Jerry's exodus and, framing it as his "civic duty," convinced Jerry to decamp to Toronto where there was a thriving ex-pat community. Once there, Jerry was to await further instructions from his Svengali.

After several weeks in Canada, Jerry boarded a British Airways flight from Toronto to London, after which he would take a train to Coventry and await further instructions. Jerry was in the sedate English Midlands, almost 100 miles from London, certain this could not be his final destination, wondering what would happen next.

The Coventry area was made famous by that great Victorian lady of letters, Mary Ann Evans who, under *the nom de plume* George Eliot, wrote *Adam Bede*, *The Mill on the Floss* and the incomparable *Middlemarch*, establishing her in the pantheon of great novelists. Her fame could not save her from the scandal of living openly with a married man and insisting that he was her husband.

After a few days, Jerry was visited by someone from the University of Leicester and learned that he would be joining a British archeology team led by the renowned Prof. Phineas Popenjoy. He was astounded to learn that their destination was Kathmandu, the ancient city in Nepal.

"I trust you won't get mixed up with that crowd on Freak Street, Jerry," Eyesmore said with a dismissive laugh. "Freak what?" Jerry asked. "You'll find out soon enough," Eyesmore replied, no longer laughing.

Eyesmore knew that he was putting a great deal of faith in Jerry Kosinsky but he owed the young man a great deal for encouraging him to forsake his country with no prospect for return in the foreseeable future. The Brits had promised to keep a watch on him after Eyesmore explained that while he did not distrust his protégé, he worried that Jerry was naïve and susceptible to anything new.

As THE DC-3 from Kabul circled the bowl-shaped Kathmandu Valley, some 4600 ft. above sea level, preparing to land on the airstrip below, Jerry Kosinsky looked out the window, his mouth agape at the Ganesh Himal and Lantang, sub-ranges of the Himalayan Mountains located northwest of the fabled city.

Jerry had started reading Thomas Merton's *The Seven Storey Mountain* on the flight from London to Afghanistan and was filled with excitement about the images that the Trappist Monk created and which now awaited him on the ground below. "I'll be the mystical archeologist, a rare breed," Jerry said to himself before he had spent a day in Nepal.

Jerry saw himself back at Pythian College one day, the

successor to Prof. Eyesmore. He would be the molder of young minds, having experienced first-hand the esoteric world of the ancient mystics. Wasn't this the role that Eyesmore was grooming him for even if he had never articulated it? Jerry believed it and saw Kathmandu as an important step, a prelude to that destiny.

The Vietnam War couldn't go on indefinitely and when it was over, Jerry could return home triumphant, his own man on his own terms.

NEPAL'S THIRD LARGEST city was undergoing a transformation of its own - a clash of two cultures – and Jerry would be in the middle of it all in Kathmandu. For some adventurers and interlopers who overstayed their visit, it would end badly but like so many others, Jerry Kosinsky was oblivious to it all as the plane settled onto the runway.

THE BRITISH ARCHEOLOGY team, part of a larger group under the sponsorship of the United Nations, was stationed in a guesthouse just outside the downtown area of Kathmandu. Their assignment was to examine and catalog the numerous religious temples in and around the city, many of which lined the Bagmati River that separated the cities of Kathmandu and Patan. Through the efforts and influence of Prof. Eyesmore, Jerry had been assigned as an "adjunct advisor" to the British team. It was a nebulous, made-up title but sounded official enough and no one deigned to question it.

There was a dingy café connected to the guesthouse and the exhausted travelers had a dinner of rice, lentils, chickpeas and hunks of Tibetan bread. Cows roamed the streets but no beef was served. After dinner, Jerry got his first tutorial on Kathmandu from a seasoned veteran on the British team. He was briefed on local customs and cautioned about the notorious hippie gathering area that the locals had nicknamed Freak Street. First the warning by Prof. Eyesmore and now this admonishment from an uptight Brit. Jerry was amused.

Back at Pythian College, Jerry had avoided the nascent drug scene that emerged in his senior year, preferring to get his stimulation from Genesee Cream Ale or whatever beer was on sale that weekend. Jerry knew he had work to do for Prof. Eyesmore and felt confident that he would not be sidetracked by the lure of a hippie gathering place.

First thing in the morning, he would stop at one of the shops in town and buy a few postcards. One would go to his parents and the other one to Woody Meacham. They deserved to know that he was alive and safe in Kathmandu.

CHAPTER ONE:
Casting A Wide Net

It was late May of 1977 and the gaggle of middle school kids had ridden out early on the Thimble Island ferry, some full of nervous energy, others lethargic or feigning indifference, but none of them knowing exactly what to expect on their final field trip of the year. They had been granted a day of relative freedom and relished it. Some boys were still revved up from the release a few days earlier of *Star Wars*. The final exploding star scene in the movie where Han Solo and Luke Skywalker save the day was all the rage. "The force be with you" could be frequently heard in solemn or mocking tones during the short boat ride. Meanwhile, the girls took a back seat to Princess Leia.

The group's destination was DeCourcy Island, one of the inhabitable islets out of a total of 365 outcroppings of an archipelago off the Connecticut coast. The Thimble Islands, as they are collectively known, have a rich history, both real and apocryphal.

Most residents of the area didn't bother to delve into the true history of Capt. William Kidd, the Scottish buccaneer who, in the 1600s, supposedly buried treasure on one or more of the Thimbles that separate New York from Connecticut. Was he a legal privateer, sanctioned by the British crown, or a pirate who deserved to be hung for his alleged crimes on a pole overlooking the Thames River? Kidd initially had friends in high places – including King William III – but they all turned on him in the end when politics made it expedient to do so. Over two hundred years later, no one felt sympathy for Kidd but some treasure seekers still wondered – and hoped – that he had left a valuable prize behind.

Most of the Thimbles were small and under water except at low tide. DeCourcy Island was one of the larger ones, almost eleven acres, with an educational pavilion and classroom dedicated to teaching impressionable young students about the importance of conservation and respect for their natural habitat. The island was owned and managed by the prestigious DeCourcy Institute and today's outing was under the direction of Gretchen Cadwallader, a project volunteer.

By late morning, after a classroom session that went too long and was as much propagandizing about man's abuse of the planet as it was educational, the kids were assembled in small clusters at the rocky shore. The usual pinching, punching and shoving occurred along with an occasional yet hesitant flirtation between a few of the more advanced 13-year olds. At least a few boys were looking for a princess.

Gretchen had left the classroom early and had positioned dragnets at various spots along the shore for each group to use. Guidance was provided on how to drop them in the tide pools and collect a cross section of crabs, starfish, bait fish and plankton. School chaperones stayed back at the pavilion, glad to be relieved of their pubescent charges for a few hours, while volunteers from the Institute monitored each group of kids to help them identify and then catalog what was captured in the nettings.

Overhead, a few puffy clouds dotted an almost clear azure sky. Even the indolent kids started to show animation as they inspected their trappings and learned what they had caught. Amidst the scattered laughter there came from one of the tide pools a sudden shriek that pierced the air and caused an eerie silence. In the sky, a majestic osprey soaring above seemed to pause in mid-flight to look down, as if it were receiving a call for assistance from a fallen comrade.

A chubby, freckle-faced, towhead in khaki shorts and a blue shirt emblazoned with the Barchester School logo had stumbled back from the edge of the water, digging her heels frantically into the ground with her hands still tangled in the dragnet, pumping her legs furiously as if trying to escape from some unseen attacker.

Gretchen rushed to the girl's side and knelt beside her, smoothing down the child's hair while freeing her hands from the netting.

"What is it Dorothea? What frightened you?" asked Gretchen. The girl's mouth was gaping. She was trying to speak but only hoarse, unintelligible sounds were emitted. She finally managed to point into the netting with one outstretched, shaking arm while clutching Gretchen's shoulder with the other.

Gretchen acted annoyed. She had warned the other volunteers that there were always a few kids who hyperventilated over the most mundane discovery. It happened on almost every outing she supervised.

Dorothea was inconsolable while the other kids gathered around. Some scoffed and laughed. She continued to point frantically and then Gretchen saw it. Tangled in the netting, next to a starfish, pointing back at them, almost in an accusatory way, was a pale bloated, ringed finger with a faded insignia.

Gretchen waved her arm furiously, motioning for the other kids to stay back while she hugged the girl tightly with her other arm. She wanted to pluck the finger from the netting and cover it before there was a general panic but then a boy's raucous voice pierced the air. "It's a friggin' finger," he yelled out gleefully. Most of the girls shrieked and turned away quickly before cupping their hands over their mouths in disgust. The boys surged forward to enjoy the moment, perhaps inspired by the intrepid Han and Luke.

Gretchen heard her name and turned to see one of the other volunteers hovering above her, looking for guidance. "Get these damn kids back in the pavilion," she barked. She caught herself and added, almost in a whisper, "Then, someone had better call the police."

A day earlier and only a short boat ride away, a fire broke out on Quarry Island in the offices of the company that was mining the pink granite unique to the Thimble Islands.

CHAPTER TWO:
FREAK STREET

WHEN JERRY KOSINSKY landed in Kathmandu near the end of 1967, it was a magical time for the hippie invaders. Eventually, they would run out of money or wear out their welcome and would be forced to emerge from their self-induced hazes. In the late 60s and early 70s, such a possibility seemed remote or irrelevant. For now, the flower people reveled in their own special Neverland.

When our adventurous neophyte sauntered into the Tibetan Blue Café on Freak Street just south of Durbar Square, he was grinning broadly until the thick, overpowering smoke caused him to gasp for breath. Jerry Kosinsky squinted and rubbed his eyes while involuntarily inhaling thick, potent plumes. Through the haze, he saw that the walls were covered with hand-made, banal signs like "Make Love, Not War" and "Keep The World Beautiful – Stay Stoned."

Regulars knew a virgin had walked in the door and those who hadn't already descended into a late morning stupor looked up in amusement at this man-child in preppy attire. Someone pushed a wooden pipe toward him but he motioned it off with a flick of his hand. It would take Jerry a while to understand that he had stepped across a threshold into a seductive hippie heaven.

Word quickly got out on Freak Street that Jerry was connected to the British archeology team. That first visit to the Tibetan Blue had him pegged as an amusing outsider but someone the regulars needed to keep an eye on. Anyone wearing khaki pants and a blue, button-down shirt was immediately suspect, an interloper if not a spy from the establishment. Paranoia went with the territory.

When Jerry asked someone in Tibetan Blue about the best local beers, he was treated to bewildered looks and smirks. When he asked where the bathroom was, the café regulars erupted in uproarious laughter. It was not the auspicious beginning this neophyte adventurer, who had stepped through the looking glass into an alternate universe, had expected.

Jerry Kosinsky had left behind the pampered academic life of Pythian College and small-town Parlor City. He was ill-prepared for what lied ahead.

LESS DIGNIFIED THAN its proper name of Jhochhen Tole, Freak Street in Kathmandu was the name given to this narrow thoroughfare by the locals when wild-eyed, long-haired young Americans and Europeans started flooding into their ancient city in the 1960s. Before long, it became a geographical icon, much like Haight-Ashbury in San Francisco and Greenwich Village in New York City.

The hordes of aliens came for a variety of reasons, principle among them: the best and the cheapest cannabis – hashish or marijuana - on earth. There was an overland route that became known as the "Hippie Trail," beginning in London and eventually winding through Afghanistan and India before arriving in Nepal. Adventurous trekkers went on foot via what became known as the Annapurna Circuit, an often-treacherous passage through the Himalayas. The less adventurous travelers boarded the charter buses that left London and Amsterdam on a regular schedule and, for about $150, would deposit you in Kathmandu.

Flower power was the rage and hippies, successors to the beatniks of the 50s, were considered to have put Nepal on the tourist map for the youthful disenchanted. It wasn't long before nicknames for Kathmandu abounded: the *Mecca of Hippiedom*, the *New Jerusalem*, the *Amsterdam of the East*, the *Capital of the Aquarian Age*. Whatever you called it, Nepal was the "happy land" in the Orient, the mythical Shangri-La so many disaffected youths were so desperately seeking.

In reality, many of them were myrmidons, feckless acolytes and devotees to the fashionable anti-establishment creed of the day. They feigned an attachment to mysticism but eschewed the hard work of actually studying the world's great religions, instead relying on a smattering of knowledge, some convenient catch phrases, to carry them through. In the end, they were content to rely on a vague, hashish-induced cosmic vision of peace and love.

Into the 1970s, Kathmandu remained an open and inviting town. It was a destination for naïve idealists, young spiritual seekers, drop-outs and drifters, counter-culture adventurers and budding mystics dramatically characterized by the "Dharma bums" with their shaved heads. The pseudo-intellectuals and unsophisticated, many inspired by Jack Kerouac, Ken Kesey, Allen Ginsberg and Herman Hesse, left vacuous, slothful lives behind and raced to the promised land. Many were eager to join like-minded drop-outs in a permissive, non-judgmental world where you could stay high all day and all night.

Alongside the harmless innocents, you had your crusty-armed, hard-core drug addicts and criminals who came for the panoply of cheap black-market drugs like opium, heroin, pure morphine and methedrine. Nepalis had become accustomed to the exceedingly polite and sedate "blue rinse" tourists of the 50s, as the elderly set were known who dominated tourism in Kathmandu prior to the youthful invasion. Now, the citizenry was forced to adapt again.

To accommodate the hippie influx, Freak Street – also known as "Backpackers Central" - grew from three government-run hashish shops to over thirty enterprises in a confined downtown area. If you could make it to Kathmandu, it was said that you could live on $1 a day while smoking yourself into an eternal fog. Entrepreneurial Nepali quickly opened up shops, guesthouses and cafes catering to the youthful, budget-minded outsiders. They capitalized on the influx of the alien masses at a time when other Asian nations were less accommodating. There was a unique societal fissure in Nepal between abstinence and permissiveness which couldn't be found elsewhere on the continent. As a result, the cultural rebels from within and without took full advantage of it. While some of the English daily newspapers wrote complimentary pieces about the hippies, as if giving up Western conveniences was a laudable sacrifice worthy of press notice, others in Kathmandu looked at the interlopers with contempt for corrupting their youth and culture – not to mention driving up prices.

The disillusioned invaders saved up money or sponged off their parents with the singular goal to get to this nirvana in the foothills of the Himalayan Mountains. It wasn't just Americans who flooded into Kathmandu, even though they seemed to be the overwhelming contingent of "time travelers" who had prompted locals to give an ancient Nepalese street its discordant nickname. Peripatetic youth from Europe, Australia and New Zealand also came to enjoy the perpetual party. Unlike older tourists, they stayed for weeks, even months and years, until outside events intervened and shocked many of them back to reality.

Living was cheap once you arrived. You could sleep in a dormitory for $1.50/month or luxuriate in a private room for $4.50/month. Then, there were the crash houses that accommodated dozens at a time and had a revolving clientele. For 30 cents, you could get a meal consisting of buffalo steak, tea and a hunk of Tibetan bread. The locals even had a sense of humor and, with a nod to McDonald's, offered a "YakBurger" with a flavor akin to bison.

Musicians added to the transcendental aura of Southeast Asia in general and Nepal in particular. While the Beatles never made it to Kathmandu, they did get as far as India, where they holed up in a luxury ashram near New Delhi.

It was said, most likely apocryphally, that the singer/composer Cat Stevens, later known as Yusuf Islam when he converted to the Muslim faith, wrote "Katmandu" (he spelled it without the "h") while sitting in the Tibetan Blue Café. Rumors persisted that Bob Marley had stayed at a guesthouse not far from Freak Street and carved his name on the wall. And if Janet Joplin, John Lennon and Bob Seger never actually visited this counterculture utopia, Kathmandu made it into all of their songs.

A SHORT WALK from Freak Street was Pig Alley with its cluster of pie and cake shops catering to the sweet tooth of the hippie throng, incessantly eager to cure the "raving munchies." If you could look past the open sewers and the back alley rats the size of cats while deprived of the amenities of western culture – no electricity or indoor plumbing - Kathmandu was heaven on earth.

For Jerry Kosinsky, it almost turned out to be hell.

CHAPTER THREE:
A MODERN DAY DON QUIXOTE?

~

AT THE BEGINNING of 1968, Jerry kept his distance from the more notorious cafes on Freak Street, focusing on several research projects for Prof. Eyesmore on the Hindu and Buddhist temples around Kathmandu.

The professor also sent Jerry to study the Buddhist pilgrimage center in Lumbini, a bumpy seven-hour bus ride from Kathmandu. The novelty of Nepal had not yet worn off and Jerry relished the uniqueness of his surroundings. A bus ride that would have been torture back home was now part of the charm. Tradition says that Buddha's mother touched a tree in the garden at Lumbini and then gave birth to the spiritual leader of 350 million followers around the world.

East of Kathmandu, Jerry explored the *Changu Narayan*, one of the oldest Hindu temples in Nepal, dedicated to the god Vishnu. The two-tiered pagoda was an architectural marvel that mesmerized visitors from around the world. Jerry had no shortage of temples to visit. It was estimated that the Kathmandu Valley had more of them than private homes. Jerry was the proverbial "kid in the candy store."

One of Jerry's favorite days was the 5-mile bike ride to Boudhanath where he could study the 5th century Buddhist *stupa*, a dome-shaped religious shrine, and visit the open-air market to buy fresh vegetables and fruit.

On a regular basis, Jerry went to the Poste Restante, the central post office in Kathmandu, and sent meticulous, long-hand reports, accompanied by photographs, back to Pythian College. He was determined to impress Prof. Eyesmore.

Jerry also made side trips to Calcutta and Bangkok to study and photograph various ancient shrines designated by Eyesmore. All in all, the professor seemed to be quite pleased with Jerry's work during their monthly calls.

1968 WAS A transformative year for Jerry and convinced him that he had done the right thing in fleeing the United States, particularly when he heard firsthand the horror stories coming out of Vietnam as deserters showed up in Kathmandu after making the long trek across Cambodia, Thailand and Burma. He worried that Woody was there and fantasized that he would see his friend walk up Freak Street one day.

Jerry increasingly bought into the theory that his country had started an irreversible decline, beginning with the assassination of Pres. Kennedy in 1963, followed by his brother Bobby and then Martin Luther King. The song "American Pie" wasn't just about the plane crash that killed the singer Buddy Holly. It captured the decade of death and decline, the loss of the idyllic, which seemed to presage the inevitable riots, looting and burning of cities both large and small.

After finishing *The Seven Storey Mountain*, Jerry immersed himself in all of the other writings of Thomas Merton, the Trappist Monk, mystic poet and social activist. It was a heavy blow to him when Merton was found dead under suspicious circumstances in a suburb of Bangkok in December of 1968. Conspiracy theories abounded involving the CIA since Merton was an outspoken critic of the Vietnam War. When word got out that Merton's body was flown back to the United States on a military plane that was also transporting dead soldiers, the dark rumors and speculation increased. Jerry's mood started to darken.

As THE MONTHS slid by into 1969 and then 1970, a disillusioned and disheartened Jerry became a regular on Freak Street and over in Pig Alley where he favored the banana cake and apricot pie. He ditched his khakis and blue shirt in favor of a beige, collarless shirt known as a *kurta*. He adorned it with a string of beads and wore matching pajamas to complete his ensemble. One of the Brits snickered that he was on the verge of joining the brotherhood of love. Walking through town, he laughed at the stoners who huddled in groups, some incoherent and others struggling to speak. When referring to one particular Buddhist shrine, *Swayambhunath*, the idlers simply gave up trying to say it and thought it was amusing to call it the "monkey temple."

Jerry had gradually let his hair grow down to his shoulders and now sported a beard to accompany a mustache that reached his lower lip, giving him an almost inscrutable look. He appeared god-like as he strode through town, towering above the locals and most of the Americans. Jerry was on the verge of giving up on beer. It was imported from India and he tired of its bitter taste. Finally, he succumbed to the omnipresent temptation and had his first pull on the wooden pipe – known as the *chillum*. For Jerry, it was as if he was in the Garden of Eden and had yielded to the soothing, sensual voice of the serpent.

ONE DAY IN early 1971 while sipping tea at the Tibetan Blue Café, Jerry was befriended by Dickie Carlyle and his younger sister Leila. On most days, they stationed themselves at the same corner table. They had been in Kathmandu for about a year and seemed much more mature and under control than the stoners roaming Freak Street and loitering outside the nearby temples where they made a ritual of ringing the bells to clear their heads. The Carlyles described themselves as purveyors of rare books with customers around the world for the growing interest in any literature connected to mysticism and the Orient.

One evening, Leila pulled Jerry aside and asked if he might perform a small favor. In keeping with the times, she was wearing no make-up but her smooth, milky complexion needed no adornment. Leila wasn't Joni Mitchell but close enough. She was wearing a loose-fitting shift and when she leaned in, Jerry couldn't help stare. She was braless and her fulsome, upturned breasts were almost completely exposed and seemed to be peaking up at him invitingly. The titillation was almost overpowering but Leila didn't appear to notice Jerry's flushed cheeks.

It seemed that her brother had a recent run-in with the clerk at the post office and didn't want to return there until tempers cooled. Would Jerry be nice enough to mail a package of books for them to a customer in Chicago? Leila stroked Jerry's arm a few times, gave him a few dreamy looks and then squeezed his hand for good measure. Of course, Jerry said he would be glad to oblige them. As it turned out, Dickie's relationship with the post office never seemed to improve and Jerry was always there to help out.

Jerry was now hopelessly pulled into the Carlyle orbit, enthralled by Leila and her suggestive eyes. Whenever Jerry left Kathmandu, for side trips to Goa on the southern coast or to

Bangkok or Calcutta, Leila had a delivery request for him. After a few late-night assignations at the guesthouse, Jerry would have walked on hot coals for Leila Carlyle.

JERRY WAS SPENDING less and less time with what he considered the unenlightened and priggish British team. He had grown tired of their preaching about the dangers of what he considered the harmless Freak Street crowd and rarely accompanied them on any of their excavation projects. He took umbrage one day when confronted and chastened by Prof. Popenjoy.

What Jerry didn't know was that the British team leader was having regular conversations with Prof. Eyesmore and had, on more than one occasion, referred to his prize student as a gullible "jackanape." Eyesmore was furious. "Just keep an eye on him and get him out of there when you leave, Phineas, and I'll ask no favors again. He doesn't know it but he will be freezing his ass off soon if he doesn't straighten up." Popenjoy didn't accede to Eyesmore's request and wasn't convinced that it would do any good to intervene.

LYING IN BED late one morning in the Spring of 1971, Jerry was awakened by Prof. Popenjoy and another member of the British team who informed him that they were headed to the Black Sea the next day. Jerry listened intently as he heard the news that a vessel had been found in the waters off Bulgaria, possibly dating back centuries when trading colonies dotted the coast.

When he heard the news that he would not be accompanying them, Jerry feigned indifference but his heart sank. He had alternately ignored or rebuffed the Brits for several months but was always comforted by their presence. Now, he would be left to his own devices.

"I know you're sick of hearing it but you're playing a dangerous game with this Freak Street crowd, Jerry. There are some unsavory characters mixed in with the innocent stoners and I'm afraid that you're too naïve to tell the difference. I informed Prof. Eyesmore this morning exactly why we're leaving you behind so you will have to deal with him on your own now." When the professor stopped talking, Jerry got out of bed and loomed over him with a menacing look on his face which only made the Brit smile. Jerry was not a violent man and the ephemeral glare was the only show of indignation that he could muster.

As he was leaving, Popenjoy turned at the door and said, "Not that it will matter to you but the word from our embassy folks is that the Nepali rulers will not be tolerant of Kathmandu much longer. I've given your name to our attaché' and asked him to help you any way he can if you get yourself in a bind. I told him you're a decent sort, just easily mislead. You're not a Brit so frankly I wouldn't count on him if I were you. I must say, though, that if there is anyone who has exhibited such a combination of idealism and naivete since Don Quixote, I have not met him yet. Well, good luck, old chap."

YEARS LATER, THE professor would be Sir Phineas Popenjoy, knighted by the Queen for his work in the Black Sea, just off the coast of Bulgaria. in an area known by the ancient Greeks as the haunted sea. It was a 13th century Venetian trading vessel laden with grain and textiles bound for Europe that earned Popenjoy his immortality – not a temple dig in Nepal. History was made 3600 miles from Kathmandu and Jerry Kosinsky missed it all.

Jerry had seen the small, wiry boy loitering outside the Tibetan Blue Café, strumming a guitar. He would catch Jerry's eye, smile and then look away diffidently until one day he was motioned over. His name was Ganesh and he was a 14-year old intrigued with all things American. They would talk and Jerry would give him a few rupees. Then, he would bow, smile shyly and quickly disappear.

Ganesh always seemed to show up when Jerry was on Freak Street or at one of the pie shops in Pig Alley. In his "Nepalese English," he told Jerry that there were bad people in Kathmandu and he would keep watch over him. Jerry was amused and patted Ganesh on the back.

There was a loud banging on Jerry's door and he heard the frantic voice of Ganesh telling him to open up. He had learned that the Carlyles had been arrested for drug smuggling and Jerry had been implicated as their courier. "It's impossible, Ganesh. They're book dealers. It must be a mistake," Jerry insisted. Ganesh was shaking his head and looked dour. "What is it, Ganesh?" Jerry asked. "She not his sister. I saw them together more than once in alley. They not kiss like brother and sister."

It was as if a bolt of lightning had struck Jerry and in a single moment purged his brain of all the mush that had accumulated there over the last several months. He thought about all the books he had mailed for them and was gripped by fear. If they weren't book dealers, what was in the packages? Jerry knew the answer but didn't want to accept it.

"No time to lose. Come with me now" Ganesh said. "I will hide you," he said, while pulling on Jerry's arm. One hour later, they were in a shack on the outskirts of Kathmandu.

It turned out that the drug smuggling Carlyles, man and wife, had also been dealing in forged travelers checks on the black market, an enterprise that first caught the attention of the local police. When an informant revealed that they were also smuggling Nepali temple balls out of Kathmandu inside of carved-out books, the police could not believe their good fortune. The temple balls were polished hashish spheres worth their weight in gold in the United States. It didn't matter to the Carlyles that Nepali Buddhists considered hashish a ritual sacrament. The dope dealer community was an inventive, creative group when it came to smuggling their precious cargoes out of Kathmandu. Someone else had come up with the idea to hide hashish in a jelly jar for resale in the West and it worked so well that the name "Kandahar Jam" caught on. The Carlyle scheme took a literary bent.

The Carlyles of the world had an almost unfathomable incentive – namely, that a $10/kilo price in Nepal for top grade hashish could be sold for $5000/kilo back in the United States. The Carlyles were two-bit operators in comparison to the big-time smugglers but they generated very handsome profits and, of course, Jerry Kosinsky, their innocent pawn, was oblivious to it all. It would take a while for him to accept that he had been groomed by Dickie and Leila Carlyle and that what he thought was his first sexual conquest had been a dope-dealing married woman who bedded him as part of her job.

Ganesh was a clever and resourceful kid. He liked Jerry Kosinsky and would not take advantage of him. With the Brits gone, Jerry was reluctant to call Prof. Eyesmore but knew that he couldn't put it off indefinitely. Then, he remembered the name of the individual at the British consulate provided by Popenjoy. He wrote a note to him and sent Ganesh on his behalf, hoping for the best. While he waited for a response, he snuck out at night and called Eyesmore.

WHEN GANESH WENT back to the consulate two days later, there was an envelope waiting for him. In it, there was an unsigned, hand-written note on plain paper which read: "Too late to help you. Turn yourself into the police and tell your side of the story."

When Ganesh heard the message, he cried out. "No, not good. You will be locked up for many years. I get you out of Kathmandu, Jerry. You innocent, I know, but I think you very stupid, yes? Must get you across the border or it all over with you. Not even Booch Cassidy or the Sundancing Kid can help you if you stay," he said with a broad grin, proud of his knowledge of the characters in the popular American movie.

That evening, Jerry shaved off his beard and mustache in preparation for the long donkey cart ride to the Nepal border town of Birgunj. Ganesh's family had relatives there who would sneak Jerry into the nearby town of Raxual, India. Once there, Jerry would be met by an emissary of Eyesmore who would accompany him on the train to New Delhi.

It was a long, hot trip across eastern India but Eyesmore's agent was phlegmatic, as if he shared the professor's disdain for the wayward student. When they arrived in New Delhi, Jerry was handed exit papers and an airline ticket with a destination of Stockholm. Eyesmore had worked furiously to arrange the paperwork for Jerry's flight. He would have left him in Kathmandu if he could but the professor had a reputation to protect.

CHAPTER FOUR:
FROM BAD TO WORSE

Jerry's contact in Sweden was Hugo Olafsson, a professor on the campus of Lund University in the coastal city of Malmo.

He would study under Professor Olafsson, who had been a visiting professor at Pythian ten years earlier and had co-authored numerous papers with Eyesmore. Olafsson lived alone and was a frequent sponsor of students from all over the world who wished to study abroad after completing college.

A short train ride from Stockholm brought Jerry to Malmo, the southwestern port town situated on the Oresund Strait separating Sweden from Denmark.

While the country was officially neutral during the Vietnam War, it was not hospitable to Americans in general even though many Swedes cut draft dodgers some slack. It didn't help that Jerry arrived in Malmo when a recession hit Sweden, destroying shipbuilding and manufacturing jobs. The locals were in no mood to humor an American.

Quickly discouraged by the lack of empathy and the language barrier, Jerry concluded that the Swedes were as icy as the breezes blowing into Malmo from the Baltic Sea. He missed the warmth and openness of Kathmandu before what he considered bad luck in friends had forced him to flee the country like a criminal. Prof. Olafsson, with whom he was now lodging, was open and engaging, even solicitous to a point that made Jerry uncomfortable. As a protégé of Eyesmore, Olafsson assured Jerry that he could stay indefinitely and things would get better once a course of study had been established.

One week into his stay, Jerry awoke near dawn to a strange sensation. Something was slithering, snake-like and warm, between his legs. He sat up abruptly and, throwing off the covers, saw a shadowy figure laying on the bed. Jerry flipped on the light and gawked at the naked professor posing on one elbow with a lascivious smile on his face. Jerry leapt up as Olafsson, with his free hand, beckoned him back to bed.

"*Dumhuvud*," Jerry screeched, deploying a slang word he had picked up upon his arrival in Stockholm when he bumped someone at the airport with his luggage. It was Swedish for a number of derogatory names – including asshole - but Jerry wasn't satisfied and added "faggot" for good measure. The professor scowled and backed off the bed and out of the room, watching Jerry intently to guard against any sudden attack.

LATER THAT DAY, Jerry was in a hostel on the outskirts of Malmo. He called Eyesmore and learned that Olafsson had already provided the professor with a lame excuse, even implying that Jerry had behaved suggestively earlier in the evening. Jerry was dumbfounded and outraged. In fact, Eyesmore had heard rumors about Olafsson's proclivities in the past and could no longer dismiss them.

"You let me down in Kathmandu, Kosinsky," Eyesmore shouted into the telephone. "Perhaps, I miscalculated and you can't flourish outside the protective academic cocoon. It's time to grow some backbone. You're no longer a damn kid." It pierced Jerry to the core. The professor had never called him by his last name before or spoken with such vitriol. The sympathy over the incident with Olafsson was short-lived. Eyesmore's voice was harsh and Jerry was too dumbfounded and chastened to react.

One week later, Jerry Kosinsky, dispirited and disillusioned, and still bewildered by the axiom that consequences are pitiless, arrived back in Toronto where he had begun his fanciful odyssey. It was 1971 and he was starting to question himself after four years on the run.

CHAPTER FIVE:
LEAVING TORONTO

~◯~

Jerry Kosinsky returned to North America at the age of 26, a troubled man with a broken spirit. On the long flight from Stockholm to Toronto, he looked out the window as the plane chased the fleeing sun. He thought back on his wasted years in Kathmandu and cursed himself, concluding that he had played the part of the self-inflated puppet to perfection.

Recalling the few intimacies with Leila Carlyle, he had to confess that her apparent attraction to him was all an act, just part of the job. While he was dallying with a married woman, he missed the chance to join the British team in the Baltics. When he groaned out loud, the passenger next to him asked if he was okay.

Jerry went to the bathroom, locked the door and wished he could stay there until the plane landed. He covered his mouth with both hands and, consumed by shame and self-pity, cursed his existence. The roar of the plane's engines muffled the outpouring of his grief.

~◯~

OTHER THAN THE draft board and the district attorney back in Parlor City, who was looking for Jerry Kosinsky? Who even suspected he was in Toronto? He had occasionally sent postcard to his parents from Kathmandu, Bangkok and Calcutta, ostensibly to let them know he was still alive but also to impress them. He felt guilty for his negligence and sent them a postcard from the Toronto airport. Maybe it would make them rest easier knowing he was so close to home. The war in Vietnam was still raging and he was still a criminal. He had just let four years of his life drift by in a fog with nothing to show for it.

AFTER HIS OUTBURST during the telephone call from Sweden, Eyesmore was now conciliatory and counselled patience. He reminded Jerry that he was still destined for great things but this time, the promise rang hollow.

Exactly what was Eyesmore's notion of great things? Throughout that summer of 1967, after his graduation from Pythian, when Jerry was in Parlor Harbor consumed with the fate of his best friend who might go to prison for life on trumped up murder charges, Eyesmore, in his calm and reasoned style, had warned Jerry that his life was at stake as well. Thinking back now, Eyesmore had shown no sympathy for Jerry's best friend – or him - during any of their conversations. When Woody was finally cleared, Eyesmore had pressed his argument and finally persuaded Jerry to cross the border into Canada.

Eyesmore had never explained to him, and he didn't ask, what the end game would be for a draft dodger like him. How and when could he return home? Would he be teaching at Pythian and someday be Eyesmore's successor? The professor had more than once implied such a future. Jerry laughed scornfully now at the impracticality of it all and wished he had been wise enough to ask back then, "So, Professor, Jerry Kosinsky is to be granted a PhD for resisting the draft, roaming the world, visiting ancient sites and writing up reports? Is that how it's going to work?"

Jerry said nothing of the sort and quickly realized that he had no choice but to stay in Toronto for the time being and find a way to start his life over – with or without the help of Prof. Eyesmore.

Jerry had settled somewhat comfortably in the Yorkville section of Toronto, a disparate community of American ex-pats whose initial motivation, above all else, despite the vocal posturing about the evils of war, was not to fight and die in Vietnam. It turned out that thousands of draft dodgers and deserters had decided to make Canada their new home with no intention of returning to the United States under any circumstances.

IT WASN'T LONG before Jerry's sedate if unrewarding existence in Toronto was disrupted. Prof. Eyesmore suffered a stroke that left him unable to speak. Already, unbeknownst to Jerry, Eyesmore's influence at Pythian College and elsewhere was waning. Now, his almost total incapacity left him helpless – not just to himself but anyone else. Jerry's application for the PhD program at York University, which seemed to be on the fast track, thanks to Eyesmore's influence, was no longer being considered. Jerry's dream of studying in Canada and then returning to Pythian as a lecturer or even as an associate professor evaporated overnight. In a startling flashback to 1967, Jerry saw himself crossing the New York border into Canada and shuddered.

Jerry audited some courses at York and picked up part-time work at a bookstore and a restaurant while the months drifted by.

IN 1974, PRES. Ford offered conditional amnesty to draft dodgers but with the caveat that two years of community service were required. Jerry was not prepared to give in yet, despite the pleadings of his father and the stern rebuke of his still authoritarian mother. To do so would be an admission that he had not only done something illegal but also a confession that he had no moral convictions. And so, Jerry Kosinsky hung on in Toronto and the weeks dragged on.

SITTING IN A pub one day in 1975, sipping a Molson Ale, Jerry heard the scratchy voice of Bob Seger singing "Katmandu" and almost fell off his stool. Under altered circumstances, the lyrics would have created a nostalgic moment but Jerry was wiser now and knew that he was lucky to get out of Nepal when he did. It made him think of Ganesh and smile.

A few years earlier, as Prof. Popenjoy had predicted, the Nepal government outlawed the buying and selling of cannabis, causing the cafes and hash shops around Freak Street to close down overnight. Hippies with expired visas were rounded up by the police in droves and those not arrested were trucked to the border and deported. To discourage additional hippie throngs, new dress codes for tourists were instituted. It wasn't just because of pressure from the United States and its new Drug Enforcement Administration. The people of Nepal had simply grown weary of the alien invaders.

"What, they don't sell Jenny Cream Ale north of the border?" Jerry heard the question and recognized the voice immediately, spinning around on his bar stool to face Woody Meacham. He jumped down and embraced his childhood friend in a prolonged bearhug. "How the hell did you ---------" Jerry blurted out before Woody Meacham waved him off.

"A little birdie told me you were in Toronto. Don't ask any questions, okay? Once I got here, it wasn't too difficult to find a big lug like you," Woody said. Jerry figured that his father had coughed up his whereabouts but didn't ask. He was overjoyed that he did.

The boys from Parlor City had a great deal of catching up to do after eight years and it would take time, more than one reunion. Not everything would come out right away. Woody started by telling Jerry about his time in Virginia after leaving the Army. He described Pudge McFadden, the Irishman who owned the pub where he worked for a few months, before he decided to head home to Parlor City for a visit. He left out the heartbreak story of Nellie Birdsong and his aborted attempt to rekindle a relationship that began years earlier.

Jerry regaled Woody with stories about Kathmandu and the colorful characters on Freak Street but left out his almost disastrous relationship with the Carlyles and his narrow escape from Nepal. And there was no mention of his brief sojourn in Sweden before his return to Toronto.

They both found it more comfortable to reminisce about those idyllic childhood days growing up in Parlor City, finding a gun in a park, their run-ins with wannabe teenage hood Rudy Gantz and his twin enforcers, the Clintock brothers. "Don't forget the calendar in my dad's workshop, Woody," Jerry said, punching his friend in the arm. Woody laughed. "Yeah, later on I pegged that day as the beginning of our growing up. We thought Marilyn Monroe was a goddess, a symbol of pure beauty and perfection, didn't we? How long has she been dead? And the revelation that she was JFK's mistress, wow."

The old stories and cajoling went on into the wee hours and ended with Woody sprawled on the couch in Jerry's apartment for the remainder of the night. The next morning, the two were sober and serious.

"I'm not coming back right now, Woody. It doesn't feel right doing community service under Ford's plan. It essentially means that I confess to doing something wrong. Just not ready to do that."

"Listen, I came up here to make sure you were okay – and you are. Sure, I'd like you back home but understand it has to be on your terms. But at least now I know where to find you. Eight years of silence is long enough," Woody said.

BEFORE WOODY LEFT Toronto, it was agreed that he would talk to Jerry's parents and reassure them that their son was okay. During his drive north, Woody had made the decision to join the Parlor City police force. He hadn't informed his stepfather yet but Billy Meacham, Jr. would be ecstatic when he heard the news.

"So, the tradition continues, kid, and that's good, but you realize that it's one more reason why I need to stay in Toronto a while longer," said Jerry. Woody looked puzzled and Jerry laughed. "Hey, I don't relish the thought of walking back into Parlor City and having you slap handcuffs on me."

IT WAS EARLY in 1976 when the saucy and flirtatious Missy Grisham arrived in Toronto and Jerry's life perked up. She had come north after graduating from Vassar College, a pampered, trust fund debutante from Greenwich, Connecticut in search of adventure. Unlike some of her sisters at Kappa Kappa Gamma, becoming a rock band groupie was not the ticket for Missy. She had been an inveterate war protester on campus and was now on the hunt for a draft dodger she could call her own. Missy's parents were apoplectic but she was defiant – and could afford to be. She was an adult now, at least legally, and the trust fund left by her grandmother was inviolate.

It didn't take long for her to corral the vulnerable Jerry Kosinsky. Missy Grisham helped assuage Jerry's bitter disappointment but she wasn't enough to sustain him. He grew moody and despondent, causing the effervescent Missy to look elsewhere for companionship. When she cheerfully announced that she was moving to a commune in Vancouver with one Leo Skimpole, Jerry felt shock and relief at the same time. He protested weakly but Missy was undeterred. "We're going to have a family of war resisters, Jerry," Missy said, while patting her stomach and smiling broadly, adding enthusiastically, "He's not just some draft dodger, Jerry. He's a deserter, the real deal." Jerry looked at her dumbfounded and Missy pouted. "You don't want me here when the baby comes, now do you? It's probably not yours," she said, looking down with feigned modesty.

It was the Spring of 1977, two years after Woody's visit, and Jerry Kosinsky had his pardon after a decade on the run. Pres. Carter offered unconditional amnesty right after he took office and Jerry, convicted of draft evasion *in absentia* while in Kathmandu, was now free to return to the United States.

For many of those in Toronto who Jerry got to know, feelings of vindication were expressed after Carter's amnesty edict. Many were bitter and defiant but for Jerry it was more a sense of relief – and the fact that he had his freedom back.

With Eyesmore warehoused in a nursing home, drooling and incoherent, and Missy producing babies for the cause in Vancouver, Jerry felt increasingly unmoored. The old-timers and veterans in Parlor City would shun him but he decided that he wanted to go home.

NOT EVERYONE LIVING in exile would get pardoned and not everyone wanted to leave Canada. Those who were AWOL were not eligible for Pres. Carter's grand gesture. Soldiers on the run would face court martial proceedings if they were caught reentering the country. One such deserter was Percy Hoole. When he heard that Jerry was leaving the Yorkville conclave to return to the United States, he came to him with an urgent request.

Percy explained that no one in the family had heard from his father for several days. He had traveled from their Vermont home down to Connecticut to check on a quarry operation he co-owned with a local investor. There was some issue with the business partner but he didn't know the details. The local police said there were no reports of highway accidents and no hospital admissions in the area. The father had simply vanished.

"He's a good man, with the proverbial heart of gold, Jerry," Percy said. "After my older brother died in Nam and I took off from Ft. Dix, halfway through boot camp, my mom had a nervous breakdown. With me here, he's all she's got. There's no way he would abandon her. If I go looking for him ………" Hoole's voice trailed off but Jerry understood.

"I need to spend a few days at home first, then I'll go over to Vermont to see your mother before driving down to

Connecticut. You understand, I'm no detective so it may be futile. I'll do it but you are going to have to give me more information," Jerry said.

Percy gave Jerry a picture of his parents and explained that his mother had called the business partner, Elwyn Grex, who insisted that the father had never showed up. Jerry learned that the quarry was located at a place called the Thimble Islands off the Connecticut coast. The partners had actually bought the island and the quarry came with it. Somewhat hesitantly, Percy explained his father's infatuation in recent years with the legend of Capt. Kidd. "He always joked that Kidd's buried treasure would be discovered one day and he had a dream that it would be on his island."

Percy stopped and let it all sink in. Jerry didn't want to say it but couldn't help thinking that perhaps the father had entered a fantasy land, a second childhood. He remembered reading about Capt. Kidd when he was a child but the details were sketchy. And of course, there was *Treasure Island*. It was over twenty years since Jerry had read the Stevenson classic and the thought of it brought back fond childhood memories when he was comfortably ensconced in the Parlor City Public Library surrounded by piles of books. Had Kidd really anchored off the coast of Connecticut and buried treasure there, Jerry wondered? Had the father gone looking for it and met with disaster? Of course, there was the possibility that the father had gone off the deep end and simply taken off, leaving all his cares behind him.

BEFORE HE LEFT Toronto, Jerry wrote a letter to Phineas Popenjoy, now an emeritus professor at the University of Leicester. In it, he acknowledged that he had done the right thing in leaving him behind in Kathmandu, depriving him of participating in the historic Black Sea expedition. He had missed a momentous opportunity and could no longer deny it. It was a humbling admission but Jerry felt that a blackmark on his reputation had been at least partially expunged when he dropped the letter in the mailbox.

THE NEXT DAY, Jerry took the bus across the border and transferred in Buffalo for the rest of the trip to Parlor City. It was late May and he was entering the United States for the first time in over a decade with no clue how to restart his life. He would have a long talk with his old friend, Woody Meacham, certain he would give him sound advice. Woody had joined the police force and was already rapidly moving up the ranks.

He felt a little foolish but he had promised to go looking for Percy Hoole's father and he would keep his commitment. He gazed out the bus window and laughed when he tried to picture the Thimble Islands. It sounded like some place out of a fairy tale, a land inhabited by miniature people, like the munchkins that populated Oz. And what did that make Jerry, a modern day version of Robinson Crusoe preparing to descend among the Lilliputians?

Jerry Kosinsky had spent a decade on the lam, tossed off ten years of his life with nothing to show for it except for some articles on Nepal's ancient treasures for which he didn't even receive academic credit or even a byline. What did it signify to take a few weeks or even a month to go off on what was most likely a wild goose chase to a place called the Thimble Islands?

CHAPTER SIX:
Picaresque Man

~~

Jerry stayed with his parents the first few days back in Parlor City but his mother, who had made such an outward display of affection and compassion in front of others when he was on the run, turned autocratic and caustic in the confines of her domain, as she had been all through his youth. Some of the town folk who did recognize him shrugged, stared or glowered when he walked by on the street. His father warned him that he would be a pariah for many, especially the older veterans. One straggly-haired man wearing an olive-green army jacket looked at him fiercely and gave him the finger. Did he know him from high school or was it more likely that the word was out that a draft dodger had the temerity to return to the town that he had fled? He had that wild look that Jerry had seen at times with the stoners wandering aimlessly around Freak Street. "I guess he won't be inviting me to the VFW for beers," Jerry mumbled darkly.

He was galumphing around, partly due to his depressed state of mind, his oafishness the outward manifestation of his troubled spirit. He had lost the self-confidence that had been nurtured at Pythian College and which he had brought with him to Kathmandu ten years earlier at the commencement of his grand adventure. A presidential pardon turned out to be more of an albatross in Parlor City than Jerry expected and he knew he had to get away as quickly as possible.

After a few tortuous days at home, Jerry was sleeping on Woody's couch. During the day, he retreated to the one place where he found solitude all through his childhood, the Parlor City Public Library. He spent hours researching the history of the Thimble Islands and their formation off the Connecticut coast during the Ice Age. The granite rocks became home for migrating seals as well as terns, plovers and osprey. The Mattabesec Indians called the islands *Kuttomquosh* – or "beautiful sea rocks." If the legend was true, the islands were eventually named by early settlers after the thimbleberry, a rarely seen fruit akin to a black raspberry.

The granite quarry on one of the islands first opened in 1852 and produced the seemingly indestructible stone with the distinctive pinkish hue that would be used to build the Lincoln Memorial, the Brooklyn Bridge, Grant's Tomb, the Statue of Liberty and many other historic structures. When train and trolley services commenced along the Connecticut coast, the Thimble Islands became a popular tourist destination. Even President Taft maintained a summer home there in the early 1900s.

Jerry also took time to research Capt. William Kidd who, it turned out, even had one of the Thimble Islands named after him, even though the Scotsman's connection to the Connecticut coastal islands might be questionable. Jerry remembered the comment by Percy in Toronto about his father being a dreamer so he understood how Ellis Hoole might be intrigued by such a swash-buckling character. Maybe the father imagined that Kidd had buried treasure near his quarry and was searching for it when some sort of tragedy ensued. Maybe he actually found something. Could that explain his disappearance?

Reading up on Kidd and the Thimble Islands energized Jerry

for his trip. Yes, he was on a mission to locate Percy's father but he would spend some time exploring the area even if he didn't get to see all of the islands in the archipelago. "365 islands. Guess I'll have to stay a year," he chuckled to himself.

INITIALLY RELUCTANT, JERRY was convinced to spend one evening with Woody's stepfather. Billy Meacham, Jr. had resigned as chief of the Parlor City police shortly after Woody joined the force. Billy's excuse was arthritic knees but those who knew him well felt certain that he had tired of the increasing bureaucracy and, most importantly, would not have his stepson's career tainted by even a hint of nepotism. He was still, and always would be, revered in town as the "boy wonder" detective who had solved several crimes that had rocked the city in the 1950s – not to mention exonerated his stepson when he was framed for murder in 1967 in the family vacation town of Parlor Harbor.

Billy could see that Jerry's "homecoming" was weighing heavily on him and the Korean War fighter pilot was not one to pile on. He objected to Jerry fleeing to Canada but his views on the Vietnam War had changed since then. That conflict was certainly nothing like the two world wars to save the world from tyranny. Even the Korean War was viewed as a necessary step to thwart the spread of communism in Asia but this poorly-executed and politicized Vietnam debacle, and that's how Meacham came to see it, had riven the country. As a result, he had gradually come to agree with Pres. Carter's pardon edict. "The country's moving on, Jerry, and so must you. Woody tells me you have a bit of a detective assignment on your hands down in Connecticut. Hey, you weren't so bad back there in Parlor Harbor in '67 when I needed your assistance tracking down Rudy Gantz and his boys on that tourist boat. Gantz didn't last long in Strathmore. I thought he might eventually die in prison but the Mexican cartel wasted little time in getting to him. You take their drugs and you pay the ultimate price.

"Anyway, help that friend out in Toronto and I promise that you will feel better just for making the effort. If you get stuck, give us a call." Meacham stood up slowly on cranky knees and wrapped his right arm around Jerry's shoulders while walking him to the door. It wasn't a full bear hug but it was enough.

It was Memorial Day and the parade festivities would dominate downtown Parlor City with its salutes to the veterans who had fought in that century's wars, many of whom still called it Decoration Day even if Congress had mandated a name change in 1971. There would be some war protesters but they would be quickly shuttled off by edict of the town elders. Jerry had no argument with either side but without urging by either Woody or Billy decided to stay inside that day and avoid provocation. Jerry had shown discretion but it saddened him when he heard the booming sound of the marching bands and the cheers of the crowd. It had always been a day of delight when he was growing up but that was all past now. It was time that he moved on.

AFTER A WEEK in Parlor City, Jerry borrowed a beat-up 1966 Ford police cruiser that Woody Meacham had acquired at auction and hit the road. Before he left, his father handed him a fat roll of bills wound tightly with a rubber band. "Been saving this for you, son," he said before they hugged.

Eschewing the main highway, Jerry drove east on country roads through a series of small New York towns, many of which memorialized the state's heritage and its early citizens. He recalled 7th grade New York State history class as he passed through Pompey, named after the Roman general and statesman. He stopped in Nelson for coffee and learned that it had been named for the famed English admiral Lord Nelson who died at the Battle of Trafalgar during the Napoleonic Wars.

After leaving Nelson, Jerry decided that he would be in no hurry as he meandered over the forgotten roads that were the backbone of the colonies, the main thoroughfares during a time that was so vital to the establishment of the eventual union. His next stop was West Winfield, named after General Winfield Scott, a hero of the War of 1812 and later Commander In Chief of the Army. In 1852, he was the Whig candidate for president, losing to Franklin Pierce. The townspeople wanted to name their village Scott but the name was already taken so they settled on Winfield. Today, who could name this brave man and who would reverence his exploits, Jerry wondered? And if Winfield Scott was long forgotten, except by scholars, historians and few locals, what did that foretell for him?

Further on, he came upon a giant teepee that seems to appear out of nowhere on the outskirts of Cherry Valley, where Samuel Morse tested and developed his telegraph machine. It was also the site of a horrific massacre during the Revolutionary War where residents were slaughtered by British loyalists, with the support of Iroquois Indian tribes.

He made a pit stop in the village of Esperance, long enough to learn that in 1818 it was named for the French word meaning "hope". He imagined that the settlers needed a large dose of it back then and for some reason it spurred Jerry on.

When he saw the sign for Howe's Cavern, Jerry suddenly detoured south toward the village of Cobleskill. He had always meant to go back to this "cave of wonders" since his childhood excursion in 1955 with his cub scout troop. It was the genesis of his interest in geology and archeology but he didn't know it then. He was simply in awe of nature.

Jerry leafed through the brochure describing the history of the glowing limestone walls dating back to the Silurian and Devonian periods of the earth's formation. First explored by

Lester Howe in 1842, it was described by some as a "subterranean palace", a netherworld worthy of the pagan gods. Jerry was mesmerized and yearned for those simpler, childhood days. He wanted to linger in the caverns but he was a man on a mission and so he moved on.

Jerry turned back north and headed to Saratoga Springs, for two centuries known as the "Queen of the Spas." Well-heeled socialites made the trek regularly from Boston and New York City to "take the cure" in the only naturally carbonated mineral waters east of the Rocky Mountains. Jerry was more intrigued by the fissures that created the springs during the Paleozoic Era and vowed to return to do some in-depth research.

The next day, Jerry arrived at Port Kent, a hamlet on the New York side of Lake Champlain. Amtrak had just opened a seasonal station for vacationers going across the lake to Vermont. The Adirondack, as the train was known, went from New York City to Montreal in 11 hours. Jerry stopped and picked up a train schedule, curious about the towns along the route and saw that Rouses Point was a few stops north of Port Kent. It was at Rouses Point where Jerry had crossed the border into Canada a decade earlier, excited about beginning his odyssey of hope. "Esperance," he said aloud, in a self-mocking tone.

That afternoon, Jerry took the car ferry across the majestic Lake Champlain, the site of the Battle of Valcour Island. Valcour was not visible that day and Jerry knew nothing of its history as a strategic island during the Revolutionary War and the War of 1812. Two hundred years later, it was a tranquil retreat, a popular place to anchor your boat while sailing on its historic waters.

Within an hour, he was back on shore, just south of Burlington, Vermont. Jerry had been energized by his two-day trip from Parlor City and each stop along the way has instilled in him a sense of humility. Prof. Eyesmore had built him up all the way back to his undergraduate years at Pythian College and, with little or no self-reflection, he had drunk it all in. Woody's stepfather was right. It was time that he step outside himself and do something for someone else. He was no Winfield Scott or Samuel Morse but he had something to prove – if only to himself.

JERRY KEPT THE promise to Percy Hoole that he would stop in Burlington to see the mother before heading down to the Thimble Islands, if only to reassure her that someone was trying to help the family. Mrs. Hoole was a meek, retiring woman. She sat with her legs close together and her elbows on her lap as she clutched a handkerchief with both hands. A cane leaned against her chair. It almost seemed that she was too overly guarded for a frail, lonely woman who was anxious to get help in finding her missing husband. After an awkward hour, Jerry learned that her husband was in charge of finances for the quarry and he was concerned that the partner might be embezzling funds. He was going down to confront him.

"He called from some place called the Brightwood Motel outside of New Haven. It was last Friday, to be exact. He sounded nervous about how the partner, a man named Grex, would react. Apparently, he has a bad temper. He was checking out the next morning and would be in touch. That's the last time I heard his dear voice."

Back in the car, Jerry drove south through Vermont, thinking of Longfellow's poem about the "forest primeval" as he gazed at the abundant pines and hemlocks in swarms along the highway. Everything he had seen since leaving Parlor City seemed to be taking him back to prelapsarian times.

When he crossed the border into Connecticut, Jerry wondered if he was on a futile mission. He had made a commitment and would do his best to find any information that would shed light on the whereabouts of Ellis Hoole. Woody had laughed at his childhood friend when he expressed his reservations and had simply echoed what his stepfather had said. "It'll do you good to get away from here. Maybe you'll forget about yourself for a while and stumble upon something worthwhile."

CHAPTER SEVEN:
A LITTLE ENCOURAGEMENT GOES A LONG WAY

THAT EVENING, JERRY checked into the run-down Brightwood Motel on a frontage road just outside of New Haven, Connecticut where Ellis Hoole had stayed the last night anyone in his family had heard from him. The dim bulb over the office door gave off just enough light to reveal a line of cabins in dire need of repair. He wondered if the dilapidated structure had ever lived up to its name.

The lanky, pimply-faced night clerk with the sullen expression was slouched over a comic book called *Inhumans* and looked up dead-faced. He acted offended when Jerry asked when Hoole had checked out. "The constable's office up in Graniteville called here and asked for that information. Of course, it was official business so we gave it to them," he said with a smirk, returning to his comic.

Jerry wanted to throttle the clerk but just scowled. He had studied a map and knew that Graniteville was a coastal village only ten miles north that overlooked the Thimble Islands. After his inauspicious start with the mother and the motel clerk, Jerry was tempted to call the Meachams for help.

THE NEXT MORNING, Jerry walked up the creaky steps of the Thimbletown Inn in Graniteville, catching his shoe on a raised nail and stumbling forward before regaining his balance. A porch wrapped around two sides of the white, clapboard structure and Jerry noticed that the floor sloped down as if it was completing its own aging process.

As Jerry opened the screen door, he looked to his right and saw an elderly man with snow white hair and matching beard sitting in a rocking chair. He was smoking a pipe and the only sign of life was a slight sucking in motion of the cheeks which produced puffs of smoke that billowed toward the roof of the porch. Then, Jerry noticed the old man's head was tilted slightly down as he stared into the book open on his lap. "That's me some day, hopefully," Jerry mused to himself as he opened the door.

Jerry had visited the Graniteville constable's office first thing that morning and the girl sitting at a desk near the door was more helpful than the insolent motel clerk. She confirmed the wife's story that Hoole had stayed at the Brightwood Motel and checked out the day after speaking on the telephone with his wife. As Jerry was leaving the station, the girl smiled and said, "You could check down at the Thimbletown Inn. Everybody going out to one of the islands passes through there at one time or another. They have a great little café. Who knows, maybe Hoole ate there on occasion."

The Thimbletown Inn had a café on the right side overlooking Long Island Sound and a sitting area to the left. The walls were paneled and stained a deep mahogany. Along with the heavy, dark curtains and the dim lighting, Jerry felt like he was entering a cavern. Upstairs, there were a dozen rooms with the prized ones overlooking the water. Jerry wondered if Hoole had checked in here after leaving the Brightwood Motel, possibly using an alias. He chuckled to himself as he looked around. "Here I go, getting conspiratorial with absolutely no proof," he said to himself.

When he approached the desk, a middle-aged woman with a name tag that read "Tillie" looked up and smiled warmly. Yes, Tillie had heard about Ellis Hoole but was certain he had not checked into the Inn under his own or any other name. And if he ate breakfast in the café, she would have noticed.

"Everyone around here is talking about the finger," she said animatedly. Jerry had a quizzical look on his face so Tillie told him the story about the schoolgirl who trapped a finger in her netting during a field trip to DeCourcy Island a few days earlier. "They sent the finger up to the state crime lab for examination. It's the darndest mystery we've ever had down here. Why -----." Tillie stopped and looked past Jerry to the screen door while cupping one hand over her mouth. Jerry turned to see the white-haired man puffing on his pipe, sending up smoke signals.

Tillie lowered her head and started moving papers around the front desk. As Jerry started to talk, she held up her hand to stop him. Jerry looked back and the white-haired man was gone. As Jerry started to walk away, Tillie said, "I always talk too much, even to strangers. If there's anything to know, you best speak with Cyrus. I'm sorry."

"So, where do I find this Cyrus?" Jerry asked softly. "You were just looking at him. He's my brother, Cyrus Trowbridge. We own this place. He knows everything that happens in Graniteville but says little – especially to strangers. Sometimes he reminds me that I do enough talking for the both of us. And I'll warn you now, if you call him Cy, you won't hear a peep out of him even if you wait until the cows come home."

Jerry looked to his left as the screen door clapped loudly behind him. It made him jump but the old man, back in his prior pose, book open and pipe emitting a steady upward stream of smoke, didn't seem to notice. Jerry was intimidated and his first inclination was to walk away. Then, he stopped. It was only a few days and he was already at a dead-end in his search for Ellis Hoole. Shrugging, he decided that he had nothing to lose.

Jerry slowly approached the old man, cleared his throat and said, almost obsequiously, "I'm here on behalf of the Hoole family. The father has disappeared and anything you might know about his whereabouts would be greatly appreciated." He watched as the cheeks puckered and smoke ascended from the bowl of the pipe. Otherwise, the old man's face was immutable.

Exasperated and intimidated at the same time, Jerry was ready to turn away when he looked down at the book on the old man's lap. It was closed now and Jerry could see that it was *The Invisible Pyramid* by Loren Eiseley. "I read it in college. It changed my life," Jerry said haltingly. There was still no acknowledgment from the old man so Jerry turned away dispirited when he heard, "Find the blonde and you'll find the father."

Jerry looked back and noticed that the book was open again and the old man's pipe was furiously pumping smoke. He wasn't going to push his luck but he did say, "Thank You, Sir," before continuing down the steps.

No one would have noticed but Jerry had a slight bounce in his step and the faintest of smiles on his lips as he got into his car. He had something to build on – a mysterious blonde, no less. He was happy that he hadn't called the Meachams so soon. "Who knows," he said under his breath, "Maybe I won't need anyone's help after all."

CHAPTER EIGHT:
JERRY STARTS DIGGING

~~

AFTER LEAVING THE Thimbletown Inn, Jerry stopped at a nearby drug store and bought the local paper along with the *New Haven Beagle*, quickly spotting the story about the severed finger caught in the netting on the shore of DeCourcy Island. There was a grainy photograph of a young woman walking away with the caption: "Get lost. I have no comment."

Jerry spotted a telephone booth in the back and called the Thimbletown Inn. He recognized Tillie's voice and since he hadn't given her his name earlier, she had no idea who he was. He could have gone back to make the reservation in person but that would have been an opportunity for her to make some lame excuse and say they were booked up. Also, he was reluctant to confront Cyrus again so soon. Tillie was clearly cowed by her brother so Jerry expected very little else from her after the warning stare she received.

Jerry wasn't automatically buying Tillie's pronouncement that Cyrus was the oracle of Graniteville. Perhaps, she was confusing stoicism with wisdom. In any event, Jerry speculated that his comment about the Eiseley book had most likely broken the ice with Cyrus and given him some credibility in the old man's eyes. For his part, he decided that anyone who read Eiseley must be a person who had a curiosity about the origin of life and thought deeply about things.

What about the blonde that Cyrus mentioned? His tone seemed to suggest that Hoole had run off with her or that they were holed up somewhere. Maybe on one of the Thimble Islands? If so, it would be a time-consuming task to find them. And hideaway for what reason? It just didn't make sense to Jerry. He did know, however, that sooner or later he had to take a boat out to the Quarry Island and talk to the business partner.

As he thought of the blonde, Jerry had a flashback to when he was just 12-years old and snuck a peek at the Marilyn Monroe calendar in his father's workshop. Woody had reminded him about that incident when he came to Toronto, how they trembled with unfamiliar feelings as they ogled the goddess, lying on red velvet, in her birthday suit. Then, he recalled the blonde vixen who came to Parlor City when he was just a kid. She was somehow involved in a murder and extortion racket uncovered by then Det. Billy Meacham, Jr. The memory of it, vague as it was, gave Jerry a sudden chill.

JERRY DROVE BACK to the Graniteville constable's office, now prepared to ask questions. He wanted to quiz the girl about the mystery blonde but now she looked stern and quipped, "Sorry, on-going investigation" as someone walked by.

When Jerry turned away, he heard "psst" and looked back to see the girl smiling as she whispered, "That was Deputy Constable Buffle, a real pant load. Everything is hush hush with him. He says we don't talk to outsiders." Jerry nodded, thinking of Cyrus. "Look, if I were you, I'd pay a visit to Gretchen Cadwallader. She volunteers at the DeCourcy Institute part-time but her job is at the New Haven public library. Some sort of historian – or whatever. She was right there when the schoolgirl spotted the finger in the netting. She's out here quite often as a volunteer. Maybe she saw Hoole or the blonde around town. It's a long shot but worth a try, right?"

"Is she a blonde? You can't tell from the picture in the paper," Jerry asked. The girl looked quizzical and then shrugged before saying loudly, "Get lost. I told you I can't give out confidential information." Jerry was momentarily stunned but caught on when he looked across the room and saw Buffle staring menacingly at him, hands on his hips, as if he might have to draw his gun at any moment. Jerry knew to play along. He huffed and said, "Thanks for nothing" and stalked out of the office.

JERRY DROVE OVER to the Brightwood Motel on his way to New Haven and sat in his car in front of a cabin with a cleaning cart parked in front. When the maid came out, he quickly approached her and pulled out the picture of Ellis Hoole. "Remember him? I'm a friend of the family. He's gone missing and they're terribly concerned," he said in his most sympathetic voice.

She was wearing a front and back pullover apron, a drab gray shirt and stained gray sweatpants. The gloomy expression on her face matched her outfit. Her hair was in a net and Jerry could see an unsightly mishmash of mossy green strands mixed in with dirty brown locks. Not the kind of nest anyone would attempt to run their fingers through. A Virginia Slim cigarette was hanging precariously from her mouth, forcing Jerry to suppress a chuckle. He had seen the magazine ads and commercials for the cigarette depicting beautiful, stylish professional women on the go. If anything, the maid was a parody of the image the manufacturer was trying to portray. He wondered from which cabin she had lifted the cigarettes.

The maid stood mute and stared out of slit eyes until Jerry

pulled a $5 bill out of his wallet and dangled it in front of her. "Did you see him at all? Did anyone visit his room?" Jerry asked softly.

The maid stared at the money and her eyes opened a little wider. Even the Virginia Slim perked up. "I didn't see nobody come or go – just caught a glimpse of him once. After he checked out, I found a hairbrush that he left in the room. I took it but will call you a goddam lying bastard if you repeat it. Now, can I have the fin?" Her voice was raspy and low as she reached out and grabbed the end of the bill. Jerry smiled and let go.

"As I said, you ain't getting the hairbrush. It doesn't exist, if you catch my drift. But I do got something else that might interest you." The maid went to her cart and came back with a book. "You can have it for $2 more. Found it under the bed," she explained, dangling it out in front of her. It was *The Gold Bug* by Edgar Allen Poe. Jerry had read *The Pit and the Pendulum* and *The Murder in the Rue Morgue* in junior high school but never heard of this story. He knew it could be a con but for $2 he was willing to take a chance. Poe was worth at least that much.

The maid smirked and pushed her cart to the next cabin. Jerry would have liked to get his hands on that hairbrush if for no other reason than to have tangible proof that he was making progress. He imagined the maid going home that night and taking off her net before using her purloined hairbrush. It made him wince.

Jerry sat in his car and pulled out the picture of Ellis Hoole to confirm what he already knew. Why in hell would a bald man – with only a very modest fringe of short-cropped, grey hair around the circumference of his head - need with a hairbrush? Jerry grinned. He was starting to feel like a detective. Hey, maybe Poe will inspire me to keep digging, he said to himself as he pulled out of the parking lot.

As Jerry drove to the New Haven Public Library, he wondered if this Gretchen Cadwallader would even be working on a Saturday. He had already decided that the mystery blonde mentioned by Cyrus had been in Hoole's room at the Brightwood Motel. The father certainly didn't look like a Don Juan type and Jerry had trouble imagining some sort of sexual liaison – unless it involved a "lady of the night."

The front desk lady at the library directed Jerry to the rare book room where Gretchen Cadwallader worked. Looking through the glass panels, there didn't appear to be anyone else inside except for a girl, probably in her mid-twenties he guessed, with rounded cheeks and a clear complexion. She had chestnut hair cut just below the ears and curled in at the ends, exposing a pristine alabaster neck. The hair was lush and the neck was enticing – but she wasn't blonde.

Jerry explained his mission and Gretchen listened intently but with a skeptical look on her face. "So, some broad at the constable's office sent you down here because one of my students found a finger and my picture was in the paper? That's it?" She puckered her lips and squinched while holding up her hands with the palms facing out, as if to emphasize her annoyance.

Jerry was flummoxed and gulped before saying, "Look, I read the article that went with the picture of you and it gave the impression that you are around the islands quite a bit. So, I took the chance that you might have seen him. I'm trying to do a favor for a friend who is out of the country and can't come down here himself. All I've got so far is a motel where he stayed, an Inn where he might have eaten and some blonde he might have shacked up with. The locals aren't talking so, as I said, I took a chance coming down here." Jerry's earnestness seemed to have some effect.

"Hey, I'm sorry. It's been a rough day and I've got some

cataloging to finish up. Sometimes I can be a bitch. If you want to hang around, we can have a beer after work. I'll tell you everything I know. There's a new Irish pub a few blocks over on State. It's called Pudge McFadden's. Say around 5:30?"

Gretchen was standing up now. Her face had softened and she had an engaging smile which revealed perfectly-aligned teeth right up to the gum line. Jerry noticed the tight-fitting jeans, a little too snug on her plump but curvaceous frame but enticing all the same. She might not be drop dead gorgeous but she was cute. A spirited girl with brains. Yeah, temperamental but still worth pursuing, Jerry said to himself.

JERRY HAD SEVERAL hours before he could meet Gretchen at Pudge McFadden's so he decided to continue his research on Capt. Kidd. If he could find solid evidence that Kidd was indeed in Connecticut – and on the Thimble Islands in particular – it would help explain Hoole's apparent fascination with the Scotsman and might provide a clue, no matter how sketchy, about the father's whereabouts. Jerry's stomach was growling. He would grab some lunch and then head for the library stacks.

CAPT. WILLIAM KIDD lived the good life in New York City when he wasn't enticed by another sea adventure. He married a rich widow, lived in a mansion on Wall Street and even enjoyed the prestige of owning a pew at Trinity Church. But his greatest passion was as a privateer.

A perspicacious man, Kidd planned ahead and was alleged to have hidden booty in various places, including the islands off the coast of Connecticut and New York.

It was Kidd's misfortune to be on the high seas when the distinction between privateer and pirate blurred. He had left England somewhat of a hero with patrons and financial backers in high places who shared in the wealth that privateers could seize. When he commandeered a ship owned by Mukhlis Khan, then the Great Mogul of the Indian Empire, it was a fatal mistake. Khan complained to the British government and, eager to stay on good terms with him, Kidd was quickly branded a pirate. It was a classic double cross.

Kidd's last days on earth in 1701 were in Newgate prison in London, a far cry from his opulent mansion in New York. After his capture in the colonies, he was sent to England where he was found guilty of piracy and murder. On the day set for his hanging, the chaplain found Kidd drunk and incoherent in his cell to the point that he was almost incapacitated.

At the gallows, the rope broke and Kidd fell into the mud as the crowd cheered. He was hung again, this time successfully, after which his body was placed in a cage overlooking the Thames River. His fetid, rotting corpse was a warning to other would-be or aspiring pirates. For years, the bones hung over the river even as the memory of Capt. William Kidd faded from the memory of most Londoners.

AFTER RESEARCHING KIDD, Jerry opened up *The Gold Bug* and breezed through the novella in less than an hour. In it, a servant finds a scrap of paper with a code that reveals the location of Kidd's buried treasure. Poe invented the word cryptology for his story and used it to effectively advance the plot. It was *The Gold Bug*, not his other stories so well-known to schoolchildren, that made Poe an international sensation and generated huge audiences when he went on a lecture tour.

Jerry found it a compelling read. The main character,

William Legrand, might well have been the first cryptographer in literature. If not, it was still fascinating how he de-coded the ancient parchment in his successful effort to locate Kidd's buried plunder.

Of course, it was fantastic but had Hoole been taken in by it all? A businessman, part owner of a quarry with valuable rock deposits, fixated on a fairy tale-like story at a time when he is suspicious of his partner? Sure, it featured a real-life privateer in Kidd – a pirate if you prefer – but the notion that something valuable might be discovered in the Thimble Islands seemed preposterous. Legrand's best friend in the story thought he was delusional right up to the moment the treasure was found. Was Hoole, like Legrand, crazy like a fox or some misguided dolt looking for a little adventure?

WHEN JERRY CHECKED his watch, he was surprised to see that it was a few minutes before 5. The hours had flown by, as they always did when he was in a library. He decided to head over to Pudge McFadden's and loosen up with a pint of Guinness before Gretchen showed up. He hoped she wasn't in a foul mood.

CHAPTER NINE:
PUDGE MCFADDEN'S

~~

When Jerry walked into Pudge McFadden's, he was greeted at the door by a life-size plastic leprechaun, grinning and tipping his hat. The leer on his lips suggested that he had just polished off a few pints. The walls were Kelly green and thick with white shamrocks, cascading down like snowflakes. Pipe and fiddle music was emanating from the sound system. It was tacky, not what Jerry expected, even though he wasn't sure what an authentic Irish pub was supposed to look like.

It appeared to him that the place was prepared for a perpetual St. Patrick's Day party – American style. Jerry looked ahead and spotted the bartender in a white shirt set off by green arm bands and a matching hat. The paste-on red beard completed the comical ensemble. Shortly, he would be subjected to a fake brogue.

Sitting at the bar, it came to him. When Woody made his visit to Toronto, he mentioned that it was at Pudge McFadden's in Alexandria, Virginia where his rekindled relationship with Nellie Birdsong came to an abrupt and unexpected end. He had a feeling that his friend was still not over Nellie after all these years. He remembered their kibitzing back in Parlor Harbor that summer of 1967 when they debated good-naturedly whether or not Nellie was more like Joni Mitchell or Jackie DeShannon. Yeah, maybe we're both still chasing those youthful dreams of the idealized girl and just won't let go, he said to himself.

IF PUDGE MCFADDEN had walked into the New Haven saloon bearing his name, he might have croaked. There was such a man, now in his 50s, who had opened an eponymous "shot and beer" bar in the Old Town section of Alexandria, Virginia some years ago. The place became popular and he expanded his little empire to five Irish pubs in the Washington, DC area. When he caught the eye of a visiting Texas entrepreneur with a vision – and plenty of papa's oil money to throw at it – the offer to sell was too lucrative to turn down. Within a few years, the new owner had franchised the Pudge McFadden concept of an "authentic" Irish bar to eager restauranteurs in several cities around the country.

It was the Texan's idea to sell franchises in college towns and there he had been prescient. Another nascent chain, TGI Friday's, was growing like gangbusters and starting to dominate the big city singles market. This Lone Star entrepreneur had similar ambitions for a Pudge McFadden's near every major university campus.

Pudge had his regrets when he heard from an old friend in Philadelphia that his homely pubs – with the obligatory picture of an old Irish shebeen over every bar – had been turned into caricatures of the ebullient but always besotted Irishman. He told the friend that the cowboy had turned his joint into "McPub" and he was embarrassed. Pudge had walked away with a cool $1M to assuage his disappointment, along with his measure of guilt, and was enjoying his leisure time in Key West, Florida, waiting for his restrictive period to expire so he could open up another bar. The Texan hadn't garnered any franchisees in South Florida and that's where Pudge would make his come-back. He had sold his name and the Texan had defiled it. That still hurt but he vowed to find a way to correct two wrongs. "I'll have the last laugh over that *Gombeen*," Pudge insisted.

WAITING FOR GRETCHEN to arrive, Jerry enjoyed his Guinness and surveyed the scene from his bar stool. It was the beginning of happy hour so the place was only sparsely populated. A few salesmen in three-piece suits, vests unbuttoned and ties pulled down, slouched over the bar and stared into their drinks, working half-heartedly to get appointments and despairing over not making their monthly quotas.

Jerry noticed a guy at the end of the bar in a white linen suit with an open collar who was gesticulating wildly to a few people who were laughing uproariously at whatever he was saying. At the end of his spiel, he grew louder and Jerry heard, "Well, excuuuuuuse me," after which laughter erupted again.

Gretchen had dolled up before meeting Jerry. He noticed right away that she had put on bright red lipstick and her cheeks had a pinkish hue. She was smiling and looked good. He wondered if it had all been done for his benefit or if it was her normal preparation when leaving the library behind.

Gretchen sat down next to Jerry and almost immediately the bartender put a drink in front of her. "I don't have to order," she said, glancing up at Jerry as she took a sip of her drink. "Double Jameson neat," she added. "Did you grow up here?" Jerry asked, hoping something trite would get her to open up. Gretchen hesitated for a few seconds and said, "Nope, Ohio. Down near Cincinnati." "Big Buckeye fan, I would guess," Jerry responded with a grin. "Huh?" she asked, looking confused. "Ohio State Buckeyes. I figured everyone in the state was a football fan."

Gretchen took a sip of her drink and looked away while she said, "Nah, not really into sports."

She abruptly turned her face back to Jerry and without encouragement, launched into the dramatic discovery of the severed finger on DeCourcy Island. "You could say I was in charge, as the lead volunteer of the group. I had all the kids sent back to the pavilion as we waited for the police to arrive. When I was alone, I pulled out my Kodak Instamatic and took a bunch of pictures. Didn't tell the constable, though. My souvenirs. They were going to do their thing no matter what, right?" Gretchen was talking and drinking rapidly and when she finished her story the Jameson was gone.

Jerry didn't know where to begin. He wanted to see the pictures but was hesitant to ask. Gretchen filled the void by asking, "So what's the deal with the missing husband and this mysterious blonde?"

"Well, she was seen by more than one person but no other description than the blonde hair. I'm thinking it's a distinct possibility that the old man ran off with her and didn't have the heart to confess to his family. I guess blondes have that power," Jerry said with a half-hearted laugh.

"What is it with you guys and blondes? It makes me sick," she said, while signaling the bartender to hit her again. "Maybe it all started when I was a kid and I got a look at a calendar of Marilyn Monroe in the buff," Jerry said, laughing uncomfortably. He thought making a joke about a pubescent schoolboy enamored with the blonde movie star would placate her.

"I can just picture you drooling over her boobs. What's wrong with these," she demanded, cupping her petite breasts outside her blouse. "Not big enough for the average guy. You're an average guy, right? Or are you looking for some lusty babe built like a brick shithouse?" Gretchen scowled and took a slug of her new drink. Then, she smiled maliciously and said, "Right. You all want some big-titted woman running around in a teddy

61

with her jugs ready to pop out. I'll bet you think all blondes automatically put out and that you can get into their pants on the first night."

"You have a dirty mouth – and a dirtier mind," Jerry said, shaking his head. "Why did you bother to meet me anyway? What have I said or done to offend you?" Jerry stared at Gretchen but she was now looking down and refused to make eye contact. He thought of Leila Carlyle back in Kathmandu and then Missy Grisham in Toronto. They were angelic compared to her. Was this his destiny with women, he wondered?

"Sorry, cub scout. I'm on the rag," she blurted out. "I get kinda weird around this time of the month." Jerry couldn't believe it. Was there nothing this girl wouldn't say?

Jerry finished off his Guinness and got up from his stool. Gretchen started to open her purse when Jerry said, "I'm buying. It's been an interesting afternoon. I don't mind paying for the entertainment – and the education." Gretchen laughed and said playfully, "Hey, I said I was sorry. Want to see my pictures?"

GRETCHEN WAS ROOTING around in her purse and the guy in the white linen suit was now regaling a larger group at the end of the bar. "So, what's your specialty?" Jerry asked, eager to find a non-controversial topic. "Antiquities," she said softly, not looking up. "Mainly 15th and 16th century Italian and Greek pieces. After you left, I was studying a medal bearing the face of Hieronymus Scotus, the alchemist and sorcerer. Interesting character." Jerry smiled. For some reason, it made him think of Capt. Kidd and buried treasure.

Gretchen pulled out a picture from a cache held together with a rubber band. "Here, you can keep it. Consider it a peace offering from the bitch." She smiled broadly and Jerry found this version of her captivating. He glanced at the picture and noticed the ring on the finger. It was more distinct than in the newspaper photograph but still blurry. Eager to forgive her, he said, "It's all forgotten. Say, what do you know of all the Capt. Kidd stuff and his supposed connection to the Thimble Islands? Is it all a myth?"

"A bunch of treasure hunters get all excited when the newspaper hypes the legend from time to time. Amateurs come out of the woodwork with their maps and make fools of themselves. I guess it's good for tourism but the locals sure as hell don't like it. The influx of outsiders drives them batty. My guess is that you found that out already," she said, shaking her head as if disgusted.

"I wonder if that includes my friend's father," Jerry mused, hoping to get a reaction. "Could be. Who's to know. What did you say his name was?" she asked nonchalantly.

Before Jerry could answer, there was a roar of laughter at the end of the bar and Gretchen turned her head. "Oh boy, he's on a roll now. C'mon, Jerry, I'll introduce you to Twitchy when he gets done emoting. Someone made the mistake once of telling him that he was just as hilarious as Steve Martin."

R.J. Hurley developed a twitch sometime in his youth. If he got excited while talking, he would jerk his head sharply to the right in a quick, almost imperceptible movement. You had to be around R. J. for a while to see that it was no illusion. At some point, his friends started calling him Twitchy and the nickname stuck. Twitchy didn't seem to mind at all.

Gretchen and Jerry walked to the edge of the crowd around Twitchy that had now grown to around 8 when she said, as if disgusted or offended, "Oh jeez, he's doing his turd museum routine again." All Jerry caught was, "Hey, some of that crap is worth a lot of money" followed by a burst of laughter.

Jerry noticed that Twitchy's hair was a combination of grey and white and looked as if it had been frosted into place. This character is fully committed, Jerry said to himself. In an unnaturally low baritone voice, Twitchy said, "I bought me a gasoline-powered turtleneck sweater" and the crowd, feeling the effects of a collective buzz, laughed even louder. "I think he gets most of it from Martin's latest comedy album. Twitchy can be pretty entertaining when you catch him for the first time," Gretchen suggested. Jerry smiled and said, "I guess he better hope that Martin keeps coming up with new material."

Twitchy turned his back and fumbled with something. "Is that an arrow he just put through his head?" Jerry asked. "Yeah, sometimes he wears floppy bunny ears or a balloon hat," she explained. There was a louder roar than previously when Twitchy put on a serious face and said, "I just appeared on Celebrity Assholes."

Twitchy's routine varied but if you came into Pudge McFadden's often enough, you would hear bits of his repertoire a second or third time. Regardless, according to Gretchen, he rarely had to buy a drink when a newcomer picked up his schtick for the first time.

Jerry looked at Gretchen and asked, "So does he do this Steve Martin routine often?" "Too often, if you ask me. Tonight, he's relatively cerebral. On occasion, he'll go slapstick and launch into a vaudeville routine with crazy dancing and pencils hanging from his nostrils. He added his own creative touch by stuffing green olives into his nose and waiting for someone to say ugh. Then, he would do a fake sneeze and the olives would go flying. He's particularly proud of this comedic adaptation. Unfortunately, he can't play the banjo or ad lib like the Real McCoy or he might get a gig at the local comedy club."

"So, you know him from here?" Jerry asked, wondering if

he had competition but not sure if he even wanted to be in the game. "I know Twitchy from the bar scene. We sorta dated a few times but it was strictly platonic – at least for me. He's a harmless sort. Lives with his mom. Sometimes, I feel like the big sister. He's a loveable guy but this is all he's got going for him right now," she said, nodding her head toward the Steve Martin wannabe.

Twitchy held up his hands to signal that he was finished and the gathering dispersed amidst clapping and backslapping. "You were in rare form tonight, Twitch. I want you to meet, Jerry. He's in the area looking for a man who seems to have disappeared around the Thimbles and his family is concerned. May have taken off with some blonde bimbo. Somebody from the constable's office up in Graniteville had the bright idea to send him to me."

Twitchy was wiping his brow with a lavender handkerchief that he stuffed into the breast pocket of his suit coat as Gretchen was making her little speech. After the men shook hands, Jerry said, "I understand that it's customary for a newbie here to buy you a drink after watching you. I'd like to adhere to that tradition." Twitchy laughed and went into a series of contortions that almost nailed one of Steve Martin's antic routines.

When Twitchy wasn't imitating his comedic hero, he seemed to withdraw into a shell. Gretchen had gone silent as well so Jerry told them about his sojourn in Kathmandu, leaving out his ignominious departure and his relationship with the Carlyles. Later, he regretted how he had embellished his experience with the British archeology team.

AN HOUR LATER, the threesome walked out of Pudge McFadden's together and Gretchen pointed Jerry toward the Temple Street garage where his car was parked. Twitchy started to walk away when a wino rushed toward them yelling gibberish. He lunged at Twitchy, who caught sight of his pursuer in time and went into a full sprint. The wino's right hand was covered in white bandages stained with dirt. He held it aloft like a torch as he staggered after Twitchy but not before pausing and giving Gretchen a puzzled look.

Gretchen's face was ashen after the vagabond stumbled away but Jerry was watching the fleeing duo and didn't notice. When he turned back, she looked at him and said, "Not sure what a drunken hobo would want with Twitchy. He pushes some drugs with some of the college crowd but nothing big time. Well, one never knows about Twitchy," Gretchen shrugged.

Jerry felt it might be his last chance so he asked Gretchen if she ever visited any of the other islands. "Why would I?" she snapped, as if his question was provocative and offensive. Jerry was thinking of Quarry Island but said nothing. Gretchen had a way of shutting down a conversation, avoiding an inquiry she didn't like by asking another question.

After an awkward silence, Gretchen said, "Well, you know where to find me now, Jerry, but I wouldn't be surprised if we never meet again. I don't have a lot of male admirers and the ones I get don't last long. I guess you've figured that out." She shook Jerry's hand and Jerry just nodded. He didn't feel like lying so he said nothing.

ON THE DRIVE back to the Thimbletown Inn, Jerry thought about the relationship between Gretchen and Twitchy. It seemed like she was trying too hard to make it appear casual, even inconsequential. But if so, why would she describe herself as his "big sister"? He hadn't pressed her but he didn't miss the fact that she had been evasive when he asked her if she had visited any of the Thimbles besides DeCourcy. All she had to say was no.

Jerry wasn't inclined to think ill of anyone, even those who had done him wrong. Maybe it was because he had endured the barrage of criticism from his mother while growing up. But he did agree with Gretchen's own assessment that she was a bitch – a first class version, perhaps. He wondered who had done her wrong along the way. Certainly not Twitchy. More likely, the opposite was true.

Jerry had been deceived by the Carlyles back in Kathmandu, essentially turned into their lackey. And then the break-up with Missy in Toronto which seemingly came out of the blue but, in reality, had been developing right under his nose. He had to admit that he wasn't that taken with Gretchen Cadwallader in the first place. She was cute but not special and her mercurial personality was unnerving. No, she was right. They probably wouldn't see each other again.

JERRY WONDERED IF he would see Cyrus rocking on the porch when he got back to the Inn. He needed someone to talk to, help him sift through all that had happened that day. Would the old man be receptive? The Meachams were always available, a convenient crutch, but he wasn't ready to grab it. Maybe he wanted to prove something to them as well as to himself. He decided he would start by showing Cyrus the picture of the severed finger that Gretchen had given him. Yeah, that would be an excellent way to re-engage with the old man, he decided.

CHAPTER TEN:
CYRUS TROWBRIDGE

~

Jerry stopped at Johnny's Diner just off the highway exit for Graniteville and wolfed down the meatloaf blue-plate special before heading to the Thimbletown Inn.

He was tired when he walked up the steps to the inn. Initially disappointed when Cyrus wasn't in his chair on the porch, he decided it was just as well. He would have the evening to decide how to sort through the day's events and decide how to approach him – if at all.

When Tillie saw Jerry walk in, she tensed up. "We're sold out for the evening. You should have booked a room when you were here earlier. Terribly sorry, young man," she said fretfully. Jerry wasn't sure if her display of consternation was genuine or just an act.

"No rooms at all?" Jerry asked politely. "Only for those with reservations. They have until 9:00 to show up before the rooms are released but that rarely happens on a Saturday when the weather is nice like it is now," she said. "Would one of those reservations be for a Jerry Kosinsky?" he asked. "Well, we don't give out guest information, that's confidential and ……" "I'm

Jerry Kosinsky, Tillie, and it's not 9:00 yet," he said, pointing at the grandfather clock in the corner and pulling out his wallet.

Cyrus wasn't around and Tillie's basic good nature and sense of propriety took over. Her face softened and she said, "So, you were the gentleman who called this afternoon. That was very clever, I must admit." Tillie was smiling and there was no rancor in her voice. Tillie radiated kindness and gentleness, a person you could warm to quickly and feel comfortable near. Affection or pretense were not words that anyone who knew her would apply to Matilda Trowbridge Chivery.

TILLIE MET ARTHUR Chivery when she was well on the way to spinsterhood. He was a confirmed bachelor when a shocking event brought him back to the Graniteville Methodist Church after an absence of many years. A linesman for the Southern New England Telephone Company, Chivery had a near-death experience when he was zapped by an electrical surge while working atop a pole. Coincidentally, he "found Jesus" the next day.

Tillie and Arthur met at a church social shortly after his reawakening, two gentle souls who deserved each other, and they were married a year later. Their little risqué joke was that Tillie had to behave herself while Arthur was repairing telephone lines high above the streets of Graniteville because she could never be sure when he might be eavesdropping on her conversation. A heart attack took Tillie's husband to an early grave and while she grieved, she would tell anyone who would listen that Arthur Chivery had provided her the five best years of her life.

At breakfast Sunday morning, Cyrus sat down at Jerry's table unannounced, as if he had been expected or needed no invitation. Cyrus said, "Well?" and, with that terse prompt, Jerry proceeded to summarize yesterday's events.

Cyrus listened intently as Jerry told him about his encounter with the maid, his meeting with Gretchen Cadwallader at the suggestion of the girl at the constable's office, his Capt. Kidd research at the New Haven library and the encounter with the wino outside Pudge McFadden's.

"The girl's friend who was chased by the wino – did the bum just appear out of nowhere? You left something out, didn't you?" Cyrus asked. After Jerry described Twitchy's comedic fixation and his relationship to Gretchen, Cyrus mumbled "Hmm" and then "Okay," as if to say he had heard enough for now.

Jerry went on to provide a Clift Notes version of *The Gold Bug* and finished by saying, "I wasn't sure if the maid was shaking me down for more money. She could have found the book anywhere but for two bucks I was willing to take the gamble. When I got to the section on Capt. Kidd, I was convinced it came from his room. I'm starting to believe that the father was obsessed with the Scottish privateer and the possibility that treasure could be buried on one of these islands – maybe even his own."

Cyrus listened intently but showed no emotion. He puffed on his pipe and finally said, "Sounds like you had a pretty productive day yesterday, even if you didn't find anything on the blonde. What's next?"

"I want to get out to the Quarry Island and meet the partner. The family said there was bad blood between them and suggested embezzling might be the reason. "Do you know anything about this guy?" Jerry asked. "Nobody comes here without me knowing all about him, young man. His name is Elwyn Grex. Came down here about ten years ago from New Bedford. Heavy drinker and belligerent as hell when he gets into his cups. An all-around misanthrope. He's easy to find when they're not digging up granite on the island. Go to any tavern in the area and you're liable to spot him with Reginald Buffle, our part-time constable. Now there's a pair to behold. They look like Laurel & Hardy until they get drunk and turn nasty. Then, there's nothing comical about them. No telling what prompted this Hoole guy to go into business with the likes of Grex. Maybe they knew each other. Everyone has a past. Listen, you'd be a fool to go out there alone. It's best if I come with you. Unless you object, I'll arrange it for tomorrow. Grex is a booze hound and no doubt got lit up on a Saturday night. He'll be in no shape to engage in a civil conversation today."

Jerry nodded his acquiescence and, feeling emboldened since Cyrus had somewhat opened up to him, asked, "Any ideas on the blonde that was most likely in the motel room with the husband?" Cyrus sucked in his cheeks and both of them watched as smoke bellowed toward the ceiling. "Well, she's no local girl, that's for sure, or someone would have recognized her. When your friend's father disappeared, so did she. So, the hypothesis that they took off together is not illogical even if they are a very unlikely pair. He would have to be offering something other than his good looks, right?" Cyrus smiled and for some reason, it made Jerry ask, "Foul Play?"

Cyrus chuckled. "If you're thinking about making a connection to the father and the severed finger that washed up on the shore of DeCourcy Island, you're diving into murky waters. Are you ready for it? By the way, the appendage in question is now up at the state crime lab being looked at by forensic experts. My sources tell me the ring on the finger will undoubtedly provide an important clue as to the identity of the owner. Unfortunately, the tip of the finger was chewed or ripped off so they won't be pulling fingerprints from it. The big question is, of course, where is the rest of the body? If there was a murder and if the body was thrown into the water, it could be downstream by now as far as New York City." Jerry's fork had been hovering over a pancake and Cyrus could see that he was getting uncomfortable if not queasy so he decided not to speculate any further. "I can probably get us an appointment at the lab. Off the record, of course," Cyrus explained.

Cyrus' mention of the ring on the finger reminded Jerry about the picture given to him by Gretchen. He pulled it from his pocket. Cyrus studied it for a few moments and said, "Well, you can't pick up the necessary details from this photograph but the crime lab will have some quality shots – including some close-ups of the ring."

"I'd like to talk to the partner as soon as possible," Jerry said, happy to change the subject. Cyrus nodded and Jerry went on. "Listen, I'm grateful and all that but you were pretty standoffish yesterday. Why so accommodating and helpful today?"

"Yesterday, I thought you might be some greenhorn private dick or rookie insurance investigator who was nosing around and acting naïve as a ploy to get information. I've dealt with that kind and it grated on me. But then I figured that anyone who read Loren Eiseley couldn't also be a neophyte gumshoe. Too incongruous. Listen, I'm not going to push myself on you but it struck me that you needed an assist. These locals won't open up if someone like me isn't at your side.

"One other thing. This girl in New Haven that you met. Did she bother to tell you that she got canned the next day by the DeCourcy Institute? Apparently, she used abusive and vulgar language around the school children and the parents complained. Plus, some supplies and tools were missing after her last excursion to DeCourcy Island. In case you haven't figured it out already, I've got connections everywhere." Jerry wasn't entirely shocked by the news of Gretchen's firing. It was almost as if she egged people on until they revolted against her.

Cyrus pulled a small metal tool from his pocket and cleaned out the bowl of his pipe. Then, he reached into his pocket again and extracted a pouch of Borkum Riff bourbon whiskey tobacco. After stuffing some fresh leaves in the bowl, he tamped them down, struck a match on the underside of his seat and slowly lit his pipe, never for a second taking his eyes off Jerry. Cyrus looked almost benign as he took a long draw and exhaled with his mouth forming a perfect oval. His eyebrows went up and the smoke billowed toward the ceiling in small, concentric circles.

Jerry watched as if entranced, then smiled and reached across the table to shake hands. "I'm Jerry Kosinsky from Parlor City in Upstate New York. Went to Pythian College." Cyrus stuck out his hand and smiled warmly before saying, "I know."

CYRUS TROWBRIDGE WAS a 7th generation member of an English clan that emigrated to the United States around 1750. After a short stay in the Boston area, the family moved southwest into the upper Connecticut Valley in search of lush farmland, eventually settling in the coastal area near the Thimble Islands.

Trowbridge Farms had been sold long ago but, in an earlier time, had a prominent role in the area, growing an array of vegetables and fruits. When Cyrus McCormick invented the reaper in 1831, so farmers could harvest their crops mechanically, it was revolutionary and the inventor was hailed as a genius. The Trowbridges couldn't afford a reaper but the father was so impressed with McCormick that, after his death in Chicago in 1886, and against the wishes of his wife, he insisted that they name their son after him.

Young Cyrus went off to Thorndyke College at the age of 18 and then straight into their law school after graduation. After 20 years in the local state's attorney office, he tired of the constant plea-bargaining charade and the new-fangled concept of "restorative justice" which seemed to be gaining favor with some judges, the theory being that the perpetrator and the plaintiff were both somehow "victims" of society and could amicably arbitrate their grievances. Consequently, he turned down a promotion and went into private practice.

He bought the Thimbletown Inn with his sister when it was announced in the local paper that it might be demolished by a developer from New York City with plans to build a sleek, cookie-cutter motel. Tillie had been widowed a few years prior to the purchase and, truth be told, Cyrus believed that managing the ramshackle inn and its adjourning café would do wonders for his disconsolate sister. He was right.

After he closed his law office, Cyrus retreated to a small, isolated cottage on the water a few miles north of Graniteville. When he moved in, he made arrangements with the owner of the gas station a mile away on the access road to receive messages and then had the phone in the cottage disconnected. Cyrus Trowbridge thought a great deal about the past. He liked his isolation and his solitude.

He was on the cusp of his 80th birthday and suffering from Huntington's Disease, a debilitating ailment that was kept a secret from everyone, including Tillie. It had been a few years since his diagnosis and Cyrus could feel the subtle signs of the disease's progression. He never flipped the hourglass on his mantle anymore. He already knew that his clock was ticking faster each day and, according to the specialists down in New Haven, there was no way to slow it down.

Cyrus spent his good days on the porch of the Thimbletown Inn, weather permitting, doing the reading that his legal career had forced him to postpone for far too long. Delving into Loren Eiseley had certainly made him more philosophical and reflective. Even Tillie detected a gentler nature but said nothing for fear that she might ruin it. And then there was the arrival of the outsider, Jerry Kosinsky. Cyrus almost instantly liked the young man but refused to show it during that first encounter on the porch. If Jerry came back, he had already decided he would help if asked. It seemed as if Eiseley had orchestrated this particular moment for him to get out of his rocking chair.

CHAPTER ELEVEN:
QUARRY ISLAND

THE QUARRIES AROUND the Thimble Islands dated back until the mid-19th century, eventually employing hundreds of men, mainly immigrants from several European countries.

It was arduous and dangerous work in those early years, many of the laborers maimed by falling stones or debris, with others killed by the dynamite used to reveal the precious pink granite. Once a suitable seam was found, the granite had to be carefully extracted. The pieces weighing several tons were lifted out by derricks, then hauled to cutting sheds for shaping and polishing to the customer's specifications. And these weren't ordinary customers with mundane demands. Pink granite from the area quarries adorned a number of august places in the United States and even Europe.

Mechanization gradually reduced the need for manual labor and by the time that the two unlikely partners bought Quarry Island, the market for quality granite had receded and was dominated by big operators. The glory days for the small entrepreneur were a distant memory.

It could be tricky navigating the waters around the Thimbles so Cyrus had arranged for a skilled waterman to captain a skiff for the short ride to Quarry Island. As they approached the shore, Jerry gazed up at the imposing rock formations and marveled at the history behind them. Millions of years ago, these stone walls were formed out of volcanoes that never erupted and here they were staring down at him. He thought of his trip across Upstate New York with stops at Howe's Cavern and Saratoga Springs. Here was another reminder that he didn't have to go to Nepal to study the wonders of history.

As the boat was being tied up, Elwyn Grex lumbered down to meet his guests. Cyrus had pegged him correctly. He was a tall man with an immense girth. At the belt line, his stomach protruded from beneath a faded and stained black Judas Priest tee shirt with a ferocious, fire-spewing dragon across the front. His face was greasy and flush under a two- or three-day growth of beard. His head looked like a speckled pumpkin ready to explode. A few scattered tufts of black hair dotted a shiny scalp. Jerry thought he might be coming off a bender when he noticed the can of Falstaff beer in his hand. "The hair of the dog," Jerry said to himself. He'd been there a few times.

"I'm pretty damn busy here, Trowbridge. What's the urgency and who's this cream puff, your bodyguard?" Grex asked with a menacing grin. He was above them on an incline glaring down at Jerry as if itching for a fight. Grex took a slug of beer and wiped his mouth with a meaty paw, waiting for one of them to react.

Jerry seized the moment and walked up next to Grex so they were on an even level. "I see you're a man of Falstaffian proportions without the roguish wit and charm of Sir John," Jerry said calmly while pointing to the beer can.

"What in Sam Hill you talking about? Hey, you cracking

wise with me, knucklehead?" Grex said fiercely, flushed and confused as he inspected the beer can for a clue as to what Jerry meant. He felt that he had been insulted but didn't know how and it infuriated him. Grex had never backed down from a chance to brawl and had the scars to prove it. With Cyrus there, he showed rare good judgment and decided it wasn't worth it to pummel this outsized kid with a witness only a few feet away.

"Never mind," said Jerry, suppressing a grin, which only inflamed the big galoot. Deciding it was imprudent to poke the bear any further, Jerry turned serious. "Listen, this visit was my idea. I'm a friend of the Hoole family. I know your partner came down here to see you about something that was troubling him with respect to the business. And now he's disappeared. I just want to confirm that you didn't see him and have no clue as to where he is."

After a brief stare down, Grex grinned at Jerry and then turned to Cyrus. "I've already been interviewed by the constable's man. My partner never made it here to the island – at least not when I was here – and that's what I told him. End of story. One more thing, fellas, since you're so damn inquisitive. The day my partner supposedly disappeared, I had a fire out here in the wee hours. Destroyed almost all the contents of the office. Why isn't that incident being investigated? You tell me. Now, get the hell off my island."

"Like you implied, maybe your partner came out here without you knowing it and is still here. Mind if we look around?" Jerry asked, ignoring Grex's diatribe.

Grex waved an arm behind him and barked, "Sure, take a look from right here. Ain't it beautiful? Now, I've got to get back to my crew. We finally got an order and my bunch of Portuguese misfits who pretend they don't understand English only work when I have eyes on them. So, shove off or I'll file a complaint for trespassing. Oh, and if you see my partner, tell him to haul his ass out here and pay the boys. He issues the paychecks and they're getting mighty antsy."

Jerry was getting hot and Cyrus grabbed his arm. "You think carousing with Reginald Buffle qualifies as an official interview? That's priceless. Guess you've never been grilled by the boys in the state's attorney office. Don't be surprised if someone with real authority looks into your dealings with your business partner and his untimely disappearance. For instance, who stands to gain from it? Well, no problem, right? Buffle will run interference for you." Cyrus was smiling when he finished and Grex's face turned dark. He crushed the empty beer can in his hand and slammed it to the ground.

"Just one last question before we leave," Jerry said. "I understand it's dangerous work in the quarries. Did one of your people lose a finger in an accident in the last couple of weeks?" Grex exploded. "Get the fuck out of here before I lose my temper, sissypants. You don't want to see that."

Cyrus tugged on Jerry's sleeve and whispered, "C'mon, don't take the bait." In a few minutes they were back in the skiff for the short ride back to the mainland. "I'm sure you can handle yourself, Jerry, but you're a gentleman and Grex wouldn't have fought in accordance with the Marquis of Queensbury rules. Nice touch with the Shakespeare reference, though," Cyrus said.

"Thanks. It just popped into my head when I saw the beer can. I was pretty sure he wouldn't get it. Hey, based on what you said yesterday about these two guys, I now know who Laurel is so Buffle must be Hardy," Jerry said, causing Cyrus to burst out with unaccustomed laughter. He was starting to like this stranger.

BACK AT THE Thimbletown Inn, Tillie noticed a change in her brother when he walked in with Jerry. She wouldn't say anything but was pleased by what she saw. The twinkle in his eye that had been missing for some time was now back.

Uncharacteristically, Cyrus opened up to Jerry and told him that he had been a government lawyer for over twenty years after which he went into private practice. He didn't want it to be a mystery as to how he knew so much about what went on in the area and how he had such extensive connections. Plus, he understood that this openness would prompt Jerry to be more forthcoming himself.

"I'll arrange for us to visit the crime lab tomorrow. I don't know about you, but I'm excited as hell to see what they've discovered about the finger and the ring. I'd be shocked if it's one of that asshole's laborers but you never know. Word would have got out and he would have received medical treatment. As for our clown on Quarry Island, someone more demanding than Buffle needs to hassle him to flush out any useful information that he might be hiding," Cyrus said while scratching his head.

"What do you make of Grex's comment about a fire. Do you think he set it?" Jerry asked. "Well, if he was embezzling funds, it could have been a clumsy attempt at a cover up. It's odd though, that Grex didn't seem at all concerned about being implicated in his partner's disappearance. Maybe just false bravado. We'll just have to wait and see, kid. Whatever the outcome, it doesn't change the fact that Elwyn Grex is a wretched soul."

"I'm going to hit some of the local bars tonight, just nose around. I'd love to run into that girl from the constable's office and see if she might open up away from work. She was pretty helpful until Buffle walked by. And don't worry, I'll be on the lookout for Laurel and Hardy," Jerry said.

"You won't have much luck with the local boys, Jerry. Be careful. I'm anxious to read *The Gold Bug* if you wouldn't mind lending me your copy. It will keep me out of trouble tonight. You'd better do the same."

CHAPTER TWELVE:
DEAD MAN'S FINGER?

~⁀

CYRUS HAD WARNED Jerry about the insular nature of the local populace and he was right. Jerry was met with suspicion in the three bars he hit that night. Shouting over the music of Dolly Parton blasting from the juke box, only one bartender vaguely remembered Hoole but couldn't say he was with anyone – blonde or otherwise. Jerry felt silly but he scrutinized every woman with any shade of light hair that he saw, eliciting some icy stares and even a few "come hither" looks. In no mood for romance and not willing to invest the time in scoring a one-night stand, he went back to the Thimbletown Inn with a buzz but nothing else. Well, at least he hadn't run into Buffle and Grex, all liquored up and itching for a fight.

He flipped on the television in his room and caught the end of *Laverne & Shirley* . The next thing he knew, he was watching a commercial for Fotomat which reminded him of Gretchen Cadwallader pulling out her pictures at Pudge McFadden's. Frustrated and discouraged, he decided it was time to call it a night. As he closed his eyes, images of ash, golden, platinum, silvery, buttery, frosted and even sickly yellow hair danced in front of him.

JERRY DROVE TO the crime lab on Tuesday morning with Cyrus riding shot gun. Trowbridge had *The Gold Bug* on his lap and was tapping it lightly with his fingers as he looked out through the windshield. "It's a good read, Jerry. Typical Poe suspense, right? I can see why someone in a certain state of mind could be drawn in by it. The Legrand character turned out to be a very sharp fellow. We see our treasure seekers with their maps show up from time to time whenever the Capt. Kidd history is resurrected by the press but this is the first time I've encountered the possibility that Edgar Allen Poe was the likely motivation." Jerry laughed. "And I thought only kids yearned after buried treasure."

"El Tapado," said Cyrus, almost absentmindedly, causing Jerry to say, "What?" "Oh, it's a Vegas joint in one of Chandler's novels. I think it was *The Long Goodbye*. It's Spanish for something hidden from view, if I'm not mistaken. You just made me think of it. Strange, I haven't read any of his novels in years," Cyrus said, his tone soft and contemplative.

"It's still hard for me to square, though," Jerry said. "The father is a businessman, probably went to college, has a family – and then veers off into fantasy land. I'm learning that I don't know a great deal about human nature." Jerry was thinking about his ill-fated adventures since leaving Parlor City as a brash and cocky young man, an overconfident and naïve adventurer, who just happened to be breaking the law.

"Don't be too hard on yourself, young man. Part of wisdom is admitting that you are not as smart as you think you are. It's a humbling experience when it first dawns on you and for some people it never does. For others, it's a new beginning. Try not to be too cynical since it has clearly already dawned on you. Hey, the turn off for the lab is coming up soon. Get ready to meet Ward Babbidge. You're in for an education."

THE CRIME LAB was a unit of the state police but run independently by the talented and autocratic Fenster Butterwell, considered by most of his employees as a demanding perfectionist but, nonetheless, a benevolent dictator. He was no politician which happened to suit most fair-minded prosecutors, defense lawyers and police since they always knew that the purity of the analysis coming out of the crime lab was unquestionable.

Back in 1935, when it was established, the lab focused on fingerprint and photographic analyses. Over the years, as technology improved and the lab's budget increased, analytical capabilities were mastered in firearms, sera, trace evidence and other areas. Today, Butterwell was at the state capitol, smoothing the way with key legislators for an even richer appropriation for the coming fiscal year.

When Trowbridge and Kosinsky walked into Babbidge's office, he stood up and said, "Greetings, Uncle Cyrus. It's always nice to see you for an 'off the record' chat." Jerry looked quizzically at Cyrus who smiled but said nothing.

Cyrus introduced Jerry, briefly describing his mission, and then asked, "Strictly off the record and not for attribution, can you tell us anything about the finger found at DeCourcy Island? Jerry simply wants to give the family some peace of mind that the father can be excluded so his search can be continued elsewhere."

Before Babbidge could respond, Jerry reached into his pocket and said, "I came into possession of this photograph. It doesn't reveal much except there appears to be a ring on the finger. We thought it might be a clue as to his identity."

Babbidge studied the grainy photograph for only a few seconds and said, "Amateur day. Must have been that girl from the Institute. I'm surprised it hasn't made it into the newspapers already. Of course, it's useless for our purposes," he said dismissively. He then pulled out a large manila folder and plopped it on the desk for emphasis.

"We'll be notifying the constable's office of our findings later today or in the morning. We've got a man's right-hand finger, consistent with where he would wear a ring. The bad news is that we were unable to pull prints even though our analysis indicates that the finger had only been in the water for a short time. Maceration had occurred- that's a softening and breaking down of the skin tissue – but we might still have pulled a partial print if the tip hadn't been chewed off, probably by a prawn, shellfish or some other form of marine life. We've pretty much ruled out tampering by humans."

When Babbidge stopped, Cyrus asked, "Tampering?" Babbidge laughed and said, "You wouldn't believe what people do to remove fingerprints and avoid detection, some of it self-inflicted mutilation. I'm talking about dousing the hand in acid or setting the fingers on fire. John Dillinger was a famous case back in the 30s. Of course, if foul play was involved, it would be quite unpleasant, assuming that the victim was still alive. But like I said, no indication of foul play of the human sort, at least with respect to the tip of the finger."

"You're not toying with us, are you Ward? You keep qualifying your comments. C'mon, what are you leaving out?" asked Cyrus. "Okay, sometimes I forget you're a lawyer and like to cross examine. We're not positive but it looks like the proximal phalanx was cut through with a serrated tool, something as basic as a steak knife."

"We're not in one of your lectures for new recruits, Ward. Translation, please?" Cyrus asked, trying to sound peeved but smiling at the same time. "Sorry, force of habit. It's the finger bone right below the palm," Babbidge said.

"Okay," said Cyrus, "So, you're implying that before the fishies got to the finger, someone could have cut if off. That leads to a lot of different speculations about a possible crime, which then begs the larger question – where is the *corpus delicti*?

"So, are we going to get any clue as to the victim's identity today?" Jerry chimed in, not waiting for an answer. "Actually, yes, rather a good one and, in fact, it didn't require any forensic acumen," said Babbidge, adding, "It's a school ring on the finger and it's from your alma mater, Uncle Cyrus. Thorndyke College."

Babbidge opened the folder and pushed the blow-up of the whitened and wrinkled finger across his desk for Cyrus and Jerry to examine. The skin appeared to hang loose on the finger and part of the nail was missing from the mangled tip. "Some of the older analysts still refer to it as 'washerwoman skin,'" Babbidge said, as the other two hovered over the photograph. Babbidge handed Cyrus a magnifier and the name Thorndyke was faded but still visible on the ring below the large T.

"Was there any inscription on the inside of the ring? Jerry asked. Babbidge looked at his uncle before saying, "I've gone far enough already. Maybe too far. If Butterwell was here today, there would probably be a reprimand in my file by the end of business. Any additional information will have to come from the constable's office."

"And the rest of the body? Care to speculate?" Cyrus persisted. Babbidge laughed. "Okay, let's theorize. The body, possibly dismembered first, was dumped into Long Island Sound and sunk to the bottom where the finger was somehow bitten off – but not eaten - by some sea creature. Eventually, gases would be expelled from the corpse after which it would float to the surface during decomposition. Next, the appendages and head would separate from the body and you would be left with just the trunk. Of course, King Neptune could have arranged a buffet for his minions in the watery depths as this whole process unfolded. Listen, the Sound is an estuary with ocean saltwater mixing with fresh water from our rivers so different things occur here that you won't find in the Atlantic. Another more plausible possibility to consider is that, based on the currents at the time, the whole body – minus the finger – floated all the way to the East River and is now the property of New York City.

"Or, consider another theory. Maybe only the finger made it into the water and our victim is walking around with a mangled hand as we speak. We've already checked with the local hospital and no one with such an injury has been admitted." Babbidge was enjoying himself, having metaphorically speaking taken off his lab coat. His listeners were transfixed.

Cyrus knew that they had pushed to the limit but did get his nephew to give them a copy of the enlarged photograph of the finger. "Once Buffle gets his hands on it, especially with the chief gone, it won't be long before you see it in the newspaper. In the meantime, it's confidential, right?" Babbidge asked, thinking of Butterwell.

AT THE DOOR, Babbidge had a troubled look on his face. "What is it?" Cyrus asked. "Putting aside all the speculation, I just can't fathom how the finger survived and made it to DeCourcy Island. Why wasn't it eaten? Logically, it makes no sense to me. That takes me back to my original hypothesis, namely that the finger was cut off and dumped in the water close to shore. Guess that's up to the constable to figure out, right?"

"So now what, Uncle Cyrus?" Jerry asked with a tinge of sarcasm when they were back in the car. Cyrus was chewing on his thumb, staring straight ahead, as if in a trance. When Cyrus hadn't responded after a minute, Jerry volunteered, "Hey, my best friend Woody Meacham went to Thorndyke, graduated in the Class of 67." He wondered if Woody had purchased a ring but said nothing.

"Cyrus finally jerked his head as if startled and said, "Mine's in a jewelry box with cuff links, tie tacks, collar stays and eyelet pins. I remember wearing it for a few years after graduation but it just felt too clunky so I threw it in the box. We can't say anything about this information until Buffle releases it. However, what's wrong if I contact Thorndyke and find out if Hoole went to school there? If he did, it's not good news for the family and your search is probably over." Cyrus was holding the enlarged photograph and had a puzzled look on his face.

Jerry looked over and asked, "What is it?" Cyrus shook his head and said, "I don't know, Jerry. Something about the ring. I need some quiet time to think."

It was late morning and Cyrus sounded distracted and tired. When Jerry looked over again, his eyes were closed. Cyrus was wearing a golf shirt and Jerry noticed that the arms were taut and the skin wasn't loose or baggy but he could see the crepey wrinkles above the elbow and it made him realize that even though Cyrus was sharp, the years were inexorably catching up with him.

They rode silently the rest of the way.

THAT AFTERNOON, CYRUS got in his car and drove to his doctor's office in New Haven. Unbeknownst to him, Jerry was heading to the city as well.

CHAPTER THIRTEEN:
NO MORE TWITCHING

WHEN JERRY WALKED into the offices of the DeCourcy Institute, it reeked of opulence. The heavy solid oak door was inlaid with triple insulated glass in an ornate design. He hesitated as he reached for the glistening gold doorknob. It had now been several generations since Chester DeCourcy had accumulated massive wealth through holdings in coal, timber and real estate. Up to the end, he had lived as modestly as he was born in Brittany before migrating to America, no more charitable than the poorest family living in one of his numerous tenements that dotted cities along the Southwestern Connecticut coast. No one dared call him a skinflint or asked him why he was living on the cheap, destined to leave the spoils of his labors to later generations who might not be as austere as him.

He would not have been happy had he walked in the door of the DeCourcy Institute with Jerry Kosinsky that day. DeCourcy's progeny stood against everything he had valued and achieved. They looked back on him with unspoken contempt as a plunderer of the earth's precious assets, while all the time living grandly on his money.

Jerry told himself that he didn't doubt Cyrus but was mindful that a competent detective always checked and double-checked his information. The chatty girl at the front desk confirmed that Gretchen was no longer affiliated with the Institute and also volunteered that Gretchen had probably been at the pavilion on DeCourcy Island before the class field trip when the finger was discovered. "It's standard Institute procedure to make a preparatory visit to ensure that everything is in order before any student excursion," she said authoritatively, as if imparting critical information. She smiled mechanically and her mouth froze in place, displaying sparkling teeth that looked like rows of Chiclets.

"Was she at the pavilion often?" Jerry asked, hoping to elicit any additional information. "No idea. I didn't know her except by sight but I hear she could be real nasty at times. Not exactly lady-like, if you know what I mean." The girl was certainly prim and proper, a perfect prop for the entrance to the DeCourcy Institute, as conscious of its image as much as its mission. She was wearing a pleated, pattern skirt with a white blouse and navy cardigan sweater buttoned halfway to the neck. Her blonde hair, held in place with a blue headband, had a sheen to it that reflected the ceiling lights and hung down in curls to her shoulders, enveloping a round face with an upturned nose. As Jerry gazed at her, he decided that she was a caricature of the model receptionist. She was perky and polite, but her manufactured smile was certain to grate on anyone who stood in front of her for too long.

Jerry knew he had nothing to lose but still felt foolish as soon as he asked her if she knew Ellis Hoole. The girl frowned and looked baffled, causing Jerry to make a hasty exit.

JERRY STOPPED AT a luncheonette near Union Station and purchased a copy of the *New Haven Beagle* from the vending machine on the way in. As he sat at the counter flipping through the pages, he came upon a picture of Twitchy in his cream-colored suit. Below the photograph was an article with the headline EARLY MORNING TRAIN DEATH. Jerry quickly read about an apparent accident the prior morning in the very early hours before sunrise. The victim was identified as Ronald J. Hurley. Someone had been interviewed who said Twitchy had been at Pudge McFadden's the night before the accident and didn't leave until closing hour. The article speculated that he was drunk and somehow stumbled onto the tracks in front of an oncoming train.

Jerry left his half-eaten lunch and headed over to Pudge McFadden's. The place was almost empty and the bartender had nothing to add to the newspaper article. He worked days and knew that Twitchy was an evening fixture in the bar but could add nothing more.

OTHER THAN THE gift of mimicry, Twitchy had little else to offer. He had no inspiration to create something himself but was content to feast on the talent of others. In short, he was a parasite – and he knew it. It hounded him during those late-night hours when he was all alone with no one to entertain, no audience to puff him up, to inflate his sense of self-worth. And Gretchen had never been any help. Quite the contrary. She had derided and abused him at every turn. He laid in bed many nights and heard the freight trains rumble through in the wee hours, when those with a clear conscience (or no conscience at all) were in deep sleep mode. There had been many nights, in a fog or dozing off temporarily, when he didn't know whether he was asleep or awake.

In his confusion, he would pick up the distant sound of a train growing louder and would look over at his glowing clock. Sure enough, it was 4:02, or a minute either way. Right on schedule. That night, after coming home from Pudge McFadden's, where he got a less than respectful response to his latest Steve Martin routine, he laid on top of the bed fully-dressed, fiddling with the buttons on his cream-colored jacket as tears trickled down his cheeks.

It was 3:45 when he rose slowly from the bed, looked in the mirror and straightened his rumbled jacket as if he was tidying up before going on stage. He slipped out the door without waking his mother and headed to the trainyard. Across the yard, he could see the hobo encampment, lit up by a few flickering fires to ward off the early morning chill. He wondered if the wino who had chased him outside Pudge McFadden's was there, passed out or fast asleep. No doubt, even his dreams were more tranquil than Twitchy ever had. As he climbed up the embankment, shivering and shaking, the roar increased and the ground trembled as Twitchy stepped in front of the 4:02 Penn Central freight train barreling toward New York City.

HE HADN'T INTENDED to see Gretchen that day and had no desire to do so, but with Twitchy's death, Jerry had a compelling reason. When he got to the rare book room at the library, he could see her sitting at a small table in the corner talking to a man in a dark suit with his back to the door. When he knocked on the glass, she quickly came to the door and stepped outside before closing it, looking back furtively at her guest.

"I just found out about Twitchy. It was the next night after we were together. Was it really an accident?" Jerry asked. Gretchen scowled and said, "Beats me. Kinda strange. His mother is already bugging me with phone calls. Listen, I told you he had his issues, didn't I? Maybe it was an accident like the paper says. More likely a death wish, if you ask me. Hey, I'm real busy here," she said, reaching for the doorknob. She had been irritated by Jerry's questioning but now her voice was suddenly flat. No emotion. Here was someone, by her own admission, who had been close to, even dated Twitchy, and she sounded completely indifferent to his death, even speculating that he had committed suicide.

She started to open the door and Jerry grabbed her arm. "I was over at the Institute. Why didn't you tell me that they let you go?" Gretchen glared while pushing Jerry's arm away. "Because it's none of your goddam business. We met for a few hours after you foisted yourself on me. And I'm supposed to open up to you? Get lost!"

The door was open now and something made Jerry say, "I'm still curious about that wino that chased after Twitchy. Care to open up about that?" Gretchen slammed the door shut and the man turned to look. His hair was dark and curly with sideburns well below the ears. His bushy mustache had a Groucho Marx fulsomeness, making it impossible to decipher the look on this face. He could be smiling or growling as far as Jerry could tell. He didn't have the look of a rare book collector or historian, Jerry decided as he walked away.

WHEN HE GOT to his car, Jerry stretched his arms out across the roof of the car and stared straight ahead. He acknowledged that he was on a horrible losing streak with women and most of it was his own doing. Not that he had anything going with Gretchen but he had briefly entertained the thought that she might be worth pursuing. Now, he knew she was dark and impenetrable. He hated the idea that she might think he was hot for her and wished he could disabuse her of that notion. Jerry had taken a few basic psychology classes in college and disliked it when others used such scant knowledge to engage in amateur analysis.

And yet he felt that Gretchen exhibited the characteristics of narcissism and psychopathy. She might even be dangerous in a Machiavellian way. Was she at least partially responsible for Twitchy's slide into depression?

Leila Carlyle and Missy Grisham were no keepers either. They had treated him poorly but were absolutely charming in comparison to this harridan. He had told himself earlier that he would not see Gretchen again but now he wasn't so sure. If he did, it would be strictly business, of that he was certain.

As Jerry drove back to the Thimbletown Inn, he reflected on everything that he had learned that afternoon. He looked forward to discussing it all with Cyrus.

CHAPTER FOURTEEN:
WOODY PROVIDES COUNSEL

When he got back to the Thimbletown Inn, Jerry saw Tillie signaling for him to come over to the front desk. "Cyrus is under the weather and asked me to let you know. Said he'd see you in the morning at breakfast," she said, sounding apologetic. Tillie was one of those sensitive souls prone to express regrets for things she didn't say or do. It was just her nature to let others know that she shared their disappointment even when she didn't cause it. In Tillie, it was an endearing trait.

Jerry smiled weakly. He felt the need to talk to someone so he decided in that moment to call his best friend. Talking to Woody Meacham always seemed to lift his spirits and the afternoon in New Haven called for an emotional boost.

"Sounds like you dodged a bullet with her," Woody said, when he heard about Gretchen and her reaction to Twitchy's death. "I haven't a scintilla of proof but can't shake the idea that she knows something about Hoole's disappearance," Jerry said. "Sometimes your instincts will lead you to solid evidence if you are just patient and persistent, Jer. Just be careful that you don't get too invested in a theory and get blinded by it, okay? It's easy to be suspicious of people we don't like," Woody cautioned. "Boy, do you sound like the boy wonder himself," Jerry exclaimed, alluding to Woody's stepfather.

Woody laughed and Jerry went on the describe yesterday's visit to Quarry Island and the crime lab meeting that morning. "It's not unreasonable to focus on Grex," said Jerry, adding, "If anyone had a motive to get rid of a partner, Grex would have to be at the top of the list. Maybe he's too obvious to be a suspect – assuming foul play was involved." When Jerry finished, Woody said, "I'll run Grex through the federal database. If anything pops up, I'll let you know but there's no guarantee that Massachusetts entered it in the system even if there is a record on him."

After Jerry summarized the meeting at the crime lab, Woody said, "Fascinating stuff. I know your hands are tied temporarily but once the lab findings are public information, fax me a copy of the enlarged photograph of the finger with the ring on it. I'd like to study it and show it to Billy. Who knows, we might catch something. I agree, though, that if he attended Thorndyke and if there is an inscription on the inside of the band identifying him, it would seem to be bad news for the family. Sure, he could still be alive – minus a finger – but I would not be hopeful."

Jerry was starting to believe that the crime lab results would prove ominous but still he felt better after hanging up the telephone. He had waited too long before calling his best friend. Maybe all those years on the lam had made him forget how close they had been since childhood. He wouldn't make the same mistake again.

THERE WAS A light knock at the door and then Jerry heard, "It's Tillie," come softly from the other side. When he opened the door, she was holding a tray of food with steam emanating from the hole on top of the silver dome covering the plate.

"You looked out of sorts when you came in so I made the assumption you wouldn't be going out again. Sometimes, I get in a funk and don't want to be around anyone," she said haltingly, as if she had perhaps assumed a little too much and intruded a bit too far.

"You read me correctly, Tillie," said Jerry, stepping to the side and giving Tillie passage into his room. She put down the tray and nervously straightened down her flower print dress before saying, "You have already figured out that my brother is a very private and cautious man. Not sure he told you but he lives alone in a cottage just a few miles up the coast. Anyway, he's taken a liking to you in just a few short days and that is not like him. It had done him good to be around you and I just wanted you to know it."

Tillie's brief soliloquy sounded rehearsed but it was still genuine and in no way were the sentiments contrived. She bustled out of the room so quickly that when Jerry said, "Thank you, Tillie," she was already closing the door behind her.

THAT EVENING, JERRY was determined not to turn on the boob tube until the late news came on. He pulled a copy of *The Adventures of Augie March* from his suitcase. He had bought it a few weeks before leaving Toronto upon learning from Woody that Doc Sauer had died.

Sauer's death caused Jerry to recall that the dentist had carried around a copy of the Saul Bellow novel that summer in Parlor Harbor. The joke was that he used the novel as a surveillance prop but never actually read it. Well, Jerry would read the novel, as a sort of a belated tribute to the avuncular character.

The dentist had fitted porcelain caps on Woody's front teeth after a basketball mishap his senior year at Thorndyke College had turned the bottoms of those most prominent of incisors to dust. Sauer came over to Parlor Harbor that summer of 1967 when Woody was falsely charged with murdering a college classmate. His amateur detective sleuthing helped clear his best friend. Sauer had befriended Jerry at that time and, looking back, he realized that Sauer had been as much a mentor to him as Prof. Eyesmore.

.

JERRY HAD READ some of the great picaresque adventures but never thought of himself as a man on a quest. Early in the pages of the Bellow novel, he was reminded of the sheer joy he got from *Don Quixote*, *Tom Jones*, and *Tristram Shandy*. Maybe he was on the road to discover something – perhaps himself – and this simple inquiry on behalf of an acquaintance in Toronto made Jerry realize that he had been energized, in some way renewed. He had met some interesting characters and, he was pretty sure, had established at least a tentative bond with the most unlikely of men, Cyrus Trowbridge.

CHAPTER FIFTEEN:
THE REG AND EL SHOW

~~~

GRANITEVILLE CHIEF CONSTABLE Homer Tulk was at a law enforcement convention in Las Vegas, accompanied by his wife, after which they would be vacationing at Lake Tahoe. The chief was comforted by the fact that, in his absence, his niece would serve as his mole and gadfly.

The office of constable was an English tradition that dated back to at least 1650 throughout New England. While most constabulary positions were civil in nature, towns had the statutory authority to appoint or elect constables with legal powers akin to sheriffs. By ordinance, Graniteville had given Constable Tulk law enforcement authority after his first municipal election victory in 1952. He was one of the rare constables still extant in the state who was not limited to routine civil duties.

While Tulk had some police training over the years, he was a humble man and knew his limitations. With his jurisdiction restricted to the town's borders, he was never hesitant to seek outside help. In addition, Tulk knew his days were numbered. It had been confided to him that Graniteville would soon have its own police department and his authority would evaporate. At best, he would be like an appendix, an extra part of the body politic that no longer served a useful purpose. The convention in Las Vegas was his "last hurrah," a token of thanks from the town elders. Homer Tulk would officially retire when his term expired the following year.

NOMINALLY IN COMMAND while the constable was away was part-time deputy Reginald Buffle, or "Reg with a soft g," he reminded people. Buffle liked to think he took his limited civil duties seriously and performed them admirably. It never dawned on him that his professional image, such as it was, was in any way tarnished by late night carousing with his erstwhile drinking buddy, Elwyn Grex.

Prior to taking the Graniteville job, Reg had been with the sheriff's department where his pedestrian duties included transporting prisoners, providing security detail at court and serving warrants. His detective skills were not just weak, they were non-existent.

It was Wednesday morning and the chief had been gone for only 24 hours. Buffle had a raging headache and his second cup of black coffee was no anodyne. Grex and he had been out the night before, ostensibly celebrating the chief's departure and his temporary elevation to leadership of a department which was comprised of the Tulk, Buffle, the niece and a part-time school crossing guard who also functioned as a department factotum.

The "Reg and El Show," as the beefy pair were known when on a bar-crawling tear, had been center stage the night before when they were observed merry-making into the wee hours with two equally inebriated out of towners. The bovine-like divorcees – or so they claimed – were down from Boston on vacation. One of the hefty ladies confided to Grex that they were deprived and neglected back home and soon the romp was on. After a night of debauchery, the two overweight lotharios mocked their out-of-town conquests as they drove home, as if they were themselves prize bull calves who had latched onto a couple of aging Holsteins on a lark for just one evening.

WHEN THE NIECE announced that a courier had just delivered the crime lab report on the severed finger, Buffle cringed. "How soon do you want to issue a statement to the *Graniteville Gazette*?" she asked, grinning broadly. Buffle grumbled and wanted to crawl under the desk. If he ever succeeded the chief, she was a goner. His desk in the cramped, two-room office abutted and faced her. Tired of her condescending smirks and snickering comments, he retreated to the chief's glass-paneled office and closed the door.

Buffle leafed through the report but was having trouble focusing. He managed to comprehend that no fingerprint analysis could be completed due to the mangled condition of the tip. As he read, Buffle had his hands pressed into the sides of his head as if it would dissipate the throbbing pain. Without knocking, the niece came in and said, "Mind if I take a look?" Buffle growled and pushed the report across the desk without a word. He had to admit that she was sharp and might pick out something that would be useful to him. He would quiz her later.

She was back in front of Buffle after a few minutes and clapped the report on the desk. It sounded like thunder to him. "Says here that the ring was from Thorndyke College with the initials *EH* on the inside of the band. There's also a date of *6/10/51* inscribed. Must be when he graduated. Heck of a clue, wouldn't you say, Reg?" She lingered over the soft g and strung it out. Buffle's eyes showed a flicker of life through the streaks of red. He missed her mocking tone and managed to say, "Okay, get a hold of the school and ask them to go through all their records for that date and identify anyone with those initials. Can you handle that?"

The niece smiled but didn't move. Buffle's mouth dropped open and his eyes went up. "So, what are you waiting for?" he snapped, exasperated and throwing up his arms. She covered her mouth to stifle her laughter and then finally forced out the words. "Uh, Reg, these are the initials for Grex' missing partner. As in the guy from Vermont. You filled out the wife's missing person's report, remember? Sure, I can confirm with the college. That's easy enough by just giving them his name without asking them to search all of their records. But don't you think you need to get Grex in here right away? That's what the chief would do."

Buffle's face went ashen and he felt bile rising in his throat, making his eyes water. He swiveled the chair around to face the wall, hoping to force back down whatever might gurgle up. "Just call the damn college. I'll handle Grex my way," he managed to sputter.

JERRY WAS ATTACKING a mountain of pancakes with a side rasher of bacon when Cyrus walked into the café. "Looks like Tillie has taking a liking to you, feeding you as if you were a hungry lumberjack," he said, laughing and pointing to the plate. Jerry's mouth was crammed but he forced an embarrassed smile.

"Brace yourself for some bad news," Cyrus said, his tone now serious. "I heard back from Thorndyke. Grex' partner did graduate from there, class of 1951. Unfortunately, they don't keep records of who buys class rings. It's handled by some outside company." Cyrus paused to let the news sink in and then went on. "We still need to learn if there's an inscription on the inside of the ring band but it's looking worse all the time." Jerry had pushed the plate away. His appetite was gone. "How soon can we head over to the constable's office?" he asked.

"Just got off the phone with my nephew. The crime lab report was sent over first thing this morning. Let's slide over there in an hour. By then, Buffle should have digested it, to the level of his capability. With the chief gone, he's going to exercise his temporary authority to the hilt, I can promise you. It should be interesting. In the meantime, tell me what you were up to yesterday afternoon, if anything."

When he heard about Twitchy and Gretchen's reaction, Cyrus shook his head and said, "She's pure poison, kid. Lethal."

BUFFLE WAITED UNTIL he saw the niece on the phone and called Grex on the other line. He didn't sound good and felt even worse when Buffle told him about the Thorndyke ring with Hoole's initials. Instructed to come in for a formal interview, he slammed down the phone, sending a piercing pain through his best friend's forehead. The night before, they were swearing undying fealty to each other as they drank and canoodled with the buxom babes from Boston. It was only six hours later and the *bon homme* had evaporated.

THE NIECE INTENDED to but had not yet called Thorndyke. Instead, she placed a call to The Mirage in Las Vegas and woke up her uncle. After a brief chat, she pressed down the receive button, let go, and dialed the operator to get the Thorndyke switchboard number.

Buffle wondered if Grex would show up and what he would do if he didn't. He heard the phone ring and the niece yelled out, "It's for you, Acting Chief."

He was certain it was the local paper so he cleared his throat, gathered what little fortitude he had and introduced himself in his best baritone voice. "I'll bet you're acting, Buffle. More like posing and puffing yourself up in my absence. Please tell me that you haven't done anything in the last 24 hours to embarrass the department." Buffle heard the booming voice of Constable Tulk and choked up, wondering if he already knew about last night's dalliance.

Getting no response, the chief continued. "Listen closely. I called the crime lab a few minutes ago and they summarized their findings for me. There's going to be a full investigation now and we're in no way equipped to handle it. You'll get a call shortly from Lt. Ladislaw over at the barracks. The state police boys are taking over this case as of right now and you need to zip your lips about it. No interviews, no opinions, no late-night blabbing in the bars. One more thing, stay away from your pal Grex. As of now, he's a person of interest in his partner's disappearance. Could end up being a suspect. I'm leaving for Tahoe in the morning and even though I might be 3000 miles or so away, don't think I won't hear everything that's going on there until my return."

Buffle barely got out a weak, "Yes, Chief" when he heard the click on the other end. For a few moments, he'd forgotten about his raging headache but now the full force of it came roaring back. He popped a handful of aspirin and took a sip of water, gulping hard to force them down. Grex was probably on his way and there was no way to stop him. No doubt, the staties would show up soon and take the crime lab report. He knew a few of the boys at the barracks and they invariably gave him a hard time when they saw him around town. Their visit would not be a pleasant one.

Buffle's mind was not so addled that he couldn't wonder about the timing of the chief's call. And how was it that he had also called the crime lab that morning? He looked out and saw the niece's hair. As if on cue, she lifted her head slightly and peered out under raised eyebrows with an impish grin. Buffle felt the blood rush to his temples.

A few minutes later, the telephone range. The niece put her hand over the receiver and yelled, "It's the press, Acting Chief."

Buffle had hoped it was the chief calling again so he could explain that he had asked Grex to come in before his earlier call. Now, the chief would hear the niece's or Ladislaw's version, if it came to that. No, he wouldn't give the little tart any more ammunition to use against him. He heard the mocking sound of "Acting Chief" again, louder this time, and finally blurted out, "Tell them no comment."

WHEN CYRUS AND Jerry walked into the constable's office, the niece smiled and said, "Hi, Mr. Trowbridge." Turning to Jerry, she said, "I see you've made a friend since your last visit. You chose excellent company."

"This is Jerry Kosinsky, Fanny. He's here on behalf of that man's missing partner," Cyrus said, pointing into the chief's office where Grex was standing inside the door next to Buffle. They appeared to be in a heated conversation.

"My uncle called from Vegas about an hour ago. He contacted Lt. Ladislaw. The state police are taking over. With Grex now a potential suspect in his partner's disappearance, Reg should understand that he needs to step away but he doesn't get it," she said in a disgusted tone.

"I must say it's a sly way of confirming that the ring probably belonged to Ellis Hoole," Cyrus said. "No comment," said Fanny. Before they arrived, she had called Thorndyke and confirmed Hoole's graduation date.

There was an awkward silence while Grex and Buffle stared out at Cyrus and Jerry. "They won't come out until we leave,

Jerry. The blustering we saw on Quarry Island is restricted to his own domain or the saloons," Cyrus said.

"The staties will be hear shortly and will want to interview Grex. My guess is that they'll conduct a thorough search of Quarry Island. Could get interesting, Mr. Trowbridge," Fanny said.

Cyrus nodded and said, "They'll want to notify the wife even without a body, is my guess. Looking at Jerry, he added, "I've known Lt. Ladislaw for years. Let's pay him a visit."

As they headed to the door, Fanny offered, "I scanned the crime lab report after Buffle tried to decipher it. If you want to guess the initials that are on the inside of the ring band, I'll tell you if you're wrong." Jerry gave her Hoole's initials and they waited. "Well," said Jerry but Fanny said nothing, only smiling demurely. "Thank you, young lady. We'll be going now," said Cyrus.

OUTSIDE, CYRUS SAID, "Clever girl. She should go into politics. Plausible deniability." Jerry shook his head and grinned. It finally dawned on him that she hadn't said anything because, of course, he had guessed correctly. "She's also as cute as a button," he quipped.

"If you are intent on calling the wife, Jerry, let Ladislaw know first and make sure you tell her it's not conclusive and that she will be hearing from the state police." Jerry nodded agreement and said, "Did you see the looks of their faces? I know there's nothing to link Buffle and Grex directly to any crime but they definitely appeared to be concerned about something."

"I'd love to see Grex squirm when Ladislaw's interrogators start grilling him. And you better believe the staties will go over every square inch of Quarry Island with a fine-tooth comb. If there's a body buried there, they'll keep digging until they find it. The fun is just starting," said Cyrus.

"Even then, Cyrus, it wouldn't explain how only a finger made it into the water." Cyrus chuckled and patted Jerry on the back. "Well, listen to you now, talking like a cagey and cynical detective who has seen it all."

CHAPTER SIXTEEN:
FLETCHER LADISLAW

~

FLETCHER LADISLAW WAS an upright citizen who happened to be a career trooper. It was well known that he played everything by the book. Cyrus had gotten to know him when he was with the state's attorney office. Ladislaw's ramrod posture and perfect flat top were viewed by some as a façade, a form of deception, a way to hide an uninspired and intellectually vapid persona. They were wrong. Ladislaw was a reserved, laconic man who thought deeply about things. He was no Tesla or Einstein but he was nobody's fool. What people saw were simply the outward symbols of his rectitude.

"I know you'll contact us if you fellows stumble on anything of interest," Ladislaw said, after hearing Jerry describe his connection to Hoole's family. "Quite frankly, while the circumstances are highly suspicious, we don't even know yet whether a crime has been committed. Right now, we have a finger with a ring – and a missing person. We knew about the blonde that the partner was seen with around the time he disappeared but now both of them have simply up and vanished."

Ladislaw was waiting for his team to meet with Buffle and pick up the crime lab report so Cyrus told him they had received indirect confirmation that the initials on the Thorndyke class ring matched the missing partner's. Ladislaw's brow furrowed and he seemed to be deep in thought. He finally said, "Hmm, the chief didn't mention that fact when he called this morning. Guess he figured I would find out soon enough. It's certainly a game-changer."

Cyrus then described their confrontation with Grex on Quarry Island and Ladislaw laughed. "Whenever he has a beer in his hand, he's itching for a fight. He won't like it when we start to dig into his relationship with his partner and start snooping around the island. Rumor is that the quarry was in financial trouble so that's an angle we will be pursuing. We're talking off the record, of course."

"Here's a picture of Hoole in case you want to make a copy. Any problem with me calling the wife with news about the ring? I can tell her that your office will be contacting her when further details are available," Jerry added.

"No problem at all. And we've got a picture of Grex and his partner together which appeared in the local paper when they acquired the quarry," said Ladislaw, standing up to signify that their meeting was concluded. The lieutenant shook their hands and crunched some fingers. He didn't mean anything by it. He had learned the iron grip from his father and never gave it a second thought.

WHEN THEY GOT outside, Cyrus said, "I was a little surprised that you didn't mention your adventures in New Haven." Jerry scratched his head and said, "Well, the initials on the Thorndyke ring seem pretty conclusive, right? Ladislaw sounds like a competent, no nonsense guy who will steam roll right through Buffle and Grex if he has to. My amateur sleuthing would probably seem pretty irrelevant right about now."

"In all fairness, you were sent on a hopeless mission by the family and you did the best you could. After you call the wife, are you going to head home or hang around a little longer to see what happens?" asked Cyrus.

"Yeah, I'll give it a few days. Truth is, I'd love to be here if Ladislaw's boys nail Grex – assuming he's complicit. It would be worth it," Jerry said.

"Every investigation has its lull, its dead time. The search of Quarry Island and the nearby waters could take a while. Why not explore our little library? It's nothing like the one in New Haven but I think you'll enjoy it all the same." Thinking of Jerry's latest confrontation with Gretchen, Cyrus looked stern and added, "She's a bloodsucker, Jerry, a vampire who drains people of their humanity. Look how she reacted to Twitchy's death? She's capable of anything." He didn't intend to give Jerry a warning. It just came out.

CYRUS HEADED TO his cottage for what Jerry now figured was a ritual afternoon nap. Jerry went to the Inn and was pleased to learn that Tillie had a fax machine in her office behind the front desk. He sent the enlarged photograph of the finger with the Thorndyke ring to Woody Meacham, wondering if it was a futile effort and he was just going through the motions.

He had not been entirely honest with Cyrus when they parted earlier. Of course, he wouldn't interfere with Ladislaw's team but he wasn't willing to give up yet. It seemed like interest in the mysterious and elusive blonde was fading as fast as a late spring snow. And what about the potential New Haven connection? Did the self-described bitch know one or both partners? Jerry didn't like Gretchen Cadwallader but couldn't stop thinking about her. And Twitchy's death, accident or suicide, a day after fleeing from the wino – was it just a coincidence? And the man in the dark suit huddling with Gretchen when he dropped by the library. Was he really suspicious looking or was Jerry just chasing shadows?

No, he had invested too much in this adventure and Woody would chide him for walking away too soon. Jerry understood that there was likely no connection between the missing partner and what he had discovered in New Haven. Maybe he had it in for Gretchen like he did for Grex and was fabricating a conspiracy. He could acknowledge that it was a very thin thread, ephemeral at best, but he just wasn't ready to let go.

CHAPTER SEVENTEEN:
THE POE ENIGMA

~~

Of course, almost any library could seduce Jerry Kosinsky. When he walked into the quaint, two-room Graniteville Library, the respectful, hushed atmosphere gave him a warm, soothing feeling. It took him back to his childhood in Parlor City where he would bury himself in the stacks, sometimes hiding when he spied his best friend approaching to drag him outside.

Jerry decided before he walked in that he wanted to learn more about Edgar Allan Poe. After reading the encyclopedia entry on the writer, he found a Poe biography and settled in with a contented smile on his face.

Poe was a literary man of considerable talent as a short story writer, poet, editor and critic. Known for his acerbic tongue, he castigated more than one writer, earning him the moniker "tomahawk man."

Born in Boston in **1809**, he was not one of the Brahmins but would do battle with the city's literary elitists years later. Orphaned as a child, he was taken in by wealthy Virginians John and Frances Allan after his mother died while in Richmond. Later, he took their last name as his middle name.

In **1827**, he dropped out of the University of Virginia when John Allan refused to pay his exorbitant gambling debts or provide financial assistance. That same year, he lied about his age and enlisted in the Army using the fictitious name "Edgar A. Perry," successfully rising through the ranks to Sgt. Major. During the year, he published his first work, *Tamberlane and Other Poems*.

After a brief reconciliation, John Allan used his influence and secured Poe's release from the Army and an appointment to West Point. Early on at the Academy, Poe decided to sabotage his nascent career as an Army officer and was court-martialed in **1831**. He was now estranged from his foster father who later left him out of his will.

In the next few years, Poe submitted various pieces to magazines but all are rejected. When he won a writing contest in **1835** for *The Manuscript Found In A Bottle*, Poe finally got a job. The next year, he married his cousin Virginia. She was only 13-years old.

With the publication of *The Murder in the Rue Morgue* in **1841**, he was considered by many to be the creator of the modern detective story. In **1843**, *The Gold Bug* won an $100 prize in Philadelphia and brought Poe considerable recognition but it was his poem "The Raven" that garnered him international acclaim two years later.

While nominally a native of Boston, Poe had no use for the likes of Longfellow, Emerson and Thoreau and what he considered their highly stylized, moralistic writings. He nicknamed them "Frogpondians," a play on the Frog Pond in Boston Commons. The contempt was mutual but the iconoclastic Poe had touched a sensitive nerve.

By **1849**, Poe had been through a succession of literary jobs in New York, Philadelphia, Richmond and Baltimore. His drinking and erratic behavior were a constant source of trouble over the years. Back in Richmond and, two years after the death of his wife, he successfully courted his childhood sweetheart, Elmira Royster, now a wealthy widow by the name of Mrs. Shelton.

After their engagement, Poe decided to travel north to Philadelphia to edit poetry for an acquaintance then proceed to New York City to bring his aunt back to Richmond for his wedding to Elmira. Poe was suffering from some undiagnosed illness and departed Richmond by ferry or train despite the protestations of his physician and Elmira's plea to delay his journey. For some unexplained reason, he ended up in Baltimore.

It was a rainy day in early October of **1849**, only a week after he left Richmond, when Poe was found lying in the gutter outside Ryan's Fourth Ward Poll, a public house in Baltimore that also served as a polling place for that day's sheriff election. Poe, dressed in shabby, second-hand clothes that were not his own, was delirious and only semi-conscious when recognized by a worker from the *Baltimore Sun*. Four days after his arrival in Baltimore, Poe died after saying, "Lord, help my poor soul."

While the official cause of death was listed as phrenitis, or swelling of the brain, Poe's demise was the stuff of mystery and conspiracy theories abounded. He had battled alcohol demons all of his adult life, apparently lost one fiancé because he refused to give up liquor but had recently joined "Sons of Temperance" in Richmond. Many surmised that he fell into a drunken stupor or had succumbed to the illness that dogged him when he left Richmond.

Another theory that gained credence was that Poe was the unfortunate victim of a practice known as cooping, a technique made infamous by vicious gangs during election season. At the time, voter fraud was rampant in Baltimore, particularly so at the Ryan's location. Coopers, as they were called, kidnapped their victims and, after plying them with booze, forced them to vote for a favored candidate – sometimes several times. To perpetuate and facilitate the fraud, victims were forced or encouraged to imbibe to excess and frequently change their outfits. If Poe was a victim of cooping, it would explain not only the scruffy outfit in which he was found but also his apparent drunken state. Poe's biographer received several letters blaming the writer's death on a cooping scheme.

When he put down the biography, Jerry realized that Poe had led a remarkable if ill-fated life and that his death shrouded in mystery to this day was somehow apropos. He had never thought of Poe as a serious writer, assuming incorrectly that he was a second-rate hack with a talent for constructing clever mysteries and macabre horror stories. But this man, educated in the classics while living in England with his foster parents, had a keen intellect and a broad understanding of literary tenets. It was no wonder that he had the temerity to challenge the erudite titans of Boston.

Jerry had trouble believing that Ellis Hoole had any deep love for Poe's writing or knew anything about his tortuous history. *The Gold Bug* had probably been nothing more than a quick read to stoke his interest in buried treasure intrigues. Like Poe, would Hoole's end be shrouded in mystery, he wondered?

For Jerry, it would be a different quest than exploring ancient shrines in Nepal, but after he was finished in Graniteville, he was determined to learn more about this mercurial and tragic man of letters. As he closed the Poe biography, Jerry decided that it was too soon to leave Graniteville. First, he had to be convinced that Ellis Hoole was dead.

CHAPTER EIGHTEEN:
"What's The Word?"

After returning from the library, Jerry sat in his room, picked up Bellow's novel and then put it down without opening it up. The enigmatic Poe was on his mind and he was getting antsy, his head now full of conspiratorial musings. He knew that snooping around Graniteville would be improper with Ladislaw's team launching their investigation.

His thoughts turned to the demise of Twitchy. He felt bad for a guy he hardly knew, partly because Gretchen had been so callous and dismissive. The newspaper article on his death was speculative, not factual, and he wondered what kind of investigation had ensued, if any. He tried to picture Twitchy stepping in front of the train voluntarily and it made him cringe. Plus, the confrontation with the wino was still bugging him.

On impulse, he decided to drive to New Haven in search of Twitchy's antagonist. He slapped the steering wheel and joked, "I'll go to Gretchen. She'll be eager to help me." He didn't think the police would be of any assistance to some stranger and decided that a saloon was his best option. Bartender's always know what's going on in the neighborhood, he reasoned.

Jerry found the Belly Up Bar only two blocks from Union

Station. As he walked in, he was reminded of the two infamous joints back in Parlor City, Crater's and Devils Corner. They were demolished or boarded up before he was old enough to imbibe but he remembered the stories of mayhem and despair surrounding those two notorious saloons. They had contributed to the ruin of many a local family.

Belly Up was a tired, blue-collar dive bar with no pretensions, catering to workers in and around Union Station, including train crews coming off their shifts. The red beer signs in the soot-covered windows were flickering when Jerry pushed open the door.

There was a pin ball machine in one corner flashing lights and the Wurlitzer juke box a few feet away was blasting a twangy country song. The singer was debating the relative value of his girlfriend and his dog. Jerry wasn't sure but it sounded like the canine carried the day. A large Schlitz beer sign hung behind the bar. Shaped like a globe with deep blue seas, it was surrounded by ornate gold leafing, inviting the patrons to a world unknown to them and beyond their reach. The bartender, a middle-aged guy with furtive eyes and slicked-back gray hair, had a grimy bar towel flung over his shoulder. He pushed a mug of draft beer down the bar to Jerry before turning back to the small television mounted precariously on the wall. The "$20,000 Pyramid" was making the studio audience manic but the bartender just shook his head desultorily.

Jerry took a gulp and announced that he was doing a sociology paper on transient populations in various cities. "Finding them is the easy part," the bartender said, eyeing Jerry languidly and pointing over his shoulder toward the train tracks. "Getting them to talk to someone like you is the challenge. I wouldn't go down there without a gun or a baseball bat myself," he cautioned, holding up a Louisville Slugger that had been hidden below the bar. "You'll find a bunch of them across the tracks. Been there for as long as I can remember. Some hop a freight and move on. Others hang on here and die off. Once in a while, one will stagger in the door and stagger out when I introduce them to my friend. It's a Johnny Bench signature. I'm from Cinci," he said, tapping the bat and grinning for the first time.

Jerry had his opening and grabbed it. "I read where some guy fell in front of a train a few days ago. You don't think foul play was involved, do you? I mean with the transients."

"You must be thinking of the guy they call Twitchy," the bartender said. "Used to hang out at Pudge McFadden's and do some stupid Steve Martin routine. Nah, they wouldn't have pushed him on the tracks without first stripping off all of his clothes, especially that cream-colored suit of his. Unless one of them went bananas. Listen, these guys live for T'bird. Gotta be pushing 20% alcohol content. They say it causes temporary insanity and violent behavior. If you've ever been on skid row in any city, you would know what I mean."

"You lost me with T'bird," said Jerry. The bartender was taken aback, almost as if he was offended by Jerry's naivete. "It's known as The American Classic, young man, like the car. I've been told it came out the same year that Ford introduced the T'bird so the makers piggy-backed on the car's popularity. Known as bum wine for the hobo, transient, vagrant, whatever you call them. It's the beverage of choice for many of them. They have nicknames for it like Pluck, Thunderchicken or just plain Bird. The more sophisticated refer to it as brown bag vino. Haven't you heard the phrase, 'What's the word?'" Jerry looked lost and the bartender laughed and went on. His eyes were bright now and he was having a good time. "You shout out that phrase in some low-rent area with a liquor store nearby and you'll most likely hear "Thunderbird" shouted back at you and not even know where it came from. That country singer, Billy Joe Shaver, recorded a song last year with that title. Commercials all over the radio. You been living in a cave the last ten years?"

Jerry was tempted to mention Nepal but didn't. If the bartender was a veteran, it might get unpleasant. He was getting a tutorial and enjoying it. Here was a real bar, with a genuine bartender, not some amusement park like Pudge McFadden's. "Any more advice if I decide to head down there?" Jerry asked. The bartender scowled and said, "You look like a nice guy and are probably big enough to handle yourself one on one but if a bunch of them go loco and jump you, it won't be pretty. Hey, I'll lend you my bat if you promise to bring it back." Jerry declined and the bartender said, "Okay, then stop at the liquor store across the street and pick up several bottles of their beverage of choice. You can get them for 80 cents or so. Some places sell a smaller version that the boys call shorty but you'll impress them with the big ones. They'd sell their mothers' souls for that sweet rot gut. I've got a strong stomach but almost threw up when I took a taste of that swill on a dare."

Jerry reached out his hand but the bartender ignored it and started toweling down the bar. When Jerry was at the door, he heard, "Good luck to you, kid. Look for the purple and black lips and you'll know you've found the T'bird fan club. If you make it out of there in one piece, stop back in and then I'll shake your hand and buy you a drink."

Jerry paused while holding the doorknob, then walked back to the bar and leaned over. "On second thought, I'll take Johnny Bench with me," he said, pointing to the bat.

THE LIQUOR STORE clerk looked bewildered when Jerry put six bottles of Thunderbird on the counter. "Having a bum vino party?" he asked. He thought he'd seen everything but clammed up and just shook his head when he noticed the baseball bat that Jerry was leaning on.

Jerry walked over the same embankment that Twitchy had

traversed only a few days earlier in the pre-dawn hours of his last day on earth. He saw what looked like a camp or make-shift shelter in the distance, on past rows of tracks that threaded and crisscrossed in a complex network through the train yard. As he got closer, he could see a few disheveled men stumbling around with others laying on the ground, passed out or asleep. Debris was everywhere. Discarded food wrappers, empty cans of beans but mainly discarded bottles. He noticed the distinctive Thunderbird label and knew he was in the right neighborhood.

Someone from the camp spotted him and, yelling something unintelligible, aroused a few of his comrades from their stupors. Jerry pulled a bottle of Thunderbird from the bag and held it up high. "What's the word?" he shouted. There was a few seconds of silence and then the encampment came alive with a cacophonous chorus of "Thunderbird!" Damn if that bartender wasn't right on the mark, Jerry said to himself.

At the edge of the camp, Jerry halted and put down the bag. A shirtless man, scarred and tattooed, was squatting nearby, swigging from a bottle inside a paper bag. Jerry recoiled from the stink of vomit. The reek of Thunderbird seemed to be absorbed into every piece of ragtag clothing laying about the ground.

He wriggled the bat on his shoulder to make sure that everyone could see it. "Help yourselves, gentlemen. The T'bird is on the house. All I ask in return is a little information and I'll leave you to enjoy yourselves." Jerry stepped back a few steps as there was a rush at the bag. The twist caps came off quickly and the chugging began in silence. In a different time, Jerry would have been guilt-ridden and ashamed of himself. Today, he looked on this detritus of humanity and knew it was impossible to deny that most of them were beyond redemption.

After a few minutes of watching the party, Jerry said, "I've got a couple of bucks for anyone who can help me find someone with their right hand wrapped in a bandage. He's not in trouble and I'm not a cop. He just has some information that would be helpful to me."

A few of the group wandered away with their bottles while eyeing Jerry suspiciously. Then, he heard, "You lookin for Smitty? He ain't here and mightn't be coming back soon, mebbe never. He at the hospital. Hand real bad."

Jerry tossed a few dollars to the man who stuffed them in his pocket as someone from behind lurched for them. "What hospital?" Jerry asked, stepping back and assuming a batting stance when he noticed some of the group whispering.

"He be at Good Shepherd. Now, you best move along before the Bird make some of us act crazy. He not like some of this crew. Smitty'll talk to you. When he does, do him a solid, man." His mouth was open and his tongue was black. The lips had a purplish tinge that Jerry hadn't noticed earlier. The bartender was right again. T'bird could quickly turn this crew into mad men.

Jerry started backing away toward the embankment when he saw 3 or 4 of the men get up and start to stumble toward him. He reached in his pocket, pulled one-dollar bills from his wallet and threw them into the air. As they fluttered to the ground, the pursuit stopped and the scramble was on.

When he got to the street, Jerry sighed deeply and wiped sweat from his brow. He remembered the old saying, discretion is the better part of valor, and kissed the baseball bat. He thought of the Clintock twins, two hoods from his childhood days in Parlor City and Elwin Grex on Quarry Island. He was certain that they would have gladly taken a few swings at the winos and done some damage. Jerry Kosinsky could have knocked them down like so many bowling pins but he was still the gentle giant of his youth without a vicious bone in his body. The American Classic, he mumbled to himself. What a sad commentary.

JERRY WALKED BACK into the Belly Up with the bat on his shoulder. The bartender grinned and before he even got to the bar, a shot and a beer were waiting for him. The bartender was inspecting the bat as Jerry drank and said, "Well, no blood stains to wash off. I guess the sight of Johnny Bench was enough to tame those animals. You're a lucky guy, all the same."

"Where's Good Shepherd?" Jerry asked. "It's roughly ten blocks north, just off Park. Can't miss it when you get close. Say, are you sure you didn't put one of those alkies in the hospital?" the bartender dead-panned, pointing to the bat.

"Not a chance. They called me the Gentle Giant when I was growing up. Still am, I guess," Jerry said as he got up from his bar stool. "You take care now and good luck with that project of yours," the bartender said. He reached over the bar and this time gave Jerry's hand a vigorous shake.

WALKING OVER TO the hospital, Jerry couldn't stop thinking about the outcasts he had just encountered – or had they dropped out voluntarily, just said the hell with it all? Even if some of them were victims of some tragedy that no one knew about, they were now pariahs, modern-day lepers to be avoided if not shunned by society. At least one of them had spoken up for Smitty. He had shown a flicker of humanity in a sea of lost souls and might be roughed up for doing so.

Jerry entered the crowded emergency room at Good Shepherd, a charity hospital dating back to the Civil War. Prior to then, it had been an almshouse serving the urban poor with shelter, food and medical care. It was a depressing place, under-staffed and ill-equipped, with a physical structure that had already deteriorated beyond the point of repair.

In a corner sprawled on the floor, Jerry spotted Smitty,

grimacing and rocking back and forth while holding up his right arm. The hand was wrapped in the same dirty bandage he had seen outside of Pudge McFadden's. Jerry approached gingerly and said, "Smitty." The wino was startled. He looked up and gasped, before saying, "You gotta help me doc. It's killing me."

Jerry struggled for a moment but decided to prevaricate. If Smitty realized he wasn't a doctor, he would most likely clam up. "Tell me what happened so I can help you. How did you hurt your hand?" Jerry said, conjuring up his most sympathetic voice. Smitty stared at Jerry and pulled a bottle from his pocket. It was a Thunderbird "Shorty" for winos on a budget. Poison on the cheap, Jerry thought.

Smitty took a slug and held the bottle between his legs while screwing the top back on. He looked around suspiciously as he stuffed it back in his jacket. He brightened up for a moment, invigorated by the potent hit, and gurgled before saying, "Damn Twitchy double-crossed me and now I can't find him. I'll crack that bastard's head open when I catch him." Smitty had taken the bottle out again and was waving it in the air. A nurse was walking by and snatched the bottle in mid-stride and disappeared down the hall. Smitty was energized by his loss and sprung up, pursuing her in a frenzy while yelling unintelligibly. Jerry had lost his moment but now he knew where to find Smitty. He had also learned that there was some arrangement between the two of them and that Twitchy had reneged before his death.

"What's your interest in the bum?" asked someone standing behind Jerry. He turned around to see a young guy in short-cropped brown hair in full preppy attire, a throwback to the 60s with his khakis, penny loafers, blue blazer and madras tie. He was grinning as if he had said something clever. "And you are?" Jerry replied, peeved at losing his moment with Smitty and taking instant dislike to his interlocutor. "Boyd Mandeville, city desk at the *New Haven Beagle*. My editor sent me down here to check on the wino. Got a tip he was here and might know something about the character who jumped in front of a train a few days ago. Sounds like a wild goose chase, it you ask me, but here I am."

"You're referring to Twitchy," Jerry said. "Yeah, you know him, too? Did you call in the tip? What's going on, anyway? I don't mind telling you that I could use a scoop, preferably something scandalous or juicy. It can be off the record if that's what you want. I just need the skinny," Mandeville said, sounding desperate.

Jerry needed some help. If this guy was legit, it might be his best bet. He didn't have to like him. Jerry asked to see his press credentials, looked them over and said, "I met Twitchy a few days ago over at Pudge McFadden's. He's friends, or used to be, with a Gretchen Cadwallader who works at the library. That night, outside the bar, Smitty appeared out of nowhere. When Twitchy saw him, he took off with Smitty in pursuit. Today, I went over to the hobo encampment at the trainyard. One of Smitty's compatriots told me he came here."

Mandeville's eyes brightened. "Wow, maybe you should be the reporter. You're not a detective, are you? Maybe a private eye?" he asked, eagerly. Jerry laughed and said, "Just curious, that's all," not ready to say more.

"Listen, if you think of anything else, would you give me a call? This is my first job out of college and I ain't exactly a Woodward or Bernstein, if you know what I mean." Mandeville pulled out a card and handed it to Jerry, then said, "If I learn anything, I'd be glad to share it with you. Not supposed to but it only seems fair."

Jerry smiled. Maybe he wasn't such a jerk after all, he thought. "I'm from out of town. Staying at the Thimbletown Inn up in Graniteville for a few more days. You can get a message to me there. Smitty knows something about Twitchy. He just told me that Twitchy double-crossed him before the nurse snatched his

Bird. You saw the rest. Maybe their conflict's not connected to his death but whatever it is, it made Twitchy run from the wino."

Jerry heard "catch you on the flip side" as he walked away. He had been close to getting something out of Smitty and then he had to wave the damn bottle of Thunderbird in the air like a warning flair. It was a decent gesture from the reporter but Jerry was discouraged. He had trouble putting faith in the investigative skills of the sophomoric Boyd Mandeville who was now trying to figure out what the Bird was.

CHAPTER NINETEEN:
BURIED TREASURE

Ladislaw's team commandeered the chief's office to interview Grex, sending Buffle slinking back to his desk across from the niece.

Reg had borne the barely-disguised smirks of the troopers as best he could, having no ability – or courage – to retaliate. But he could not hold back from unleashing a torrent of invective on the girl. "They're here because of you, you conniving little snitch. I was handling everything fine myself before you called the chief behind my back. I directed you to contact the college but instead you get on the blower with your uncle. Don't bother denying it."

Fanny just smiled, further enraging Buffle. He stood up and pounded on his desk, causing one of the troopers to open the door to the chief's office and ask, "Everything okay out here, Miss Tulk?" Fanny just grinned. She liked to provoke Buffle and knew that anything she said, no matter how innocuous, would drive him closer to the edge. She had concluded long ago that he was all hot air and feared no retribution except more of his airy rage. That she could handle easily. "Grex doesn't look too happy in there, Acting Chief, and I'm guessing it's not just due to his hangover. You might want to consider how to distance yourself from your drinking buddy and lay off me."

Self-preservation suddenly became more important to Buffle than the friendship with his beer-guzzling buddy. He would never acknowledge her point but did immediately take it to heart. What if Grex was in serious trouble, had actually played a role in his partner's disappearance? Grex had castigated the partner more than once and had told Buffle that he wished he had never met the man. It was unthinkable until that moment but now Buffle wondered what the troopers would find when they searched Quarry Island. He thought about the severed finger with the partner's college ring still on it. If it had drifted over to DeCourcy Island, then where in hell was the rest of the body? He looked into the chief's office and could see Grex shaking his head violently back in forth as the lead trooper hovered over him. It sent shivers down Buffle's spine.

As the day progressed, and to anyone who would listen, Buffle talked as if he hardly knew Grex, might even walk past him on the street and not even exchange hellos. He would paint a picture of their relationship as mere acquaintances who occasionally had a beer together, teammates on the Graniteville softball team. Of course, it was laughable but then everything that Buffle did outside of the strict protocols of the constable's manual was looked on with either bemusement or ridicule.

GREX INSISTED, AS he had earlier with Cyrus and Jerry, that he had not seen his partner in over a month and, as far as he knew, he had not set foot on Quarry Island during his recent visit to the area. He had started the interview with the troopers haughty and indignant, almost bellicose, but after an hour of questioning was starting to wear down.

When Grex learned that the ring on the severed finger

belonged to Hoole, he slumped in his chair and started feverishly rubbing his temples. The troopers knew about the previous night's escapade with Buffle and were keeping the pressure on. Grex was not a quick-witted or insightful man but it dawned on him that he was now a likely suspect in his partner's disappearance.

"Did you guys have any survivor insurance policies?" one trooper asked. "What the hell is that?" barked Grex, not liking the sound of things. "Let me explain, Grex. One partner dies and the surviving partner gets to collect money. You guys have anything like that in place?" It sounded even worse to Grex now. If he was the survivor, then the implication was clear. Hoole would have to be dead.

"Listen, the business was in big trouble. I had bid low on a few granite jobs just to keep the crew busy and, quite frankly, we couldn't deliver. Shit, we were losing our shirts. Yesterday, that Portuguese bunch took off just because we were a few weeks behind with the payroll. Hoole was supposed to come down and straighten things out. That's his job. I know it may look bad but I might as well tell you guys now. I borrowed some money from petty cash to tide me over. My ex back in New Bedford got a court order against me for delinquent alimony and child support. I didn't embezzle, damn it. It was an advance that I was going to put back somehow. But I swear to god that I know nothing about my partner's disappearance or any damn insurance policy."

Grex was bent over with his hands covering his eyes. He looked pathetic and his burst of candor garnered no sympathy from the troopers. They all knew Grex. Even if part of what he was saying was the truth, the whole thing didn't sound kosher. "We'll have a court order this afternoon to visit Quarry Island, Grex. Until we complete our work there, you're not allowed back on."

"I can go back tonight, right? I have no place else to stay,"

Grex pleaded. "Hard to say, El. We'll let you know. Maybe those babes from last night are still in town and they'll make room for you. Or, you could stay with your best friend out there. That's your problem." The lead trooper immediately regretted his sarcasm but he couldn't help himself.

Grex ignored the taunt, a comment that would normally make him pounce, and cleared his throat. "Not sure how much you'll find in quarry records. We had a fire," he said plaintively. He realized as he said it how bad it made him look.

Armed with a court order, the troopers descended on Quarry Island. It was early afternoon and they hoped to complete their investigation before dusk. They picked through the charred remains of the two-room quarry office and carefully packed up the few items that had survived the blaze. According to Grex, the missing partner had handled the business and financial aspects of the enterprise and Grex's job was strictly bidding and production. In theory, it was a good arrangement.

After the troopers left, Buffle holed up with Grex in the chief's office as Fanny looked on. Buffle took a contrived, official tone that Grex had never witnessed before and didn't like. No, Grex couldn't stay at his place that night because Buffle might have family coming in from out of town. When Buffle offered to spot him money for a motel room, Grex angrily grabbed the twenty from his hand. "I wouldn't recommend getting sloshed tonight, El. You're going to feel even worse tomorrow morning than you do now," Buffle said, feigning sympathy. While his advice was sage, Grex saw through it and stormed out.

Grex headed to the bar where Buffle and he had encountered the two women the night before. He couldn't remember what they looked like except for an abundance of teased hair and glossy red lips. He had no carnal urges at the moment. He was simply intent on relieving his mental and physical anguish. Getting obliterated was the only way he knew how.

A PLAINCLOTHES TROOPER sat in a corner booth of the bar sipping a coke, watching Grex order a shot with a beer chaser. Grex would grow increasingly morose as he pondered his life. He had left New Bedford officially a bankrupt but had siphoned enough cash out of his cement company in its waning months of solvency to start over in Graniteville. As luck would have it, or so he thought at the time, his ad for an investor in the quarry operation had brought him together with Ellis Hoole. Grex had some nefarious partners in the past who could have disappeared and no one would have given a damn. This time, he had the misfortune to pick an investor with an inquisitive family.

Grex inventoried his problems and it made him knock down another shot. Bad teeth, bad ticker and bad arches. His former wife had turned the kids against him and now Buffle was distancing himself. In a moment of false bravado, he said he didn't even care if those fuckin troopers found Hoole's body buried on Quarry Island.

IT WAS LATE Wednesday afternoon on the far side of the island away from the quarry office, one of the troopers came upon a patch of fresh dirt spread in a small rectangle like a miniature grave. After a few minutes of digging, he came to a black plastic bag with a tie at the top. He thought of the severed finger and braced himself for the possibility of discovering more body parts. Another trooper was called over to witness and corroborate the moment. When the bag was opened, they found a man's shirt and a pair of pants with a wallet in the back pocket. Inside the wallet were family photos, a few one dollar bills and a receipt for a stay at the Brightwood Motel with the missing partner's name on it.

The sun was setting and the immediate area was quickly searched for another spot of freshly-turned dirt and, quite possibly, a grim discovery. Nothing was found and the troopers would have to continue the next day.

The lead trooper radioed the mainland and Ladislaw authorized the arrest of Elwyn Grex who, at the moment, was having trouble staying upright on his bar stool.

CHAPTER TWENTY:
CASE CLOSED

WHEN JERRY GOT back to the Thimbletown Inn, he had a message from Woody. He called back but his friend was unavailable. The mystery of the ring had been solved so he didn't really need Woody's help in that respect. He just wanted to hear his friend's voice and engage in small talk, if nothing else. When Jerry asked if he could be reached elsewhere, he learned that a sensational murder had occurred that very afternoon. "Biggest event in Parlor City since those murders over twenty years ago. It's crazy here but I'll try to get him your message," he was told. She sounded thrilled, as if Parlor City was overdue for some excitement.

Jerry was hesitant to tell Cyrus about his latest adventure in New Haven but with Woody unavailable, he needed someone to talk to. He had no coherent theory with respect to the connection between Twitchy and Smitty – except for the mysterious blonde. He was just uncomfortable and suspicious. He went to the front desk and Tillie informed him that her brother would be coming over to the café for dinner, then added, "The news is spreading like wildfire. Mr. Grex has been arrested. The state police found his partner's personal items buried on Quarry Island. They're going back tomorrow to search for the body. I hope that awful man gets his due." She was excited and nervous at the same time, as if relating what was now public information might somehow be a breach of propriety. It made Jerry chuckle inwardly. Tillie clearly abhorred Grex but still called him mister.

Jerry wasn't shocked by the news. Grex was easy to suspect of almost any crime you could mention. It had been speculation before but now there was physical evidence that seemed to link him to his partner's disappearance. Jerry's afternoon encounter in New Haven with Smitty and the rest of the wino brigade suddenly seemed inconsequential.

LADISLAW'S TEAM SPOKE to all the watermen around Graniteville. They showed the picture of Grex with Hoole but no one remembered taking the missing partner out to Quarry Island in the last month. The troopers were all confident that they had their man and that he would eventually confess when the booze wore off. Still, they were baffled as to how Grex lured Hoole to the island and no one saw it.

GREX WAS TRANSPORTED to the county jail, the constable's office having nothing more than a storage room to secure a suspect. He was so drunk when they shuffled him out of the bar, they could have put him in stocks and planted him in the town square and he wouldn't have objected.

Over at the barracks, one trooper was reviewing and cataloging the files that had been salvaged from the quarry office fire. In one folder, an insurance policy was discovered like the one Grex had been questioned about earlier. If one partner died, the surviving one received a cash payout of $25,000. It was noteworthy that the policy had been taken out only two months earlier. As the evidence piled up against him, Grex was passed out in his cell, oblivious to it all.

TINY GRANITEVILLE WAS abuzz with the apprehension of Elwyn Grex. He was well known as a brute and a bully, not a candidate for sympathy and compassion even among the most devout, God-fearing Christians in town. No one entertained the possibility that he might not be guilty or that there might be mitigating circumstances, say an argument between the partners that grew heated and resulted in accidental death. How could Grex offer a plausible explanation for the Hoole's personal items buried on Quarry Island, if reports were accurate? The wallet was enough for most people – even without a body.

THAT EVENING, SITTING in the café picking at the pot roast special, Cyrus and Jerry both expressed puzzlement over Grex's apparent obtuseness. "Why didn't he just erect a neon sign above the plot of dirt with a blinking arrow pointing to the ground? As I see it, assuming that Grex killed him, he had to have dismembered the body on the island. That's the only logical explanation for the finger washing up on DeCourcy Island," said Cyrus. "Why cut off only one finger, the one with the college ring no less? So, he dumps the body parts in Long Island Sound and the finger floats ashore. And not just any finger but the one with the Thorndyke ring which immediately implicates Grex. It makes no sense to me," Jerry said, frustrated with his own logic.

"You're starting to sound like a real detective, Jerry. Your friends back home would be proud of you. Maybe you've discovered your avocation here in Graniteville," Cyrus said. Jerry shrugged and Cyrus went on, "Grex's elevator doesn't go all the way to the top floor, Jerry. I agree that if your theory is correct, it was quite a blunder on his part. It surprised me, too. Maybe he panicked. Trust me when I say that even highly intelligent people do stupid and impulsive things in stressful circumstances. And don't discount Grex's temper, especially when he's liquored up. You've already seen that side of him on display."

Jerry shook his head and chewed on his lower lip. It was futile to speculate further about Grex until Ladislaw's team completed their work. He decided to tell Cyrus about his afternoon adventure in New Haven.

Cyrus was taken aback and almost dropped his fork. He wiped his mouth with his napkin and said, "What the hell possessed you to go down there all by yourself with only a baseball bat for defense. This obsession with Twitchy and the wino has nothing to do with the partner's disappearance. Tell me, is it because of the girl at the library? I know she got under your skin but is that it?"

"Maybe," Jerry said. "You know, she was out here a few days before the finger was found, ostensibly to prepare for the kids' field trip. Don't you think Ladislaw's team should at least talk to her, especially if they don't find a body on Quarry Island? Sure, it's a long shot, but perhaps she saw something. And just for the record, I do feel that she was complicit in Twitchy's death. Yes! She tore him down constantly, by her own admission. Maybe he'd still be alive if she was more supportive, a true friend."

Cyrus smiled warmly. "You're a good man, Jerry Kosinsky. If it'll make you feel better, we can go over to see Ladislaw in the morning. Tell him what you learned and let his boys handle Gretchen, okay? Now, Tillie's been watching us; let's attack this pot roast before it gets cold.

JERRY SAT IN his room, hoping that Woody got his message and would call back that night. Cyrus had been supportive, even complimentary, but it wasn't enough. He needed to call the wife and give her the latest news but had procrastinated so long that he felt certain that Ladislaw's team had already done so. He would confirm that in the morning.

He was sitting on the end of the bed and flipped on the television. *Barney Miller* came on but he was in no mood for canned humor so he clicked to the next channel and saw *The Man From Atlantis*. Not a science fiction fan, one more click brought him to *Hawaii Five-O* and when he heard Detective Captain Steve McGarrett say, "Book'em, Danno," he thought of Grex. He watched for a few minutes until a commercial break with dancing cats singing "Chow Chow Chow" made him turn off the set and fall back on the bed.

He glanced over at the nightstand. There was *Augie March* staring at him. He grabbed the Bellows novel and propped up a few pillows. Damn, he was a writer of the first order, he said to himself. He felt better while reading about the fictional Augie who, on a quest, was combatting feelings of alienation and helplessness.

Later on, laying in the dark with only a slit of light emerging from under his door, Jerry decided that he would only hang around Graniteville for a few more days – unless something dramatic happened to dissuade him. He wasn't ready to go back to Parlor City and had pretty much decided to drive down to Baltimore. He had gotten into his head the idea to visit Poe's grave and it wouldn't go away.

CHAPTER TWENTY-ONE:
A NEW TWIST

WHEN CYRUS CALLED Ladislaw Thursday morning to arrange for a meeting, he wasn't sure the lieutenant would have time to indulge them. Calling in a favor on the slim evidence that Gretchen had visited the Thimble Islands right before the finger washed ashore might be seen as inconsequential – particularly in light of the Quarry Island discovery.

"Come in, Cyrus. I'll listen to what your friend has to say. Matter of fact, your call was timely. Our prisoner has clammed up and now says he'll talk only to you. Still a member in good standing at the bar, right?"

"Yes, but I haven't had a client in years and I'm not looking for one now, especially the likes of Grex. He'd be advised to look elsewhere," Cyrus said.

"Not even sure he knows you practiced law in the past. In fact, he hasn't even requested a lawyer. Come by and let's talk before you say no. It would be a favor to me," Ladislaw said. He was not pleading but there was a tone in his voice that indicated tension and Cyrus picked up on it immediately.

So now the tables were reversed and Cyrus felt he had no choice but to oblige the lieutenant.

Ladislaw folded his hands and listened politely as Jerry described his first meeting with Gretchen and his subsequent visit to the DeCourcy Institute where he learned that she had been to the Thimble Islands shortly before the finger was found. He left out any mention of Twitchy or Smitty.

"I'll get one of my boys to contact the girl and bring her in for questioning. It makes sense to tie that detail down even if we are feeling comfortable with our circumstantial case against Grex. I don't like loose ends and maybe she saw something that she didn't tell Buffle. We'll go down to New Haven to accommodate her, if necessary." The mention of Buffle had everyone smiling, even the undemonstrative Ladislaw.

"I did not contact the wife after the ring was found. Guess it was a fortuitous delay, in light of the discovery of the wallet," Jerry said. "Ah, yes," said Ladislaw, "Thanks for bringing that up. We have tried to reach her repeatedly at her home in Vermont without success. Any clue where she might be?" Ladislaw asked. Jerry was hesitant to suggest Toronto, thinking it was widely perceived as a hotbed of unpatriotic war protesters and deserters. He was in a sea of state troopers and something told him that most, if not all, of them were veterans. Instead, he simply said, "I can check a few places if that would be helpful." Ladislaw nodded yes and added, "Just keep us posted."

"Grex?" Cyrus asked, reminding Ladislaw of his request. "Yes, well he's in a great deal of pain after last night's bender. Not as if anyone is sympathetic. As for his mental state, it's self-induced agony and I have no pity for that either. Unlike a lot of drunks, he's not remorseful. Just miserable. Anyway, he's been causing a ruckus over at the jail, Cyrus. Before he does some damage to himself or one of the deputies over there, I'd love to get him to open up. You might mention that we found an insurance policy and he's a beneficiary if Hoole is dead.

"You know me, Cyrus. We're not going to coerce a confession out of him. I will not sit still for that tactic. But if he'd just relax and let go of his anger, who knows what details might spill out?"

Cyrus didn't respond and Ladislaw went on. "I understand we made the papers in New Haven and Providence – even up in Boston since Grex is from up that way. The state representative from this area has been barking up the chain of command and my bosses have made it clear that they want this story off the front pages as soon as possible."

Cyrus felt bad for Ladislaw. He was a straight shooter but not immune to political pressure. "Call over to the jail and make sure he agrees that we meet on condition that Jerry accompany me. I don't want anyone, including Grex or some public defender, saying later on that there was some sort of attorney/client privilege as a result of our little chat. I will warn Grex myself before we sit down that he shouldn't say anything remotely incriminating or even exculpatory that can't be repeated in public." When Cyrus finished, Ladislaw picked up the telephone and started dialing. "I'll pass on the conditions, Cyrus, and let them know you are on the way."

GREX GRUMBLED WHEN he saw Jerry even though he had been advised that his presence was a condition of the meeting. The prisoner was holding a paper coffee cup and his hands were trembling. Going without booze after a binge was a new experience for Grex and he craved a Falstaff bracer to ease the transition.

After Cyrus' cautionary admonition, Grex said, "I didn't

see him and I damn well didn't kill him. Believe it or not, our business arrangement was pretty stable until about six months ago. Soon, bills started piling up and creditors hounded us for payment. He only came down every few weeks so the pressure landed on me to field a bunch of angry calls. When he showed up, the last time was about a month ago, he said not to worry and that he would take care of things. Then, we're out to dinner one night and he's all over me about the petty cash account. It was a bad time for me with the ex. I was behind on alimony and child support so I took an advance and he caught it. Sure, I shoulda told him but I was embarrassed but I did put a note in the cash box. We were in public and he wouldn't let it go. It was like he wanted to provoke me so others would witness it. Said he might have to notify the police. I lost my temper, reached across the table and grabbed him by the collar. I'm sure a few people in the restaurant witnessed it. Hey, I'm no lovable teddy bear. Don't you think I know that? But I'm supposed to have killed my partner over a few lousy thou? C'mon!"

Cyrus and Jerry were thinking the same thing. Sure, Grex wasn't likable but his story about the petty cash wasn't absurd and might even be true. Cyrus spoke next.

"You can be sure that investigators already know about the restaurant incident or will know soon enough. If everything you say is true, how do you explain the insurance policy payout to the surviving partner? The troopers found it and it is probably worth a hell of a lot more than two thousand dollars."

Grex looked startled and started stammering. "I know nothing about some survivor insurance policy. Ladislaw's boys already grilled me about it. Kept pressing me to trip me up. If there is a policy, he took it out without asking me. If he had, I would've said use the money to pay some quarry bills instead. My two businesses back in New Bedford went kaput. Along with the booze, they cost me my marriage. The quarry operation was my last chance."

"And the partner's personal items buried on the island?" Jerry asked in a neutral tone, hoping not to provoke Grex. It didn't work. Grex jumped up and the guard standing at the door moved toward him quickly. "Sorry," Grex said softly, sitting down with a thud as if all the life had been drained out of him.

Grex started whispering, fearful that another outburst would end the session. He had a point to make when asking to see Cyrus and he got to it now. "It's a frame-up, I tell you. Why would I kill my partner and then bury his wallet where a blind squirrel could find it? Shit! It's easy to paint me as the bad guy. I would. But Hoole's no choir boy. What about that blonde I saw him cavorting with? She was young enough to be his daughter. Him with an ailing wife back in Vermont. I'm no Prince Charming but he ain't exactly a saint. And how about the fire that woke me up one night? Guess I started it and then put it out instead of letting it burn. Now, I hear about some insurance policy. I tell you, there's something fishy here and I'm probably going to get railroaded. Maybe it's what I deserve for being a jerk most of my life."

As he listened to Grex, Jerry was reminded about his own ruminations the night before at dinner. And now the blonde was back in the story. He looked at Cyrus who seemed to be deep in thought and turned to Grex. "Any idea where to find her? The blonde, I mean," Jerry asked, not expecting any help. "Not a clue. I only saw them together once, in a booth at a diner in the next town over. They were sitting close together until they saw me. I can't say she was a gold digger but Hoole looked like a puppy dog. It was disgusting."

"Do you consider yourself indigent, Elwyn? Cyrus asked. "If you mean mad, hell yes," Grex said. "No, it means that you can't afford an attorney. If that's the case, the state is required to provide you with one," Cyrus said.

Grex dropped his head into his hands and moaned. He brushed a hand across his eyes and said, "Yeah, I'm practically broke, in case you didn't already know. What a system. The government boys are after me for a crime I didn't commit and now the very same government that pays them is going to pay an attorney to defend me. Tell me, am I to believe that someone is actually on my side?"

Cyrus reminded Grex that he had not been officially charged with any crime but it seemed imminent. "My advice is simple. Talk to no one except in the presence of legal counsel. If there is any information that will help exonerate you, even if it's embarrassing personally, share it with your attorney."

Jerry and Cyrus stood up when the guard said, "Time's up." They looked down on Elwyn Grex, clutching the empty paper cup like a lifeline. He looked much smaller than the belligerent man looming over them just a few days earlier on Quarry Island.

At the door, Cyrus turned back and said, "Remember, zip locked lips except with your attorney. Perhaps we will talk again. Oh, and ease up on the sheriff deputies. It'll go better for you."

Jerry felt compelled to say something encouraging and, half-smiling, added, "I've been trying to find that blonde since I arrived in Graniteville. Haven't given up yet."

A muffled "thank you" could be heard as the door clicked shut. Grex had no beer can to crush to relieve his frustration. He started pulling at the coffee cup and ripped it apart.

WHEN THEY GOT outside the jail, Cyrus and Jerry didn't speak for several minutes. Finally, Jerry said, "Not exactly a sympathetic sort of guy. But ------" "Right!" interrupted Cyrus, with more animation that Jerry had seen before. "Grex looks as dumb as an ox but, in my judgment, he's not that stupid. His arrogance surfaces when he feels cornered. Finding the partner's personal items was too easy; he's got a point there. I gotta believe that

Ladislaw knows it, too, and it's why he was hoping that Grex would open up to us. Maybe he thought Grex would blurt out a confession even after being warned to keep his mouth shut. At this point, I'm not judging whether he's guilty or innocent. Maybe there's another clue in those office records besides the insurance policy. If there is, Ladislaw's team will search like hell for it. Without a body, all they've got is a circumstantial case to take to a grand jury."

"And the blonde?" Jerry asked quickly before Cyrus could go on. "She just keeps popping up and this time it wasn't me who invoked her name. And with all the focus on bad boy Grex, what do we really know about Ellis Hoole? My whole theory has been based on the assumption that he was a decent family man, maybe a bit naïve, who got duped by an unscrupulous partner."

"Well, he probably looks like Bishop Sheen compared to Grex, Jerry. I'm not necessarily buying the story Grex laid out for us, at least not all of it, but it didn't seem rehearsed or contrived. He actually showed some humanity, even some humility. And assuming he's broke, he'll get a public defender assigned – if he wants one. I hope he's not dumb enough to think he can act as his own counsel."

Jerry was hardly listening to Cyrus' last speculation. He was thinking of the blonde again. Had she seduced this receptive, middle-aged man with a sick wife back home, as Grex had suggested? What did she have to gain and who else might have seen them in that diner to corroborate Grex?

"When Ladislaw's team interviewed the watermen, they presumably asked them if anyone had recently taken Hoole out to Quarry Island. That we can take for granted," Jerry said. "Okay, don't laugh, Cyrus. What if we ask them about the blonde – or anyone else during the period in question. The blonde would certainly be remembered a lot more vividly than a middle-aged, non-descript balding guy."

"If you want to get cynical and morbid, Jerry, let's say that the blonde met the same fate as your middle-aged guy and is either buried on Quarry Island or fish food in Long Island Sound. More likely, she was hustling the man, played around with him for a few days and, when she realized he wasn't going to be a big score, simply took off. But just to satisfy what I fear is your insatiable curiosity about mysterious blondes, let's go see if one of the watermen remembers her."

CYRUS AND JERRY had spoken to all but one of the watermen and none of them remembered giving a ride to Hoole or the blonde. "There's old Crinkett, our last shot, Jerry. He's been navigating these waters for as long as I can remember and he's even longer in the tooth than me. Can still handle a skiff, though. You wouldn't get two words out of him if you approached him alone." Jerry laughed. "Islander code of silence, I get it."

Crinkett was sitting on a bench gazing out at the water and chewing on a soggy cigar. "Ne'er seen him nor some blonde hussy, Cyrus. I still have an eye for the girls and woulda remembered a looker. Troopers didn't ask after her. What gives?"

"Probably just a wild goose chase, Crinkett. The missing partner was seen with a blonde a few times and they appeared to be pretty chummy, if you know what I mean. We figured she might know something if we could just find her," explained Cyrus.

"If this guy Grex is as evil as people around town are saying, she could be down there right now with the partner – what's left of her, that is." Crinkett chortled as he pointed to the water.

Jerry was flustered and desperate. He reached in his pocket and took out the newspaper article with the picture of Gretchen at the shore of DeCourcy Island, the netting at her feet with the finger tangled in it. She appeared defiant, looking up into the camera.

Jerry unfolded the article and put it in front of Crinkett. "Ever give her a ride?" he asked. Crinkett studied the picture for only a few seconds and laughed. Then, his eyebrows went up and his mouth flew open. "Darned if there ain't something in her look that reminds me of little Betsy what's her name. Used to spend summers here as a kid. That scamp never had no need for my skills, young man. She could navigate like an old salt," he said, handing the article back to Jerry. "Betsy practically grew up on these waters. She knew where all the rocks were, low or high tide, and would cruise the safe channels day or night with ease. Her aunt owned that big house on the hill overlooking the water just a stone's throw from the Thimbletown Inn. You know, Cyrus. It's now the community center. Why am I struggling with the damn name?"

"Cruikshank," said Cyrus, as if distracted. "Leticia Cruikshank. Everyone called her Letty." Crinkett perked up. "Yeah, that's it. She was a gorgeous lady, weren't she now, Cyrus? Wasn't you sweet on her? Darn if I don't remember you calling on her. Died an old maid, poor thing."

Cyrus didn't react and Crinkett went on. "Betsy was a feisty, red-headed devil. Swore like a sailor. Made some of the experienced boys envious but not me. Everyone thought Letty would leave the place to her when she died but she up and donated it to the town. Darndest thing, now that I think about it." He was rubbing his deep brown, gnarled hands as if he might force some more distant memories out of them.

"What happened to Betsy?" Jerry asked anxiously. "Can't help you there, son. She showed up every year to stay with her aunt. Wherever she is now, my guess is that she's raising Cain," he said.

"You've been a big help, Crinkett," Cyrus said somberly. "I don't reckon how but you're welcome all the same," he said. He was chewing on his cigar and looking out on the water. He had done enough talking to last him a month.

AS THEY WALKED away, Cyrus said, "Let me see that article again, Jerry." He held it close to his face then moved it back in forth with a perplexed look on his face. "Not sure what old Crinkett saw in the photograph that reminded him of little Betsy. I sure as hell don't see it."

Jerry didn't say anything. He was more interested in Leticia Cruikshank than her firebrand niece. Was she Cyrus' true love from the past, the paramour that got away?

CHAPTER TWENTY-TWO:
ON THE ROAD AGAIN

~~

AFTER LEAVING THE old waterman, Cyrus and Jerry plopped down in two oversized chairs in the lobby of the Thimbletown Inn. Jerry didn't ask but he assumed that Cyrus was about to disappear for his ritual afternoon nap. He was worried but reluctant to intrude into his personal life and ask a direct question about his health. It would do no good to inquire of Tillie. Cyrus looked paler than when Jerry first met him and he seemed to drift off from time to time, not in a daze but deep in thought and far away.

"Old Crinkett has got me thinking. I've got a contact in vital records, Jerry. It shouldn't take long to get information on Betsy Cruikshank. I'll have him check under Elizabeth as well. She hasn't been seen around these parts since before her aunt died. She must have been twelve or so at the time. Probably about your age now, maybe a bit younger. Like Crinkett said, she was a real fireball and she had a mouth on her, too. Letty was a refined woman and it didn't sit well with her. Funny to remember these things after all these years. I don't know why it didn't dawn on me earlier but the Cruikshanks are from Burlington just like the missing partner. Interesting coincidence. Well, anyway, remind me to tell you about the Cruikshank family history all the way back to England. There was one particularly famous progeny that will interest you."

Jerry wanted to press for more details and ask about his relationship with Letty Cruikshank but something in Cyrus' voice dissuaded him. Instead, he said, "One of these days, I'm going to ask you to provide a list of all your contacts, Cyrus. While your secret agent is checking on Betsy, could you get him to search for information on Gretchen Cadwallader?" Cyrus smiled and said, "Still fixated on that girl, huh? Sure, let's see what we can dredge up."

JERRY WENT BACK to his room and called Vermont but had no more success than Ladislaw. He didn't understand how somehow so anxious to get updates on her husband's disappearance didn't own an answering machine. What if Hoole wasn't dead and was trying to reach her?

It was an intriguing coincidence that both the Hooles and the Cruikshanks were from Burlington but what did it signify anyway? Jerry Kosinsky, wayward detective on a mission to nowhere, he laughed to himself.

Jerry was pacing the room, eager to do something but frustrated because he was at the mercy of other people. He tossed his suitcase on the bed and threw in *Augie March*, a change of clothes and his toothbrush. At the front desk, Tillie had stepped away and the maintenance man stood there on temporary duty, looking awkward and out of place, hoping the telephone wouldn't ring. Jerry left a message for Tillie to tell Cyrus that he would be in Vermont for a few days.

JERRY WASN'T THE only one exasperated that day. Ladislaw's team didn't exhume a single piece of new evidence on Quarry Island and Grex made it clear that he would still talk to no one except Cyrus and Jerry. Ladislaw was hardly surprised when calls to over two dozen harbor towns between Graniteville and New York City confirmed that no bodies, intact or in pieces, had washed ashore. He was starting to feel uncomfortable about the strength of his circumstantial case against Elwyn Grex. Ladislaw was respected as a straight shooter but he knew it would get him only so far with his superiors if he started to express doubts about the guilt of his only suspect.

IT WAS EARLY Thursday evening when Jerry pulled into the Hoole's driveway. He remembered that a car had been parked there on his first visit. It was near dusk and he peered through the windshield at a darkened house. There was no answer to his knock so he walked around the house and peeked into a few windows but saw no activity. As he walked back to his car, he saw the blinds move in a window next door and saw a pair of eyes staring at him through the slit. Jerry waved, trying to look friendly and casual.

Maybe she's out shopping, Jerry thought. He decided to call again that evening and stop by again first thing in the morning. A mile away, he saw a bright red sign for Teddy's Diner and pulled into a parking spot. Slumped forward on a stool at the counter, he looked to his side and saw a telephone booth in the corner. The hinged door was half open and he noticed the hanging telephone directory. As he leafed through it, he saw a George Cruikshank listed. He looked around and no one was watching so he tore out the page and stuffed it into his pocket. He couldn't suppress a grin as he walked back to his stool.

Burlington was not a small town so Jerry wondered what

the chance was that the Cruikshanks and the Hooles even knew each other. He stared at the open menu without reading it and picked up the sound of crackling gum. When he glanced up, the waitress had planted herself in front of him. She was wearing one of those white, one-piece outfits that button up the front, set off by pink lapels. From a distance, you might have mistaken her for a nurse. Close up, Jerry noticed the crusty pink lips and pancake cheeks covering a bumpy complexion. He guessed she was in her mid-thirties but she had the mileage of a 60-year old written all over her face.

She looked down at Jerry through large, pink-rimmed glasses with small inlaid stones and pulled a pencil from a nest of teased, yellow hair not worthy of being called any respectable shade of blonde. "What'll it be, Hon?" she asked sharply between smacks. Jerry looked up but her eyes were diverted as she held up her pad. Figuring if he didn't decide now, she might punish him and never come back, Jerry closed the menu and ordered the cheeseburger special.

Waiting for his food, Jerry rested his elbows on the counter and suddenly felt silly. Here he was, back in Burlington, running around playing detective, acting deadly serious like Jack Webb, surreptitiously tearing pages out of telephone books. It was something Woody and he might have done as kids back in Parlor City. Sure, he was trying to find Hoole but that effort had been futile. He was looking for conspiracies and plots everywhere, first with Gretchen then with Twitchy and Smitty. He was starting to wonder if Grex knew anything about Hoole's disappearance. If the husband had run off with the blonde, he did so missing a finger. That made no sense. And how soon before she ditched him?

And now he was going to deliver bad news to Hoole's wife and then pay a visit to the Cruikshanks – and for what? Sure, maybe they would tell him about Betsy's whereabouts and he could pass the information on to Cyrus. He was starting to get that feeling like he had when leaving Kathmandu and Malmo. A pathetic failure. Jerry was snapped out of his doleful reverie by the sound of popping gum and "Get you anything else, Hon?"

THE WAITRESS FOLLOWED Jerry over to the cashier stand and stood where she could eyeball his wallet as if to compel him to increase whatever tip he planned to leave. He paid his bill and handed her a few bucks. When he asked where Beresford Drive was, she said, "That's the hoity-toity part of town up along the lake, Hon. You got friends in high places?" She was adjusting her pink glasses and peering up at him as she stuffed the bills into her breast pocket. Inexplicably, she started rolling her tongue around her mouth and Jerry caught a glimpse of the wad of pink gum she had been working since he walked in. Was this her way of coming on to him?

"Just a friend of a friend," Jerry mumbled as he turned toward to the door. "I'm working a double tonight. Stop by later for a piece of home-made rhubarb pie if you get hungry and need some company," he heard her say. To Jerry, it came across more as a warning than an invitation.

JERRY CHECKED INTO the Lakeview Lodge, tucked in a recess off the highway. With its log cabin facades and tall pines in the back, it was a bucolic setting designed to relax any weary traveler. When he reached Tillie on the phone, she sounded anxious. "Cyrus has been lingering in the café hoping you'd call. I'll get him."

"Got ants in your pants, Jerry?" he heard when Cyrus got on. He sounded almost cheerful and Jerry was pleased by the cajoling tone. Jerry told Cyrus that the wife wasn't home but that he would go back in the morning. "Probably the best time to catch her, Jerry, if she's there," Cyrus said. "If you'd seen her when I first stopped here, you would've thought she was home-bound she acted so meek and fragile. Very odd. Makes me wonder if it was an act," Jerry said.

"Maybe you should check with the neighbors if she's not there in the morning," said Cyrus. "Read my mind. They were spying on me when I dropped by this afternoon. Probably thought I was casing the joint," Jerry said with a chuckle. "Any news from your end, Cyrus?" he asked.

"Crinkett's comments prompted me to take a trip down memory lane with the Cruikshanks," said Cyrus. "I'd forgotten that Letty's brother, George that is, married the young nurse who tended his wife in her dying days at home. She moved quickly on the widower, some say she took advantage of his grief, and they tied the knot six months later. They had the one child, Betsy. When she got older, little Betsy was shipped down to Graniteville to spend the summer with her aunt. Betsy went to college out west somewhere and basically dropped out of sight."

"You said George, right?" Jerry interjected. "Yesiree, why?" Cyrus responded. "I found a George Cruikshank in the telephone book. Apparently, he lives in some posh neighborhood on the lake not far from downtown."

"Damn, that's got to be him. I'll bet he's ninety years old if he's a day. I just assumed that he had died," Cyrus exclaimed.

"Not even sure why I checked, Cyrus. Guess I was just curious and bored after not finding Hoole's wife at home so checked the telephone book on a whim. Maybe I'm nosing around too much, just playing amateur detective and making a fool out of myself."

Cyrus ignored Jerry's self-flagellation and said, "Hey, as long as you're there, try to see Letty's brother. It'd be a favor to me to find out what happened to Betsy. Probably raising hell on the beaches of California."

"Anything on Gretchen?" Jerry asked. "Nothing on your girl except a Connecticut driver's license. It's not that surprising there's nothing else as she might not even be from these parts. What was a strange coincidence, though, is that there was another Gretchen Cadwallader born not far from here. Died years ago at the age of 5," said Cyrus.

"Another dead-end. Guess I need to get used to it," said Jerry. "Don't give up yet," urged Cyrus. "You might luck out in the morning and catch the wife at home. Who knows, maybe she heard from her husband and Grex is off the hook. It doesn't explain the severed finger with his ring but stranger things have happened. And don't forget, you're doing me a favor by paying a visit to the Cruikshanks. It would be nice to hear that Betsy is doing well, wherever she is."

Jerry was ready to hang up when Cyrus said, "Wait a second. I almost forgot. Spoke to Ladislaw. No luck reaching Gretchen in New Haven. Nothing else found at Quarry Island and Ladislaw is feeling the heat on what was supposed to be a slam dunk case only yesterday. His team got overconfident, thinking they would find a body. Oh, and Grex wants to see us again. You heard me right. Both of us. So, get yourself back here for dinner tomorrow night or I'll be forced to eat alone again."

Jerry felt better when he hung up the phone. The two of them had come a long way since that first chilly encounter on the porch at the Thimbletown Inn. Cyrus Trowbridge actually missed him and enjoyed his company.

CHAPTER TWENTY-THREE:
THE CRUIKSHANK CONNECTION

∽

As Jerry approached the Hoole's house Friday morning, there was no car in the driveway. It was only 7:00 a.m. and he had gone over early to catch the wife before she went out for the day, on the tenuous theory that she had come home late the night before. He had called from the lodge the previous evening and got no answer.

He pulled into the driveway and stood by his car, looking at the darkened house, knowing that it was useless to knock on the door. Then, he heard a disembodied voice from the house next door. "You wasted your time coming back again. She's been gone for a few days."

Jerry looked over to see a middle-aged woman in a drab yellow housecoat standing in the doorway. Her hair was populated with large round curlers and she had a coffee mug in her hand. "Almost called the cops on you yesterday but you looked harmless enough. Bill collector or friend of the family?" The mug was now up to her lips and her eyes were lowered.

"You could say I'm an acquaintance doing the family a favor. Do you know them well?" Jerry asked. The lady smirked and said, "The Hooles are stand-offish folks, been that way since they moved in some 15 or so years ago. An occasional cook-out but that's about it. When the oldest son died in Vietnam and the younger one deserted and bolted to Canada, the parents seemed to go into hibernation." She stopped abruptly, took a sip of coffee and asked, "So, who in the hell are you, anyway?"

Jerry decided that a little honesty might keep her talking so he said, "I know the son. He's living in Toronto. I was here a few weeks ago because the father disappeared and the family asked me to help find him. I'm no detective or investigator, just a guy trying to help out. They thought he might be in Connecticut so I went down there first. No luck."

The woman scowled. "My husband served in the Marines. He'll kick that boy's ass from here to China if he ever comes around here again. Hey, you're not one of them deserters, too, are you? My man is pushing 60 but he wouldn't back down from the likes of you either," she said, sizing Jerry up and pointing a finger at him.

"No, I am not," Jerry said. He thought later that day on the drive back south that he could have really gotten her going by saying, "No ma'am, I'm not a deserter. I'm a draft dodger who just received a presidential pardon for not fighting in that damn war. Was on the run for ten years, first in Nepal and then in Sweden before ending up in Toronto. How do you like them apples?"

The woman knitted her brow and peeked at Jerry through narrowed eyes, holding her mug to shield the lower part of her face.

"Any idea where she went?" Jerry asked, motioning to the Hoole's house. The woman shook her head. "Does she have family in the area she might be visiting? I've been trying to reach her on the telephone for several days without success. With her fragile health, I assumed she would be practically home-bound."

The woman had been looking Jerry up and down as if it

might provide a clue to his character. When she heard Jerry's description of the wife, she jerked the mug and spilled coffee down the front of her housecoat. "Fragile what?" she barked accusingly, as if Jerry had uttered an unforgivable falsehood. "She was outside weeding and watering plants the day before she took off, buzzing around like a busy bee."

She saw the puzzled look on Jerry's face and was enjoying the prospect of setting him straight. "She's a feisty little lady. I don't know what kind of act she put on when you were here but don't let her size and age fool you. Ask me, she ran that family with an iron fist but you can't control everything, now can you? That milquetoast husband of hers, hah! He was gone most of the time but when he was here, she bossed him around loud enough for all the neighborhood to hear. When she's in her cups, she can get real nasty. Likes her gin. All the bullying. I can't figure how he puts up with it. When I step out of line, and it ain't often, Harold will cuff me around a bit to show he's the man of the house. Course, as he says, he never hits me where it shows.

"After news came of the older boy's death, Buddy Hoole that is, she got into it right there in the front yard with his girlfriend. It was a time for grieving but those two went at each other like alley cats. The mother ripped the necklace off the girl's neck and then walked into the house. The girl went down on her hands and knees screaming. The husband came out and joined her. Turned out they were looking for a locket given to her by the boy before he left. Word is that the girl blamed the mother for encouraging her son to enlist. Whooee, she a fiery little redhead. Husband tried to stand up for the girl more than once and the wife lit into him, too."

"Guess she's not off visiting the girlfriend," Jerry said, thinking a little dark humor would keep the woman talking. She didn't catch Jerry's sarcasm and said, "That'd be a laugh. She's from one of those wealthy families living large up on the lake. Her family was incensed that she was dating a local boy.

Let me tell you, Buddy Hoole was a dare devil with his motorcycle and black leather jacket. Nothing like his father. More like my Harold. It must have driven those blue bloods crazy, her riding on the back of his bike all over town. Anyhow, the parents threatened to disown her and sent her away to school. Betty was her name if I'm not mistaken. After that free-for-all on the lawn, she was never seen around her again."

"Betsy Cruikshank?" Jerry suggested. "Damn if that's not the name. How in the hell did you know? Hey, you playing games with me, egging me on? Hank always tells me I don't know when to shut up. You sure you're not police or some private dick?"

"No, no," Jerry said reassuringly, deciding to prevaricate again. "I had a talk with the brother up in Toronto. He told me some of the family history and mentioned some girl that had dated his dead brother and upset his mother. He probably told me the name and it popped into my head when you said Betty. You know, the mind recalls buried stuff like that."

The woman eyed Jerry suspiciously. She wasn't buying his psychology lingo and slipped inside the door without saying another word. He heard the lock click as he walked toward his car.

JERRY STOPPED AT a gas station and got directions to the Cruikshanks. As he drove, he tried to decide how to best get Cruikshank to talk. He worried that even though he might still be listed in the telephone directory, he could be dead. At the very least, he wanted to return to Graniteville with Betsy's address.

He passed through a stone-pillared entrance and, as he rounded the circular drive, caught a glimpse of immaculate, terraced gardens sloping up a gradual hill behind the house.

There was a white-haired man sitting in an Adirondack chair with a blanket covering the lower half of his body. He was not moving and seemed to be staring off into the gently undulating trees lining the back of the property. Off to his left and down through the hill sprinkled with tall trees, Jerry could see a dock and the sparkling water of Lake Champlain. The Cruikshanks weren't just well off, they were rolling in dough, Jerry said as he exited Woody's jalopy.

A maid in a black and white outfit with a small matching cap answered the door. "I'm a friend of Cyrus Trowbridge and am visiting the area. He asked me to pay his respects to Mr. Cruikshank," Jerry said. He was getting comfortable with dissembling. All for a worthy cause, he decided.

Jerry stood in the foyer for a few minutes until a silver-haired woman in an elegant, flower-patterned silk dress came out from a side room. "I'm Mrs. Cruikshank. My husband is indisposed but I will pass on Mr. Trowbridge's best wishes unless there is something in particular that he wished to convey." Her tone was officious and condescending. Perhaps, she saw my car through the window, Jerry thought, and decided I was not worthy of her attention. She was certainly a very handsome woman, probably a beauty in her time, and Jerry could easily imagine how George Cruikshank had, amidst his grief, succumbed to the physical charms of this young nurse some thirty years ago.

She bowed her head slightly and turned away but Jerry wouldn't give up that easily. "Cyrus wanted me to ask after Betsy and see if you could tell him how to reach her. Would you be kind enough to provide an address or telephone number." Mrs. Cruikshank turned back with narrowed, fierce eyes and said, "Our daughter was a major disappointment to us for many years. I emphasize the word was because we no longer have any contact with her. We sent her off to college and she disappeared after graduation. We didn't disown her, as some have suggested. She deserted us – and our way of life. As to her whereabouts,

Cyrus' guess would be as good as mine. She called here once quite some time ago and asked that some belongings be shipped to an address in California. We didn't save the address. Is that sufficient to satisfy Mr. Trowbridge's insatiable curiosity about our family?"

Beneath the refined exterior was a severe, tightly-wound woman who was clearly used to getting her way, a nurse who had worked her way into the Cruikshank's world and was now firmly ensconced. It reminded Jerry of Cyrus' description of Betsy and he wondered if the mother understood what she had wrought. Her condescending tone grated on Jerry, prompting him to persist. "Would it be possible to deliver Cyrus' best wishes in person. Am I mistaken or wasn't that Mr. Cruikshank sitting out back when I arrived? It will only take a few minutes."

Mrs. Cruikshank's face reddened. Then, she took a deep breath, as if exasperated but also resigned to the fact that she had to tolerate this impudent intruder a little bit longer. Her tone was calm and pedantic as she said, "Cyrus Trowbridge tried to worm his way into this family until my husband put a stop to his flirtation with his sister Leticia. I'm guessing that he didn't tell you that the magnificent house in Graniteville overlooking the water was actually owned by my husband. Leticia was warned that the house would be sold if she did not end her unseemly romance with that two-bit lawyer. Good sense finally prevailed with her and she was allowed to live there until she died. As for any outsider seeing my husband, you might as well pass this information on to Cyrus so he doesn't send you or any other emissaries back here again. Mr. Cruikshank is in the late stages of dementia. Most of the time the dear soul doesn't even recognize me. Now, I've told you more than you deserve to know. It's time that you left."

Jerry was tempted to defend Cyrus but let it go. It would only unleash a torrent of invective that would prove nothing.

Instead, he forced out the words "Thank you for your time." He would be polite, for Cyrus' sake.

After Jerry left, Mrs. Cruikshank walked out into the garden. "I heard a car. Did we have a visitor?" he asked softly. "Oh, just some man looking to do yard work, dear. You would think he could have seen that we have a full-time gardener," she said, dismissively.

JERRY LINGERED OUTSIDE his car, looking down at the lake. He had suspected that there was some romantic connection between Cyrus and Letty so there was at least a grain of truth interlaced with what were no doubt a fabric of lies spewed by the wife. Cyrus the Golddigger, that was a laugh. She should take a hard look in the mirror. He now understood what kind of mother could send her daughter off to Graniteville every summer and why the girl would flaunt a boyfriend like Buddy Hoole in front of her. She was no doubt an unruly, defiant child reacting to a cold, heartless mother.

He tried to imagine what Mrs. Cruikshank had been like as a nurse. Certainly, no Florence Nightingale or Clara Barton, dedicated to relieving human suffering. Or like Woody's mother, the gentlest and most compassionate woman Jerry had ever met. Jerry had seen *One Flew Over the Cuckoo's Nest* recently and decided he had just been face-to-face with a real life Nurse Rachid. He wondered what Cruikshank's first wife thought while she lay dying. Did she see through the woman who would replace her and take that depressing image to her grave?

ON THE RIDE south to Connecticut, Jerry's initial ruminations were dominated by his confrontation with Mrs. Cruikshank. He had quickly dismissed the aspersions cast at Cyrus but now understood his old friend's distraction after the meeting with old Crinkett. Cyrus must have a lot of memories to rummage through. There was nothing to gain from repeating her spurious accusations as they got Cyrus no closer to locating Betsy. No doubt, those same insults had been hurled at Cyrus himself back then.

Jerry turned his thoughts to his conversation with the Hoole's neighbor. She was a busy body, for sure, but what would be her motivation to lie? If what she said was true, why had the son and then the wife led him to believe that she was feeble and practically helpless? He didn't relish the idea of going back to Canada, the land of his original exile, but he would call Percy Hoole. First, he needed to get insight from Cyrus on what he had discovered in Burlington. Despite the fact that the severed finger was wearing the husband's Thorndyke ring, Jerry was starting to entertain the possibility that Ellis Hoole wasn't dead after all.

CHAPTER TWENTY-FOUR:
THE RING OF TRUTH

~

When Jerry walked into the Thimbletown Inn, Tillie looked up and anxiously motioned for him to come to the front desk.

"I wrote your friend's message down carefully, word for word, so here it is," Tillie said, handing Jerry a folded piece of paper. Jerry expected some dramatic news based on the fretful look on Tillie's face but all he read was, "The fax clouded the details of the ring but something struck me as strange. You can reach me at home tonight." Strange was enough to send Tillie's heart atwitter.

Just then, Cyrus walked in and the two men retreated to an alcove next to the café. Jerry started with a recap of the Cruikshank meeting while Cyrus just shook his head. "I never knew about Letty's house. Maybe she was too embarrassed to tell me she didn't own it. George was a decent even if a covetous man but the nurse brought out his baser instincts. Some people were suspicious early on when the wife's health deteriorated rapidly after the nurse showed up. Next thing you knew, she was the next Mrs. Cruikshank.

"Sounds like she's in total control now. You can be confident that Betsy has been completely written out of the will – if she was ever in it to begin with. I noticed that you left out the vitriol Cruikshank's wife most assuredly heaped on me. That's fine." Cyrus finished and rubbed his hands back and forth, as if, Letty exempted, he was washing off all the remnants of his connection to the Cruikshanks of Burlington.

"You're going to love what I tell you next. It makes the husband's disappearance – even his presumed death – all the more complicated, if not questionable," Jerry said, watching Cyrus' face and eager to change the subject.

When Cyrus heard the bizarre tale of the front yard cat fight between the partner's wife and Betsy Cruikshank, his eyes lit up. "There's more," Jerry said excitedly. He went on to relate the neighbor's description of a very active and domineering wife, nothing like the meek and terrified woman Jerry had met on his first visit. "But why the act?" exclaimed Cyrus. "It makes no sense to deceive you unless it had been planned in advance with a particular goal in mind. And her disappearance, being incommunicado, it is all inexplicable behavior for a grieving spouse. Either something happened to her or, I'm sorry to have to say it, the son and the mother played you, Jerry. Of course, how could you possibly know?"

Cyrus sensed that he might have been misconstrued and added, "Everyone has a secret life, Jerry. That means you and me. Now, some are more benign and harmless than others. I would put Letty in that category. Others are more diabolical and those are the ones who carefully guard their sinister intent."

Jerry looked grim. He had already decided that being the trusting sort had not served him well since his graduation from Pythian. "Exactly what I chewed on all the way home, Cyrus. That would mean that the son in Toronto was complicit in the deception as well and, let's be honest, possibly the father. Why was I sent on a wild goose chase? If it wasn't for the damn finger and ring, I'd say Hoole isn't even dead."

Both men sat quietly for a while as if stymied into silence. Jerry handed Cyrus the message from Woody and said, "I'll call him after dinner. Very curious about his comment regarding the ring."

Cyrus looked nettled while he read the note. "I spoke with Ladislaw today. His team tried again but has been unable to reach Gretchen Cadwallader. He was pretty blunt about her not being a material witness to anything except the discovery of the finger. He said she's a low priority right now since all she can do is regurgitate the description of the incident with the schoolgirl on DeCourcy Island."

"Where did your connection in vital records check on her? I mean, in which states?" Jerry inquired. "Well, here in Connecticut to start and then the rest of the New England states when nothing was found except a driver's license, which was issued in December. Why?" asked Cyrus. "I just remembered a brief exchange when we first met in the library and I was making small talk with her, still pretty nervous playing detective. Anyway, she tells me she's from Ohio and I ask her if she's a big Buckeye fan. She looked at me like I'd asked if she could speak Swahili." Jerry stopped and Cyrus looked puzzled.

Jerry laughed and went on. "I'm guessing you're not a college football fan. Even if you're not, you'd have to be in a coma growing up in Ohio not to know the existence of the Ohio State football team. Hell, Ohio's nickname is the Buckeye State. As for football, it's as big as god out there. A friend at Pythian told me what Fridays were like all over the state the day before the big game with the University of Michigan. Everyone, even casual fans, wears Buckeye scarlet. I'm talking sweaters, jackets, shirts, socks, maybe even jockey undershorts – you get the idea. Not to be aware of it would be like walking into a department store at Christmas, seeing a child on Santa's lap and asking, 'Hey, who's the fat guy in the red suit with the white beard'."

"Sort of like a naturalist or a paleoanthropologist not

knowing who Loren Eiseley is?" Cyrus asked, smiling broadly. "I like that analogy better," Jerry said.

Turning serious, Cyrus said, "Ladislaw needs to know what you learned about Hoole's wife. It's important. Don't forget, it's a two-way street with him. He won't admit it but he feels foiled and needs all the help he can get – even from a couple of rank amateurs like us. I'll have my contact check Ohio records for Gretchen. Now, let's go into dinner and not let this latest enigma regarding the partner's wife ruin a good meal. I'll tell you what I learned from Letty about a famous Cruikshank from the past."

CYRUS TOLD THE story of the original George Cruikshank, one of the great caricaturists and illustrators of the 19th century. Among his many works, he provided drawings for editions of *Paradise Lost*, *The Pilgrim's Progress* and the first English translation of *Grimm's Fairy Tales*. His political cartoons were so devastating that King George finally paid Cruikshank to stop satirizing him. Cruikshank collaborated with Charles Dickens on *Oliver Twist* and it was said that he had done as much to bring his characters to life as the famous author himself. Later on, the two masters, once friendly, had a bitter falling out.

A drunkard in his youthful years, Cruikshank joined the National Temperance League and became a fervent advocate for total abstinence. Some say he became somewhat of an insufferable moralist and when he died in 1878, it came out that he had eleven illegitimate children with his maid.

Jerry listened intently as he tackled the immense slab of blueberry cobbler that Tillie had placed in front of him unannounced. He finally put his napkin over the plate, signifying his surrender. Cyrus had pulled out his pipe and was loading it for action. "I'm not much of an art connoisseur, Cyrus, but

Cruikshank was a fascinating man, to be sure. Would love to see some of his work," Jerry said.

"Letty gave me a copy of *Oliver Twist* for my birthday one year. It's a rare first edition for which Cruikshank did all of the sketches. She told me at the time that some antiquarian book collector would pay me big bucks for it if I was ever in need of cash. I'll bring it by one day to show you. Before she died, she also gave me a painting by Cruikshank called *The Worship of Bacchus* which hung in her foyer for years. After Cruikshank gave up booze and joined the temperance movement, he came up with the idea for a panoramic oil painting depicting every imaginable debauchery resulting from drunkenness. It's a virtual panoply of the besotted. You gaze at the sorrowful, ghastly images long enough, Jerry, and you might even swear off booze. I sometimes thought that having it on her wall turned Letty into a teetotaler herself."

When they parted, Cyrus reminded Jerry that he would have someone check vital records in Ohio for Gretchen Cadwallader. He was certain that something would be found and Jerry could stop obsessing over a girl who he hardly knew and who had been nothing but trouble to him.

WHEN JERRY REACHED Woody, it felt good to hear his friend's voice. Before he unloaded his own burden, Jerry was eager to hear about the excitement back in Parlor City.

"You're going to love this one, Jerry. Even Billy was stupefied and he's seen it all. You remember Mayor Wattle, of course. Went away to prison along with his wife for accessory to murder. Well, he had placed all his assets in the hands of his daughter and son-in-law – including the chain of funeral homes. When he came out, the town shunned him and his daughter turned her back. Wouldn't give him a plug nickel. He left town a broken man and was never heard from again.

"After the son-in-law put the Conklin name on all the funeral homes, he started acting like a playboy. Plain-looking guy but fancied himself a ladies man. When he doesn't arrive home for dinner, his wife goes looking for him and spots his car parked behind one of their parlors. She walks in on hubby and some babe going at it in any empty casket, naked as jay birds. Coroner called it *flagrante delicto* which I guess is a fancy way to say they got caught doing the deed in the nude. The wife proceeds to pull out a gun and put one bullet into the back of poor hubby's head. She spared the girl. Then, she turns and calmly walks out, leaving her dead husband on top of his lover.

"Lord love a duck," Jerry almost shouted, trying unsuccessfully not to laugh. "There's more, Jerry," Woody said, "So fasten your seatbelt. The wife walks into the police station shortly afterwards, lays the gun on the desk and calmly confesses. When officers got to the parlor, they found the girl traumatized, trapped under the body and babbling like a child."

"Sounds like an open and shut case, Woody," Jerry said. "Most likely, Jer. But there's always some angle to play. Temporary insanity, something like that. And you can bet that if it goes to trial, she'll get a lot of sympathy from the female jurors.

"Anyway, the titillating part came out the next day when the babe came in and gave a detailed statement. According to her, this Conklin character had a fetish – the department psychologist called it a compulsive sexual fantasy – that the wife refused to indulge. Get this, the girl says Conklin kept pressing her to join him in a sexual act with one of the corpses that hadn't yet been embalmed but she resisted. Said she had her scruples. Ha! A frolic in the coffin with Conklin was fine but she was too classy a girl to go any farther. His perversion is called necrophilia – another word I learned this week."

"Well, it's sure nice to see the girl had some sense of

propriety, Woody," Jerry said in a solemn tone before busting out laughing. "You have no idea how much good your story did for me, pal," he added.

"You probably don't remember, Jerry, but when my stepfather sold his beloved sports car before he married my mom, his only disappointment was that Mayor Wattle's son-in-law bought it. Billy didn't like Conklin but had to admit that he kept that car in mint condition. Maybe it was enough to attract the girlfriend with mutually kinky sex cravings and look where it got him. Now, enough about sin city, what's going on with you?"

Jerry described his trip to Vermont and Woody listened without saying a word. He could tell from Jerry's voice that his friend was frustrated so at the end, he said, "You know what 'Wonder Boy' Billy Meacham, Jr. would say, don't you, Jerry? He'd say you're on to something – keep digging. By the way, people still call him 'Wonder Boy' or 'The Wizard' around these parts after all these years and it embarrasses the hell out of him.

"Hey, sorry I never got to it but do you still want me to check on that guy from the quarry?" Woody asked. "You mean Grex. Don't bother. The staties already combed through his background. He's a pretty pathetic character but I'm not convinced he's a murderer," Jerry said. "Staties, you say," Woody exclaimed, stifling a laugh. "The troopers must get a kick out of you talking their lingo."

Jerry was about to mention Gretchen but stopped himself. He wanted to see what Cyrus uncovered and he was concerned that Woody would chastise him for being distracted. Instead, he asked Woody to explain his comment about the ring.

"I know it's not practical but would love to get a better image or see the ring in person, Jerry," Woody said, adding, "I know it's been verified as a Thorndyke ring but ------." Jerry jumped in with, "I just had an idea. Cyrus still has his Thorndyke ring. We can compare it with the crime lab photograph that was faxed to you and see if we catch anything. The partner's initials are engraved on the inside of the band along with his graduation date so we know it's his ring. Still, something tells me he may not be dead. Sure, wish you were here to help, old buddy."

"Well, I probably saw nothing. Just some grainy distortion in the fax. Listen, you're doing better than you realize, Jerry. The suspicious conduct of the partner's wife isn't trivial. You uncovered it by being inquisitive and persistent. Keep questioning everything until all doubts are erased. It's the only way," Woody said.

AFTER HE HUNG up the phone, Jerry said out loud, "Hell yes, I'll be persistent and that includes finding out who in the hell is Gretchen Cadwallader."

CHAPTER TWENTY-FIVE:
THE WIFE'S LAMENT

THE NEXT MORNING, before going to the trooper barracks to see Ladislaw, Jerry told Cyrus about his conversation with Woody the night before. "I wonder what he might have seen. I'll bring my Thorndyke ring over later along with a magnifying glass. We can examine it side by side with the crime lab photo you faxed to him," Cyrus said, before laughing and adding, "Parlor City is a hotbed compared to Graniteville. All we've got here is the mystery of the severed finger and a missing person. Kind of hard to compete with murder in a casket in the midst of illicit carnal pursuit."

WHEN CYRUS AND Jerry arrived at the barracks, Ladislaw's office door was closed and they were told that he couldn't be disturbed. Ten minutes later, the door opened and Hoole's wife walked out slowly dabbing her eyes with a white handkerchief. Ladislaw was wearing a sympathetic expression, cultivated and refined over the years, as he guided her out.

When she noticed Jerry, she smiled faintly and whimpered,

"I expected to hear from you but came down when I heard the terrible news. It's almost more than I can bear right now. He was such a sweet and gentle man. Thank you for trying to be of help. The lieutenant has assured me that the Coast Guard will be making an effort to recover the body – if that scoundrel of a partner didn't bury him on that damn island."

Ladislaw tried to explain that there was no guarantee that her husband was dead or that Grex had anything to do with his disappearance but she waved her hankie at him and groaned.

"I went to your house yesterday, Mrs. Hoole, after calling several times without success. Where have you been?" asked Jerry. There was an exasperated edge to his voice but she ignored it. "I was on my way to Toronto to visit my son when I decided to come down here instead," she said meekly, looking at the floor and patting her nose with the handkerchief.

Ladislaw stepped forward and said, "I'll have someone drive you to your motel, Mrs. Hoole. We'll bring you back to get your car when you feel up to driving. Now, as soon as we have more information, I will be in touch."

Cyrus and Jerry watched as Mrs. Hoole , followed by a trooper, shuffled toward the door like a feeble octogenarian. Ladislaw glanced at Cyrus and Jerry. When he saw the bemused looks on their faces, he said, "Okay, what's going on, fellas. Something about her misery touched your funny bones at the same moment? I'm surprised you can't show some compassion for a woman who is clearly distraught."

After Jerry summarized his visit to Burlington and the conversation with Mrs. Hoole's neighbor, Ladislaw scratched his head. "Doesn't sound like the same person who just left. Assuming the neighbor is trustworthy, why the ruse? She did mention that she has hired an attorney in New Haven and has asked him to petition for the issuance of an early death certificate on the presumed death theory. I have no idea if the ringed finger is enough evidence for the courts but she seems to know her stuff and is wasting no time."

"Interesting that she showed up now. Does anyone believe that she was on her way to Canada and impulsively switched directions and drove down here? And the lawyer thing, it had to be planned in advance. After being incommunicado, she suddenly appears on the scene without notice, several days after filing a missing person's report. How did she know that her husband's belongings were found buried on Quarry Island? Not the kind of story that would make it into the Burlington papers, is it? She must be in communication with someone down here. One more thing – it sounds to me like she's being coached," Jerry said, shaking his head. "Are you sure you're not a private eye, kid?" Ladislaw asked in a mock serious tone. Jerry tried not to smile but couldn't hide his pleasure at the lieutenant's comment, even if it was uttered half in jest.

"Life insurance?" suggested Cyrus. "Good question. We don't have access to his personal records yet so all we have so far is the quarry policy that, as you know, implicates Grex. Miraculously, it's one of the few documents that survived the quarry fire intact."

"Looks like the evidence is piling up nicely against the poor bastard. Coming together in a neat little package," Cyrus said.

"What's that supposed to mean?" Ladislaw asked, His jaw clenched when he picked up on Cyrus' sarcastic tone.

"Just an observation, Lieutenant, that's all. You're a busy man. We'll leave you to your work." Cyrus was inscrutable and it rubbed Ladislaw the wrong way. He had his own reservations about Grex but didn't like to be baited.

Outside the barracks, Jerry asked, "Why did you try to provoke Ladislaw?" Cyrus smiled and said, "Because he needed it. He can take a little tweaking. He's receiving pressure to solve the case and he's getting ahead of himself. He probably knows it, but just in case he didn't, I wanted to remind him."

When Cyrus and Jerry got back to the Thimbletown Inn, Tillie hurried over with a message left by her brother's contact in vital records. Not a single document, not even a birth certificate, was found on a Gretchen Cadwallader in the state of Ohio.

Cyrus looked at Jerry and said, "I know what you're planning to do and I'm going with you."

Jerry guided Cyrus up to the historical section of the New Haven library where Gretchen worked. The lights were on but the door was locked and no one could be seen inside. Jerry saw someone pushing a cart stacked with books but he just shrugged when asked where Gretchen might be. "Well, it is a Saturday, Cyrus, and maybe she has the day off," Jerry speculated.

Downstairs at the information desk, they learned that Gretchen was no longer employed by the library. When pressed for details, they were directed to the personnel office, located in cramped, dank quarters in the basement of the building. Miss Thwaite was polite but reluctant to provide any details on Gretchen's departure. Jerry was frustrated and about to lose his temper when Cyrus spoke in a soft, pleading tone. "I'm her uncle. We've had a family tragedy and I drove here all the way from Ohio to inform her. We went to her old apartment but apparently, she moved with no forwarding address. Can't you bend the rules just this once?" Cyrus coughed and stared beseechingly into the woman's eyes. It was a beautiful performance. The woman's face softened. She looked sympathetically at Cyrus, then walked to a cabinet and pulled out a file. In a minute, she had scrawled down an address near Union Station.

As they were leaving, she said, "As her uncle, you might want to give her some fatherly-type advice. Calling your supervisor a foul name which I won't repeat, in front of others no less, is a fool-proof way to get yourself fired. Gretchen is a bright and industrious young lady but her vulgarity and temper will not get her far. Sorry about the family situation. Good luck."

"Where did you learn to ad lib like that?" Jerry asked when they got outside. He was grinning broadly and patting Cyrus on the back. Cyrus just chuckled and said, "Desperate times require desperate measures."

GRETCHEN LIVED IN a faded three-story brick building a short walk from the trainyard where Smitty and the boys held court. Jerry hit the buzzer in the hallway below a nameplate that read "G. Cadwallader" but got no response. He pushed it a few more times for good measure without any luck.

"Maybe she left town," Cyrus suggested. "Yeah, she probably went home to Ohio to visit family," Jerry quipped.

"I don't have the energy for a stake-out this afternoon, Jerry, if that's what you have in mind," said Cyrus. Jerry had remarked to himself that Cyrus had looked energetic earlier but now he looked wan and his face was drawn.

"Well, now we know where she lives. I can come back another time. Let's head back," Jerry said.

As they walked to the car, Jerry pointed out the wino encampment in the distance across the tracks. They passed the

Belly Up bar where Jerry had borrowed the baseball bat. "Shall we grab some Thunderbird and join them?" Jerry said, pointing to the trainyard. "Some other day," Cyrus said quietly.

Back at the car, Jerry asked, "Do you mind if we make a quick stop at the *Beagle*, Cyrus? I'd like to learn if the reporter I met at the hospital has any update on Smitty." Cyrus waited in the car and Jerry was only gone for a few minutes. Boyd Mandeville was out on assignment so Jerry left the number for the Thimbletown Inn.

THE TRIP TO New Haven had been a bust. Except for getting Gretchen's address and learning that she had been fired, it was a day of dead-ends. Both men were dejected and rode back in silence. As they approached Graniteville, Jerry said, "Maybe we should tell Ladislaw all that we've learned about the mysterious Gretchen Cadwallader." Cyrus didn't respond and Jerry looked over to see his eyes closed with his head leaning into the window.

THE FINANCIAL EXPERT on Ladislaw's team was not encouraging. "Okay, only fragments of the business ledgers survived the fire so it's difficult to piece things together. The team found absolutely nothing for the current year. We'll have to get the court to issue a subpoena directing the bank to release records of payments made and income received in the current year. We know that an insurance policy was purchased but that's all." Ladislaw looked almost mummified and the trooper started to fidget. "Get the damn subpoena," he finally muttered.

LADISLAW LOCKED HIS hands behind his head after the trooper left. He had lost his temper again and was not proud of himself. He clenched hard and shook his head. Elwyn Grex was the ideal perpetrator. He fit the Hollywood mold of a genuine bad guy, rough-hewn and obnoxious, easy to despise, but what did Ladislaw have on him? The confrontation in the restaurant plus the personal items of the missing partner buried on Quarry Island were not enough to hold him indefinitely. He would get someone from the fire department to confirm arson. Grex might be thick-headed but could he be so asinine as to set a fire and then leave behind an insurance policy and Hoole's belongings that pointed the finger directly at him?

Ladislaw respected Cyrus but was not happy that he had reproached him. Maybe he deserved it but why not do it privately instead of in front of Kosinsky? He had to admit that the kid was smarter than he had originally thought. His observations about the wife had the ring of truth. He was sure the duo were still snooping around and normally it would bother him. Not now.

CHAPTER TWENTY-SIX:
A LITTLE REPRIEVE

~~

AFTER CYRUS LEFT for his cottage, Jerry trudged off to his room, not sure what to do with himself. It was a few hours before dinner and something told him that Cyrus wouldn't be back that evening. Even so, it wasn't like they had a standing arrangement.

Jerry was not very far into *Augie March* and decided he should dive back in. It would take his mind off the elusive Gretchen Cadwallader, the missing partner, the mysterious blonde, the disingenuous wife and all the perplexities surrounding the severed finger.

Augie was still in high school and had already determined that he couldn't let other people, including his older brother, manipulate him. No matter how benevolent their motives might be, Augie decided that he had to be his own man. It made Jerry think about Prof. Eyesmore and his own tendency to subjugate himself to the will of others.

After an hour, Jerry closed the novel and gazed out the window, catching the last slice of a reddish orange sun as it slid below the water in the western sky. It was a serene, almost idyllic scene, the calming sensation reminding Jerry of those first few moments when he looked out on the majestic Himalayas before his plane touched down in Kathmandu. He sat propped up in bed and was embarrassed to think of that 22-year old man-child, naïve to the hilt and oblivious to the deceit and treachery in the world that awaits the uninitiated. He liked to think that if nothing else, he had learned since then to be not cynical but rather skeptical while still holding on to his essential humanity. Maybe it was just wishful thinking.

His mind drifted to the dustup with the partner's wife that afternoon. What game was she playing, he wondered? She was clever enough not to take his bait in front of Ladislaw. He was convinced that she had put on an act for the lieutenant, just as she had done for him on his first visit to Burlington. It made him mad enough to jump off the bed, put on his shoes and head out the door. He wanted to catch her off guard, certain that she wouldn't reveal herself without some sort of surprise provocation.

HER INN WAS just a mile outside town, a garden bower nestled behind some giant horse chestnut trees. When he knocked on Mrs. Hoole's door, he heard a harsh female voice from the other side ask, "Who is it?" It was a voice he didn't recognize and made Jerry think she must have a guest. After he announced himself, the door opened only so far as the chain lock would allow. Mrs. Hoole peaked though the opening with a distraught expression on her face and Jerry caught a shadow of someone moving away in the background. "What is it, young man? I'm awfully tired from my trip. Do you have news regarding my husband?" It was the frail, timid woman talking now, the third time for the poseur. He wanted to castigate her at that moment. Tell her to knock it off.

He decided to take a gamble, knowing that she might

call Ladislaw and lodge a complaint. "Sorry, Mrs. Hoole. Any further news on that front would come from the lieutenant. It wasn't much but I did all I could but, as you know, I'm no detective, not by a long shot. Actually, I was hoping you might shed some light on the whereabouts of Betsy Cruikshank. My friend Cyrus Trowbridge is trying to locate her. I understand that she dated your older son and the two of you became quite close after his death in Vietnam."

Mrs. Hoole's eyes darkened and her mouth tightened, as she stared at Jerry. "I know nothing of that scamp and haven't seen her in years. Close to that little slut, you say? Who have you been talking to and how dare you bring her up at a time like this? I'm sorry that my son ever enlisted your help. You'd be advised to stay away from me or, by god, I'll file a complaint with Lt. Ladislaw. Now, put that in your pipe and smoke it." Her words were sharp and full of vituperation as she pushed the door shut.

Jerry stood outside the door for a few seconds and smiled. He knew that he had done something cruel to agitate her yet it had been worth it. He didn't even care if she contacted Ladislaw. The neighbor had pegged her correctly. This was a fierce, domineering woman with a vengeful personality. He wondered if she cared about her husband at all. If not, she had ulterior motives in coming to Graniteville and engaging an attorney to secure a death certificate even before her husband's body was found. Was she In it strictly for a potential insurance payout?

He was certain that it was her gruff voice that he heard through the door after he knocked and caught her off guard. But who was it lurking in the shadows?

JERRY WAS SMUG and rather proud of himself as he drove away from the inn. He had tried a ruse and it had worked. He didn't expect that she knew anything about Betsy Cruikshank's whereabouts and, if she did, certainly wouldn't tell him. There would probably be another catfight if the two every met up again and he would love to be a bystander for that battle.

He had worked up an appetite and decided to head over to Clive's Diner out near the highway. Before doing so, he checked in with Tillie to confirm that Cyrus had not shown up.

JERRY PATTED HIS stomach as he walked out of Clive's. It was not even eight o'clock and he wasn't ready to spend the rest of the evening alone in his room – even in the company of Augie March. He pulled into the Graniteville Saloon and sidled up to the bar. He pressed his hands into the cold brass rail below the mahogany top. It had no doubt kept many patrons upright over the years, he decided.

Jerry tilted his head back to knock down the remainder of his second Falstaff and caught a glimpse of himself in the mirror over the bar. Behind his image, he saw a girl waving him over to her table. He turned to see Fanny Tulk, the constable's niece.

She was sitting with a guy wearing a blue denim work shirt with the name Earl stitched in red on the pocket. A mesh trucker's baseball hat sat atop a mop of brown hair. The sleeves of his shirt were rolled up and Jerry could see part of a cast on the left arm with names and salutations scribbled all over it. "Sit down and help us finish off this pitcher. Jerry, right?" she said, smiling warmly. Earl frowned and filled a glass and slid it over in front of Jerry without saying a word.

"Don't mind my brother. He's in a constant sour mood until the cast comes off and he can climb back on his Harley. Hey, I heard the missing partner's wife showed up in town and laid a sob story of the lieutenant. You met her once, didn't you?" she asked.

"Cyrus and I got there as she was leaving today. Been wondering what brought her down here without telling anyone that she was coming," Jerry speculated. He didn't think it was prudent to share his earlier confrontation with her and decided to go fishing instead. "She seemed to have the lay of the land before she arrived."

Fanny smiled and said, "Buffle talked to her first when he completed the missing person report. It had to list her contact information. No one else talked to her before today, best of my knowledge. I mentioned it to the troopers when they walked in on Reg and El sweating like overworked oxen."

Jerry looked at her more closely than he had during their brief encounters at the constable's office. She had a pleasant, round face with a pure complexion that revealed a smattering of faded freckles, all set off by saucer-like blue eyes. Her lower lip was full and gave her a slightly pouty expression no matter what her mood. Her pale brown, tawny hair was pulled tight in a ponytail and she was wearing a sleeveless white top with a vee cut that showed off the smooth, tan skin of her sleek neck and arms. Jerry was titillated. He had heard guys say, almost brag for some reason, that they were boob or leg men but Jerry was invariably drawn to the exposed neck. She turned her head slowly and Jerry decided that it was definitely a neck worth kissing.

"How much longer will you be in town?" she asked, almost coyly. If it came off like a come-on, it wasn't meant that way but it made her brother frown and stand up. "I'm walking home now. *Mork & Mindy* comes on in about thirty minutes," he grumbled.

Fanny looked at her brother, then at Jerry, and said, "I'll hang here a bit longer. You go on ahead."

"Deacon Blues" came on the jukebox and she smiled. "I

like Steely Dan, too. Maybe I'd better get another pitcher," Jerry said. "Excellent idea," she responded. The alien and the earth girl would have to wait.

Two hours later, the two incipient lovers came through the side door of the Thimbletown Inn, avoiding the diligent eyes of Tillie. Both of them were eager with anticipation. There was a lot of fumbling with shoes, buttons and zippers but eventually they dove naked under the covers with only the light from a half open bathroom door revealing the gyrating pair.

They had talked freely at the bar without pretense or affectation, establishing early on that there were no current paramours creating obstacles or regrets. Neither one could say with any certainty or conviction whose idea it was to leave together and how they gravitated to Jerry's room. No one had instigated anything; it had just happened and it didn't matter. Maybe it was that third pitcher of beer or the mellifluous sound of Steely Dan that prompted hot, lustful urges. Both of them had been deprived of late and it was an innocent, serendipitous moment that took over.

Jerry confessed to being somewhat out of practice since his break-up with Missy in Toronto but Fanny didn't seem to notice. In a different time, they might have dated and paced themselves but the truth was that they both sensed that they had no future together. They hit it off and, without pretense or regrets, let libidinous instincts govern their actions.

For one evening, Jerry forgot his own self-doubts and the cast of assorted characters who had drawn him to this coastal town hundreds of miles from Parlor City.

Without trying and quite by accident, Jerry had learned that Reg Buffle was probably the one feeding information to the wife, prompting her hasty trip to Graniteville. Was there anything in it for him – other than to get back at the constable, the niece and the state troopers?

CHAPTER TWENTY-SEVEN:
SMITTY'S REVENGE

~

JERRY LOOKED UP from his eggs Benedict Sunday morning as Cyrus walked into the café, holding up his right hand and pointing to his Thorndyke ring. Jerry was starting to wonder it Cyrus somehow timed his arrivals to catch him wolfing down one of Tillie's signature dishes. Cyrus was almost jaunty and his color looked healthy, almost like he had a buzz or had put on make-up. After his amorous rendezvous the night before, Jerry was in a buoyant mood and somewhat aglow himself. He woke up feeling that anything was possible.

"Got thinking about *The Gold Bug* again last night, Jerry," Cyrus said as he sat down. He pointed to some yolk on Jerry's lip and smiled. He watched Jerry frown and wipe his mouth, then continued. "If the missing partner had the fanciful notion in his head that Capt. Kidd's treasure might be buried on Quarry Island, he would probably have done some digging before he disappeared. Surreptitiously, of course. We should ask Grex about any other freshly-dug spots without mention of buried treasure."

Jerry wiped his mouth again and pushed his chair back from the table. He was about to tell Cyrus about Buffle likely being the wife's contact when he noticed Boyd Mandeville standing at the café entrance, waving tentatively, like a timorous schoolkid reluctantly raising his hand to answer the teacher's question. Jerry walked over and, after a brief chat, brought the reporter back to the table.

"I mentioned earlier that Boyd's with the *Beagle*, Cyrus. You remember that I met him at the hospital when I tracked down Smitty – the wino with a taste for Thunderbird. He has some news to share with us," Jerry said.

Mandeville fumbled with a small spiral notepad that he had pulled from his jacket and read through his notes before saying, "I got the message that you stopped by the newsroom yesterday. Probably shouldn't be here, journalistic ethics and all, but I owe you an update after you gave me the scoop. I called this morning and was told you were still here so, since it's my day off, decided to drive up."

Mandeville stopped as if reluctant to proceed. "Thank you, Boyd. Please go on," Jerry said gently. Mandeville began haltingly. "Okay, after you left the hospital, I hung around and got chummy with one of the admission clerks. Turned out she's friends with the nurse that took Smitty's bottle. Told me to come back later and she might have some information for me. Turns out, security grabbed Smitty just as he was accosting the nurse. Probably just trying to get his bottle back. Anyway, they wrestled him to the ground and he apparently had a seizure or some sort of attack right there on the floor. Took him to ER where he was suddenly lucid and started babbling about a guy named Twitchy who owed him money plus a weekly bottle of the Bird. Course, you guys know he meant Thunderbird wine. Then, he starts moaning about his hand so they proceed to unravel the dirty roll of gauze wrapped around it. As they did, Smitty said something to the effect that the blonde bitch said it would heal up in a few days." Mandeville was flipping through his notes and stopped, then started to shake his head and wince, as if he was trying to purge a disturbing image. "And?" said Cyrus.

"Keep in mind that I am relating what the clerk told me. She talked to the nurse and also got a look at the medical file. The hand looked like something out of a horror movie. Gangrene has set in. The odor was revolting and brown pus was oozing out everywhere. The hand was covered with red and black splotches and was swelled up to almost twice its normal size. Here's the kicker: the nurse and doctor were so distracted that they didn't see it right away but a finger was missing, chopped clear off right down to the palm. The doctor asked what happened but Smitty had already drifted off. It was too late to amputate; the gangrene having already spread through his body. Turned out he also had diabetes and a fried liver. He didn't have a chance."

Jerry's head was flooded with ideas and images vying for attention. It would take a while for him to sort everything out. He was staring straight ahead, as if in a trance, when he heard Mandeville say, "My story runs in the *Beagle* this morning. My first byline, thanks to you. It will describe Smitty's grudge with Twitchy and speculate about his apparent suicide. The hospital notified the police so there's going to be some sort of investigation but no one at the *Beagle* thinks they will dig too deeply into the rantings of a dead wino. My editors were quick to doubt his babbling about some blonde chopping off his finger." Everyone stood up as if on cue and solemnly shook hands. Not another word was said as Mandeville walked out of the Thimbletown Inn.

IN A WAY, Jerry felt good for Mandeville. He was having a hard time of it and now he had his break. Time would tell if he was just lucky or if he had the necessary grit and tenacity a reporter needs when no one was there to give him a boost. Mandeville had been gone for several minutes and Cyrus and Jerry sat across from each other without talking. Cyrus finally broke the silence and said, "I know what's racing through your head, son, but don't get carried away too quickly. It's probably an extraordinary coincidence – two mysterious blondes and two severed fingers not that many miles apart. Then again, you know the old saying, 'truth is stranger than fiction'."

"Mandeville didn't say how prominent she would be in the article nor did he seem curious about who the so-called blonde bitch was. I wonder if he was being coy or just didn't understand the lead staring at him? Maybe they're saving her for a follow-up story after the reader is sucked in." Jerry said with an exasperated look on his face.

Cyrus took a deep breath and sighed. He sensed that Jerry wanted high drama, with a shady character always lurking in the shadows. He wanted to bring him down a notch without dashing his hopes entirely. "This elusive blonde – or blondes – has me perplexed too, Jerry. Yeah, it's possible that they're one and the same person but how probable is it that she knew the wino and the missing partner? I know, in case you're thinking about her, that Gretchen is a self-described bitch but she isn't a blonde. And didn't you say that Thunderbird makes these winos go berserk. Maybe Smitty was hallucinating or one of his pals who held a grudge went loco and chopped it off when he was passed out."

Jerry's morning effervescence had faded clear away and he looked defeated, prompting Cyrus to say, "It's now time for a little detective work. Let's see if we can find out what troubled your friend back in Parlor City when he examined the photograph of the finger." Cyrus pulled off his Thorndyke ring and took a magnifying glass out of his pocket, handing it to Jerry. He then laid the crime lab photo of the ring on the table and smoothed it out, laying his ring next to it. "Okay, kid. You take first crack at it."

CHAPTER TWENTY-EIGHT:
Two Fingers?

Jerry and Cyrus took turns with the magnifying glass, going back and forth between the ring and the crime lab photograph. They zoomed in and out several times, both of them finally dropping the magnifier down on the table in frustration. Both of them were distracted by Mandeville's revelation of Smitty's death and another severed finger.

"Woody admitted that the fax was grainy and distorted, Cyrus. It was probably some defect in the transmission line, or even one of the machines, that made him think that he saw something strange. Let's give it a rest. I need to tell you what I was up to last night," Jerry said.

When he finished, Cyrus said, "So, after all of her posturing, the wife could be nothing more than a cold-hearted mercenary, not at all bothered by her husband's disappearance. We know she's already proceeding as if he's dead but that could be just for show, meaning that it could well have been the husband's shadow that you saw. Are we to believe that everything she does is a calculated act of deception? I agree that she leaves a bad taste behind but focusing on her doesn't necessarily get us any closer to finding him. Your stratagem worked but I can't believe that you thought to poke the bear with that allusion to Betsy Cruikshank."

Jerry shrugged as if it was inconsequential. He had no intention of mentioning that after leaving the wife he ran into Fanny Tulk at the Graniteville Saloon. Still, the thought of last evening's feverish rendezvous caused Jerry's face to redden.

The two of them sat in the alcove, looking forlorn. Occasionally, they glanced at the ring and the photograph but said nothing. Tillie walked over and broke the silence. "Lt. Ladislaw just called. He wants to see you now," she said, pointing at Jerry.

"Do you want to guess who called me?" Ladislaw said, twirling a pencil and staring at Jerry. "I was at the Graniteville Saloon last night and made fun of Buffle. Did he hear about it and file a complaint?" Ladislaw dropped the pencil and scowled. "Don't get cute with me, Kosinsky. It's supposed to be a day of rest but here I am dealing with your shenanigans. Don't forget, you're privy to certain information only because of the good graces of Cyrus. You two have helped me out and I appreciate it – but stay away from the damn wife. She sounded like she was on the verge of a breakdown when she called here this morning. If you want her to contact my boss, just say so because that's her next step."

Jerry slouched in his chair and said, "Sorry, Lieutenant. I can assure you it won't happen again. But if you had heard her last night, you'd agree that she's putting on one helluva act. Plus, I'm almost positive that there was someone else in the room." Ladislaw didn't respond but a faint smile creased his lips. He was thinking of Reg Buffle but didn't say anything.

"Tell him about the visit from Mandeville, Jerry," Cyrus

interjected, anxious to change the subject. "Oh, you mean about the other severed finger down in New Haven, Cyrus?" Jerry quipped.

Ladislaw was looking back and forth, waiting for someone to explain. Cyrus motioned for Jerry to go on. It was his show and it might put him back in the good graces of the lieutenant. He would jump in if necessary.

To make sure Ladislaw had a complete picture, Jerry started back to when he first met Gretchen Cadwallader, then the subsequent meeting with Twitchy at Pudge McFadden's and finally the incident outside the bar with the wino who turned out to be Smitty chasing after the Steve Martin wannabe.

"So, a few days later, Twitchy is dead – an apparent suicide by stepping in front of a freight train and Smitty died yesterday, complications of gangrene and who knows what other maladies."

"And the finger?" Ladislaw asked, sensing that Jerry was dragging out the story for dramatic affect. "Oh yeah. Apparently, it had been chopped off for money and booze. The last thing he said before dying was to blame Twitchy and some mysterious blonde. I have a hard time believing he was either hallucinating or making it up. Quite a revelation. You can read it in the *Beagle* today," Jerry concluded with raised eyebrows.

Ladislaw stroked his chin and then asked, "Which hand?" "Right," said Cyrus. "Which finger?" Ladislaw pressed. Cyrus and Jerry looked at each other with mouths agape. "Damn, I never asked," said Jerry.

"Get a hold of that reporter and confirm which finger it was. Keep it under your hat. You know where I'm going with this, guys. If confirmed as the wino's right index finger, I'll get the crime lab to run some more tests. Don't get excited. It's a bizarre connection to make and it's a long shot to be sure."

As Cyrus and Jerry were leaving, Ladislaw burst out laughing and said, "Now stay away from poor Mrs. Hoole, even if you think she's the greatest actress since Theda Bara. I'm calling as soon as you leave to let her know you have been chastened."

When they got outside, Jerry asked, "Yogi Berra's wife is an actress?" Cyrus shook his head and started laughing. "That's a good one, Jerry. I like your sense of humor, assuming that quip was meant to be funny. For the record, Theda Bara was a silent film star. Gorgeous woman but a little bit before your time."

Jerry didn't have a way to reach Mandeville so he decided to drive to New Haven and track him down. "Not without me," Cyrus said, adding, "I need to keep an eye on you now." Cyrus' eyes were twinkling and Jerry caught the faux warning. We're really starting to mesh, he said to himself.

CHAPTER TWENTY-NINE:
THE STAKE OUT

On the ride to New Haven, Cyrus was in an upbeat, jaunty mood. "I'm thinking of heading down to Florida to pick up the quest for the legendary Fountain Of Youth. It could be my last great adventure – not that I've had many, mind you. Never was much of a traveler or risk-taker, for that matter."

Jerry was racking his brain. He got his Spanish explorers mixed up and asked, "DeSoto?" Cyrus laughed. "No, he discovered the Mississippi River, among other things. You meant Ponce de Leon. He was frustrated in his search for the legendary fountain but it's my shot at immortality. You'll understand when you get old. Trust me."

Cyrus turned his head away from Jerry and gazed out the window, fiddling nervously with his chin and suddenly withdrawn and distant, the vigor of a few minutes earlier suddenly sapped. When Jerry looked over, he caught a wistful expression reflected in the window. He knew Cyrus was joking about heading down to Florida yet there was something plaintive in his voice and Jerry wanted to say something comforting. He just couldn't find the words. And would unsentimental Cyrus even want to hear them?

The two drove on in solitude. Cyrus had closed his eyes and Jerry had a pit in his stomach.

WHEN THEY ARRIVED at the *Beagle* offices, it dawned on Jerry that Mandeville wouldn't be there. He sweet-talked the receptionist into giving up Mandeville's home telephone number on the pretext that he had vital information for him relative to that morning's wino expose'. His story had made it below the fold on the first page of the second section of the paper, accompanied by a photo of the trainyard. The cub reporter was starting to get some faint nods from the seasoned scribblers, as if to concede that he wasn't just some annoying part-time stringer or hack. Nothing dramatic or overly encouraging, just acknowledgement that he existed and wasn't held in contempt. It was enough to put a strut into Mandeville's step when he walked into the coffee shop near his apartment to meet Jerry and Cyrus.

"Never asked which finger but I can probably find out. The girl in admissions is sweet on me," Mandeville said boastfully, in response to Jerry's inquiry. "Hey, I ventured down to that wino encampment but didn't have your luck. Couldn't get any information on the blonde that Smitty cursed out before he died. Had a few security guards with me," he added, embarrassed by his lack of fearlessness. He was certainly no Walter Cronkite, the venerable and much-loved news anchor at CBS, who left his comfortable life in New York City behind and went to Saigon to report on the progress of the Vietnam War. It was said that Cronkite's subsequent broadcast questioning the ability for the U.S. to win against the fierce yet undermanned Viet Cong changed the course of history, even prompting Pres. Johnson to forego re-election.

"Bringing a couple of guys in uniforms down there is a sure fire way to get them to clam up. You might try again with a bag of Thunderbird shorties and have the guards stay back. You got anything else on the blonde?" Jerry asked.

"Dead ends everywhere. Called on Twitchy's mother and went to a few of his hang-outs. His home base, so to speak, was Pudge McFadden's and no one remembers seeing Twitchy with a blonde. I'm convinced that both Twitchy and Smitty knew her. Still, it's as if she's a phantom. She vanishes and they're both dead. I gotta tell you, though, that the boys upstairs are still skeptical that she even exists." Mandeville looked bewildered and Jerry wasn't going to help him anymore. If he wrote anything new because of Jerry, Ladislaw wouldn't be happy and, besides, Mandeville had to earn his next scoop.

Mandeville promised to leave a message for Jerry at the Thimbletown Inn once he talked to his hospital contact. On the way out, Cyrus looked at Jerry and said, "His first story and he's already sleeping with a source. Quite a muckraker, that kid."

"IN THE MOOD for a stake out?" Jerry asked, as they got into the car. "Sure," said Cyrus. "I assume you mean Gretchen's apartment. How about you surveil and I nap? Let's grab some lunch on the way. Feel like I could use a drink from that Fountain Of Youth right about now." Cyrus hadn't recovered since their ride into town and Jerry was still reluctant to pry.

JERRY FOUND A parking spot on Gretchen's street a half block down on the opposite side. Her building was on the corner and Jerry angled his rear view and side mirrors to watch the entrance. If no one showed up after a few hours, it was agreed that Jerry would go in and knock on her door.

Cyrus was nibbling on a tuna sandwich and watched with bemusement as Jerry tore into a loaded pastrami and swiss with miscellaneous condiments oozing out the sides. "You'll never make it to 40 eating that way, son. On top of the eggs Benedict this morning, you're a heart attack in the making." Jerry raised his eyebrows mid-bite and smiled.

"Are you going to confront her like you did Mrs. Hoole?" Cyrus asked. Jerry took a long pull on his Nehi Orange soda and wiped his mouth. "Damn, right, Cyrus. What's she going to do? Punch me in the gut? Complain to Ladislaw? Seriously, it's the only approach she'll respect. She treated Twitchy like dirt because she could. Hell, she had me on my heels the first time I met her. Don't worry, I'll start off gentle."

Cyrus smiled. What a change from the insecure guy who stumbled up the porch of the Thimbletown Inn that first day. He wondered if Jerry appreciated his own transformation.

AN HOUR LATER, Jerry was glancing in the side mirror and nudged the dozing Cyrus, prompting him to jerk his head and look out the back window. They saw Gretchen and a middle-aged man enter the corner building and disappear. "That's her, Cyrus. And the man looks like the one she met with in the library when I went back a second time."

Cyrus started to get out of the car and Jerry grabbed his arm. "Pull the car around in front of the building and wait for me. I don't expect she'll even give me the time of day, let alone invite me in. Still, because of the guy and since you preach caution, we need to be ready for a speedy departure." Cyrus looked glum as he pulled his door shut and slid over to the driver side as Jerry got out. "I know you are a big galoot, Jerry, but just be on guard. You know nothing of this man and what he might be capable of." Cyrus had rolled down the window and was peering up at Jerry with an anxious, pleading expression on his face. Jerry reached in and squeezed his shoulder. As he walked toward Gretchen's building, he realized that his simple gesture, an unplanned display of comity, was his first intimate contact with the old man.

As HE CLIMBED the stairs, Jerry thought about what he would say to Gretchen. He knew that events rarely unfold the way we script them but he was determined not to provoke her right away – if that was even possible. He knew she was mercurial but also shrewd and wily. He just hoped he could catch her off guard.

When the door opened, Gretchen showed surprise for a fleeting moment before flashing her trademark scowl. "You got nothing better to do than stalk me?" she said with a malicious grin. She had swung the door open just far enough to lean her outstretched arm across the frame and extend it to the very top. She then leaned across the entrance in a nonchalant manner, effectively blocking his view.

"Did you see this morning's *Beagle* with the story on Smitty?" Jerry asked, almost *sotto voce*. "Who?" Gretchen demanded; her eyes narrowed to slits. "Of course, you remember him, right? The wino who chased Twitchy that first night outside Pudge McFadden's. Turns out that Smitty and Twitchy had some deal working that involved a mysterious blonde who now appears to have vanished. Being as you were so close to Twitchy, I thought you might know who she is."

"You like playing detective, Jerry? You realize that you'll make a horse's ass out of yourself, right? If Twitchy knew some mysterious blonde, it's news to me. Got it? Now stop bugging me or I'll find some way to make your life miserable. Is that simple enough to get through your thick skull?" Gretchen's face had reddened and she was firing words at Jerry from tight lips that seemed to turn white as she pressed them against her teeth.

And just like that she cooled as quickly as she had heated up, smiling almost benignly as she started to close the door. "Who's your friend? Want to introduce me?" Jerry asked. Gretchen glowered and Jerry said, "You know, the guy you walked in with just a few minutes ago."

"There you go again, Sherlock. Another tenant happened to walk in at the same time as me. I don't even know his name and I'm not even sure what floor he lives on. God, you're pathetic," she said sneeringly as she slammed the door shut.

Jerry was smiling as he walked down the stairwell. Her lie at the end was worth it all. It begged the question: Was everything Gretchen Cadwallader said part of a dissembling web, one prevarication woven and interlaced with another? She was a cool customer alright but she had slipped up, forgetting that Jerry had seen the so-called neighbor in the library with her, someone who she now claimed not to know. Yeah, he was an amateur sleuth but not half bad, he said to himself.

Jerry was sure that If Cyrus and Ladislaw met Gretchen just one time, they would be motivated to dig deeper into her past. He was convinced that she knew at least one of the blondes who had disappeared without a trace.

CHAPTER THIRTY:
A LIGHTNING BOLT

~~

THE CAR WAS idling at the curb when Jerry exited Gretchen's building. Cyrus slid over to the passenger side and breathed a sigh of relief when he saw the grin on Jerry's face.

"She's still an icy bitch with her guard up all the time, Cyrus, but I caught her in a lie right before she slammed the door on me," Jerry said excitedly. "Bold-faced harpy," Cyrus chimed in. "I've got to meet her one of these days. What about the man?"

"That's just it. Denied even knowing the guy who walked in with her. Said it was a coincidence – some other resident. I tell you it was the same man with the curly hair and mustache from the library. He was in her apartment, I'm sure of it. She literally blockaded her doorway when I tried to look in. Why lie about it, Cyrus?"

"A lot of plausible reasons. Maybe he's her lover and he's married. Let's get moving – unless you want to stick around and resume the stake out," said Cyrus. "No, she's too clever to come out for a while and when she does, I'd bet anything she'll be alone. If she sees me again, she'll never let down her guard. Let's go."

W<small>HILE</small> G<small>REX WAS</small> languishing in jail, Ladislaw was now seriously entertaining the possibility that this chronic loser had been duped by his missing partner, possibly with one or more accomplices besides the wife. But the damn finger with the class ring was complicating everything. Why would you maim yourself and fake your own death to pull off a scam? Another theory started to form in the lieutenant's head, namely that one of the accomplices did Hoole in, in cahoots with the wife, leaving Grex as the fall guy if and when the finger washed ashore.

It would not be a popular theory with his team or the bosses so Ladislaw kept it to himself. He would wait to see what Cyrus and Jerry confirmed with respect to the wino's finger.

W<small>HEN THEY GOT</small> back to the Thimbletown Inn, Tillie handed Jerry two messages. One was from Fanny which he quickly folded and put in his pocket, avoiding Tillie's penetrating gaze.

The second message was from Mandeville and simply read, "Left hospital and heading back to the *Beagle*. I've got your information."

The two men walked away from Tillie, ever curious but afraid to ask what was up. Jerry was holding the pink message slip in front of him and his hand was trembling. Cyrus took it and said, "Says here that he called 30 minutes ago. He should be back at the *Beagle* by now."

Jerry went to the phone booth in the alcove and wedged himself into the undersized seat while Cyrus held the hinged door open. The call with Mandeville was brief. Jerry hung up the receiver and turned to Cyrus, shaking his head and smiling. "Right ring finger. It's confirmed, Cyrus."

When Jerry came out of the booth, Cyrus grabbed him in a bear hug. "Call Ladislaw, son. It's not conclusive but you're about to make his day – if not his entire year."

WHEN LADISLAW HEARD Jerry's news about the wino's finger, all he could say at first was, "Stunning. A goddamn finger for sale." He promised to call the state crime lab immediately to see what tests, if any, had been completed, prompting Jerry to mention that Smitty was a drunk infected with gangrene and also suffering from diabetes. "Hopefully, this information impacts their analysis, Lieutenant. The lab might also want to contact the doctors at Good Shepherd who tried to save his life. They probably ran a bunch of tests that might be helpful."

"All good points, young man. Don't get too enthralled yet with the idea that the wino's finger somehow turned up on DeCourcy Island and was found by some schoolgirl. Remember, the missing partner's ring was on the finger and he is still missing. Odds are that it is a bizarre coincidence and we still have two fingers."

Jerry hung up the phone from Ladislaw, somewhat deflated but not discouraged. Of course, the trooper was being practical and cautious. That was the standard MO, right? But Jerry couldn't shake the thought that two severed fingers and two elusive blondes would have to be some sort of fantastic coincidence. What were the damn odds? He was glad he hadn't brought up his latest confrontation with Gretchen.

Cyrus was sitting in any easy chair in the alcove, holding his right hand close to his face and turning it back and forth. In his other hand, he held the crime lab photo. He was frowning at his Thorndyke class ring as if it was intentionally holding back a secret. When he saw Jerry walk up, he said, "Still can't see anything, Jerry. Want to give it another look?"

Jerry shook his head no and recapped his conversation with Ladislaw. Cyrus listened and then said, "Maybe we give all the speculation and intrigue a rest until the crime lab finishes its analysis of the finger. I'm heading home, son. Forget all this for one night. Go out and have yourself some fun."

THAT EVENING WITH Fanny was not going to be a reprise of their spontaneous coupling a few nights earlier. Over dinner, she confessed to having a boyfriend, later described as an "almost fiancé," who was an Army corporal stationed in Stuttgart Germany. He had not written or called lately but would be home by Christmas.

Sensitive to Jerry's feelings, she made clear that while she bemoaned her discretion, she did not regret their evening together. It was a delicate balancing act which she pulled off beautifully and Jerry thought none the less of her. No one had been coerced, prodded or even seduced. He was glad she did not ask him if foreknowledge of her relationship with the soldier would have changed anything.

The evening was not, however, without its rewards. After dinner, and certain that he could trust her, Jerry opened up about the second blonde, the one who allegedly sliced off Smitty's finger. When he finished, Fanny looked pensive for a moment and then said, "Have you considered the possibility that there is only one blonde?"

Jerry's face broke out into a broad grin. He wanted to kiss her. He had hoped that she would see what to him was a distinct possibility – even though no causal relationship had been established. "But Jerry, why not go a step further with your theorizing? What if your single blonde isn't a blonde at all?"

Jerry had a stunned look on his face and Fanny went on.

"What are the chances that two blondes, both of whom vanish, are connected to severed fingers just 20 or so miles apart and occurring within a few weeks of each other? Sure, it's possible but I'd be strongly tempted to lay my money on a single woman wearing a wig. That would explain her – or their – disappearance without a trace. If true, that means your blonde could be right under your nose."

Fanny shook her ponytail and arched her eyebrows, as if to say, "Go ahead, tell me I'm wrong." Jerry looked at her and stroked his chin. "Your finance' will never get away with anything," he said, smiling broadly.

Outside the restaurant, there was a lingering hug which might have led to another dalliance but which was forestalled by Fanny's earlier confession.

As Jerry drove back to the Thimbletown Inn, he wondered what might have developed between them in a different time. That hug outside the restaurant was still with him. Perhaps it was his imagination but she seemed reluctant to let go. "*Carpe diem*," he muttered to himself.

Back in his room, Jerry thought through his conversation with Fanny. He was grateful and relieved that she had given validity to his conspiracy theorizing, without any prompting by him. Hell, she had even expanded on it with her suggestion about a possible blonde wig. Then, it hit him like a ton of bricks. There might be a way to test Fanny's theory. It was right there where he started his quest - at the Brightwood Motel.

CHAPTER THIRTY-ONE:
THE COLOR OF MONEY

~♂

JERRY SAT IN his car outside the Brightwood Motel on Monday, scanning the row of identical dingy, peeling facades. He had waited until late morning when most of the departing guests would have checked out and the cleaning crew would be commencing their daily drudge.

When he saw the purple-tinged hair now complemented by streaks of lime and orange, he quickly exited his car and approached the cleaning lady.

"What the hell do you want now? That man ain't been back, I don't mind telling you that. No charge," she snarled, grinning at her own levity and exposing a bottom row of stained, rotting teeth. She was holding a pack of Winston cigarettes in one hand and jiggled it just enough to shake one loose. As it popped up, she leaned in toward the pack and grabbed the cigarette between her lips, flipping open a silver lighter with the other hand.

"You're looking very colorful today. Gave up on the Virginian Slims, I see," Jerry said, eyeing the pack of Winston's. He was certain that she smoked whatever brand she could lift while cleaning, most likely reasoning that no one was going to report missing smokes.

The lighter looked expensive, with some sort of ornate, raised carving on its face. She was no doubt smart enough not to take anything of value from a room whose guest hadn't already checked out. "Under a bed?" he asked, pointing to the lighter. The maid scowled, not quite understanding but always on the defensive. "Just curious where you found the lighter. Guess you'll be turning it into lost and found after your shift," Jerry offered.

Her eyes almost closed as she absorbed Jerry's insult. She lit the cigarette and said, "Beat it" through a cloud of smoke. As she turned away, Jerry cleared his throat. She looked back as he pulled a five dollar bill from his pocket, dangling it in front of her.

"How's your memory?" Jerry said, smiling. "Better'n yours, kiddo," she snapped. "Okay, if you can remember the color of hair on the brush you took from that man's room last week, this here five spot is yours. But before you say anything, be aware that I already know the correct color. I just need you to verify it. Just a double-check, got it?"

The woman frowned, as if insulted by Jerry's warning. Then she smiled slyly and said, "I knowed you were a private dick all along. Guy's in a lot of trouble, ain't he? Got caught screwing the wrong babe. That makes it worth more. Double sawbuck and I'll confirm what you already know." Jerry reached into his pocket and pulled out another five. "I could stop by the front desk and let them know you'll be turning in the lighter. Now, be reasonable. A sawbuck is all you get. Take it or leave it."

After a brief stare down, the woman said "brown – but it weren't her natural color" and grabbed for the money. "Positive?" Jerry pressed. "I know my tints, mister. Went to beauty school once," she sneered. Jerry pulled back his hand and said, "Why didn't you tell me this when we met the first time?" She smiled scornfully and said, "You didn't ask."

Of course, she was right and Jerry was chastened into silence.

She tugged at the bills in his hand and this time he released his grip.

Humbled by the cleaning woman, it took Jerry a minute to absorb the significance of what he had learned. Of course, she could have been lying or guessing but her more logical prevarication – or gamble – would have been blonde hair. No, he was sure that she was telling the truth.

So, Fanny had been perspicacious and most likely right about the blonde wig. She had been good for him in more ways than one and he would find an opportunity to thank her. It seemed clear now that there was at least one woman involved in the missing partner's life wearing a disguise. But who and why?

The only two women Jerry knew in the area with brown hair were Tillie and Gretchen. At their first meeting, Jerry thought of Gretchen's hair as brown with a hint of red. There had to be a name for that shade. Jerry laughed. Maybe he should go back and consult the beauty school expert. He wanted to say Gretchen Cadwallader with assurance but couldn't bring himself to do it. There was still a frustrating mystery to unravel but Jerry was anxious to share his latest discovery with Cyrus and Ladislaw.

As Jerry was driving back to the Thimbletown Inn, information was now flooding into Ladislaw's office. Unbeknownst to Cyrus and Jerry, the lieutenant had authorized a background check on the missing partner. It revealed that prior to his quarry venture, Hoole had been the long-time comptroller at the Red Clover Insurance Company based in Montpelier, Vermont. Company records confirmed that he had left after what was termed some "financial irregularities" had been uncovered at one of its operating units over which Hoole had supervisory authority. The company would not provide further details without a subpoena but Ladislaw did the translation himself, to wit: funds had been embezzled, the evidence was circumstantial but not ironclad and a mutual departure was the compromise.

Jerry's discovery regarding the wino made Ladislaw anxious to get the crime lab analysis on the finger. If it wasn't for the class ring, he was ready to believe that there was no way it was the Hoole's finger found at DeCourcy Island which, in turn, meant that the missing partner was most likely still alive. Had this non-descript, mild-mannered insurance man orchestrated a complex con job that had been designed to set up his hapless partner for a murder rap? Even Grex didn't deserve such a fate. It bothered Ladislaw that such a scam meant that elaborate steps were taken to lure in a wino and then use him as disposable collateral damage. But what was the con? Right now, he had zero evidence.

Ladislaw knew that the son was in Toronto and, practically speaking, out of reach. But the wife now had some explaining to do. He had not heard from her in the last few days but he would now bring her in for questioning. If she pulled the timid routine on him again, he would rake her over the coals.

CHAPTER THIRTY-TWO:
DISAPPEARING ACT

~~

WHEN JERRY GOT back to the Thimbletown Inn, Cyrus was sitting in the lobby, puffing on his pipe and reading the *New Haven Beagle*. He looked up when he saw Jerry and said, "Usually don't read this rag but wanted to see if there was a follow-up story by our intrepid reporter. Nothing."

Jerry told Cyrus about his confrontation with the maid, causing him to slap both knees and exclaim, "Damn! A bald man with a hairbrush led you to the facile conclusion that he had a blonde female visitor. I never entertained the possibility of a wig. Great thinking, kid." Jerry should have demurred. He felt guilty taking credit for Fanny's insight but felt a greater obligation to protect her privacy. So, he accepted the unearned encomium with a diffident shrug.

"I know only two people with brown hair in the area, Cyrus. Your sister and Gretchen. We know that Gretchen spent time out here so it's not a wild-assed theory that she ran into Hoole and went to his motel room at some point. It doesn't explain why she would be wearing a blonde wig, but --"

Cyrus interrupted him with a hearty laugh, causing Jerry to

frown. "Oh, I was just trying to imagine Tillie in a blonde wig. But seriously, you're forgetting someone else." Cyrus paused and Jerry looked bewildered. Cyrus said, "Well, she's not from here but she's here now. You omitted the wife." Jerry cuffed his forehead and asked, "So, are you suggesting that the wife came down here and put on a disguise to secretly aid her husband?" Cyrus took the pipe from his mouth and waved it in front of his face. "It's not far-fetched. You said she's the bossy, domineering type, right? Maybe she didn't like the slow progress of things and wanted to expedite issuance of the death certificate. Sounds just like the wife you described. I'm just encouraging you to stay open to all possibilities and not get fixated on one person who you find distasteful and who, quite frankly, treated you like dirt. That's all." Jerry screwed up his lips and looked thoughtful for a few seconds before saying, "touché."

Cyrus had made his point and wasn't going to dwell on it. "Let's call Ladislaw. He'll want to hear your story about the maid. Hell, he might even want to make you an *ex officio* member of his team," he said. The two were standing side by side and Cyrus put his arm over Jerry's shoulder, letting it linger there.

"THAT SON OF a bitch isn't dead," Cyrus blurted out after hearing Ladislaw describe Hoole's questionable departure from the Vermont insurance company. "His disappearance and supposed death has the odor of a classic insurance scam," he added, when no one reacted immediately to his outrage. He was sitting with Jerry and Ladislaw in the lieutenant's office hashing over all the information that had come in that morning.

After hearing about Jerry's latest encounter with the maid, Ladislaw said, "We'll get a statement from her. You gents will be pleased to hear that I'm bringing the wife back in today. If there's a scheme, she is likely a part of it. Can you picture her teamed up with Grex to dispose of the spouse? It's laughable. More likely a husband and wife job. As a matter of course, we asked her earlier about any life insurance policies on her husband but she professed total ignorance. Could be some of her play-acting. Called her at the inn twice this morning but got no answer. Sent a trooper over there already to watch her movements. Her car is still there so she hasn't bolted." Ladislaw stopped and sat back in his chair, forming a steeple with his hands before proceeding. "Now, I've been very accommodating so far but you're free-lancing has got to stop. Believe me, I appreciate what you've discovered but I do wonder what you might be holding back on me. If you are, that would be a mistake." Ladislaw was looking intently at Jerry, his face a mask of steely resolve. He had used this technique successfully before and today's results were no different.

"Well, I did do a little checking up on Gretchen Cadwallader yesterday. You might even say that I staked out her apartment. Caught her in a lie, lieutenant. Twice now, I've seen her with this middle-aged man with curly hair and a bushy mustache, sorta like the Eliot Gould character in *Mash*. You know, the movie not the tv show. If you're suspicious of the wife, you ought to be concerned about her as well. I know there's no proof but something tells me she knows the missing partner." Jerry spoke earnestly and Cyrus noticed that Ladislaw's face had softened.

"Your speculation seems like a stretch but we'll make a renewed effort to interview her. Don't be offended but some young women have a thing for older men. Sometimes, according to the department psychologist, it's a father replacement thing. I will say that the fact that there's no information on her is puzzling. DMV did issue a license to her but the story about growing up in Ohio doesn't hold water, as Cyrus discovered. Still, wanting to keep one's past a secret is no crime, Jerry. We all have things we don't want out there, right? Well, let's see what my boys can get out of her. We thought we had our man and still may but, hell, even a loser like Grex deserves a fair shake, right?" Ladislaw stood up and folded his arms across his chest. He was smiling but his posture was authoritative. "Remember, no more free-lancing. If you have an idea or a theory, come to me. Play ball and I'll keep you two in the loop. And by the way, I loved Gould in that movie. Maybe Gretchen fell for this guy because he looks like Trapper John."

Outside, Jerry said, "We should have asked him about the crime lab analysis of the finger, Cyrus. I'm starting to worry that he might not share the results with us. It'd be my fault if he doesn't." Jerry was thinking about Ladislaw's veiled comment about the secrets people keep and wondered if it was a direct reference to his own past. The man had broad investigative powers and why would Jerry be exempt from them? Still, it felt like a sucker punch. Images of Nepal and Sweden floated before his eyes and made him cringe. Who was Jerry Kosinsky to question the mysterious past of Gretchen Cadwallader – or anybody else, for that matter, he asked himself? Still, it bothered him that Ladislaw might think he was fixated on Gretchen because she might have rejected him in favor of some old fart that looks like some character in a movie.

To the best of Jerry's knowledge, Cyrus had never pried deeply into his background, probing for things dark and disreputable. Cyrus didn't strike him as judgmental but he certainly could have wondered where Jerry was when a good portion of his generation were dying in rice fields and jungles 8000 miles away.

Loren Eiseley's book had bought him some credibility with Cyrus on that first day. Maybe that was all it took. Jerry couldn't have known, right when he walked up the steps of the Thimbletown Inn, that Cyrus needed some purpose at that particular time – besides watching over Tillie. It struck him in that moment that the old man had turned out to be much more of a mentor that Prof. Eyesmore had ever been. He knew then that Cyrus deserved some explanation when this caper with the missing partner was resolved. Perhaps, it would even bring a measure of expiation with it.

Cyrus interrupted Jerry's introspection with a light-hearted laugh. "Let me remind you that you need to understand a guy like Ladislaw, Jerry. He's a career trooper and you're coming up with information that his team should be uncovering. It stings a bit but he'll get over it. He's no Buffle, carrying a grudge for every slight, perceived or real, but he is a creature of the system. As for not free-lancing, he was looking at you when he said it. What's to stop me from calling my nephew at the crime lab to say hello? There's no telling what he might say. He can be a gabby sort when the mood strikes him."

CHAPTER THIRTY-THREE:
Corpus Delicti

Cyrus and Jerry sat in the café at the Thimbletown Inn, nibbling almost absent-mindedly at their lunches, waiting for the nephew to call back from the crime lab. Jerry broke the silence by saying, "Remember what your nephew said, Cyrus. The finger found at DeCourcy Island appears to have been cut with a serrated knife or similar instrument. That explanation would be consistent with what happened to Smitty. He could very well have sold his finger – and his life – for $100 and what he imagined would be an unending supply of Thunderbird. That bartender at the Belly Up knew what he was talking about. People do crazy things when they get hooked on that rotgut."

Cyrus shook his head slowly before saying, "And some sicko took advantage of his craving. It makes my blood boil. From your description of Twitchy, it's obvious he didn't act alone nor was he even the instigator. Just a pliant, useful tool for someone with a heart of stone. I suppose it's a crime to remove a body part and use it in another crime. And if the seller eventually dies, as Smitty did, can a case for manslaughter be made? I might need to research some case law at some point, just to satisfy my curiosity."

"Well, you've only seen the wife's play-acting so far, Cyrus, but if you want cold-hearted, Gretchen makes Mrs. Hoole look like a rank amateur."

Just then, Tillie walked in and announced, "You've got a call, Cyrus. It's Bert Spooner from vital records." Cyrus was back in a few minutes, his shoulders sunk in and looking dispirited. He had received information on the girl he still thought of as "little Betsy." Spooner had located an Elizabeth "Betsy" Cruikshank in Manhattan Beach, California. Records confirmed that she had applied for a driver's license by showing a current one from Burlington, Vermont. When she didn't show up at her job, a few co-workers went to her apartment complex. A neighbor told them that she had seen Betsy loading up her car with suitcases and boxes. It was around mid-December and no one has seen her since that day. Cyrus shook his head as he looked at Jerry and said softly, almost in a whisper, "A lot of people are pulling a disappearing act. I hope she's okay."

"Some of our guests like to sleep late and we accommodate them, Lieutenant. It's inconvenient for housekeeping but that's our policy," the day manager at the inn explained to Ladislaw. He was a small, thin man with a sallow complexion, his wispy grey hair parted down the middle as if he was trying to mimic a silent film actor from the 20s. He quickly wilted under Ladislaw's stare and called the wife's room. When he got no answer, he looked at Ladislaw's immutable face and said, "But if you insist, follow me."

Ladislaw slowly turned the knob to confirm that the door was locked. He stepped back and said softly, "Knock and calmly announce yourself. Give her a chance to respond. Tell her that housekeeping needs to get in soon. Talk normal." The manager nodded and followed Ladislaw's instructions, his voice quivering slightly as if he was confronted with a herculean task. When there was no response, Ladislaw made a motion of a key turning in a lock and the manager started to perspire and shake. Ladislaw took the key and slowly opened the door while calling out the wife's name and announcing himself. Nothing but silence.

Past the narrow entrance hall, Ladislaw could see that the blinds were drawn and only a few rays of sunlight slipped through the uneven slats, just enough to expose a figure lying on the bed. The clerk was peering in and Ladislaw motioned for him to back out of the room. Before approaching the bed, Ladislaw checked the bathroom and the closet.

Mrs. Hoole was on her back, laid out neatly in her nightgown as if in a casket, her mouth open wide as she stared blankly at the ceiling. A cord had apparently been ripped off a table lamp that was tipped over on the floor. It was wrapped tightly around her neck, the plug lying against her throat like some grotesque pendant. Spittle had formed in the corners of her mouth and Ladislaw caught the foul smell before he noticed the soiled linens beneath her. There had been an involuntary evacuation of bodily fluids, no doubt occurring as the last breaths were squeezed out of her. The scene made even a veteran like Ladislaw squeamish, forcing him to briefly look away.

The body was cold and rigor mortis had set in. Ladislaw was certain that she had been dead for hours but would wait for the coroner to provide a reliable time range. Ladislaw turned and saw the manager lurking behind him. "Call for an ambulance," he said quietly.

IT WOULD BE a few hours before Cyrus and Jerry learned that the wife had been murdered the night before. Her room had been ransacked during an apparent robbery. The contents of her purse had been emptied out and whatever money it contained was gone.

The most intriguing discovery came from a member of Ladislaw's team later on and before the room was sealed off. When the suitcase on the top shelf of the closet was opened, buried at the bottom beneath a few layers of clothing was a blonde wig.

CHAPTER THIRTY-FOUR:
The Wig and the Ring

~⁀~

"Damn, never would have guessed her but you did," said Jerry, looking at Cyrus and shaking his head dejectedly, as if he had been negligent and missed an obvious clue. Ladislaw had phoned Cyrus and sounded like he was in a hurry when he passed on the news of the wife's murder and the discovery of the blonde wig. "I started to ask questions and he cut me off rather abruptly. All he would say was that it was most likely a burglary that went south. I call it a perfect example of Sod's Law," Cyrus said.

"Sounds biblical, Cyrus. What does it mean?" asked Jerry. "It could have its origins in the bible but I'm not certain. Anyway, it's a variation of Murphy's Law but more cynical so some folks speculate it came about much later. It means that if something will go wrong, it will go wrong at the worst possible moment. I would say it applies to Isabel Hoole, on the verge of collecting on her on what I'm guessing is her husband's insurance policy. If there is such a policy, Ladislaw is going to find it.

"To be sure, she was a wily, tough broad who fooled a lot of people and aggravated some others – and then she gets snuffed out during a random burglary. I tossed her into the mix because she had brown hair and you were speculating. With the discovery of the wig, we are to assume that she's the one who went into the underbelly of New Haven to negotiate with a wino to perform such a dastardly deed, all to help her husband fake his death. It's hard to grasp, but what other explanation is there?" Cyrus asked.

"Well, for one thing, the wig could have been planted in her room at the inn, certain the police would find it and jump to conclusions. Which means it probably wasn't a burglary. Ladislaw was under pressure to solve the missing partner case even before the wife's murder and now it's going to get ratcheted up. I guess we're supposed to believe that it was just a coincidence that the husband's still missing and now she's a random victim. As for Ladislaw, it sounds like he might be going tight-lipped on us, Cyrus."

Cyrus was biting his own lip and rubbing his forehead vigorously as Jerry talked. He ignored Jerry's concern regarding Ladislaw's reticence and said, "No, it makes no sense when I think it through. Even if the wife went to Smitty with a sordid offer to buy his finger, it would have to have been through Twitchy. He was going to be the on-going supplier of Thunderbird, right? There's no way a middle-aged lady from Vermont, as feisty as she might be, propositioned a wino on the street or walked into that trainyard encampment on her own and somehow teamed up with Twitchy to perpetuate the scheme. So, let's scratch my lame theory and go back to yours, namely that the murderer or an accomplice planted the wig. Ergo, it wasn't a burglary after all."

"So, if the wife wasn't wearing the wig, the mysterious lady is still out there. Maybe she really is a blonde and the wig is a clever piece of misdirection," Jerry said, grinning mischievously. He was so frustrated that he almost looked demonic as he stared off into the distance.

Cyrus knew that Jerry didn't believe what he had just said and that Gretchen Cadwallader was constantly on his mind. Now, with the wife dead, he was ready to take the kid more seriously but decided not to give him any encouragement just yet. "Let's give it a rest. Once we hear back from my nephew, we can go at this thing again with some solid, empirical evidence. Right now, we're drowning in speculation."

CYRUS HAD SENSED correctly that Ladislaw had not been entirely forthcoming when he notified them about the wife's murder. He told them she had been strangled and about the blonde wig but left out other, vital details. If he had shared his initial suspicions regarding the crime scene, Cyrus and Jerry might have rushed over to see him. He needed time to think, unencumbered and without their influence. Plus, he feared that his team would wonder, even be concerned, about his deference toward a couple of what they considered rank amateurs who had no business intruding in an official investigation.

After leaving the crime scene crew in charge at the inn, Ladislaw sat in his car and mentally recreated what he had seen. He recalled that the door to the wife's room had not been tampered with and the key slid in easily. So, it hadn't been jimmied, making it likely that the wife knew the murderer and perhaps even invited him in – unless, of course, he had a duplicate key. He had checked the windows of the ground floor room before leaving and both of them were locked.

Ladislaw felt certain that it was a murder with the intent to make it look like a burglary gone bad. It made no sense that a seasoned burglar looking for jewelry and money would ransack the room and strangle the sleeping guest, with the obvious risk of arousing other guests. No, his MO would be a quick in and out, no fuss, no muss. Murder would not be on his agenda unless something went terribly wrong during the heist. If she had a weapon, it was no longer in the room. Even then, the burglar wouldn't stage a stylized, almost ritualistic death scene.

The night clerk had been called at home and confirmed that there were no noise complaints the prior evening from other guests.

If the perp came in uninvited, it was probably sometime after midnight when the wife was likely in bed and the element of surprise would normally work in his favor. On the other hand, if she gave her killer a key or simply let him in, he could have been there for a while. The missing husband? If so, the hate built up inside of him must have been palpable. Was it because he thought that the wife was going to double-cross him? The cord around her neck had left very deep abrasions, indicating rage. Was the lamp plug hanging down the front like a necklace trinket accidental or some final cruel joke?

The suitcase appeared to have been undisturbed and that puzzled Ladislaw. In a darkened room, maybe the burglar simply missed it whereas a murderer wouldn't have cared unless he planted the wig in it. But why? It seemed far-fetched. No, the most logical assumption at this stage was that it was the wife wearing the wig.

The original case of the missing partner and the severed finger had suddenly become more complex, even melodramatic. It was one thing to have the husband's finger with his college ring wash ashore but quite another for his wife to show up looking for him and end up strangled. He expected the telephone to start ringing as soon as he walked back into the barracks. His bosses would be hounding him for answers. And the press would sensationalize the murder and up the pressure.

Ladislaw caught himself nibbling nervously on the tip of his finger and quickly pulled his hand away from his face. He didn't want to admit it but he was anxious to get input from his two neophyte detectives. He just wasn't prepared to bring them into the barracks. Others would see it as a concession that he was a fish out of water.

"He said he couldn't talk now but would be here around six," Tillie said. Jerry had retreated to his room and Cyrus was sitting on the porch, puffing on his pipe and gazing out on the calm waters of Long Island Sound when she delivered the message from the nephew. Cyrus nodded and said, "Thanks, Tillie. Please ring Jerry's room and let him know." There was a softness, almost a gentle sweetness in her brother's normally placid voice. It startled Tillie and made her hesitate for a moment. She wanted to say something as simple as, "Are you okay?" but the words got caught in her throat and she walked away.

"I delivered our updated analysis to Ladislaw just a short time ago, Uncle. Naturally, it's confidential until he releases all or part of it." The nephew was sitting in the alcove at the Thimbletown Inn across from Cyrus and Jerry.

Cyrus smiled and gestured slightly with his hands, as if to say, "Okay, you got your disclaimer and warning out of the way. Tell us what you know."

Almost everything the nephew said next was cautionary and qualified. Yes, they were certain from the outset that it was the finger of a white male, most likely middle-aged, even before the inscription on the ring was identified. They couldn't pull fingerprints and there were no tattoos or other identifying marks. "Tissue samples indicated that there was nerve damage, consistent with an alcoholic or heavy drinker. Then, there was the broken fingernail caked underneath with dirt – not exactly what we would expect to see with a businessman. Excessive alcohol intake over time results in nerve damage, causing numbness in the extremities. So, it is rather ironic that whatever pain the victim felt during the cutting might have been minimal. The drinking over time, in other words, acted like an anesthetic, deadening the finger for the impromptu surgery. It would be quite helpful to know if the missing partner imbibed excessively.

"Listen, I know what I said earlier when you visited the lab but, just to be clear, we're not 100% certain that a serrated knife or similar instrument was used to sever the finger. If the missing partner was tossed into the Sound, his body could have broken apart and been consumed - except for the finger, as we discussed before. Take the sand tiger shark, for example. It lives in these waters and has narrow teeth that could have caused the jagged cuts on the finger. Of course, the wife's murder most likely changed the police thinking on whether the missing partner is actually dead but it's not our job to speculate. Sorry, that's all I can give you for now."

Cyrus thought of Smitty and mumbled, "excessive alcohol intake" as a clinical, dispassionate way to describe a man drowning in alcohol. He fiddled with his Thorndyke ring, catching the nephew's attention, prompting him to grab his uncle's hand and spread the fingers out, palm down. He then ran his index finger slowly over the surface of the ring. "What is it?" Cyrus asked. "Something's different about your ring. Maybe I've been looking at that gruesome finger too long. What the hell is it?" the nephew said, his voice rising in frustration.

Cyrus pulled the crime lab photograph from his pocket and unfolded it. When he laid it on the table, the nephew exclaimed, "Aha!" and pointed to the ring's insignia in the picture. He grabbed his uncle's hand again and laid it flat on the table. Everyone was leaning in now, alternately scrutinizing the ring and its image in the photograph. The insignias on the rings were pointing in different directions. Cyrus' faced out toward anyone who might approach him but the one in the picture pointed to the left, toward the wearer. The insignia was faded in the picture and everyone had missed it.

Jerry smiled but the other two looked perplexed. "On graduation day at Pythian, we all turned our ring insignias out to indicate to the world that we had earned our diplomas. It's a tradition. Until then, it points inward, at you, as a reminder that your goal has not yet been achieved. I'm guessing that the same tradition is pretty much universal – including at Thorndyke."

"Can't remember that far back but is it relevant or just another clue that takes us nowhere? We confirmed that the missing partner graduated so either he followed tradition or got lazy and never rotated the insignia. Then again, he was proud enough to get the ring engraved with his initials and graduation date, right? So, sure, he would likely have done what his classmates were doing – adhered to tradition." As Cyrus was talking, he turned the insignia on his ring. It was snug but he was finally able to rotate it inward and then immediately turned it back. "Well, we can probably agree that some sea creature didn't turn it, right?" Cyrus said, looking up at the others.

"So, either someone turned it intentionally, which makes no sense to me, or, try this out, it got rotated accidentally during a struggle," Jerry offered. He tried to imagine someone pushing Hoole's ring onto Smitty's finger and it made him queasy.

The nephew seemed to read Jerry's mind. He jumped in and cautioned, "We did not say in today's report that the finger wasn't the missing partner's. Still too speculative, some would say preposterous, to suggest it was the wino's finger wearing the missing partner's ring. Hard to see the troopers going out on a limb with this theory with the risk of getting burned. The press would have a field day mocking them. The safer conclusion is that the finger still belongs to the missing partner, which means that Ladislaw's team may have husband and wife murders to solve. And now I'll go strictly off the record, Uncle, and offer my personal opinion. I don't believe it's the missing partner's finger that was discovered at DeCourcy Island. So, if it is the wino's, how in god's name did it get into the water wearing the missing partner's ring? I'll leave that conundrum to the both of you. Happy now?"

The nephew stood up, shook Jerry's hand and gave his uncle a brief hug. Before he walked away, he said, "When Ladislaw shares our report with you, assuming that he does, I know you'll act surprised. Let me know how he reacts to our findings. He looked like a very conflicted man when I left him earlier."

CHAPTER THIRTY-FIVE:
THE BONDING

AFTER THE NEPHEW left, Cyrus said, "C'mon, let's get out of here. I'm buying dinner tonight." Tillie stopped them at the door with a message from Ladislaw, saying he wanted to see them first thing in the morning. "Call back and confirm that we'll be there at 9," said Cyrus, without looking back. "He's coming here. He said it twice," Tillie said, her voice almost shrill, as if the lieutenant's repetition was somehow momentous.

Jerry squinted and Cyrus laughed. "He doesn't want to be seen talking to us so often. Bad for morale and makes him look insecure. May even have heard some grumbling from his team. That's okay, probably even better that he come here. It'll make him more forthcoming. We should cut him some slack. Hell, I'd likely do the same thing if I were him. And now, let's leave it all behind for one evening, okay?"

"WORRIED ABOUT HER?" Jerry asked. A few minutes earlier, Cyrus had mused about the disappearance of Betsy Cruikshank from her California apartment but now the old man had gone quiet. The waiter had cleared away their dishes and Cyrus was sipping his wine and looking pensive.

"More curious than concerned. She was always a free-spirit, an iconoclast of sorts, even at a young age. Probably took off for some place like Tobago or Bora Bora and will show up one day – maybe when her dad dies. The truth is that ever since your visit to Burlington, I haven't got Letty out of my mind and Little Betsy is intertwined with a lot of those memories. I remember her saying that the girl was impossible to get close to. At a young age, she had already thrown up an impenetrable wall. Her aunt showered her with affection but it didn't seem to make a difference. Letty mentioned the whispering in the family about how quickly George married the nurse after his wife died. Not only that but some thought it more than curious when the nurse moved into the Cruikshank residence to supervise her convalescence. Betsy was no normal child. She picked up on things that other kids would miss. At least, it's how Letty summed up things."

Cyrus shrugged and then seemed to brighten up. "All that talk about Ponce de Leon and the Fountain of Youth was just that – idle talk to amuse myself. Hope you didn't think I would take off. I'm no Dorian Grey, ready to make a Faustian bargain in a bid for eternal youth. No, I'd just like to roll back the clock to a certain date I have in mind and get another shot at it, that's all. Not too much to ask, is it?" Cyrus said with a self-deprecating laugh.

"No, it's not, Cyrus. In fact, I know how you feel," Jerry said, gulping noticeably as he choked out the words. Cyrus nodded, caught the discomfort and said, "Listen, if you ever want to talk, I'm available. First, I want to confess something. Did some checking on you when you first showed up here and started snooping around. I know you're no deserter but you did take off for Canada around ten years ago so my assumption is that you were avoiding the draft. I might have had a problem with it back then but not any longer. As to your motives as a 21-year old, it's not my business unless you make it so. Whatever it was that prompted you back then, well, I'd like to think that it was for a heartfelt and noble purpose. And I believe it was, Jerry. As to what you did in those intervening years, it's no business of mine either. You seem like a decent young man trying to find himself. You're not alone. I'm just glad I got to know you." Cyrus finished and tipped his wine glass to Jerry, who felt moisture forming in the corners of his eyes. It sounded like something his father or Billy Meacham, Jr. would have said and it made him profoundly sad and appreciative at the same time. A slight smile creased Jerry's mouth. He wanted to open up but something was holding him back at the moment and Cyrus wasn't one to press.

A few nights earlier, Jerry had laid in bed, unable to sleep, thinking about how he was so persuadable, so malleable, under the tutelage of Prof. Eyesmore. During the summers between classes at Pythian, Eyesmore had arranged for expeditions to the Great Plains and the Grand Canyon to test Jerry's intellectual process and stamina under real life conditions, or so he explained. Initially, he met the professor's expectations before everything collapsed in Kathmandu. Crippled since childhood by a bout of polio, Eyesmore would experience vicariously through Jerry and other acolytes the adventures he had missed. If they screwed up, like Jerry had, it was Eyesmore's torment. It had taken years for Jerry to consider the possibility that he had been used as a tool by the revered professor in an attempt to expunge a lifetime of his own frustrated expectations.

Sitting across from Cyrus was revelatory for Jerry. He had earned the affection if not the respect of a man he had grown to admire, a man who still struggled with his own self-doubts after all these years.

It was a short ride back from the restaurant to the Thimbletown Inn. Both men were silent, absorbed in their own ruminations and regrets. Neither one wanted to talk of severed fingers, murdered spouses or missing persons. For one evening, there was a tacit understanding to give it all a rest. Ladislaw would show up in the morning and it would start all over again.

CHAPTER THIRTY-SIX:
TORONTO COMES CLEAN

"We've asked the Mounties for help in locating the son but so far no luck. Thought maybe you'd be willing to help. We need someone to identify and, hopefully, claim the body." It was early Tuesday morning and Ladislaw was looking at Jerry but making side glances to Cyrus, as if his acquiescence would make a difference.

"I doubt he'll come back," Jerry said. "Assuming the father isn't dead or a suspect, maybe her murder will flush him out of his hiding place – assuming that he isn't long gone, that is." Ladislaw had a distressed look on his face and Jerry wished he hadn't been so flippant. He didn't understand that beneath the stolid trooper façade, cultivated and nurtured over many years, a man was fractured. Nothing seemed to be working out. There were no leads on the husband and the prints lifted from the wife's room were partials and of a poor quality. Ladislaw had sent the best set up to Vermont authorities to run against their database after no match was found locally.

Quiet desperation was starting to set in and you could read it on Ladislaw's face. Cyrus saw it as soon as the lieutenant walked into the Thimbletown Inn that morning but it took Jerry a little longer. Under normal circumstances, Ladislaw was unflappable, a competent investigator who handled cases by the book and rarely, if ever, doubted himself. A knife fight, a biker brawl, a domestic dispute, even a hit and run – these were the cases that dominated his resume. He had not been prepared for the tangled skein which now seemed to be dominating his every waking minute. He had never been called upon to probe the dark recesses of a killer's mind.

"If you can make contact with the son, it's more likely he'll open up to you, maybe say something helpful. Even if we do find him and he's somehow a party to this sordid affair, he'll probably clam up immediately," Ladislaw explained. He couldn't bring himself to say "please" but everything in his voice and manner said it for him.

"It's quite possible he was finagled by the parents and knows very little about their scheme. My guess is that his only task was to appeal to your good nature to get you down here, a way to give legitimacy to the father's disappearance and provide cover until their scam was completed," Cyrus said, looking at Jerry.

"I don't relish the idea of being used as a pawn but it looks like I was. I'll make the call, Lieutenant. Like you said, he might say something helpful that wouldn't come out otherwise." Jerry was thinking about what Cyrus had said yesterday regarding Ladislaw's possible reasons for no longer sharing information. Hopefully, this gesture on his part would alleviate if not eliminate that obstacle. The proof came quickly.

"I had two men in New Haven last night, watching the Cadwallader apartment from six o'clock on. Neither the girl nor her friend came in or out. In fact, the lights never went on. Around one, the boys went around to that Irish pub that she was known to frequent. The bartender said he hadn't seen her since her friend jumped in front of the freight train. You realize that we don't have a shred of evidence that links her either to the wino or the missing partner. Believe me, we're looking under every rock." Ladislaw stopped and threw up his hands, waiting for some reaction.

Sensing he was holding back, Cyrus and Jerry were both stone-faced, compelling Ladislaw to go on. "We got some information back from Vermont insurance officials. There's a $50,000 policy on the husband with the wife as the beneficiary, so it explains why she was so anxious to get the death certificate. We found nothing to benefit the husband, making him an unlikely murder suspect – unless, of course, we consider that he was motivated by pure hatred. All we have to bolster that theory are the comments made by the neighbor."

Ladislaw had opened up and Cyrus knew he was expecting some acknowledgement. He thanked him and then added, "I was almost certain that it was an insurance policy that brought her down here. And by the way, you are right not to rule out a crime of passion."

"What about the wig?" Jerry asked. Ladislaw was caught off guard and his mouth flew open. "It's being analyzed," he said cryptically. "That's all?" Jerry asked, clearly agitated and causing Cyrus to touch his arm.

Ladislaw's eyes darkened. He had been cornered and didn't like it. "After your latest confrontation with the maid, we examined the wig and found brown hair follicles on the inside. We assume they belong to the wife but, to be certain, we sent the wig along with some strands of the wife's hair up to the crime lab for analysis. Only a few members of my team are aware of this evidence. If it's not the wife's hair and the press gets a hold of it, they'll have a field day, not to mention that a story in the newspaper will tip off any suspects out there." Ladislaw finished and let out a deep breath, as if he had successfully purged his system of pent up pressure. Cyrus and Jerry knew that he had made a big leap of faith in trusting them with potentially explosive information.

"I'll make that call to Toronto this morning, Lieutenant. You'll know everything I learn, no matter how banal."

Ladislaw stood up slowly, his shoulders slightly hunched and carrying what he thought was the burden of impending failure. Cyrus felt for him and said to Jerry, "There goes a man known for his ramrod posture and unflappable demeanor, the proverbial Atlas carrying the world on his shoulders. It's sad to see this case dragging a decent man down. You have to promise me, Jerry, that anything we come up with goes to Ladislaw immediately. No goddam exceptions." Jerry looked contrite and nodded his head yes.

Cyrus was satisfied and let it go. He poked Jerry's arm and said, laughingly, "You couldn't have said trite or ordinary? The poor guy is probably sitting in his car trying to figure out what a banal is and whether it's good or bad."

ON THE THIRD try, Jerry got through to Percy Hoole in Toronto at a number provided by another veteran who had deserted around the same time. He sounded genuinely shocked when he heard about his mother's murder but there was no anguish in his voice. "My mother called me after the finger was discovered in the water down there. You had just left Toronto to go back home. Asked if I'd heard from my father. That was our last conversation," he said matter of factly, before asking, "Any word on him?"

"Nothing. The police are unsure if he's dead or on the lam. They're not even sure it's his finger. You need to understand that the cops want to question him in connection with your mother's murder. He is a potential if not an actual suspect. And why didn't she mention the severed finger when I stopped to see her? She knew by then."

"Beats me. It's just like her to keep it a secret. She only wanted you as well as me to know only so much. As to my father being a suspect, that's a laugh," Hoole said. "He's got the courage of the Cowardly Lion, if you know what I mean. Always said we were cut from the same cloth. It's no secret that my mother despised both of us."

"Not exactly how you portrayed her in Toronto when you asked for my help," Jerry said. The son laughed softly but it was self-mocking and Jerry picked up the cynical, defeated tone. "Yeah, sorry about that. She put me up to it after I mentioned I had a friend who got a presidential pardon and was heading home. She said the family's survival depended on it. I tried to press her for details but she just scoffed at my request. Told me that all you need to know is that your dad is going to fake his disappearance and it has to seem like we are diligently searching for him. When she told me later about the finger, I assumed that she had used me for something nefarious. She warned me to keep my mouth shut if anyone started to make inquiries. Guess that was an idle threat, huh?"

It was clear to Jerry that the son was a pliable tool who was on the run from his family, the Army, perhaps even the memory of his older brother whose death was the impetus for his enlistment. It wasn't hard to believe that the mother had goaded this weaker son to follow the fateful path of the favored one. In one sense, he was probably relieved to be out from under her thumb.

"What do you remember about Betsy?" Jerry asked, deciding to change the subject. There was a few seconds of dead time before he responded. "Oh, the Cruikshank girl. My brother was madly in love with her and it drove my mother crazy. Hated the competition, I guess. That girl would hang all over my brother when she came to the house, caress him suggestively in front of the family and then start laughing. After my brother's death, she went away to college and was never seen again around

Burlington. My mother accused my father of staying in touch with her. He was a real puppy dog with her, acting really foolish when she came over. My mother was right on that score; it was embarrassing."

He was no prodigal son and Jerry couldn't imagine him coming down to Connecticut to claim the mother's body. But he had to ask. "For my father, I might risk it," he said softly. "If he turns up, tell him to contact me, okay?" Jerry heard the humming sound of the dial tone before he could say anything else. He knew he had gotten all he would out of Percy Hoole.

CHAPTER THIRTY-SEVEN:
A Surprise Visitor

JERRY IMMEDIATELY CALLED Ladislaw to confirm the anticipated news that the son would not be returning stateside anytime soon, if ever. "According to Percy Hoole, she never had affection for him or his father. All of her attention was devoted to his dead brother."

"That corroborates what you heard from the neighbor and certainly provides motive for the husband. I'm assuming that he hasn't heard from his father," Ladislaw said.

"That's what he says but I wouldn't be so sure. He vaguely described some sort of scheme that involved both parents. Said they kept him in the dark as to the details – except that the father would fake his disappearance and there would be a phony effort to find him. That's where I came in as a useful tool. He half apologized for conning me. He did hear from his mother after the severed finger was found but it was only to determine if anyone had contacted him, basically warning him to keep his mouth shut. According to him, that was their last conversation."

"Anything else?" Ladislaw asked, fishing for every tidbit he could get. "No, and it seems unlikely that the parents would have found it helpful or even necessary for the son to know details of their scheme. Weak link and all."

"Sounds like the all American family. Odds are the husband is in hiding but we still can't reject the possibility that he was killed as well. With the insurance scam kaput, it's a mystery as to why someone would want both of them dead. Nothing new on this end. Still waiting on the crime lab analysis on the wig. Thanks for making that call, Kosinsky."

Jerry didn't mention the son's comments about Betsy Cruikshank and his father's seeming fixation on her. Percy's description of a tempestuous and provocative girl rang true but he wondered about the contention that his father was infatuated with a young girl to the point of making a fool of himself. He didn't see the relevance to the investigation but would share the son's observations with Cyrus.

JERRY FOUND CYRUS sitting on the front porch of the inn reading the *Graniteville Gazette* and told him about his conversations with Percy Hoole and Ladislaw. "With a wife like that, the guy was probably starved for affection and little Betsy was just the one to recognize it and manipulate him. Still, it wasn't right if what the son contends is true. Sounds like the boy was needy himself, maybe even jealous that she didn't focus her charms on him."

Jerry noted that she was still "little Betsy" to Cyrus, the 12-year old girl who had the run of the Thimble Islands for several summers under the not so watchful eye of Aunt Letty. The image of that girl, now all grown up, seducing the father of her dead boyfriend, didn't seem to register.

"Every time I hear someone describe Betsy Cruikshank, it makes me think of Gretchen, as if they were cut from the same cloth. The troopers spent hours in New Haven and couldn't track her down. Where the hell did she disappear to, Cyrus?" Jerry said, throwing up both hands and letting them flop down to his lap in exasperation.

Cyrus had pulled out his pipe and started to clean out the bowl while Jerry was talking. He looked stern and said, "Why are you surprised? She's a chameleon. There's no record of her in Connecticut except for a driver's license and she lied about her upbringing in Ohio. Maybe you need to face the possibility that she doesn't want to be found and, in fact, might be long gone by now. You're damn lucky you didn't get mixed up with her any more than you did."

Jerry didn't react and Cyrus picked up the newspaper on the table next to him. "There's an article here that says Connecticut might be adding photographs to driver's licenses soon. Sounds like New York and New Jersey are planning the same thing so we'll probably follow suit. It says that some states have already done it and it got me wondering if California was one of them." Jerry knitted his brow and Cyrus continued. "Well, we know that little Betsy did get a driver's license when she was in California. Maybe her picture is on it. I'd love to see what that scamp looks like today. Maybe then I'd stop calling her little Betsy, eh?"

"Your contact in vital records can get it for you?" Jerry asked. Cyrus nodded yes while he lit his pipe then frowned and quickly put it down. "Damn, either my taste buds are changing or I got a bad pouch."

Just then, a visibly flushed Tillie rushed out to the porch and said, "Lt. Ladislaw just called. The missing husband just walked into the trooper barracks."

CHAPTER THIRTY-EIGHT:
ALIBI IKE

JERRY JUMPED UP at the news of the husband's unexpected appearance, as if it was a call to action. "Ladislaw's true to his word, Jerry, but we can't go over there now. It wouldn't look good for him even if he did have time to see us. He'll tell us what he can – when he can," Cyrus said calmly. Jerry plopped back down heavily and said, "Don't you wonder if the son or someone else tipped off the father? Quite a coincidence that he shows up now. Damn, I'd give anything to be there and get a look at his right hand."

ELLIS HOOLE WAS the kind of man you could easily forget. Put him in a police line-up and he would be quickly passed over. He was no man and everyman; the epitome of beige. He wasn't a wallflower for that would be complimentary. He was more like the wall itself.

He had a retreating, withdrawn wariness about him as if he was pulling back from some pending calamity. His face was round and plump and his chin receded into his neck. He wore rimless wire glasses which blended into his face. His khaki pants were belted high and tight a few inches above his navel, as if he were imitating one of the old time vaudevillian comics. He clutched a fedora in both hands as he walked into the trooper barracks and asked for Lt. Ladislaw.

"Why don't you start by describing your whereabouts since you left Burlington, Mr. Hoole? Then, I'll be glad to take you over to the morgue to identify your wife's body. The husband was sitting across from Ladislaw and had stated, in a calm voice, that he was there to verify if it was his wife who had been murdered.

Hoole confirmed his stay at the Brightwood Motel and stated that his wife, wearing a blonde wig, had visited him there. He then spent several days in New Haven before he drove south into Virginia and visited the Poe Museum in Richmond so as to be far away while the wife secured the death certificate. "I'm a big fan of the writer, Lieutenant. Just finished *The Gold Bug* but lost my copy somewhere during my travels," the husband explained, showing more interest in the lost book than seemed appropriate.

"And then you left Richmond," said Ladislaw, prompting the husband to continue. "Oh, yes. It was agreed that I would rejoin her – my wife, that is- around this time. I stopped just outside Connecticut and picked up a newspaper with a headline about a woman murdered in a motel near the Thimble Islands. When I saw the description in the article, I feared that it might be her even though no name was mentioned. The article said that you were handling the investigation so I came straight here. Do you have any leads yet?" he asked, squinting and looking down at his hat, as if fearful of the answer.

Ladislaw ignored the question. His wife had feigned timidity and perhaps the husband was putting on an act as well – or maybe it was just an acquired family trait. The hat was partially blocking the husband's hands and Ladislaw strained to get a look at the right ring finger. He was not surprised to see that it wasn't missing and noticed the lighter shade of skin where the Thorndyke ring had undoubtedly been worn. "My wife and I weren't close but it is heart-wrenching news for the family," the husband said, breaking the awkward silence and trying to sound compassionate.

"We have a severed finger with your college ring on it, sir. It washed ashore on DeCourcy Island and we have a pretty good idea as to whose finger it is. That individual, along with your wife, is now dead. Before we leave this room, you are going to tell me everything you know about how your college ring ended up on someone else's finger."

The husband's eyes darkened but he still spoke meekly. "My wife engaged an attorney in New Haven. I called him before coming here and he advised me to say nothing except in his presence. I've probably already talked too much. Accordingly, I will await his arrival, Lieutenant."

AFTER THE ATTORNEY consulted with the husband, Ladislaw was summoned and was told that a statement would be made after which questioning could proceed, but only in the presence of legal counsel.

What followed was an astonishing tale of a small-time insurance scam that had been concocted by the wife and to which the husband said he reluctantly agreed. The quarry enterprise was doomed and the family was in severe financial straits. Desperate for cash, the wife proposed that they fake the husband's disappearance and then collect the $50,000 death benefit on his term life policy, his wife being the beneficiary.

There had been a certain urgency to the plot since the policy was due to expire in a few months.

They figured correctly that Grex would be a suspect and, to strengthen the case against him, she took some of his personal items and had them buried on Quarry Island. His wife also took his Thorndyke ring before he left Vermont and told him it would be discovered in dramatic fashion. He was curious about her plan but she clammed up when she visited him at the Brightwood Motel wearing a disguise. He was hiding out in New Haven when he heard on the radio about a severed finger wearing a ring found by a schoolgirl during a Thimble Islands class excursion. He frantically called his wife but was unable to reach her. "I nearly had a heart attack when I heard the news report, Lieutenant. Some poor soul out there without a finger," the husband said. Ladislaw could feel the bile rising in his throat. Here was a man showing grief for a complete stranger but not an ounce for the mother of his children.

When the husband finished, the attorney said, "My client admits to using very poor judgment, Lieutenant. His actions, you might say were, conspiratorial but faking his own death did not result in a crime being committed – at least by him. His wife filed the false missing person's report and he was clearly manipulated by her. I must confess, she certainly had me bamboozled. Now, Mr. Hoole would like to put this ordeal behind him by identifying his wife's body. I trust you will be diligent as you continue to investigate her murder but my client has a spouse to bury and needs to secure a death certificate."

Ladislaw looked at the husband who nodded and, in an almost reverent whisper, said, "Actually, she always expressed an interest in being cremated. That is one request that I intend to honor."

Ladislaw looked on with amazement and disgust as he listened to the unctuous words dripping from the husband's mouth. This non-descript, bald cipher of a man was either an innocent dupe with respect to the more heinous acts committed by the wife in furtherance of this aborted insurance scam or he was a cunning manipulator who had calculated exactly how to lay the blame on his dead spouse.

Ladislaw struggled futilely to think of a crime the husband had actually perpetrated that would allow his detention. In his comments, the attorney had deftly pointed the finger at the dead wife for any action which showed criminal action He would check with the D.A.'s office for guidance. In the meantime, he admonished the husband about not leaving the area until given permission to do so.

"So, who was the accomplice?" Ladislaw asked. Hoole looked confused and the lieutenant continued. "Am I to believe that your wife paddled out in tricky waters to Quarry Island unseen by anybody and buried your personal items there to frame Grex?" Before Hoole could respond, the attorney said, "My client will not speculate on his dead wife's conduct or who she might have enlisted to abet her."

As they stood up to leave, Ladislaw asked, "So, your wife wore a disguise when she came to visit you?" The husband was momentarily startled, then said calmly, "Oh yes, Lieutenant. She purchased a blonde wig before coming down here. I thought it was unnecessary and it looked rather silly but she was into that cloak and dagger stuff which, I guess now, she had reason to be." Hoole seemed inclined to continue talking when the attorney pushed him toward the door and whispered in his ear.

As Ladislaw watched them depart, he thought of all the reprehensible miscreants he had interviewed over the years but today was the first time he wanted to reach across his desk and throttle a suspect. Not knowing about the severed finger was hard to swallow but how could it be proved otherwise? If the wife had the moxie to venture into the bowels of New Haven, she certainly could have arranged to have the husband's personal items buried on Quarry Island. If so, there was another accomplice out there. It seemed far-fetched but could she have enlisted Grex? His boys would interview all the watermen again but Ladislaw would be surprised if any of them had given a ride to Mrs. Hoole.

Maybe Ellis Hoole didn't have the stomach to wrap the lamp cord around his wife's neck but he could have arranged it. If so, that made him an accessory to murder. That possibility only prompted another question. The scam seemed to be working so why abort it? Was pure hate enough to sacrifice the $50,000 pay-off? Was Ladislaw thinking too hard, making things too complicated? The simpler conclusion was that the wife's murder had nothing to do with the insurance scheme.

With Hoole's return, there was no longer a reason to hold Elwyn Grex. Ladislaw tried to convince himself that he should be relieved that he only had one murder to solve. It didn't work.

CHAPTER THIRTY-NINE:
BACK ON THE TRACKS

~~

On Wednesday, the husband was brought to the county morgue to verify that the corpse in the cooler was indeed his wife. The attorney wasn't available and it was understood that there would be no questioning of the client.

It was a routine procedure that could have been handled by another member of his team but Ladislaw was on hand to gauge the husband's reactions as the body was rolled out and the covering pulled back. It chilled the lieutenant that Hoole didn't reveal even a flicker of emotion, prompting him in the spur of the moment to draw attention to the deep neck abrasions. "It must have been a painful and terrifying last few moments for your poor wife," he said, looking hard at the husband before adding, "It was definitely a case of overkill and it puzzles the hell out of me why a burglar would be so vicious with a complete stranger. Oh well, it takes all kinds, right?"

The husband was impervious or determined not to take the bait. "My wife always said she wanted her ashes spread on Lake Champlain. If you've ever seen those majestic waters, you'd know why. Now, how soon can the death certificate be issued, Lieutenant?"

"Very touching but it's not up to me. Probably a few days is my guess. In the meantime, we'll have you back for what should be a final interview. Very routine stuff related to your whereabouts the last few weeks. Plus, we're taking a very close look at your partner in the quarry operation. By the way, he says he had nothing to do with the fire that destroyed almost all of the quarry's business records. We're having a hard time swallowing that claim or, quite frankly, anything that he says. We need to consider all suspects in your wife's murder that have any connection to you." Ladislaw had buried his contempt and was talking in a nonchalant, almost insouciant tone but it quickly aroused the husband. "For Christ sake, could that thieving son of a bitch have done such a thing? I'm glad to see you focusing your energies on finding my wife's killer before some other poor woman is attacked in her motel bed."

"You understand that we have to scrutinize your movements around the time of her murder. Don't be offended; it's just routine. There's an old saying in our business, Mr. Hoole. When you have a murder case, always look at the in-laws before you chase after the outlaws." Ladislaw chuckled at his rare humorous quip while the husband's face ripened to garnet and then quickly cooled.

"Sorry for my burst of temper, Lieutenant. It's been a mighty blow, as you can appreciate. Of course, I will cooperate in any way I can. As for Grex, he's a congenital liar, so good luck getting anything honest out of him."

Ladislaw nodded and smiled knowingly, as if to confirm that the two men were certainly in agreement about the nature of the recalcitrant partner. The lieutenant had been determined before they walked into the morgue that he would end their time together on a positive, even congenial note. Hopefully, it would relax the husband and make him vulnerable for their next interview.

"Want me to ride with you?" Jerry asked. Cyrus was making one of his intermittent trips to New Haven and Jerry felt the urge to tag along. He was stymied and didn't know what to do with himself until Ladislaw provided his next update. "I've got family business to take care of, kid. I know you're antsy but you need to find something to amuse yourself. Have you finished that Bellow novel? I'll be back for dinner if you want to join me."

Jerry watched as Cyrus walked away, casually waving goodbye with his back turned. Jerry looked around the empty lobby of the Thimbletown Inn. Cyrus had been chiding him and he deserved it. Augie March was back in Chicago after an ill-fated road trip with an old acquaintance. He found out too late that he was riding in a stolen car. Poor Augie was a good-hearted, small-time hustler but got hoodwinked on his metaphorical quest of self-discovery. That was what it was all about, right?

Jerry couldn't concentrate. He tossed the novel to the side of the bed, discarding it as if it had let him down. His thoughts drifted to that seemingly seminal moment in his life almost a decade ago when he looked out on the Himalayas as his plane descended toward Kathmandu. He wondered if the Carlyles were still rotting away in a Nepalese jail. And he could have been there right along with them except for a near miraculous escape across the border engineered by a mere child who was savvier and had more street smarts than he ever would.

There was no way he could face Cyrus in the mood he was in. Self-pity was written all over his face and he would garner only contumely from the old man. I'd deserve it, he said to himself. He sat up and put on his shoes. He would drive to New Haven and find Boyd Mandeville. Sure, the wig was found in the murdered wife's motel room but he was still curious if the *Beagle* had dug up anything else. Ladislaw and Cyrus didn't need to know his every move.

ON THE DRIVE to New Haven, Jerry tried to picture the unlikely scenario of a middle-aged woman in a blonde wig propositioning a wino, with Twitchy as her protector or go-between. Was it also Twitchy's job to ply Smitty with Thunderbird while she performed the ghastly surgery? Was the image of Smitty's finger being sliced off enough to send Twitchy over the edge?

If Mandeville had found anything, it apparently wasn't enough for a follow-up article. When the wig was discovered in the motel room, did the paper think there was nothing else to investigate? Jerry didn't feel like he was violating the understanding with Ladislaw by checking in with Mandeville. Hell, it was most likely a waste of time but then the reporter might say something helpful that he could pass on to the lieutenant. On this slim thread, he drove on.

BOYD MANDEVILLE HAD enjoyed his moment in the spotlight with the scoop on Smitty but without Jerry and the girl at the hospital, he was out of tips and resources. When Jerry caught up with him at the *Beagle* offices, he was hunched over his typewriter, hunting and pecking like an amateur.

"Breaking news?" Jerry asked. Mandeville looked up and laughed. "Yeah, covered a neighborhood dog show over on the west end earlier. When the badge was presented to the winner, the damn dog bit its owner and scurried off. Maybe if the mutt had bitten off her finger, I'd have an interesting angle."

Jerry noted Mandeville's cynical edge and laughed sympathetically. "Time for a beer after work?" Mandeville brightened up. "You name it and I'm there." "I'll meet you at the Belly Up over near the station. It's a little seedy but I have some history with the bartender there," Jerry said.

WHEN JERRY WALKED into the Belly Up, Sid Cuttwater looked up and nodded acknowledgement. "Slumming again, kid?" he asked, pulling up his baseball bat from beneath the bar. "Another one over there bit the dust just yesterday," he said, pointing his bat toward the tracks. "I get a kick out of the experts speculating about the cause of death, as if it were some sort of mystery. The certificate should just read 'Gave up on life a while back' or something like that. Instead, they need to identify which body organ gave out first before they bury him in Potter's field and let the poor sucker start pushing up daisies."

"Except Smitty died because of gangrene, or so it appears. Not that he would have lasted much longer," Jerry offered, deciding not to mention the finger. "So now, the papers say the bitch who chopped off his finger might've gotten payback in a motel near where you're staying, right? You ever run into the dame?" Cuttwater asked.

"Yeah, I saw her around once or twice," Jerry said, not willing to elaborate. "Well, it takes a set of iron cast you know what to come down here and do what she did. I've met some dillies over the years but never met a chick like that – hope I never do." Cuttwater heard his name yelled and moved to the other end of the bar.

Listening to the bartender, Jerry felt his skepticism being re-enforced once again. He went back to the theory of two blondes, one an obvious fake and the other a natural. Life was full of strange coincidences and this one wouldn't be so preposterous. With the fake one now dead, where was the real one?

When Mandeville showed up, Jerry was not surprised to learn that the reporter's hold on his job was tenuous. "Pretty sure I'm not cut out for this line of work," Mandeville said. "All my life, I've been used to having things fall into my lap, like the Smitty story." Jerry didn't respond and Mandeville laughed softly, appreciative of the silence.

"You guys gave up on Smitty after he died. I know it wasn't your decision but does it bother you at all?" Jerry asked. "Not really. The winos weren't talking and then that woman was found dead with the blonde wig in her suitcase up your way. The big boys decided that it was time to move on. I learned that some powerful folks in the city don't like too much attention drawn to that encampment."

"But what if the dead woman wasn't the fake blonde who propositioned Smitty? What then? Aren't you at all curious? Might be another big story out there. It would get you another byline."

"You know something?" Mandeville asked, suddenly aroused and thinking Jerry might bail him out again. "No, just a hunch. Want to check it out?" Jerry asked.

Mandeville took a swig from his Falstaff and stared at Jerry who yelled down the bar to Cuttwater. "I need Johnny Bench for about thirty minutes." Cuttwater laughed and warned, "Don't forget to pick up supplies on the way."

Jerry had the bat on his shoulder and pulled Mandeville off his stool. "C'mon, muckraker. We're going to make a social call."

"It'll be getting dark in about an hour so you'd better haul ass. And don't come back in here without my goddam bat," they heard as the door was closing.

"You carry the party supplies. I need the freedom to wield my bat," Jerry said. Mandeville's face had lost its color and he was clutching the bag of Thunderbird shorties like a prized possession as he stumbled along behind Jerry.

As they crossed the tracks, Jerry said, "We need to locate Smitty's best friend. The barkeep says that someone died here yesterday and I hope the hell it wasn't him. Most of them won't answer a damn question even with this bait but he was the talkative one. Stay close to me. I'll let you know when to take one of the Shorties out of the bag and hold it over your head."

In the excitement of his first visit, Jerry had somehow missed the shanty in the back, thrown together with pieces of corrugated metal, cardboard boxes and other cast-off materials. A stained shower curtain hung in the opening in what the boys referred to as their "clubhouse." Jerry spotted Smitty's friend emerge as they approached the encampment and breathed a sigh of relief. He yelled out "play ball" and took a full swing of the bat as he did so.

The friend squinted and seemed to acknowledge Jerry as some sort of beneficiary from a foggy past. Jerry motioned him forward with the bat and said, "It's me again, the guy who was looking for Smitty. Sorry about your pal. We've got a half dozen Shorties for the boys in this bag and all we want is a simple answer to one question. Then, we'll be on our way."

A few winos on the fringe started to move forward but

retreated when Jerry pointed the bat menacingly in their direction. "No booze for you guys if you misbehave. I'll smash every bottle in this bag before you can get to it."

Smitty's friend motioned for the others to stay back and said, "Ask your damn question and move on. Some of the boys are making a run and you'll be outnumbered when they return."

"Fair enough. The blonde that mutilated Smitty – how old was she?" The friend said "Huh" like it was a trick question and Jerry explained. "You know, old, middle-aged, a girl."

"That bitch was no girl but she was young, bout your age. I'll crack one of them Shorties over her head if I ever see her again. Smitty was good people. Now, you best move on. You got your answer. Put the bag down and vamoose."

Ten minutes later, Jerry walked back into the Belly Up with Mandeville shadowing him, still a bit shaky. He smiled grimly when he handed the bat to the bartender. Jerry would brief Cyrus before passing the wino's description of the woman on to Ladislaw.

WHEN CYRUS RETURNED to the Thimbletown Inn, Tillie told him that Jerry had taken off shortly after he departed. She handed him an envelope that had been dropped off while he was gone. Inside was a photostat of a California driver's license for Elizabeth Cruikshank. Cyrus studied the picture and frowned. He would never have guessed how much "little Betsy" had changed over the years. He didn't even recognize her.

CHAPTER FORTY:
A LEGRAND TIME

THAT AFTERNOON, CYRUS took a room at the Thimbletown Inn. Something told him the end game was near and he wanted to be available on short notice for any impromptu meetings with Jerry and Ladislaw. Gazing repeatedly at the driver's license, it dawned on him that "little Betsy" was gone forever and that he had been hanging on to more than one Cruikshank memory far too long. The more immediate and important truth was that he had become accustomed to Jerry's presence and no longer treasured his isolated life at the cottage by the water.

IT HAD BEEN a small lie but it made Ladislaw suspicious. The husband had said that his wife had purchased the blonde wig at home at the initiation of their insurance scam. The tag on the inside of the wig read House Of Beauty but no such retailer could be found in the Burlington area. Next, Ladislaw had his team check area stores and discovered a shop by that name on the edge of New Haven. The husband would no doubt have some sort of lame explanation but Ladislaw felt that he now had his wedge. And there was more.

Troopers had been on the telephone to motels within a twenty mile radius of the Poe Museum in Richmond and, on the night of the wife's murder, none of them had a guest by the name of Ellis Hoole. Next, Ladislaw had someone call the museum and confirm that visitors were required to sign the register upon entering. The husband's name was not listed for the date in question.

Ladislaw was starting to feel better about himself and the case building against the husband but was still troubled by the lack of evidence from the wife's room. He had been wilting under the pressure of an unsolved missing person case but had now regained his footing with respect to the murder investigation. It would be an interesting interview with the husband the next day, even with his tough-nosed attorney in the room.

BEFORE JERRY LEFT Mandeville, he told him he now had another story to write. The reporter didn't have the courage to tell Jerry that he was reluctant to take this latest observation of a wino to his editors, fearful of being mocked. He had also been told by one of the old-timers at the *Beagle* that a few city bigwigs who advertised heavily had advised the paper that articles about the wino encampment were not good for downtown business.

Like Ladislaw, Jerry was feeling buoyant on the ride back, having implicitly accepted the wino's comment about the blonde's age – wig or no wig. Smitty's friend hadn't hesitated and didn't sound confused. Jerry opened the windows and turned up the radio. When he heard Bachman-Turner Overdrive singing "Takin Care Of Business," he grinned and pounded the steering wheel, as if the song had been played just for him. He wasn't ready to hit the sack and drove straight to the Graniteville Saloon.

WHEN JERRY WALKED into the bar, he saw Fanny sitting at a table in the corner with some friends. She had a wistful look on her face when she saw him and seemed to force a smile before looking down. He knew it would be awkward for both of them if he walked over and said hello so he stationed himself at the end of the bar away from the entrance where he could see her reflected in the mirror. Something was bothering her and he hoped it wasn't delayed pangs of guilt over their recent tryst.

Jerry saw Grex at the end of the bar with Buffle earnestly jawing in his ear. It was early but the two were already red-faced, no doubt celebrating Grex's freedom. As if they needed a cause, Jerry mused.

Buffle scowled when he saw Jerry, viewing him as part of the imaginary cabal that had formed to thwart him at every turn. Grex, however, had an almost benevolent look on his face, even tipping his beer bottle to Jerry in a respectful salute. Before he could order a beer, a Falstaff was pushed in front of him. Jerry looked confused and the bartender nodded to Grex who saluted him again.

After a few minutes, Grex lumbered down to Jerry and tipped his bottle against Jerry's. The clinking beer bottles was a sort of sociable Morse code for Grex, a way for him to avoid uttering something stupid or inflammatory. If asked, Grex would have admitted that he had learned over the years that when he talked, it usually got him in trouble, especially when he was on a tear.

The quarryman was half in the bag and weaved side to side as he stood close to Jerry. He seemed to be searching for words that wouldn't backfire on him when he finally said, "I've got a big mouth and a bad temper. No one has to tell me but I still hate to hear it. They cost me everything. This is all I got left," he said, tipping his bottle. "Anyway, I have to admit that the old man and you treated me fairly and probably helped me with the staties. Kinda surprised me after our run-in on the island."

"Yeah, we got off to a bad start but I've already forgotten about it. When can you get back out there?" Jerry asked.

"Ladislaw's boys said tomorrow. Pretty sure they're still watching me. Wanna make sure I don't skip town in case they find anything else. Even with Hoole back, they're still treating me like a suspect. It was a damn frame-up from the start, I tell you. Just like the fuckin' wallet and clothes. In a way, I guess it doesn't matter anymore. I'm ruined anyhow you slice it." Grex downed the rest of his beer and signaled the bartender.

"Someone ought to be investigating that damn partner of mine. I wish the hell it was his finger they found in the water. Called the bank today and they said the account is empty. How is that? We get paid enough to stay afloat for a while longer but suddenly creditors are all over our back demanding payment. Should have taken that offer from the Rhode Island boys several months ago. We could have cashed out then. But no, says my big shot partner. Said he hired some firm in Delaware called Legrand and they would get us a better deal." Grex shook his head and took another pull on his beer.

"Legrand?" Jerry asked. The name sounded familiar but he wasn't making the connection. Grex had already looked away when he heard Buffle calling his name.

"Reciprocal policy your idea?" Jerry asked. "Wha?" Grex mumbled, stepping back and rubbing his eyes. Jerry shook his head and said, "Oh, no big deal. Just curious who had the bright idea to buy an insurance policy a few months ago if you guys were in financial difficulties," Jerry said, hoping it would prompt a reaction. Grex looked bewildered rather than guarded and deceptive. "No one ever accused me of being bright. No way I woulda dreamed up that idea." Grex said, looking away. He reached for his beer and heard "Grex" yelled louder from the other end of the bar. Buffle was facing them, looking annoyed.

Grex gave Jerry a week smile and said, "Guess I'd better go back and listen to motormouth." He walked unsteadily away, swaying as he went, still managing to give Jerry a final salute with his beer from over his shoulder.

There was another Falstaff in front of Jerry but when he looked down the bar, Grex and Buffle were gone. The night was early for those two inveterate boozers, once again on the prowl.

After the tipsy two left, Jerry looked in the mirror to catch a glimpse of Fanny. Her friends were still at the table but she was gone. Guess that's my signal to pack it in, Jerry said to himself.

THIRTY MINUTES LATER, Jerry was back in his room when there was a knock on the door. When he opened it, Fanny was standing there holding a six pack of Falstaff. "I was in the neighborhood," she said with mock seriousness. "Howdy, neighbor," Jerry said, pulling her in by the arm.

CHAPTER FORTY-ONE:
FOLLOW THE MONEY

~~

"T*HE GOLD BUG*, of course," Jerry said aloud, bolting up in bed. The room was dark except for the glowing green clockface on the side table that read 4:39 a.m.

William Legrand was the obsessed treasure seeker in Poe's story. Grex may have revealed something momentous with his casual comment in the Graniteville Saloon the night before. There was no chance in hell that the partner just happened to locate a company in Delaware with the name of Legrand that also, coincidentally, was in the business of brokering the sale of businesses. Grex had also said that the quarry bank account was drained. How much of it was paid to Legrand?

Jerry knew he had a great deal to share with Cyrus and then Ladislaw but it was still a while before dawn. When he got back to the Inn the night before, Tillie was still out front and surprised him with the announcement that Cyrus had checked in. He was tempted to ring his room but decided to wait.

Jerry's thoughts turned to Fanny. She had slipped out sometime after midnight. A letter had arrived from Germany that afternoon. Her putative fiancé had decided to re-up on the condition he could stay in Germany and be assigned to his current unit in Stuttgart. Near the end of the letter, he confessed that he had fallen for a fraulein who worked at the PX. "I'm not that upset, Jerry," she had said at one point after they had made love and both of them were looking at the ceiling. It sounded genuine. "Even before I met you, I tried but wasn't that anxious for his return and it made me feel guilty. But the son of a bitch could at least have been a man and called me. The Army can have him – and so can the German bimbo."

Jerry had liked the idea that Fanny wasn't available, at least on a permanent basis. She hadn't hung around until morning and he appreciated her discretion. But now, things could get complicated and he would have to think about it.

"LADISLAW NEEDS TO hear all of this before he interviews the husband," Cyrus said over breakfast. Jerry had told him about the encounter with Smitty's friend at the hobo camp and the revelation by Grex at the saloon. "Don't be surprised if he is skeptical about the wino's description of the blonde. You should be as well," Cyrus cautioned.

"WHAT DO YOU make of it, Cyrus?" Ladislaw asked. He had rushed over when Cyrus called and had listened intently to Jerry. Now, he turned to the sage.

"I would want to corroborate the wino's description, if that's even possible, but wouldn't dismiss it out of hand, especially since you don't yet have the crime lab analysis on the wig. Jerry and I agree, however, that Grex' revelation about Legrand could be significant. We know the partner read the Poe story and it would be preposterous to assume that he hired a Delaware company by the same name as the protagonist to find a buyer for the quarry operation. My first reaction is that quarry money was siphoned off into a shell company set up by Hoole. You need immediate access to the quarry bank records. Grex can help. Focus on payments and deposits in the last six months. At the same time, contact the Secretary of State's office in Delaware and request information on Legrand. Incorporation documents filed with the state will show when the company was set up plus the names of directors and officers. If my instincts are correct, you will find a newly-formed entity controlled by the husband. How's that for jumping to a quick conclusion?"

Ladislaw's eyes had widened while Cyrus was talking. He sounded excited when he said, "Wait until you hear this. We couldn't find any evidence that the husband was in Virginia on the night of the wife's murder. No motel records and no entry in the visitor registry at the Poe Museum."

"Could he be that stupid?" Jerry asked. "Maybe he didn't think anyone would have a reason to check. I would ask him in a matter of fact way where he stayed. Tell him you're checking routine items off the list. See how he reacts," suggested Cyrus.

"Yeah, if I mention Legrand, he's tipped off and on guard," Ladislaw said, looking pensive. "Why not add that you are still investigating Grex as a potential suspect in a murder for hire plot and are hoping for his help? Draw him into your confidence." Jerry suggested. Ladislaw looked puzzled so Jerry explained. "The theory would be that Grex wanted revenge for being set up by the partner so he arranged for someone to break into the wife's room and knock her off. Ask him if he knows of any nefarious Grex cohorts. The husband might eat it up, figuring all the attention was directed at Grex. It would feed his ego and buy you some time."

Ladislaw turned to Cyrus. "Worth a try if it will keep the husband in town while you analyze the quarry bank records. Isn't it ironic that Grex could end up being your ace in the hole?

If he remembered Legrand, there's probably more he can tell you – if you catch him when he's not on the sauce. Based on how much cash was drained from the quarry account and where it ended up, you could certainly have a solid motive for murder. The problem I'm having is this – If the husband is behind a quarry scam, why knock off the wife? I would have gone after Grex if I were him. Unless, of course, the husband had another plan in mind."

"He probably never dreamed that anyone would hear the name Legrand. Maybe his fatal mistake was leaving a copy of *The Gold Bug* in his room at the Brightwood Motel. If Cyrus and I hadn't taken turns reading the novel, Grex' comment about Legrand would have meant nothing at all and we wouldn't be having this conversation. Still, you're right, Cyrus. It doesn't explain the wife's murder," Jerry concluded.

"When I first saw the husband, he made me think of Don Knotts. You know, the actor on the *Mayberry RFD* television show, trembling at the mere thought of danger. Sounds like Hoole turned out to be as good an actor as his late wife," Ladislaw said, chuckling and shaking his head. "Accomplished thespians," Cyrus said, causing Jerry to laugh and Ladislaw to stare uncomfortably.

The lieutenant looked down at his watch and then stood up. "Got a date with the husband, fellas. I'll let you know what he fabricates today and what we find in the quarry bank records."

"DID GREX EVER meet your wife?" Ladislaw asked. He was sitting across from the husband and the attorney in a room at the trooper barracks. Hoole glanced at his lawyer who nodded his assent. "Not that I know of but he didn't like her." Ladislaw's eyebrows went up and the husband continued. "Well, I had made a few comments about how domineering she could be and he told me he'd slap her silly, or something to that effect. Of course, I figured it was all talk. Grex could be that way, Lieutenant."

"Right. So, since he was locked up the night of your wife's murder, we're exploring the possibility that he might have been complicit, in an attempt to get revenge and frame you at the same time. Still, we have no lead on an accomplice who he might have enlisted. Any ideas?" Ladislaw asked.

"He once described some pretty unsavory characters back in New Bedford but never mentioned any names. Sorry," Hoole said, working to sound sympathetic.

"Anything else, Lieutenant?" interjected the attorney with an edge to his voice. He had been shut out of the conversation and didn't like it. "The medical examiner informed my office that the DC can be picked up this afternoon and my client has a wife to bury. I don't mind telling you that we will be filing a wrongful death lawsuit against the inn."

The husband's eyes narrowed as he listened to the attorney. "The cremation is scheduled for tomorrow. I plan to spread the ashes on Lake Champlain the next day." The attorney mumbled an apology. It was a rare faux pas and it grated on him to be corrected, even by someone paying him a fee.

When the husband stood up to leave, Ladislaw said, "Oh, there are still a few minor items to clear up. You said stayed in New Haven before heading down to Virginia. Where exactly?" Hoole looked at Ladislaw and didn't blink before saying, "A few flophouses near the train station. Moved around and, of course, paid cash. Can't remember which ones but I could show you the area."

"We couldn't find you registered at any of the motels in or around Richmond. How do you explain it?" Ladislaw asked. He let the flimsy flophouse alibi go, deciding he could come back to it later if necessary. The husband smiled and said, "Well, I must confess to a little innocent subterfuge, Lieutenant. If you had read *The Gold Bug* by Poe, you would know what I mean. I'll blame the author for making me act mysteriously. I used the name William Legrand when I checked in. He's the main character in the story. Got the receipt right here in my pocket if you care to see it."

Ladislaw examined the receipt and it verified what the husband had said. He didn't bother to ask about the registry at the Poe Museum. His boys would check to verify his visit for the record. Ladislaw's pulse quickened at the mention of Legrand. He resisted the temptation to question Hoole about Grex's off-hand remark to Jerry at the bar and maintained his poker face.

"I realize you're just doing your job so I'm not insulted. The receipt is real. In fact, I ended up talking at length with the motel clerk. Turned out he's a Poe aficionado as well. I'm pretty sure he'll remember me."

Ladislaw was tired of looking at this man who, supercilious and obnoxious, had turned his wife's murder investigation into a game. Determined to stay in the husband's good graces, he decided not to bring up the discrepancy on where the wig was purchased and turned the conversation back to the partner. "We're having Grex back in. He thinks he's in the clear now that you've returned so we hope to trip him up with respect to your wife. If we do, we'd like to have you in one last time before you leave town. It'd be a great help to us." Ladislaw sounded so casual and deferential that even the attorney, who lived to challenge everything, failed to raise an objection.

AFTER THE HUSBAND left, Ladislaw thought he now had his big break. Hoole had admitted in front of his attorney to using the name Legrand at the motel in Virginia. How would he now explain the company in Delaware with the same name if it turned out, as Cyrus had posited, to be controlled by him? Ladislaw was convinced that Hoole's story was mostly a web of lies with a few distracting facts sprinkled in for effect. Still, he was perplexed as to how he could tie such a tangled scheme, including the Legrand deception, back to the murder of the wife.

THAT AFTERNOON, A trooper accompanied Grex to the Graniteville National Bank to request copies of the quarry bank records. Ladislaw had calculated correctly that a trooper in uniform standing beside Grex would expedite the request. In the meantime, the husband picked up the death certificate and headed straight to the crematorium to arrange for the incineration of his wife.

CHAPTER FORTY-TWO:
DON'T BANK ON IT

GREX SHOULD HAVE been prepared for bad news when he walked into the bank. He asked for a list of deposits made since the first of the year and discovered that there were none. A single check had been written during that period and it was for $2000, payable to the Legrand Corporation. None of the quarry's suppliers had been paid and yet the balance in the account was less than $300. If the trooper hadn't accompanied him to the bank, Grex might have gone berserk.

LATER ON THURSDAY, when quizzed about the quarry's accounts receivable ledger by Ladislaw's team, Grex had a blank look on his face. "When payments came in, they went into the top drawer of his desk. When Hoole came down from Vermont every other week, he made deposits and paid bills. That was our system," he explained.

"Then what happened?" one of the troopers asked Grex. "Shit, I couldn't do anything. Several weeks ago, angry calls from suppliers started coming in demanding payment. I contacted

Hoole in Vermont and he assured me that the checks were in the mail so what could I do? Right before that asshole disappeared, I couldn't make payroll and, well, you know the rest." Grex had a rash on his neck and started to scratch it aggressively, eventually drawing blood.

Unsympathetic, Ladislaw's boys pressed him about jobs completed in the last year and Grex rattled off the names of a country club outside of Worcester and an art gallery in the Berkshires. "We were down to small jobs here and there, mostly those the big boys didn't bother to bid on. We gave up on the large projects after we were constantly being undercut. If you ask me, after we turned down their offer to buy us, those brothers up in Rhode Island seemed intent on forcing us out of business. Guess they succeeded, huh?" Grex said, starting to perspire.

Grex didn't understand why the troopers were grilling him again. It didn't dawn on him that it only happened when Ladislaw wasn't in the room. They could have told him not to worry, that the focus had shifted to the partner, but they were frustrated and couldn't help themselves. Plus, they figured that if they kept badgering him, he might recall some important detail that he had forgot to mention. From memory, he provided am incomplete a list of recent quarry clients and where they were located.

Grex was rattled when he left the barracks, even after he got an encouraging tap on the shoulder from Ladislaw at the door. He was sorely tempted to stop for a beer on his way out of town but knew deep down inside it would never be just one. He had received an encouraging signal from the ex in New Bedford and didn't want to blow it. When he saw the blinking sign for the Graniteville Saloon, he glanced twice and then accelerated.

"Can someone tell me where all the money went?" Ladislaw asked, throwing his hands up with the palms out. He was in the room with his team after Grex left but there was dead silence except for the shuffling of papers. "Okay, I want you to call each of the clients mentioned by Grex. Contact every damn one. I want to know any payments made to the quarry in the last twelve months," Ladislaw directed.

Back in his office, Ladislaw was trying to decide if it was too soon to bring Hoole back in. He decided to wait for the results of the calls to the quarry clients and the crime lab analysis on the wig.

If the husband had been siphoning funds from the quarry operation, spread out over months, how could he disguise it without a record of the withdrawals? Purloining the quarry assets would explain why he would sacrifice the proceeds of a $50,000 insurance settlement which he would have had to share with a wife he detested. More importantly, if the husband planned the wife's murder, he had to have an accomplice to carry it out. Was this dumpy, effete-looking little man capable of such a cunning, cold-blooded plot, Ladislaw wondered, or would it turn out that there was no connection between the quarry scam and the wife's murder?

Ladislaw was nibbling on his finger again as he slowly picked up the telephone with his other hand. He started to put the receiver back down, hesitated for a moment, and then dialed the number for the Thimbletown Inn.

LADISLAW REMEMBERED THAT Cyrus, while with the state's attorney office, had helped crack a case involving a pizza parlor outside New Haven ostensibly owned by two immigrant brothers but, in reality, controlled by a local biker gang. Turned out they were churning drug proceeds through the joint, mixing the dirty money with the clean until it became indistinguishable. It worked for a while until greed and ostentatious spending on luxury boats and charter flights to Vegas got the attention of law enforcement.

Under the circumstances, Ladislaw felt justified in seeking out Cyrus' advice on what had been uncovered so far with regard to the quarry finances. He was bewildered by how Legrand could be linked to what appeared to be a draining of the quarry bank account. A single check for $2000 wasn't sufficient evidence. He hated to admit it but he was stumped.

"THE HUSBAND OFFICIALLY ID'd the body this morning. Looks like the attorney pulled some strings to expedite issuance of the death certificate. That means the husband can proceed with the cremation. Oh, we also got confirmation from the motel outside Richmond that he stayed there the night of the wife's murder. But get this; he used the alias of William Legrand. Signed the visitor book at that museum the same way. He was damn sure he had a record of his whereabouts when she was being strangled." Ladislaw was taking his time as he sat across from Cyrus and Jerry at a corner table in the Thimbletown Inn café.

"Loving husband," Jerry said mockingly, adding, "What a shocker. This guy seems to know exactly when to show up and when to disappear. And now he has the luxury of blaming everything on his dead wife."

"He can't point at her for everything," said Ladislaw, as he pulled a sheet of paper from his coat pocket with a list of quarry clients. "We've already verified that some, perhaps all, recent client checks were never deposited into the quarry account so clearly some chicanery has taken place – we just can't put our finger on it. All we can confirm so far is that a $2000 check was made payable to Legrand Corporation. Grex confirms that the partner insisted that it was for a broker to find a buyer for the quarry." Ladislaw was chewing on the inside of his lower lip as he finished, another nervous tic that had surfaced in recent weeks.

Cyrus leaned forward and said, "If you haven't already, you will want to confirm when and where every client check was cashed or deposited. It's highly unlikely but possible that all of them were lost or destroyed in the fire. They certainly weren't running a first class business out there. You're at a critical stage, lieutenant, and need to be careful and thorough.

"Now, assuming that it was quarry money going into the Legrand account beyond the $2000 check, it means that the husband had at least one other accomplice. Maybe the so-called burglar that murdered his wife," Cyrus said, one finger stroking his chin.

"How do you prove it, Cyrus?" Jerry asked. Cyrus was now massaging his neck, as if to force out a response. "The quarry clients will have cancelled checks sent back to them by the bank with their monthly statements. Now, the back of the checks is the key to solving this part of the mystery. If I'm right, the checks were either cashed by Hoole or signed over to a third party. One or the other will be revealed by the endorsement on the back of the check. Let's assume, for argument sake, that he used a third party. This accomplice would have deposited them into his account or cashed them, thereby providing a layer or buffer between the quarry and the husband. Not very sophisticated but good enough if you feel confident that no one is going to be digging too deeply into your financial affairs."

"Like pinning his disappearance and then his wife's murder

on Grex. Convenient distractions," Jerry chimed in. Ladislaw nodded affirmatively and Cyrus then continued. "This unknown third party then withdrew cash from his account, gave it to Hoole – or another accomplice - who then deposited it into a third account. Maybe it went to Legrand, minus a handling fee, of course."

"Son of a bitch. It could be that simple?" Ladislaw asked, rhetorically. "Dirty money in, wash it up nice and send it out clean at the other end," he added. The lieutenant was smiling and suddenly at ease, as if a tremendous burden had been lifted from his shoulders. Cyrus noticed and cautioned, "The husband is more cunning that we probably all imagined. There was a federal bank secrecy law passed around 70 that requires financial institutions to report deposits of $10,000 or more, designed to catch drug dealers and gangsters moving money around. My hunch is that the husband was working around the law. Very smart. I wouldn't expect that this third party who laundered the money for the husband knows anything about Legrand or whatever other scheme might be in the works. He or she was likely in it for the easy cash and kept in the dark about anything else. Well, that's how I see it until further details emerge."

Ladislaw stood up and said, "I appreciate your good counsel and the fact that these little sessions of ours are kept private. Now, I'm anxious to learn what my team found out about the client checks that never made it into the quarry account."

"Are you worried that bastard will try to slink out of town now that he has the death certificate?" Jerry asked. Ladislaw smiled and said, "We're watching him around the clock. He's not going anywhere. I called the crematorium before coming over. Let's just say there's going to be an equipment malfunction which will temporarily delay the disposal of the wife. She's a key part of his cover story. He won't want to leave without her ashes."

Cyrus and Jerry sat in the alcove after Ladislaw left. Jerry was the first to speak. "This third party, Cyrus, who could it be? And do you think the husband was driving down to Delaware on a regular basis, making cash deposits? If so, wouldn't the bank have surveillance footage of him? They have cameras everywhere, right? Or maybe it's the same person who's cashing the quarry checks for the husband."

"It seems to me that Hoole had – still has – at least one trusted conspirator. However, you're getting ahead of yourself. There's no proof yet that the husband took more than $2000. Right now, the back of the cancelled checks are the key and will get us closer to the truth. Now, if you supposition is correct, is the quarry money still sitting in a Delaware bank account controlled by the husband? If you're laundering money, you have a distinct purpose, a plan to execute. My guess is that the cash would be in the Legrand account for only a short period of time. If true, the next big questions is: where did it go – and for what purpose? Something tells me that Ladislaw and his team haven't thought that far ahead."

Cyrus had pondered the possibility that Ladislaw was flailing in deep waters and he felt sympathy for him. He was a good cop, quite capable of handling routine investigations by the book but seemed to have little curiosity and no instinct for digging into complex matters. Deep down, he was a decent man who didn't deserve opprobrium this late in his career.

Cyrus did not share this assessment with Jerry, fearful that it would send him off like a cynical crime story dick, looking for bad guys and conspiracies everywhere. The important thing was that Ladislaw needed help and he knew it. It was probably eating away at the lieutenant. Cyrus would help all he could and didn't care who got the credit. It was too late in life to receive succor from praise, no matter how effusive or well-earned.

CHAPTER FORTY-THREE:
BAXTER DeCOURCY

L ADISLAW HUNG UP the telephone from the owner of the crematorium who had just described a nearly apoplectic husband, incensed that his wife's ashing would be delayed for even a few days. "Maybe I shouldn't have said, 'What's your rush? She's in no hurry.' I guess it set him off."

Ladislaw was in the frame of mind to enjoy a little morbid humor, especially since it was done at the husband's expense. One of the quarry clients had gone through its cancelled checks and verified that the payment to the quarry had been signed over to and deposited into an account at a bank in New Haven. The account holder was Baxter DeCourcy Fine Art & Collectibles.

BAXTER DECOURCY WAS a flamboyant, ascot-wearing dilletante, a nephew of the great one and a lah-de-dah kind of guy, a foppish dandy who would have thrived in Edwardian England. He was one of many distant satellites orbiting the original DeCourcy moon. He had received his piece of the tribute that fell into the lap of every descendent, no matter how worthy, and it was now gone.

Baxter was not lacking in charming physical attributes. He had thick blonde hair that curled naturally in all the right places and encapsulated a finely chiseled face. His mental vacuity was not obvious until he opened his mouth.

For years, he had made a nuisance of himself at the DeCourcy Institute, where his sisters had installed him in a do-nothing promotional role that he felt did not suit his talents. When he became overbearing, he was exiled to Europe, after which he went to the Far East, returning home with a menagerie of second-rate collectibles and overpriced artwork that he used to open up a shop not far from the Institute.

Initially, the DeCourcy name garnered some attention but interest in Baxter's shop faded quickly once serious collectors discerned the dubious quality of the gallimaufry that was ostentatiously displayed. Some wag nicknamed it the "DeCourcy Faux Art Emporium" and it caught on in fashionable circles in and around New Haven. Baxter couldn't avoid the snickers when he socialized at various DeCourcy soirees and eventually stopped showing up.

Desperate for cash, he was advised by his sisters that he was tarnishing the family name and that no assistance would be forthcoming until he closed up shop or moved it to another city. Defiant, he started to look elsewhere. Around this time, the local police and the feds were onto a forgery and stolen art ring operating out of Boston. During one wiretap, the name of Baxter DeCourcy was heard but was never pursued, allowing the *enfant terrible* of the DeCourcy family to skate free for the time being. Baxter started binge drinking and could be seen around town wandering into cocktail lounges and bars, sponging drinks from not just from acquaintances but complete strangers.

It was during this period of his inveterate dissipation, weeks before the severed finger floated ashore, that Baxter DeCourcy sauntered into Pudge McFadden's. He was approached by a girl wearing the DeCourcy Institute shirt and, eager for any sort of attention, learned that she was a volunteer and had just returned from an outing to the Thimble Islands with a group of school children.

Undeterred by the reluctance of most people to share their troubles with a complete stranger, Baxter unburdened himself on the girl, describing in detail his alienation from his sisters and the financial woes at his shop. She listened sympathetically as Baxter brattled on, slurring and repeating himself. Finally, she smiled seductively, raised a hand and put two fingers to his lips. He stopped in mid-sentence and gaped at her. "I think I can help you out of your troubles and it won't cost you anything," she said.

They were facing each other on two bar stools and Baxter stumbled forward as he tried and failed to embrace her. She propped him back up on his stool and said, "I'm making you a business proposition, Mr. DeCourcy. If that works out, we will see what comes next."

Baxter grinned and said, "You're my guardian angel, my salvation, and I don't even know your name." She smiled and said, "I'm Gretchen Cadwallader."

IT WAS MID-AFTERNOON on Friday when the tan trooper sedan pulled up in front of Baxter DeCourcy's emporium. The lights were off and a large FOR LEASE banner was plastered diagonally across the plate glass window next to the entrance. Peering in, the troopers could see debris scattered on the floor. Clearly, the business was shut down. On the door, there was a sheriff's notice indicating that assets had been seized, most likely for unpaid taxes and other debts. Ladislaw would not be happy when he heard the news that his big break had possibly disappeared in a puff of smoke.

More cancelled checks payable to the quarry were pulled by clients from files and sent via facsimile to the trooper barracks. All of them had been endorsed over to the Baxter DeCourcy enterprise. When Ladislaw got the call from his troopers in New Haven, he instructed them to go to the Institute. "See if anyone there can confirm his whereabouts. Find out where he lives. And don't come back without a picture of this guy. We need to find him before he skips town."

When Ladislaw hung up, he remembered Jerry's observation about a curly-haired man with a droopy mustache that he had spotted with Gretchen – that character from the movie *Mash* – first at the library and then later entering her apartment building. He said a silent prayer that it was DeCourcy. If so, Jerry had been on to something from the start. He didn't like his style but if DeCourcy and this mystery man were one and the same, the vital link to Gretchen Cadwallader, he would grant him the credit he deserved.

The troopers did come back with a photograph of Baxter DeCourcy, pulled from one of the Institute's old promotional brochures. "Looks like quite the English gent, eh?" one of the troopers said with a smirk on his face. Emboldened, the other trooper brushed his hand across his flat top and said, "Looks like a girly boy, if you ask me. I'd love to see him make it through Parris Island." Ladislaw scowled at the former Marine and asked, "So, what did you find out?"

It turned out that Baxter had come to the Institute a few weeks earlier, half in the bag, according to one of his sisters. He told them he was fearful that his gallery would be shuttered soon and he needed to disappear for a while. He was making a scene so they gave him several hundred dollars to go away. They hadn't seen or heard from him since then.

"They gave us his address and we went to his apartment. No answer but an old lady next door peeked out and said he hadn't been seen for several days." The trooper was flipping through his notes and then went on, "I think this is a verbatim quote from the woman, chief. 'The super told me he hasn't paid his rent and is going to be evicted. If you ask me, he's shacked up with that girl. They were all lovey-dovey in the hallway.'"

Ladislaw was impatient and jumped in. "That's it? No description of the girl? C'mon guys, give me something more." He was thinking of Gretchen Cadwallader but couldn't bring himself to say it.

"I was getting to it, sir. We did ask. The old lady only saw her at night and the girl was always wearing a baseball cap, pulled down low like she didn't want to be noticed. The only description we got was medium height and, I'm quoting her, 'kinda chunky.'"

Ladislaw felt bad about his fit of temper but was in no mood to apologize. "Damn it. Everyone we want to talk to is pulling a disappearing act, except the husband who waltzes in here like he doesn't have a care in the world. Well, he does now. Good job, boys. Now, contact the New Haven police and ask for their help in locating this pretty boy. If he's desperate for cash, he must have blown through whatever he was getting as his portion of the quarry checks. You can bet your bottom dollar that once we get access to his bank records, his accounts will be drained."

The troopers were almost out the door when Ladislaw called them back in. He was thinking about the wig found in the wife's suitcase, Smitty's blonde and the girl in the hallway wearing the baseball cap. "In addition to DeCourcy, tell the boys in New Haven that we would also very much appreciate their help in finding a Gretchen Cadwallader."

CHAPTER FORTY-FOUR:
Hanging By A Hair

~

THE THREE MEN had retreated to the alcove for privacy, Cyrus and Jerry followed by Ladislaw. The lieutenant's eyes were sparkling and he had an assured look on his face, like someone who had regained his footing after momentarily slipping during a treacherous climb.

"When it rains, it pours, right?" Ladislaw said, as the other two looked at him with anticipation. "It's pretty clear now that most if not all of the quarry checks were endorsed over to a Baxter DeCourcy who, until recently, operated some sort of gallery or shop in New Haven. And, yes, he is one of the DeCourcys who run the Institute and who knows what else. We've got the local police looking for him but he seems to have disappeared. Could be on the run. How the money got transferred from DeCourcy to the Legrand account in Delaware, if that's where it ended up, is still a mystery. We have asked the bank there to provide camera footage of the lobby. I sent a man down there to urge them on. Here's what we did confirm – the husband, wife and son in Toronto are listed in the incorporation papers as the officers and directors of Legrand Corporation."

While Cyrus and Jerry absorbed the news, Ladislaw dropped another bombshell. "The crime lab analysis of the wig was completed late yesterday. The brown hairs found inside the wig didn't match the samples taken from the deceased wife. Now, it's still possible that someone, another accomplice, gave the wig to the wife to hide and we still have a burglary gone bad. For public consumption, we are sticking with that story for now. I know you understand that I am trusting the two of you with some very sensitive information. Needless to say, I feel comfortable doing so," he said, looking directly at Jerry before going on.

"There's more news on the wig which you will find intriguing. It wasn't purchased in Vermont as the husband asserted. The tag on the inside was for a shop on the outskirts of New Haven. My boys went there but they were of no help. Apparently, they sell a lot of blonde wigs in that shop and not all of them to women. When my investigator asked for an explanation, the clerk just winked. Anyway, with so much else going on, I haven't pressed Hoole for an explanation. Nonetheless, just another chink in his armor."

Cyrus jumped in before Jerry could say anything. "So, it's looking more and more certain that the wig was planted in the suitcase and my guess is that it was done so before the night of the murder – maybe when the wife was with you or her attorney. Easy enough if she trusted someone like her husband with a key. If so, he could have hidden the wig in the suitcase before he left for Virginia."

"Then, he gives his key to another accomplice who carries out the murder while he's conveniently out of town. Are you thinking this DeCourcy guy, Lieutenant?" Jerry asked.

"We don't have a complete profile on the guy yet but he doesn't seem to fit the mold. A pampered rich kid who ran through a trust fund and was recently begging his sisters over at the DeCourcy Institute for walk around money. Running from creditors and the tax man, possibly others."

"Tell me he has curly brown hair and a droopy mustache," Jerry said, his voice rising. "Sorry. I was hoping for the same thing before I saw his picture. Wavy blonde hair and clean shaven. A real pretty boy type, the kind you see in magazine ads looking off into the distance," Ladislaw responded.

"If he were capable of murder, he wouldn't settle for a pittance to launder the quarry's money. Any luck running his prints?" Cyrus asked. Ladislaw shook his head and said, "We're seeking a search warrant for his apartment. We did get some information from a nosy neighbor in his building. She saw him getting all snuggly in the hallway with some girl. Unfortunately, the girl was wearing a baseball cap and she didn't get a look at her face."

"I think we can safely assume that the wife was never in New Haven," Cyrus said. "Her role in the original scheme was simple. She reports her husband missing, the family enlists Jerry's help to find him to demonstrate they are all in earnest and she drives down here to get the death certificate. At some point, the plan changed dramatically with the introduction of the severed finger. The wife becomes expendable, even an obstacle. She didn't know it then but she was the proverbial odd man out."

"Is anyone else curious about how the husband hooked up with this DeCourcy character in the first place? He's not the kind of guy that a middle-aged man from Vermont just happens to meet and engage in a money laundering scheme. Someone had to bring them together, right?" Jerry asked.

Ladislaw looked stone-faced and said, "I've got the husband coming by in the morning. We'll be questioning him about the checks endorsed over to DeCourcy. If we ask him if he had a key to his wife's motel room, he'd probably deny it. It'll be interesting to see how much his lawyer lets him say." Looking at Jerry, he added, "Even though we have no reliable description of the girl in the hallway, the DeCourcy Institute is the logical connection between her and this Baxter character. So, let me put your mind at ease. I have asked New Haven police for their help in finding Gretchen Cadwallader."

CHAPTER FORTY-FIVE:
ANONYMOUS TIPSTER

꩜

AFTER LADISLAW LEFT, Cyrus looked at Jerry and smiled. "There's a very good chance that your instincts about that girl were right all along. Ladislaw's team could use a guy like you full-time, an iconoclast not wary about thinking beyond the obvious. You realize that he paid you an indirect compliment before leaving, right? Now, let me hear your *Reader's Digest* condensed version of the case."

Jerry was humbled by Cyrus' encomium. Of course, he knew Jerry would never become a state trooper but it felt good to absorb the praises of a man he respected. "I don't think Ladislaw is there yet but try this on for size, Cyrus. Hoole was originally spotted all cozy with a blonde around Graniteville. How they met is a mystery for now but a plot was hatched that involved a wig. Smitty and his friend weren't both delusional. It was a young woman they saw but had no idea she was wearing a wig. That same woman was somehow introduced to Baxter DeCourcy or met him through their joint affiliation with the Institute. Maybe some social event or fundraiser. At some point, she recruits him to launder the quarry money. It is the same woman seen in the hallway of DeCourcy's apartment building, the baseball cap pulled down so as not to be identifiable. We are talking about a woman who thinks two steps ahead of everyone else around her. Cautious, clever and as cold-hearted as they come. She gets Twitchy to find a wino desperate for Thunderbird - that part was easy - and convinces him to let her cut off his finger. Not just any finger, mind you, but the ring finger on the right hand. She plants the finger with the ring on DeCourcy Island where it will be discovered during a school outing. Everyone goes on a wild goose chase to find the missing husband, presumably murdered by his partner – Grex being a likely suspect if there ever was one. But then things got complicated or the scheme was altered, ending up with the wife being murdered and the husband conveniently out of town. When the husband shows up unexpected, the girl and DeCourcy disappear. That leaves one person unaccounted for – the man I saw at the library and who we both saw entering Gretchen's apartment building. One thing still puzzles me, Cyrus. How did this girl, who I clearly believe is Gretchen, meet Hoole or who brought them together?"

"Okay, we are now on the same page with respect to the woman. It's Gretchen Cadwallader or whoever she is. So, who strangled the wife and why? Ladislaw has pretty much dismissed DeCourcy but he's probably jumping the gun. That leaves this character with the curly hair and the droopy mustache, unless there's one more conspirator," Cyrus said.

Jerry looked frustrated. "If Ladislaw is right about DeCourcy, we need to find this mystery man. Damn, my head is starting to ache. This is hard work."

THE ATTORNEY FEIGNED annoyance when he sat down in Ladislaw's office with Hoole. It was all for show and it usually worked. The client would think the lawyer had his best interest at heart, agreeing to meet on a Saturday morning when he should be at his club teeing off. And, of course, he would get his billable hours. And so, the pontificating and posturing commenced.

"This better not be some fishing expedition, Lieutenant. We have been very cooperative so far but I will not have my client subjected to a barrage of irrelevant questions designed to trap him into making an honest mistake or an innocent observation that is used against him. So, let's get on with it. It is our understanding that you have questions about Grex."

Ladislaw understood the game and smiled pleasantly. "Tell me about Legrand Corporation, Mr. Hoole. Grex says that you insisted on paying them money to find a buyer for the quarry. Is that correct?"

The lawyer looked confused and started to object when the husband waved him off and said, "Yes, I did tell him that, Lieutenant, but it was a lie. In truth, it was a devious move on my part and I felt justified after he admitted to pilfering at least several hundred dollars, and possibly more, from the quarry's petty cash account."

"I see. Tit for tat between two trusting business partners. So, what is Legrand?" Ladislaw asked. "It's a newly-formed family enterprise which I set up for a business venture that I am contemplating," Hoole explained. "To do what?" asked Ladislaw. "Well, that hasn't been decided yet but most likely something along the insurance brokerage line. I've brought in a few investors already, as a matter of fact. But why is this relevant? Is Grex pressing charges against me? If so, he should be advised that he will provoke us into countersuing," he said, glancing at his attorney.

"Going into the insurance business again? Well that makes sense, I guess, since you were in it for years back in Vermont. Red Clover was the company, right? Why did you leave it and go into the quarry business, of all things?" Ladislaw asked. The husband glowered and his attorney saw his opening but Ladislaw was too quick.

"Grex informs us that client payments starting several

months ago were never deposited into the quarry bank account. Wasn't that one of your functions as the finance chief?"

"Listen, Lieutenant, Grex was the day to day guy. What he did or didn't do when I was away ought to be your concern. If checks came in on his watch, he was instructed to deposit them right away, regardless of what he might have told you. It is astonishing to me that you seem to be accepting everything that Grex says at face value. What's he going to say next, that I set fire to the offices and destroyed documents? This line of questioning is getting quite tiresome, to say the least."

The attorney could no longer hold back. He had pulled a pencil from his coat pocket and was biting down on the tip as Ladislaw and the husband went back and forth. "I warned you about fishing, Lieutenant. This line of questioning is entirely inappropriate and bordering on harassment. You are bound to regret it. Furthermore, I don't see how it has any bearing on the wife's murder. Shouldn't that be your focus?"

Ladislaw ignored the implied threat and asked, "How did you meet Baxter DeCourcy?" The husband's face quickly flushed. "I've never met a man with that name," he said softly. The attorney stood up and said, "No more questions, Lieutenant. Now, you've pushed too far."

LADISLAW JOINED CYRUS and Jerry for lunch at the Inn's café after his meeting with the husband and his attorney. Tillie noticed the regularity of the lieutenant's visits and liked the idea that he was paying homage to her brother. "He seemed to anticipate my line of questioning up to the moment I mentioned this DeCourcy fellow. It was almost like he'd been prepped. He's not going to be a pushover and, for now, he does have a point. It's basically his word against Grex – unless we can somehow connect Hoole to the missing quarry checks. One more thing

281

that struck me was the look on the attorney's face as the husband talked. Unless I'm mistaken, his client has not been open with him and he is probably furious right about now."

"Looks like he has emerged from his shell with the wife no longer around to lord over him. Either that, or someone else is pulling his strings. That problem back at his job with the insurance company in Vermont tells me that he might have had larceny on his mind before. The notion that Grex was laundering quarry checks with Baxter DeCourcy is, of course, absurd. You caught him unprepared with that last question, Lieutenant. I think you're on the right track," Cyrus said, reassuringly.

Ladislaw laughed. "Yeah, tell that to the superintendent. He called an hour after the attorney and the husband left. Wanted to know if I had good cause to suspect the husband of a crime. Guess the lawyer doesn't make idle threats."

"Any news from Delaware? Jerry asked. "My guy saw some footage of the bank lobby going back a few months. Didn't see Hoole but there was a woman wearing a baseball cap in a few of them and it makes you think of the girl seen in DeCourcy's apartment building. We're not getting records without a subpoena."

"It's got to be Gretchen Cadwallader," Jerry interjected. Ladislaw didn't object and Cyrus said, "The husband will say the funds came from investors, even if the deposits roughly match the amount of the quarry checks given to DeCourcy. How do you prove there's a link? Even if Hoole used Gretchen as a courier, it doesn't prove it was dirty money that she was depositing in the Legrand account. It's going to take more than a hypothesis to nail him. In a sense, your superintendent is right on that score. Don't forget that your mission is to first find a murderer – not a scam artist."

LADISLAW WAS NOT feeling optimistic when he returned to his office but then he got unexpected good news. An anonymous call came into the trooper barracks. It was a female voice, muffled as if a cloth was being held over the telephone receiver, announcing that Baxter DeCourcy was right under their noses, hiding at the family cottage on DeCourcy Island.

CHAPTER FORTY-SIX:
THE PATSIES

~~

Baxter DeCourcy was lounging in a silk robe with the family crescent embroidered on the left chest. He was gazing out the bay window of the cottage built by the patriarch as a modest retreat during the hot summer months. It sat on a hill that overlooked the pavilion constructed by his sisters as a monument to their beneficent efforts on behalf of humanity. He caught himself counting the Thimble Islands that dotted the landscape, wondering when he would hear from her when there was a sharp knock at the door.

He had not expected her to show up on the island. They were supposed to meet in Boston at an exact location that was being kept secret until the last minute. He didn't know why but he had learned early in their relationship not to ask probing questions. She was so clever, always plotting the next best move. There must have been some sort of hitch or a change of plans that had brought her back.

When he opened the door, Baxter was staring at a plain-clothed Fletcher Ladislaw, flanked by two state troopers in uniform. His heart sunk when Ladislaw flashed his badge. He pulled the lapels of his robe together, as if embarrassed. Something was terribly wrong and the snickers of the troopers behind the stern-faced Ladislaw didn't seem to register with the ever-sensitive Baxter DeCourcy.

DeCourcy displayed some surprising initial fortitude under the barrage of questions from Ladislaw's team. He stuck to a story that had been drilled into him, namely that a stranger came into his shop one day several weeks ago and said he had a business proposition for him, an easy money-maker. They met later at a bar and, after several drinks, the stranger proposed that he deposit in his own account a series of checks that would be signed over to him. After the checks cleared, Baxter would withdraw the majority of the proceeds in cash for the stranger and keep the remainder as a service fee to compensate him for his trouble.

"You weren't suspicious that the stranger didn't just deposit the checks in his own account and then withdraw the cash, Baxter?" one of the troopers asked. "I didn't inquire. Figured he had creditors after his assets and it was his way of evading them. I know how he feels," Baxter said, playing the sympathy card.

"Describe the man," Ladislaw said. Baxter hesitated for a second, as if he was recollecting someone from a distant past. "Curly brown hair and a bushy moustache. Middle-aged, I would guess, but the hair threw me off when I first met him. Then I figured it out," DeCourcy said.

"Figured it out?" Ladislaw asked. DeCourcy smiled knowingly, like he was now in charge. He was the kind of egoist, enamored with every inch of his own physiognomy, who would focus on Hoole's deficiencies. "He was wearing a rug. The moustache was fake, too."

LADISLAW'S TEAM TRIED in vain to get DeCourcy to talk about a girl named Gretchen Cadwallader. He stuck to his story about the stranger. She had anticipated every possible contingency and he had followed the script. She would have been proud of him, as one would a child who memorized and correctly recited the capitals of all the states. Baxter had courted many beautiful women who had been drawn to the family name, his good looks and the misguided vision of inherited wealth. None of them, however, held a candle to Gretchen Cadwallader in her ability to enchant and dominate him. It puzzled Baxter how the troopers knew he was on DeCourcy Island. It made him angry to think that his sisters, always vengeful, had probably set him up.

"IT FEELS LIKE we're investigating a damn costume party. Go back to that shop. I want to know if they carry a wig and moustache like this clown DeCourcy described. It might turn out to be the only honest thing he said today. His description sounds like the same person Kosinsky saw in the library and entering the girl's apartment building. Maybe we'll get lucky and the store clerk will describe either Hoole or the girl. Take DeCourcy's picture with you and ask about him as well." Ladislaw sent the troopers on their way. He wasn't hopeful of getting an ID but at least he now had some corroboration to go on. It all made sense. Hoole was wearing a disguise when he transacted business with DeCourcy. Two people in cahoots and both wearing disguises had recruited DeCourcy as their money changer. Had Hoole already ditched his disguise or would he be using it again? He contacted the trooper stationed outside the husband's motel. He had dogged him back and forth from the crematorium and confirmed that the husband was back in his room. No, he assured Ladislaw, there was no rear exit from the property.

Grex couldn't believe that Hoole was calling him, acting all conciliatory and sympathetic. He was asked to believe that all the client checks had been destroyed in the mysterious quarry office fire and that Hoole was as much a victim as Grex.

"Don't be fooled, Grex. These troopers are going to try and nail both of us for conspiracy to commit murder, playing us off against each other, don't you see? Listen, I'm coming into some money, an inheritance, and I'm willing to cut you in. After all, we are partners, right?"

"How much we talking about?" Grex grunted, suspicious but wanting to believe that his luck might be changing. "Does $20,000 make us good?" Grex softened at the mention of cash and his voice sounded almost boyish. "I guess so. How soon?" Hoole suddenly sounded cheerful. "A week or two max. But here's the thing, El. You gotta stop talking to the troopers or whoever else they bring in on this damn investigation. They're playing you for a sucker and the sure sign of it is when they act like your friend. Any little thing you say will be twisted and used against us. Hell, I'll bet they suggested while I was missing that you arranged my wife's murder to get back at me. If their investigation drags on, they'll be looking for someone to pin it on and we're the prime candidates. Of course, I have an alibi but they'll say I set it up – maybe even with you. Who's to say they won't plant our fingerprints at the motel? It's been done, I tell you."

"I might be going back to New Bedford," Grex said, almost in a whisper, as if he was surrendering his manhood. "Smart move to get out of here. Don't worry, though. I'll look you up as soon as the money arrives. Just be patient. And remember, any blabbing to the troopers about anything and our deal is off. Understood?"

"Yeah, sure," Grex mumbled, starting to resent the hectoring.

"Hey, buck up, partner. Soon, you'll be on the gravy train. You can buy some nice stuff for the ex. That'll put you in really good after the lights are turned off, if you know what I mean."

Grex' face was burning but he said nothing. Then, he heard, "Oh, one last thing, El. This conversation never took place so don't go doing something stupid."

The partner had never talked to Grex like this before and he didn't like it, especially the sexual allusion to his ex-wife. And what was it with calling him El like they were old buddies? Grex sat and chewed on a knuckle before deciding it was all bullshit, a cock and bull story. He wasn't buying a word of it.

GREX MADE ONE of his smarter decisions in some time and called Ladislaw. "If he calls back, tell him you're on board. Sound positive – even thankful. You have to decide who you trust right now. If it helps, we do have evidence that the quarry checks were not destroyed in the fire. That's all I can say for now. And as for the wife's murder, we did wonder early on if you might be involved but you were never a suspect."

When Ladislaw hung up, he called the husband's motel and was able to confirm that an outgoing call had been made from the husband's room to Grex's number. "You're getting careless or overconfident – maybe both," he said aloud.

CHAPTER FORTY-SEVEN:
THE SHELL

~

THE FOLLOWING MONDAY, the Delaware bank finally released details of the Legrand bank account., Like the quarry account, it was practically emptied of cash but its recent history was telling.

A string of cash deposits of various amounts totaling almost $125,000 had been made over a 6-month period. In the last few months, $15,000 in cash had been withdrawn in increments of $3000. There was a single check made payable to Mortimer Jarndyce, Esq, originally engaged by the wife. The remaining monies, the bulk of the supposedly purloined and laundered funds, had been paid via a series of checks to Caribbean Assurance Insurance Brokers in Pompano Beach, Florida.

"Hoole told Grex he would be receiving an inheritance, a dubious cover story which doesn't gibe with what he told us about investors in Legrand. Guess he figured that Grex would be taken in by the 20 grand promise and wouldn't snitch," said Ladislaw, talking to one of his troopers.

"The Legrand deposits don't match the quarry checks, Chief, but we did some quick math and they are all exactly twenty percent less than the client payments – that would likely be DeCourcy's cut that was kept back." Ladislaw nodded and asked, "What the hell is Caribbean Assurance?" The trooper threw up his hands and mumbled, "on it boss."

Ladislaw had resisted contacting Cyrus and Jerry after the anonymous DeCourcy tip and the ensuing interview with the pretty boy. He felt self-conscious and dependent when he consulted them and he was afraid that it showed. Now, he had the husband's call to Grex trying to buy him off plus the Legrand bank records showing various disbursements and, instead of forging ahead with confidence, he was anxious to get their perspective.

"ALL AT ONCE a flurry of activity. Seems like I'm getting deeper into the intrigues of the husband but no closer to solving the wife's murder," Ladislaw said, sitting with Cyrus and Jerry in the alcove at the Thimbletown Inn.

"Maybe you are but it's just not clear yet, Lieutenant," Cyrus said. Ladislaw's eyebrows went up and the old man continued. "Consider the possibility that the husband came back to Connecticut from Virginia for one simple reason – to get the death certificate and pass it on to Caribbean American. My guess is that he has already done so. As for the wife's ashes and the ceremonial spreading of them on Lake Champlain, it was all a heartless diversion but it served its purpose. It's also clear that Legrand is, or was, just a shell company, a vehicle for the husband to move money around. My hunch is that Caribbean American sells a variety of insurance products and roughly $100,000 buys you a great deal of life insurance coverage, well over a million, I would imagine. Don't forget, the husband was in the insurance business and knows his way around. Now, who was the insured and who is the beneficiary of the Caribbean American policy? If it's the wife, and the husband is due to collect, you have your motive for murder for hire. Makes the Vermont policy and the quarry money chump change by comparison."

When Cyrus finished his dissertation, Jerry said, "And the $15,000 in cash withdrawals, that was working capital for the conspirators. They'll need it to move quickly, possibly out of the country. Hey, maybe part of it went to pay for a pro to fake a burglary and knock off the wife."

"It might be time to bring in the FBI, Ladislaw. If more than $5000 in stolen money was moved from here to Delaware, that makes it a violation of interstate commerce statutes, if I'm not mistaken. That would make it federal. At the very least, the state boys here will have a potential larceny and embezzlement case. Here's another thing, now that I think of it. I would want to know if passports have been issued recently to the husband and to Gretchen Cadwallader. Better check on DeCourcy while you're at it but he probably already has one. Most likely he's been a throw away all along but just doesn't know it yet," Cyrus said.

"So, what about Hoole? He's got his death certificate along with his precious ashes and will want to go back to Vermont. At least that's his story. The D.A. says that without proof that the money that went into the Legrand account came from the quarry checks, we still don't have anything tangible to hold him on yet," Ladislaw said.

"Why not let him go, Lieutenant, but only so far. See which way he heads. Tail him but don't let him cross the Connecticut border. Find some excuse to pull him over. Changing lanes without signaling. Who cares?" Jerry said.

"Good idea to force his hand. We bring him back and put him in a line-up. Damn, should have done that already. See if DeCourcy picks him out. Put a wig and moustache on him if necessary. I'd love to search his room at the motel but doubt I could get a warrant yet."

Ladislaw went to the telephone booth and came back a

few minutes later. "I called the husband and told him he was free to travel to Vermont but that we might want him back if we developed more information on his wife's killer. Said that the investigation into the quarry finances was problematic but on-going. I threw in the comment that it was difficult to decide who to believe – Grex or him. He sounded very obliging. Probably thinks he's almost home free. I'll pull the trooper off motel surveillance before morning just in case the husband recognized his car. We'll have someone else stationed out by the road to follow him when he leaves."

Ladislaw stood up and looked anxiously at Cyrus and Jerry. "We need a break, guys. Let's hope that Hoole delivers it to us."

EVERYTHING WAS QUIET that evening. At midnight, the lights went out in Hoole's room, making the trooper more vigilant. Ladislaw was fidgety, hoping for a call from his man. It was in vain, as Hoole's door never opened.

CHAPTER FORTY-EIGHT:
Road Runner

It was before dawn on Tuesday when Hoole slipped out of his room and walked quickly to his car. He relaxed when he scanned the area and saw no movement. The second trooper positioned out on the frontage road followed Hoole onto the highway, staying in contact with Ladislaw who had slept on a couch in his office the previous night. As they approached the cut-off to head north toward Vermont, Hoole suddenly sped up and continued straight toward New York City. "Is he over the speed limit?" Ladislaw asked. When the trooper confirmed, Ladislaw said, "Pull him over and approach with caution." When he did, Hoole rolled down his window and peered up with a surprised look on his face. He was wearing the wig and fake moustache.

At the trooper barracks, the husband demanded that his attorney be called. His timing was not good. The check drawn on the Legrand account payable to the attorney had bounced and Mortimer Jarndyce, Esq. was a most unforgiving counsel.

"He's no longer my client and you can tell him that for me," he barked at Ladislaw, as if the lieutenant was somehow responsible for the husband's deceit.

DeCourcy was brought in from a holding cell to identify the husband. Two line-ups were arranged and Hoole was inserted into both of them, the first without his disguise and the second one wearing the wig and fake moustache. In both instances, DeCourcy chose the husband without hesitation. "He's got no chin, Lieutenant. He can't hide that unless he puts on a fake beard, now can he? Hey, can I go back to the island now?" DeCourcy was sure Gretchen would be contacting him soon and was afraid he might have already missed her call.

"Not quite yet, Baxter. The guy you just identified, he's in a lot more trouble than stealing cash from his company and then laundering it through you. His wife was murdered at an inn not too far from here and anyone connected to the husband is a suspect. You don't seem like the kind of guy who would strangle a helpless woman in her bed but accessory to murder is damn serious business, if you're somehow involved. And then there's the matter of the girl, Baxter. You're going to have to tell us what you know about her." When Ladislaw finished, the carefree look on DeCourcy's face had vanished. He was starting to understand that this little escapade with the checks, this lark to get some quick money and be part of the girl's grander scheme, was deadly serious. The trooper could feel Baxter's arm trembling as he grabbed it and led him away.

"No passport on a Gretchen Cadwallader or the wife, boss, but one was issued to the husband about three weeks ago. Sounds like he planned to leave his spouse behind all along," the trooper announced to Ladislaw.

The husband sat in a cell and fumed. He was mainly angry with himself. When he passed the exit on the highway that would take him north to Vermont, his emotions got the best of him and he sped up, thinking about their rendezvous in New York City. He had blundered twice, first in leaving the disguise on after departing the motel and then not going north into Massachusetts before circling back south. He was glad that he had made the offer to Grex, confident that he would keep his mouth shut and wait for his money until it was too late. The Legrand thing would blow away but it was a damn inconvenience nonetheless and she would wonder what had delayed him. And what was with the two line-ups he was forced to stand in? Did they bring someone up from the bank in Delaware to ID him? Little did he know that Baxter DeCourcy sat in a holding cell not more than 100 feet away and was about to crack.

Hoole was indignant and kept demanding to speak to his attorney. Ladislaw hadn't relayed Jarndyce's message yet and decided to let him stew in his cell for a while. First, they would focus on the pretty boy.

Left alone, it didn't take long for sheer panic to consume Baxter DeCourcy. He thought about what Ladislaw had said. He wasn't sure what it meant to be an accessory to murder but the sound of it terrified him. He thought about calling his sisters. He knew they had lawyers on call but he wasn't quite up to facing their badgering and what he anticipated would be their ultimate rejection. Then, his thoughts turned to Gretchen. He had put all his faith in her when his life was spinning out of control. He had used his portion of the quarry cash to pay off the juice loan to the thugs in Boston. Now he was destitute again.

He had been stalwart, hadn't he? It had seemed like a game to him, the way she described it. There had been no talk of murder. All he knew was that she was going to fleece this man who had tried to seduce her. They would take off together, she had promised him, and had even hinted at some place like St. Moritz or even Monte Carlo. She would reveal all the details when they met in Boston. In the meantime, he was to lay low on DeCourcy Island until he heard from her. But he needed her now, this minute, to get him out of this mess and she had given him no way to contact her. It wasn't possible that she would abandon him, he told himself.

LADISLAW MADE THE now frequent drive over to the Thimbletown Inn and told Cyrus and Jerry the news of Hoole's apprehension while wearing a disguise. "DeCourcy quickly picked him out of two line-ups, one of them wearing the wig and mustache. He didn't even hesitate," Ladislaw said.

"There can be no question now that the girl brought DeCourcy and the husband together to wash the quarry money. Hoole will stick to his ridiculous story for as long as possible," Cyrus said.

"I thought DeCourcy might crack during our interview. He was shaken when I threw out the murder accessory charge but it wasn't enough for him to immediately give up the girl. It's going to take some more persuading," Ladislaw said.

"Gretchen would only feed him what he needed to know, nothing more. He has no clue how diabolical she is. Tell him the gory details about Twitchy and the wino," Jerry urged. "Ask him if that's the kind of woman who will stand by him. Plant the idea that she might even have been the anonymous tipster who gave him up."

"I like that, kid. Maybe flavor it with a little description of prison life for a pretty boy like him. It might be just enough to season the pot. In the meantime, I'm going to let the husband sweat for a bit," Ladislaw said as he stood up to leave.

CHAPTER FORTY-NINE:
THE INTERROGATIONS

~

Ladislaw followed the script outlined with Cyrus and Jerry, holding back the portrayal of prison life until the end. "You'll be somewhat of a celebrity in the slammer, Baxter. Everyone knows the DeCourcy name plus you'll be the new fish on the block. You won't just be challenged to see how tough you are. More than one prison wolf will look on you as fresh, tender meat, if you know what I mean. You'll be locked up with some of the vilest people on earth. It won't be like summer camp on DeCourcy Island."

Baxter had been suspicious of the Ladislaw's stories describing Twitchy and the wino. He had heard that cops fabricated stuff to make people confess. Still, it sounded plausible that she could have planted the finger on the island and just didn't tell him. But wearing a blonde wig and cutting the finger off the wino and putting a ring on it, well that was way too much to believe of her. As for Twitchy, he had seen him around town but never with Gretchen.

Now, he was hearing the lieutenant's vivid description of prison life and it terrified him. He cupped his hands over his face and started rocking from side to side. He was breaking down and Ladislaw helped him along with a fatherly tone. "Who knows you were on DeCourcy Island? Don't answer. We both know the answer, don't we? The anonymous tipster's voice was muffled for a reason but it was female, I can assure you. Don't you see that you were just a small cog in the machine, used and then discarded? Time's running out for you to come clean on the check scheme before we move on to the wife's murder. My boys are anxious to grill you every which way from Tuesday; they'll do it for hours and enjoy themselves. I decided to give you one last opportunity. It's your choice."

When his hands came down, Baxter looked up beseechingly at Ladislaw and said, "I never imagined she might desert me. I fell for her almost the moment we met at that bar even though she's no beauty. We have plans for Europe – or at least we did. All I was instructed to do was deposit some checks for some guy who would come into the shop on a periodic basis. I was instructed to take out most of the proceeds after each check cleared and give the cash to her. The less you know, the better, she kept telling me."

DeCourcy stopped and Ladislaw, his voice still low and reassuring, asked, "What is her name, Baxter, and where is she now?" DeCourcy looked startled and said, "Why, you know it's Gretchen Cadwallader, right? We're to meet in the Boston area. She's to call the cottage with a specific location. Maybe she already tried. That's it, Lieutenant. You can have your boys hassle me but I've told you everything I know."

Ladislaw called in someone to take DeCourcy's statement. Of course, he knew it was her but just wanted to hear someone other than Cyrus or Jerry say the name Gretchen Cadwallader.

LADISLAW FELT HE had gotten the truth out of Baxter DeCourcy. The girl had been smart to tell him as little as possible, knowing he would crack under the least bit of pressure. He was pretty sure she had set up the poor sucker for just such a situation, hoping to send Ladislaw off on a wild goose chase to hunt her down in Boston. The idea that he had a romantic attachment to this vixen made Ladislaw cringe. The husband would be much harder to break down. He had everything to lose now.

"So, WHERE WERE you going to get the $20,000 to silence Grex?" Ladislaw asked. It was the first question he posed to Hoole when they sat across from each other in the interview room.

"No idea what you're talking about, Lieutenant. That brute can make up as many stories as he wants. Doesn't make them true," Hoole said defiantly.

"Right. That was just a social call you made to him before leaving your motel. Very cordial of you. Now, cut the bullshit," Ladislaw said.

The husband's eyes closed as he inwardly cursed his partner. So, this lieutenant was no fool after all. He had checked the motel phone records after hearing from Grex. Be careful, he said to himself.

"What's with the wig and the fake moustache? You always wear them when you launder money and go on trips?" Ladislaw asked.

"I like mysteries. That's why I read Poe. Any crime in that? As for laundering anything, I've no idea what you're talking about. Hey, did you contact my attorney? Why isn't he here yet?"

"Oh, I did just like you asked but he informed me that he no longer represents you. Asked me to pass that message on to you. Sounded upset when I called. Anyone else you may want me to contact, say Gretchen Cadwallader or Baxter DeCourcy?"

"Who? Never heard of them. Listen, you gonna charge me

with anything besides speeding and wearing a disguise? You can't hold me for that, Lieutenant. I know my rights."

Ladislaw smiled. "The FBI will decide about the money laundering charges. That's a federal offense. But this Baxter DeCourcy who you don't know, he just picked you out of those two line-ups you were in. Said he would recognize you anywhere – something about your receding chin." Ladislaw stroked the skin on his neck and the husband's face turned pale.

"So, if you don't know DeCourcy, how is it that he not only identifies you, but also swears that you came into his shop frequently, wearing your disguise? And then the quarry checks end up in his bank account in New Haven? Let me guess – Grex borrowed your disguise and did it, of course. He's your secret accomplice and this anger thing is just an attempt to throw us off track. Why didn't I think of that earlier?" Ladislaw's tone was mocking but the husband suddenly seemed impervious, staring at him expressionless.

"You realize that embezzlement on this scale is a felony, right? Could put you away for quite a while. Before you get out, that chin of yours will have disappeared entirely." Ladislaw couldn't help himself but felt cheap, even unprofessional right afterwards. His frustration was no excuse. Still, it didn't elicit any response from Hoole who now looked almost serene.

"You'll feel a lot better if you start telling the truth, Hoole. Right now, we're talking chicken shit stuff and you know it. Wait until we get to your connection to Gretchen Cadwallader, the wino's death and your wife's murder. We're only in the first inning," Ladislaw said.

Hoole smiled and said, "Did you forget? I was out of town when she was strangled. If you had anything to connect me to it, you wouldn't have taken the chance of letting me leave the motel. You would have shown your cards already. Now, as I said, I know my rights and have nothing more to say until I speak to an attorney."

Ladislaw had felt good until the husband smiled. He was right, of course. They had absolutely nothing linking him to his wife's murder. He had hoped to tease a confession out of Hoole after his success with DeCourcy but so far, the man was proving to be intractable.

"WHAT KIND OF time do you serve for money laundering, Cyrus?" Ladislaw was sitting with his amateur sleuths in the alcove of the Thimbletown Inn going over the results of the two interrogations.

"Depends on a lot of factors. If the husband was a drug dealer, for example, churning huge amounts of cash, the sentence could be severe. Length of the enterprise would be a factor, too. Here you have a case of about $100,000 or so of embezzled funds laundered for only a short period. First offense. White collar crime. No public outcry. Maybe five years, but I'm guessing," Cyrus said.

"Any word from Caribbean American yet?" Jerry asked. "Yeah," said Ladislaw. "Without a court order, they don't comment on client policies until a claim is filed. I can't get the husband's demeanor out of my mind. Hoole started out angry and defensive but at the end of our interview, he acted like he was in command of the situation. It stunned me."

Cyrus could see that Ladislaw was discouraged and said, "He thinks he has an ace in the hole and maybe he does – or perhaps he's already overplayed his hand and doesn't know it yet. Something tells me he factored in the possibility that he might be nabbed on the check scheme and is now proceeding accordingly."

Ladislaw had felt good after the DeCourcy interview but now realized that Hoole might be outmaneuvering him. His superiors would not be impressed if, instead of solving the wife's murder, he ended up handing the laundering scheme over to the feds and the state got stuck with a plea deal with DeCourcy on receiving stolen property. He felt that he was stymied unless he got Hoole to crack or he found Gretchen Cadwallader.

CHAPTER FIFTY: SLAYER BEWARE

A FEW DAYS HAD passed since Baxter's confession when the stranger strode into the Thimbletown Inn. Cyrus knew immediately that he was a foreigner on serious business. He was tall and thin with penetrating eyes that quickly took in his surroundings and dismissed what was insignificant. Cyrus guessed private investigator but not your average American gumshoe who could blend in with the wallpaper. This man had style which announced itself.

He was wearing a cream-colored linen suit, somewhat rumpled, a dark blue dress shirt and a red bowtie with white stripes. Woven tan suspenders peaked out from beneath his coat as he marched toward the front desk, smoothing the rim of his matching Panama hat.

"Looks like you just arrived from the islands. There's a Graham Greene in Cuba look and style about you," Cyrus said with a smile. The stranger returned the smile and said, "You must have *Our Man In Havana* in mind. I wouldn't want to be there now but the novel was quite entertaining."

"I'm Cyrus Trowbridge. My sister and I own this place but she does all the work. Will you be staying with us?" Cyrus asked.

"I plan to, but most likely for one night only. My business will be brief here, I suspect." Circumspect fellow with an English accent, Cyrus said to himself. Collegial but very careful what he reveals.

"Would it be presumptuous of me to inquire about the nature of your business? I'm retired from my law practice and was previously with the state's attorney office. Guess you could say I've never stopped being inquisitive and I can't help but engage a newcomer to our town." Cyrus would not normally lay out his background to a stranger but felt it might encourage him to open up. He was right.

"I'm Sedley Rawdon," he said, sticking out his hand. "On business for Caribbean American. Something tells me you might know what my presence here signifies." Cyrus hesitated and Rawdon said, "Come now, Mr. Trowbridge. It's been a long day on planes and trains. Humor me."

Cyrus grinned. He already liked this stranger. That was two in one year, he said to himself. Maybe I'm not the misanthrope some people think I am after all. Cyrus was tempted to open up to Rawdon in the hopes of getting him to reciprocate but information had been shared with Jerry and him by Ladislaw in strict confidence. Such a breach would be unforgiveable. He wanted to ask to see some identification but feared it would cause the stranger to clam up. And how was he to know that this man wasn't in cahoots with Hoole and the girl, here to ferret out information on the case against them? At this point, he would put nothing past Gretchen Cadwallader.

Ever cautious, Cyrus took the safer path. "I'm assuming you are here because of the death of Isabel Hoole. I could give you my view on the murder investigation but you will want to speak with Lt. Ladislaw of the state police. I can call him and ask that he meet you here where there will be no prying eyes. I am pretty confident that he will be accommodating. I could humor you with gossip and theories but its best that you get your information directly from the horse's mouth, so to speak."

"Excellent. I'll check in now. Please call my room when the lieutenant arrives." Rawdon tipped his hat to Cyrus and walked to the front desk.

JERRY WAS COMING down the stairs when Rawdon brushed past him. He saw Cyrus standing near the front desk, waving him over. Cyrus was unsure if Ladislaw would let them sit in on the meeting and wanted to advise Jerry of that contingency.

LADISLAW WAS FRUSTRATED and almost dumbfounded. At their next session, Hoole continued the benign, even serene attitude that had overtaken him at the end of their previous interview. He was polite while refusing to answer any of the questions posed by Ladislaw and his team. He shrugged when they asked about the $1000 in cash found in his glove compartment and the whereabouts of the $15,000 in cash withdrawn from the Legrand account. Even the mention of Caribbean American didn't seem to faze him. When the call came in from Cyrus, Ladislaw practically rushed out the door.

LADISLAW LOOKED OVER the death certificate produced by Sedley Rawdon and nodded. "Yeah, it's a copy of the one released by the medical examiner's office. It's official, if that's what you're asking."

"Thank you, Lieutenant. May I ask how your investigation is going? The wife was insured through our agency and we are about to authorize the payment of a great deal of money. Obviously, we don't want it going to anyone connected to the wife's murder. You are aware of the statutes against that, correct?" Ladislaw looked stumped and Cyrus quickly came to his rescue. "Why don't you enlighten us, Mr. Rawdon? It's been a while since I looked into this issue. I'm sure all of us would appreciate your perspective."

"It's known as the slayer statute," Rawdon began. "Sometimes it's referred to as the 'no profit theory'. It simply means that you cannot collect as the beneficiary if you were complicit in the murder of the insured. The courts have been very supportive in not allowing criminals to profit from these kinds of crimes."

"Let me be honest, Mr. Rawdon," said Ladislaw. "We believe that the husband orchestrated his wife's murder and then arranged to be out of town when it occurred. That makes him an accessory, as you know. We just haven't been able to prove it so far. I wish I had better news, believe me."

"But the girl, Lieutenant, is she implicated? She's the beneficiary on the policy, not the husband," Rawdon said. Everyone went slack-jawed at once except Rawdon, who surveyed Ladislaw, Cyrus and Jerry with bemusement. Ladislaw was thinking about his last interview with the husband and felt as if he had fallen into a dark abyss. Recovering his poise, he took a deep breath and said, "We've had an all points out on her for days. Sent her picture to police departments up and down the coast. We're almost certain that she's knee deep in a fraud committed by the husband – and that's just for starters. The monies paid to Caribbean American for the insurance policy is probably dirty but it will take us some time to prove it – if we ever can. But the damn girl, she has outsmarted all of us so far. Has Gretchen Cadwallader been in contact with your office already to collect on the policy?"

It was Rawdon's turn to look bewildered. He gazed at everyone and said, "There must be some mistake. We have no policy beneficiary by that name that I'm investigating. I'm inquiring about an Elizabeth Cruikshank."

CHAPTER FIFTY-ONE:
THE GREAT ESCAPE

CYRUS WAS THE first person to react to Sedley Rawdon's jaw-dropping declaration. He had a grim look on his face as he got up from his chair and said, "I'll be right back." Ladislaw and the investigator sat with blank expressions and said nothing. Jerry was mute as well; his mind was churning but he couldn't focus.

After a few minutes, Cyrus walked back with a paper dangling from his hand. He laid it on the table and pushed it in front of Jerry. "The missing piece of the puzzle, kid. If I'd only gone to Gretchen Cadwallader's apartment building with you that day it might have become clear much earlier. Tell these gentlemen what it means."

Jerry was staring at the copy of the California driver's license for Elizabeth Cruikshank and gasped. The girl in the photograph had red hair, just like Cyrus has described "little Betsy" more than once. But the face belonged to Gretchen Cadwallader. Jerry's girl was a phantom. Gretchen would never be found because she didn't exist.

"There's your Gretchen Cadwallader, Lieutenant," was all that Jerry could get out. "She was a troubled and damn clever girl as Little Betsy Cruikshank when she spent her summers down here as a young girl. She looks different now but inside the demons have consumed her. Good luck trying to tie her to the wife's murder," Cyrus said, looking first at Rawdon and then Ladislaw.

Rawdon stood up and said, "Well, gentlemen, unless there is evidence that Ms. Cruikshank was posing as this Gretchen Cadwallader and is linked to the murder of the insured, it appears that my work is done here. Lieutenant, unless you develop such evidence soon, Ms. Cruikshank is about to become a very wealthy young woman. I see no need to prolong my stay here and will catch the next train to New York. And now, let me bid you all a pleasant day."

AFTER THE DEPARTURE of Ladislaw and the agent for Caribbean American, Cyrus felt compelled to make the case against "little Betsy" for Jerry. Perhaps, he was hoping for some cleansing of his own soul in the process.

"Where the hell do you think she is?" Jerry asked, prompting Cyrus to expound. "The countries where we have no extradition treaties are not hospitable to most Americans. You flee to the likes of Cuba or Morocco if you're desperate. And what exactly will be the provable case against her besides aggravated identity theft? Is that worth the feds chasing her around the world?" Cyrus asked, not expecting a response.

"Then where?" Jerry persisted. "You're making me guess, so I'll say Switzerland where privacy is sacrosanct. Unless there is fraud found by Caribbean American in the application process, it may take a while but she'll eventually collect the insurance proceeds and quickly move them into a numbered Swiss account. She'll use an alias when it suits her – certainly not Gretchen Cadwallader. Remember that 5-year old girl who died? Most likely, Betsy used her birth certificate to get the Connecticut driver's license. Makes you wonder what other identities she has purloined and will use during her travels.

"As we've already seen, she won't take unnecessary risks. And you can be sure of one thing more, Jerry. Wherever she is, she won't be wearing a blonde wig or going back to her natural red for long, if at all. I wouldn't be surprised to learn that our friend Sedley Rawdon tries to track her down. Disregard his blasé attitude when he left. His agency has been scammed big time and they won't give up without a fight."

Jerry sat silently as Cyrus went on. "You're not cynical enough yet to fathom the depravity of a girl like her. Totally amoral, without feelings of pity or regret for her victims. I guess the experts would call her a psychopath or sociopath, I'm certainly not qualified to say which one applies to her. Look at her unrestrained ruthlessness and her thirst to dominate people. No remorse, no empathy, entirely narcissistic, ready to act on impulse. I don't recall any overt acts of cruelty during those summers she spent here but perhaps the genesis of it all was when she got shipped down here to get her out of the mother's way. Then, there was the death of the Hoole boy in Vietnam and the ensuing battle with his mother. Maybe they were the triggers. Was she jilted in college or victimized in a romance when she got to California? Who knows what may come out later? Whatever it is, it will make the Cruikshanks up in Burlington cringe.

"You're damn fortunate you escaped her clutches, kid. Hope you appreciate it. I would give the tip of this pinkie to find out how she hatched this elaborate scheme with the husband." Cyrus was holding up one hand and Jerry's eyebrows went up. "Oops, bad example," Cyrus laughed half-heartedly, before turning serious again. "There's something else I want to get off my chest. I have to accept the possibility that Letty chose the house on the hill and a very comfortable, independent lifestyle over a true commitment to me. Oh, she cared for me but the feelings were more lopsided than I was willing to acknowledge. It had nothing to do with Little Betsy, her brother or that wicked witch of a mother."

Jerry was shaken by Cyrus' description of Betsy Cruikshank and couldn't deny that he had avoided an entanglement that could have proved deadly. Cyrus' revelation about Letty meant that his friend was dealing with two painful Cruikshank memories at the same time. "I'm heading back to the cottage for a few days, Jerry. What are your plans?" Cyrus asked.

Jerry felt that he needed to get away as well but promised his old friend that he would return, hopefully before Hoole's trial began. He had re-read *The Gold Bug* after his visit to the Graniteville Library and decided to visit the Poe Museum in Virginia and then stop at the writer's grave in Baltimore on his return north.

"You'll stop back here before going home?" Cyrus asked. "Of course. You'll have updates for me on Hoole and I will want to give you a briefing on Poe" Jerry said. Cyrus had sounded plaintive and it gave Jerry a pang as they parted. On the way out, he left *The Gold Bug* with Tillie at the front desk and asked her to give it to Cyrus.

He thought about stopping by the constable's office to say goodbye to Fanny but it would seem so final and, he rationalized, he was coming back anyway. Her uncle had returned from his vacation and Jerry envisioned an awkward interaction between them that would raise suspicions. No, he told himself, he wasn't running from Fanny Tulk but wasn't sure he wanted to pursue her either.

As SEDLEY RAWDON was boarding a train in New Haven, Cyrus' "little Betsy" Cruikshank, her hair once more its natural, fiery red to match her passport photograph, was settling into her seat for the long flight from Miami. She hadn't decided on the color yet but would dye her hair again shortly after landing in Zurich.

Epilogue

Although Ladislaw and his team were not ready to admit it, the strangulation of Isabel Hoole was destined for the "cold case" files like a number of other unsolved murders. Gretchen's apartment in New Haven was scoured for evidence but the investigators came up empty – just as they had in Isabel Hoole's room at the inn. Even the hair follicles on the wig were a dead-end.

Over the years, fresh eyes would take a look at the file and eventually walk away frustrated and demoralized. Unlike the quarry embezzlement scheme and the foiled Vermont insurance scam, there wasn't even circumstantial evidence – unless you considered the blonde wig found in the suitcase – to link anyone, let alone her husband or Betsy Cruikshank, to the murder. The name of Gretchen Cadwallader was anathema and rarely mentioned around the trooper barracks.

Anyone who studied the case concluded that Betsy Cruikshank was almost certainly the mysterious blonde who orchestrated the grand scheme that resulted in the potential manslaughter of one pathetic soul and the murder of another. Opinion varied on whether she actually carried out that brutal and degrading final act herself. If not, then there was another accomplice still on the loose.

When Woody described the case to Billy Meacham, Jr., it made the retired detective and police chief think of Stella Crimmons, the sultry blonde who had abetted con man Winston Siebert III back in the 50s when he wreaked havoc on sleepy Parlor City. Stella was as cold-hearted as they come but Meacham decided that she would have been no match for Elizabeth Cruikshank.

WHAT CYRUS OR anyone would never learn, unless Hoole started to talk, was that Betsy had been in contact with the husband for over a year. She had called home months ago and learned that she had been removed from her father's will. Commiserating by telephone with Hoole while she was living in California, she heard that life with his wife had become intolerable but that financial problems had prompted them to put aside their mutual animosity and form an uncomfortable alliance.

When Hoole described the proposed insurance scam and his investment in the quarry operation in the Thimble Islands, her evil genius kicked into gear. She proposed to meet Hoole in Connecticut, at which time she would lay out a much grander scheme than a mere $50,000 insurance scam that had to be split with someone he loathed. Ellis Hoole was almost immediately transfixed.

By the time they met in New Haven the prior December for the first time in years, she had transformed herself into Gretchen Cadwallader and was leading Hoole around by the nose. Early on after their reunion, Hoole gave up hope that there might be a romantic relationship between them – or even a brief concupiscent encounter. He had been enfeebled by his repressed lust for the girl until they came to a tacit understanding on this point shortly after that reunion in New Haven. He then envisioned a more paternalistic role as the father figure that she had missed out on growing up. But it was even too late for that fantasy to come true and she bluntly told him so. And so, they settled into a relationship as allies against what she termed their common enemy.

When he went back in Burlington after the rendezvous with Betsy, Hoole told his wife that he had concocted another scheme that would double their payout. He would siphon funds from the quarry operation and funnel them into a new entity controlled by them. A separate $50,000 life insurance survivor policy would be taken out. The avaricious wife bought in quickly and when Hoole shuffled incorporation papers for Legrand in front of her, she signed multiple pages without even glancing at them. Two of those pages were the beneficiary and signature documents for the life insurance policy issued through Caribbean American. Shortly thereafter, a private nurse showed up at the Hoole residence to draw blood and secure a urine sample to support the felonious insurance application. On that day, Isabel Hoole sealed her fate.

The original insurance scam was simple enough. Hoole would arrange to bury some personal belongings on Quarry Island, including his Thorndyke College ring, before he went into hiding, thereby setting up his belligerent and recalcitrant partner as the prime suspect of foul play. After filing a missing person's report, the wife would come down to Graniteville to secure a death certificate so they would collect on the Vermont insurance policy. The proceeds from the second insurance scam, funded by the quarry embezzlement, would also be divided before the estranged couple went their separate ways. When the mother learned from her son that Jerry Kosinsky was returning to the states after receiving his presidential pardon, the scheme was modified to strengthen the case of a caring, distraught wife desperate to try any means to locate her missing husband.

When the wife got the call from Reg Buffle that a severed finger wearing a Thorndyke College ring had been discovered on

DeCourcy Island, she hurried down to Graniteville to confront her husband. They argued in her room that night at the inn when Jerry knocked on the door and saw a fleeting shadow on the wall behind her. Hoole refused to tell his wife how he had procured a severed finger, insisting that it was the physical evidence necessary to strengthen both insurance claims. Hoole left in a huff while the wife fumed. Little did she know that the plot had moved well beyond her by then. She would have another visitor that evening after her husband left who would make clear to her why she was expendable.

Hoole never knew how, or by whom, his wife would be killed after he left the inn. He assumed that Betsy would use some of the quarry cash withdrawn from the Legrand account to hire a professional. On first meeting Baxter DeCourcy, he was certain he was not the one. Ladislaw tried to bait Hoole with the evidence that Betsy had flown to Europe. They were supposed to meet in Mexico City and Hoole convinced himself that either Ladislaw was lying or that she had good cause for modifying her itinerary while on the run.

As he sat in jail awaiting formal charges to be filed against him for embezzlement and money laundering, he had trouble purging the image of the severed finger from his mind. Ladislaw had thrust the enlarged crime lab photograph in his face more than once and said, "If she could do this, Hoole, what makes you think she wouldn't wrap a lamp cord around your wife's neck before putting the blonde wig in her suitcase? Maybe a look at the coroner's report will open your eyes. Tremendous pressure was exerted on the carotid arteries, the trachea was crushed, extensive hemorrhaging of the eyes, you get the picture. Or would you like to see some of the photos? I know you hated each other but you've made a bargain with a worse devil than you imagined your wife to be. You're a damn fool if you don't understand that she's already forsaken you."

Everyone on the trooper team was convinced that he would eventually crack but Hoole didn't even blanch when he heard Ladislaw's dire prediction. It would take some time for them to realize that he was no Baxter DeCourcy. Betsy had helped Hoole steel himself for the possibility that if he were nabbed, he might go to jail. He still had years to live and calculated that he would serve a few years at most as a first offender. It was all worth it in anticipation of the big score. He was simply moving from one prison, a marriage to Isabel Hoole, to another. He was steeling himself to handle his likely incarceration, confident that she would take care of him upon his release.

CONSTABLE TULK'S FIRST action upon his return from vacation was to consult with Lt. Ladislaw and then fire Reginald Buffle. It was the effective end of his law enforcement career – at least in Connecticut. Buffle still had his part-time job as a security guard and usher at the local cinema where he could wear his faux uniform with its plastic badge and lord over disruptive children while he cleaned up debris from the sticky floors. Grex was now avoiding him but it didn't take long for Buffle to gravitate to other saloon regulars.

WHEN GREX MADE an unannounced visit to Ladislaw's office, jaws dropped. He was scrubbed clean like an obdurate schoolboy and his face was clean-shaven. Looking closely, you could see the numerous nicks where he had drawn blood during his diligent efforts. He was on his way to New Bedford for an inspection visit. Something in Grex's voice during his latest call home had softened the ex-wife and she had hinted at a reconciliation. Ladislaw showed him respect by inviting him into his office and closing the door. "There's no guarantee yet, but if she'll have me, we'll make another go of it. She said she could tell by my voice that I hadn't been drinking. I told her about Hoole's offer and we both laughed. Can't remember the last time that happened. Anyway, just wanted you to know I wasn't just running off. I'll come back for Hoole's trial if you need me." Ladislaw smiled and wished Elwyn Grex good luck. He made a point of shaking hands with him at the door in front of everyone. He had misjudged a number of things of late and maybe this poor soul was one of them.

WHILE ELLIS HOOLE sat in his cell, intransigent and incommunicado, some board members at the DeCourcy Institute implored the sisters to come to Baxter's rescue, if for no other reason than to spare the family name and the Institute's reputation. Attorneys for the Institute, in consultation with high-powered criminal defense counsel, would work out a plea deal resulting in house arrest and probation but no jail time for a watered down charge of unknowingly receiving stolen property. Along with a few PR hacks, they would successfully tamp down press coverage to the point that most articles on the quarry scam in the New Haven papers were pushed to the back pages and referred to a "local business owner" pleading guilty to minor charges. Baxter DeCourcy was rarely mentioned by name. Confined to the cottage on DeCourcy Island and, during the winter months, the family compound in Naples, Florida, he finally gave up waiting for the telephone call that would never come.

There was a constant buzz in Graniteville and the surrounding area about "Little Betsy" Cruikshank and her alias, Gretchen Cadwallader. The childish moniker stuck when old-timers like Crinkett, searching their collective memories, dredged up stories about her. Someone found a picture of her maneuvering a skiff near shore as a 12-year old which made it into the local paper. It was a distant shot but the red hair was distinctive. There was some dispute, however, as to whether she was simply pointing at the photographer or giving him the finger.

The fact that she was now a grown woman, a master charlatan and accomplished grifter, perhaps even a murderess, didn't seem to matter when Fletcher Ladislaw's name came up. That he had been outfoxed by "Little Betsy" was heard everywhere and it cut deeply into the proud and honorable man. His superiors questioned why he didn't vigorously pursue Gretchen Cadwallader as if it should have been obvious early on that she was Betsy's alter ego. Before he could be forced out or pushed into an administrative role, Ladislaw resigned. He had given the state his best years but would be remembered as the trooper who couldn't solve the biggest case Graniteville had ever seen.

Rawdon Sedley had been intentionally flippant in his remarks to Cyrus, Jerry and Ladislaw before leaving the Thimbletown Inn. Once he was settled into his seat on the train, he closed his eyes and plotted his next move. If the name Gretchen Cadwallader hadn't come up, he would never have thought there was a chance that the beneficiary claim could be challenged. Now, there was the distinct possibility that fraud had been committed and the contestability clause in the policy could be invoked, allowing him to start digging. He would begin with

The Severed Finger

the application and confirm that it was indeed Isabel Hoole's signature. Then, he would verify that she had completed the requisite medical exam and that a substitute had not been used. If both were valid, he would pore over the application, looking for even minor mistakes that would invalidate the claim. They could still tie up Cruikshank's claim with procedural delays, maybe until evidence emerged linking her to the Hoole murder. Sedley knew it was a long shot and prayed that Hoole or the girl had slipped up somewhere. Then Sedley thought of the agent who sold the policy to the Hooles. He had left Caribbean American after collecting his commission and would have to be tracked down. Was he part of some elaborate scam or was Sedley grasping at straws?

Sedley was tenacious and could conjure up all sorts of delays but would eventually be disappointed to learn that the application process was as clean as fresh snow on a tree limb and that Betsy Cruikshank had submitted all the proper paperwork to expedite her claim. Anticipating the possibility of a challenge, she engaged well-known insurance litigation attorney Harvey Tringle before departing Miami. Tringle lived to do battle with the staid insurance behemoths and bring them to their knees. Betsy deposited a $1000 retainer with his office in the event that Tringle needed to take action while she was abroad. Her agreement with him included a promise to pay a substantial bonus should she, because of his efforts, receive her beneficiary payout within 90 days. "Of course," she told him, surprised and annoyed by what she considered his impertinent question. "I'll take a lump sum. I'm too young to consider an annuity and who's to say I'd live long enough to collect all of it anyway?"

AFTER SPENDING A day at the Poe Museum in Richmond, Jerry headed north. His first stop in Baltimore was the Enoch Pratt

Free Library where he viewed Poe memorabilia – including a lock of hair and a piece of his coffin. It was there that he learned that Poe was moved from an unmarked grave in 1875 and honored with a marble and granite marker in a ceremony attended by Walt Whitman. Was the granite from the Thimble Islands, Jerry wondered? If so, he imagined that it would have pleased Poe.

When he got to Poe's grave at Westminster Hall, he felt for a fleeting moment, that the spirit of the dead poet had raced through him. It was a hot, muggy day but Jerry shivered involuntarily.

Afterwards, he wandered around a neighborhood known as Fells Point and drank a beer at The Horse You Came In On saloon, allegedly where Poe had his last drink. It was in the bar that Jerry learned about the mysterious visits to Poe's grave that started in 1949. Precisely on January 19th, Poe's birthday, someone entered the cemetery late at night and left a partial bottle of cognac and three roses at the grave. The ritual continued to this day and no one had yet discovered the identity of the visitor.

Nearby the saloon was Ryan's Fourth Ward Polls, later known as Gunner's Hall, where Poe was found in the gutter semi-conscious or, if you believe the alternate theory, discovered delirious inside. Did he know then he was near death, Jerry wondered? It had been almost 130 years and Jerry decided that no detective on earth, not even the renowned Billy Meacham, Jr. could solve the enduring mystery of Poe's demise.

Jerry was moved by his experience at the grave to call the Thimbletown Inn that evening to let Cyrus know that he was heading back to Graniteville the next morning. Tillie was called to the telephone and spoke in a halting, somber tone. "He died this afternoon, Jerry, sitting on the porch. He was reading that book you gave him, *The Gold Bug*, and just slumped forward. Please hurry back."

A week later, Cyrus Trowbridge had been eulogized and then buried in the small family cemetery on the edge of town. Tillie was heart-broken and consoled by Jerry and Fanny Tulk, now helping her manage the Inn. Jerry and Fanny eyed each other warily, neither one sure they wanted to make a move that would advance their relationship.

With Cyrus dead, Jerry felt out of place around the two women and would have headed back to Parlor City except for Tillie's plea that he postpone his departure until after the reading of Cyrus' will.

The prosecutor in Hoole's upcoming trial had a dilemma. Hoole was still not talking and DeCourcy and Grex were not exactly seen as stellar witnesses. Neither of them were model citizens and both had unflattering baggage that would be exposed in open court. A day before the trial was scheduled to begin, a plea bargain was reached that sent Hoole off to prison for 3-5 years. Had there been a trial, he was prepared to stick with the lame story that he had a brief liaison with a mysterious blonde he had met in a bar in New Haven, that the quarry checks were most likely destroyed in the island fire and that the cash deposited in the Legrand account over a 6-month period had come from investors who had insisted on anonymity. He knew he was going away but never gave up Betsy Cruikshank, insisting that he hadn't seen her in years. What he didn't know was that he would never see her again.

It turned out that when the Last Will & Testament of Cyrus Trowbridge was read, all of his assets had been bequeathed to his only sister with the exception of the cottage on the water, the Cruikshank oil painting and the early edition of the Charles Dickens novel given to him by Letty. All three had been left to Jerry Kosinsky.

"You can keep that damn jalopy, Jer," Woody insisted, when his friend told him he would stay a few days longer in Graniteville and then bring the car back to Parlor City.

Jerry told him about the cottage and Woody said, "He thought a lot of you, that's clear. You enriched his life at the end and it's obvious that his sister didn't object. I wouldn't be surprised if they decided jointly that you would get the best use of it."

Jerry hardly said a word more during their conversation and Woody knew his friend was dealing with a jumble of emotions that would take time to sort through. "Don't rush back on my account. Maybe I'll come down to see you instead. Things are quiet here now that the wife has entered a plea of not guilty by reason of insanity. She's up on Crazy Hill being evaluated so it'll be a while before her trial begins. Just stay in touch, okay?" were Woody's last words before hanging up the phone, not waiting for or expecting a response.

It was a clear afternoon as Jerry gazed out the large window in the front room of Cyrus' spare, two-room cottage and spotted some of the Thimble Islands to his east. Across the roughly 25-mile stretch of water that separated Connecticut from New

York, he saw the outline of trees and buildings. It seemed like a distant, alien land.

He glanced at the bookshelf against one wall. Jerry would take his time going through the collection but one book in a protective, artifact box caught his attention and he assumed it was the cherished copy of *Oliver Twist* given to Cyrus by Letty. Jerry had heard somewhere that you can tell the character of a man by the company he keeps and the books he reads. He didn't doubt that Cyrus' library would reflect well on him.

One wall in the front room was dominated by *The Worship Of Bacchus*, the original George Cruikshank's oil painting. Jerry looked at the dozens of forlorn characters, some besotted and others innocent victims of those same drunkards. It was as doleful as Cyrus described it that night at dinner when the old man unburdened himself.

Jerry's mind drifted back to what he now considered that seminal moment years ago on the Hoole's lawn, as described by the neighbor. He couldn't get used to thinking of her as Betsy Cruikshank. The girl he met and knew would always be Gretchen Cadwallader in all her devious and diabolical incarnations. Was the fight with Mrs. Hoole resulting in the loss of Buddy's pendant the beginning of the end? Did it send Betsy Cruikshank spiraling out of control? Had she subsequently done something heinous in college or California, as Cyrus had speculated, that would eventually come to light? Or was all her pent up rage reserved for that one moment of revenge?

Ladislaw had shown Cyrus and him the grisly crime scene photo with the lamp cord wrapped tightly around Isabel Hoole's neck with the plug neatly displayed, the prongs placed symmetrically, like someone was carefully adjusting a trinket on a necklace.

He wished Cyrus was there to hear his latest theory. If only he had made the connection between the two incidents earlier.

Would it have made a difference? Who would believe it now — or even care?

WHEN HE ENTERED the bedroom, he found an envelope with his name on it propped up on the nightstand next to the bed. He recognized Cyrus' handwriting. It was a brief letter, one that he would revere the rest of his life. It wasn't sappy or didactic but it struck a deep chord for our uncertain, reluctant hero. Cyrus must have known the end was near well before Jerry left to visit the Poe Museum. Was that why he took a room at the Thimbletown Inn? Referring to Tillie, he wrote, "It made her almost as happy as it did me. I hope you find both inspiration and solace here," it read at the end.

Jerry had looked forward to sharing his trip to Poe's museum and gravesite with Cyrus but would now have to content himself with imagining how his old friend would have reacted. For some reason, it made Jerry think of Augie March. He had started reading the Bellow novel again after his return from Baltimore and came upon a passage where an old acquaintance runs into Augie and learns that he is stealing books and selling them to students and collectors. He looks at Augie with a combination of amazement and disappointment before asking him, "What are you postponing everything for?" It sounded like something Cyrus might have said to him.

Jerry walked out on the dark, gravelly sand and looked at the nearly calm water, interrupted only by soft ripples of tiny waves that contrasted with the seemingly glassy surface further out. All was calm and serene. It wasn't Kathmandu and he couldn't see the majestic Himalayas in the distance but it felt good – and right.

Was this really the place, this archipelago of over 300 tiny islands, where Cyrus and he had speculated that Ellis Hoole's body parts had been dumped, chewed and mangled by sea creatures lurking in the watery depths? Had Capt. Kidd really buried treasure nearby within anyone's grasp? Was there anyone like William Legrand who could decode a secret message and knew where to look?

It all sounded so fantastical now, like something worth writing a novel about. Is that what Cyrus Trowbridge meant by inspiration?

Finis

Printed in the USA
CPSIA information can be obtained
at www.ICGtesting.com
LVHW041001210724
786093LV00028BA/422